THE LANE FAMILY SERIES

VOWS IN CORRUPTION

JOCELYNE SOTO

When it comes to my name, everyone thinks that they know who I am.

To some people, I'm the billionaire that just got named CEO of his family's company and has all the money in the world. To other's, I'm the guy that opened up his home to his brother's children and raised them as his own.

What they don't know is while I am those things, I'm also something else.

Something darker.

Something more corrupt and I will stop at nothing to get my hands on what I want.

So when a clause is threatening to take a way the one thing I worked so hard to get, I do something that I never thought I'd do willingly.

Get married.

And the kicker? My new assistant, Ella Vincent, is now my new wife.

This arrangement was only supposed to be for two years and something that benefited the both of us.

Yet circumstances are changing.

Feelings are developing.

And my perspective on marriage is changing.

But aspects of the past start to haunt us and threaten to take my wife away from me and instead of letting her go and walking away from a marriage that started out as a lie, I stop at nothing to keep it intact.

Even shedding some blood along the way.

PLAYLIST

Dark, Twisted and Cruel - Alan Wake, Paleface
Lose Control - Teddy Swims
Beautiful Things - Benson Boone
Too Sweet - Hozier
Desperado - Rihanna
Say Yes To Heaven - Lana Del Rey
Constellations - Piano Version - Jade LeMac
HEARTBEAT - Isabel LaRosa
Lust For Life - Lane Del Rey, The Weeknd
Heartburn - Wafia
After Hours - The Weeknd
Falling - Harry Styles
Swim - Chase Atlantic

READING ORDER

Please note that this story takes place a few years before the start of the *Flor De Muertos* series and *Powerful Deception*. A few things may seem out of order.

AUTHOR'S NOTE

This book does have a scene that dives into the exploration of wax play. If this is something that you are interested in exploring, please do not use this book as a guide as it could possibly lead to injuries.
Thank you.

PROLOGUE
BENNETT

When it comes to life, I know what it feels like to hit the highest of highs, where I'm able to meet with God and have him praise me, and the lowest lows of hell, where not even the devil himself could touch me.

I've suffered through death and mourning, through abandonment and loss of identity. For years, I didn't know what was right or wrong, what was up or down, or who I was, let alone who was sitting right next to me. I was lost in my own mind, and I didn't know how to get out.

At one point, I was twenty-two with all the damn money in the world, and all I wanted to do was drown myself in everything that I could think of: alcohol, women, a dark ocean that would shield me from ever seeing the light again.

Back then, anything would be better than the life I had been living.

I wanted to give up.

I wanted to throw everything away.

But then it all changed.

It changed the day I was driving up to my childhood home and saw four pairs of eyes staring back at me. That day, all the shit I was battling went out the fucking window. All the shit I had been going through didn't matter anymore.

I didn't want to drown.

I wanted to fucking thrive.

I wanted to conquer the fucking world and make life worth living again.

It was that day when I realized that there were things in the world that mattered more than anything else, and there was nothing that I wouldn't do for them.

So, that's what I did. I put those four sets of eyes before anything else, and I started to conquer the world one minuscule step at a time, and that is what I continue to do even to this day.

The world became my playing ground, Chicago my kingdom.

There is a reason why people in my everyday life call me a king, ruler of the very ground they walk on. They see me as the good guy who would do anything to help people in need.

But what they don't know is that even the king, who may seem like the godliest figure of them all, loves corruption, loves the bad, and all the deception that comes with it.

And when I want something, I will stop at nothing to get it.

1

ELLA

Five Years Before

Sweat rolls down my back as I drive away from the house and back to Chicago.

My eyes keep moving from the rearview mirror to the back seat, making sure nobody is following us and that Charlie remains asleep.

He promised he wouldn't.

He promised that if I did what I told him I would do, then he wouldn't follow us.

He promised he would let her come with me, that he would let us be as long as I kept my end of the deal.

But even if he promised, I can't help but not believe him, especially now.

It wouldn't take much for him to change his mind, to take Charlie away from me and threaten to not give her back to me until I meet his new price.

How much higher can he go?

I don't want to know the answer—I just press down on the gas and put even more distance between us and our past.

"He won't change his mind. He won't. Just take a deep breath and drive," I tell myself, trying to not only bring the sweating to a normal level but also bring down the frantic beating of my heart.

I continue the mantra for a few more miles, both out loud and in my head. I also try to think positive thoughts, but it's hard when doubt starts to creep in every few miles or so.

I don't stop looking at the rearview mirror or the back seat.

A part of me wants to be proud that I was able to get Charlie out of that hellhole. I'll be able to protect her, to give her the best life that I can. I was able to do the one thing that I set out to do since I found out about her.

The cost is something that I will live with forever, but I don't care. She's with me, safe, and that's all that matters.

I have to believe he won't come for her.

I have to believe he won't break his promise.

I have to believe, because if I don't, I'm going to spend the rest of my life looking over my shoulder, waiting for the other shoe to drop.

So, I have to believe, and I have to believe hard.

"Ella?" The little girl's voice rings out from the back seat. Somehow, I missed her waking up.

"Yeah?" I look into the mirror, catching her eyes with mine.

"Can we get something to eat? I'm hungry."

I give her the best smile I can form in the mirror. "Sure. We'll stop at the next rest stop, okay?"

She gives me a nod and closes her eyes again.

For the next few miles, we drive in silence. I should put on some music, but I don't know what kind of music Charlie likes. I also don't know what kind of food she likes or if she's allergic to anything.

I have a kid who now depends on me, and I know nothing about her.

Maybe this is a bad idea. Maybe I shouldn't have done this. What if she has a worse life with me than the one she already knows?

"Ella?" Charlie's voice sounds through the car again.

"Yeah, sweetie?"

"Thank you for picking me up. I promise to be the best little sister ever."

Tears start to take over as lump forms in my throat. I try to push it all down, but my little sister's words hit me way too hard.

Somehow, I'm able to push down the emotion enough to speak. "You're already the best little sister ever. And you never have to thank me. I will always be here for you, Charlie, no matter what. I will always be there for you."

She gives me the brightest smile I have ever seen, and it just makes my heart swell so much.

In this moment, I know I did the right thing. Taking Charlie from that environment she was in was the best decision I could have made for both of us.

It's going to be hard. I'm only twenty, and she's eleven,

but I will do everything in my power to give her the life she deserves.

Life may try to knock me down, but for her, I will try.

I will give my sister everything that she deserves.

Life. Happiness. Love.

Everything.

I may not be rich, but I will do it.

Just watch me.

2

ELLA

Present Day

I look at how much money I have in my savings account, and I let out a groan.

The number is decent, but the second the bills go through, that amount is going to dwindle, and I'm sure the new number will make me cry.

That's adulthood for you.

Whoever thought it would be a good idea to make things so damn expensive needs a good kick in the ass. Some of us can barely survive with how the economy is going.

Damn, I guess I'm really becoming a real-life adult— I'm mentally ranting about the economy and the price of things.

If I didn't have my welcome to adulthood moment years ago, this would be it.

Not wanting to get more frustrated, I close the tab and open a new window, typing four words into the search bar.

Job openings in Chicago.

Another groan leaves my body.

I love my current job. Well, I love the people I work with and the flexibility it offers me. The customers I could go without, but everything else makes it hard to want to leave.

But I have to either leave or look for a second job to help with the bills.

My hours keep getting cut more and more each week, to the point where I can't work two eight-hour shifts and be okay, especially if Charlie gets into that private school she applied to last year.

I need something more constant, steadier in the money department. A full-time job would be perfect, but I'll take a second part-time one if I can.

I just have to get over the displeasure that comes with looking through job listings.

Letting out a sigh, I press enter and let the page populate.

I don't know if I should be grateful or discouraged at the number of job openings that pop up. There *has* to be more than a few thousand listings.

My eyes travel to the time at the edge of my computer screen, and I let out a sigh. It looks like I'll be looking for something to apply to all damn night.

"I guess one sleepless night won't hurt."

Squaring my shoulders, I get to work scrolling through all the job boards I can find. From the looks of it, all of

Chicago is hiring; there are job listings for almost everything.

Dog walker.

Nanny.

Personal masseuse.

That last one makes me roll my eyes and gag at the same time.

Who the hell looks for a personal masseuse on a public job board? It's both crazy and disgusting.

I scroll away and try to look for something else. A bunch of listings pop up that I meet the minimum requirements for, so I apply to all that I can. There's even a barista position open at a coffee shop a few blocks away. I may hate the smell of coffee, but I would suck it up for a steady paycheck. I'm not going to be picky at this point.

After about two hours and fourteen applications, I'm about to give up for the night. Surely one of them will turn into something—an interview at the very least.

I should go to bed since I have a shift at the restaurant in the morning, but apparently, my mind and hand have a different idea as I click to the next page of jobs. Some that pop up are similar to the ones I found on previous pages or ads from something else. Nothing seems overly interesting.

That is, until I scroll to the very bottom.

An assistant position at Lane Enterprises.

No freaking way.

One of the most prestigious companies in Chicago, and they're hiring?

Holy shit.

I don't even take a second to think about it. I click on

the listing so damn fast, I swear my finger almost goes through the keyboard.

As soon as the post loads, I read through it and then read through it again.

I meet all the requirements.

They want a master's degree in business? I have that.

They want someone who is enthused to work? Hell, I'm very enthused.

Reading through the description of the job, I start to think I found my dream job.

It doesn't state if it's entry-level, but it also doesn't state that experience is required. *Perfect.*

Before I hit the button to apply, I check the time stamp on the listing. A few of the jobs I found tonight were posted almost a year ago and not active whatsoever, so I want to make sure I can actually apply for this job and have it go somewhere.

When I see the listing was posted only three weeks ago and is about to close, I let out a sigh of relief. I can still apply.

So without much thought, that's what I do.

For the next fifteen minutes, I fill out the whole application, add my résumé and my cover letter, and read over it about five times before I find the courage to hit submit.

When the words "thank you for applying" pop up, I have to take a second and think about what I just did. I just applied for a job at one of the most well-known companies in the world.

I don't know why, but that thought makes not only a

smile spread across my face but a giggle escape from my mouth.

"Holy shit," I say to myself between laughs. There's so much excitement rolling through me, I can't help but to do a little happy dance right here on my bed.

Who knew that applying for a job of this caliber would be so exciting? It's as if I'm high out of my mind for the first time in my life.

The excitement quickly dies down, though, once I think more about my application.

This listing has been open for three weeks; who knows how many applicants they've received? Mine is probably one of thousands.

Submitting my application is almost a fever dream, because who wouldn't want to work at a company like Lane Enterprises? It's like applying to Google or some other big tech company out in California. There's a high chance my submission won't even be seen, let alone land me an interview.

But a girl can hope, right?

Right. A girl can hope.

Who knows? That application may not get me anywhere, but one of the fourteen others I submitted tonight might, and that would be a great step in a very good direction.

I just have to keep my hopes up and fingers crossed that something comes my way.

"No more job hunting tonight," I say to absolutely nobody but myself as I close my laptop and start getting ready for bed.

Since my shift at the restaurant ran a little late and I had to help Charlie with her statistics homework when I got home, my nighttime routine was neglected.

Given the late hour, I go through it quickly, showering, changing into my pajamas, and checking that the stove is off and the front door is locked.

Once everything is taken care of, I hop into bed and wait for sleep to take me. I thought that I would be asleep the second my head hit the pillow, but no matter how much I toss and turn, sleep doesn't come.

"Great," I let out with a groan.

For a few minutes, I close my eyes and will my body to fall asleep, but it seems like my brain is wide awake.

With a frustrated sigh, I reach for my phone. Scrolling through social media should help put me to sleep. But instead of getting on social media and scrolling endlessly, I find myself on the Lane Enterprises website. I should know a little bit about the company I just applied to, right? Prospective employees shouldn't be going into any application process blind.

Then why aren't you looking up any of the other companies?

I push that thought away and continue my investigation.

You would think that after spending the last fifteen years of my life in Chicago, I would know something about one of the biggest companies the city has to offer, but I don't. All I know is the name and that everybody who is anybody wants to work there.

As I scroll through the website, it looks like the

company has a hand in a lot of things. Technology. Marketing. Security. From some of the news articles attached to the website, it looks like they're trying to get into other fields too.

I wonder what's holding them back.

After reading about what the company does, I start to look at who runs it. When I see it's a bunch of old men sitting in executive seats, I start feeling discouraged. If I get this job, am I going to be the youngest person working there? God, I hope not.

Finding the employee list a little discouraging, I head over to the history tab. Surely that's more interesting than who's running the place.

It takes a few seconds for the page to load, but when it does, it takes me a bit by surprise.

This portion of the website definitely has a different feel to it, especially once I start reading that Lane Enterprises started out as a family company, founded by Thomas Robert Lane and then later run by his son, Thomas Robert Lane the second, until his death twenty-four years ago.

That's sad.

I continue reading to check if possibly the third Thomas Lane took over after his dad died, but it doesn't say.

Interesting.

There wasn't a Lane on the list of employees I found either. I wonder what happened.

With my curiosity at an all-time high, I search the family. I've heard the name here and there, but I never really paid much attention. Just like I didn't know much about the company, I know squat about the family who formed it.

Apparently, I'm not the only one who looks up this family, because as soon as I type in the word Lane, they're second in the search suggestions.

My heart sinks when one of the first results is an obituary—not just for Thomas Lane the second, but for his wife as well.

"They died together?" I find myself whispering.

I don't know these people, but a lump forms in my throat out of sadness.

Reading how they died in a car accident on a rainy night has the lump growing, tears springing to my eyes when I read they left two kids behind: Robert, who was sixteen, and Bennett, who was eight. Robert has to be the third Thomas Lane; I wonder why he hasn't taken over the family business yet.

I scroll to the end of the obituary and find pictures of both Thomas and his wife, Catherine. They look so happy together. Did they go on a date night with all the hopes in the world of coming back to their kids?

Just thinking about it has tears falling down my face.

The tears continue as I swipe through the photos and find one of them with their two boys. They look so happy and carefree together, and all of that was taken from them.

Wanting to have something good to come from all of this, I leave the obituary behind and look up their oldest son, Robert.

Weirdly enough, nothing after his parents' funeral comes up. Did he die too?

That would make this story all the more tragic.

I really hope that isn't the case, though. Maybe he just doesn't want to be in the limelight, a more private person.

I really hope so.

After not finding anything on Robert, I move to looking up Bennett, and right away, I see that while there's nothing on Robert, there is plenty on his little brother.

Apparently, Bennett Lane is not only rich but also one of the most eligible bachelors in Chicago, if not the country. His face is on the covers of not only fashion magazines and tabloids but also tech and financial ones. The man is slated to become one of the richest men alive by the time he hits fifty—and he's only thirty-two.

What's even more shocking is that he hasn't been married yet, nor does he even have a girlfriend. From the looks of things, he is rarely seen out with a woman, and if he is, it's exciting to some and disheartening for others.

And given his looks, I can see why.

Bennett Lane is someone I don't know how to describe.

Gorgeous or handsome doesn't cut it. While he is those things, he's so much more at the same time. There's an edginess and possibly even a darkness to him that I can't explain, but I like it.

According to the news articles, he still lives in Chicago. I wonder if I've ever seen him in person, if we've been in the same restaurant or same grocery store.

I'm finding this whole family interesting, but more so Bennett. I have so many questions. I'm just chalking it up to curiosity, though, because Bennett and I live in two separate worlds. Yes, I applied for a position at his family's company, but that doesn't mean I'll actually get to meet the guy. I may never even be in the same room as him.

Feeling like I've gathered enough on the Lane family for the night, I exit out of the article I'd been reading and turn off my screen. I stare up at the dark ceiling, feeling more tired than I was earlier.

As a bit of the moonlight creeps into the room, I hope for a change.

I hope one of the applications I submitted tonight works out, because Charlie and I need it.

I hope I'm able to keep the promise I made five years ago and give my sister the best life possible.

I hope everything works out.

Sleep eventually takes me, but weirdly enough, it's with thoughts of Bennett Lane on my mind. I've never met the guy, but in my dreams, it feels like I have.

And in my dreams, just meeting him—meeting this man who is so far from reach that he's almost a god—changes absolutely everything.

If only that's what happens in real life.

3

BENNETT

It's dark outside.

As you stare out, you can't see where anything starts or ends.

The only light is coming from the house sitting behind us. Even the police car coming up the driveway has the lights off, making it seem like it's hidden in the darkness until it's only a few feet away.

Why are the police here?

We didn't do anything wrong.

We didn't break any rules, at least, I don't think we did.

Did Mom and Dad call the police to stop Robert from sneaking out of the house again? Is that why there's a police car here almost at midnight?

No. If this was about teaching Robert a lesson, Mom and Dad would be here, and they haven't come back from the party they went to earlier.

I should have told them to stay.

It was raining when they left, and it continues to rain now.

Bad things happen when it rains. I should have told them that, but I didn't want to seem like a baby. I'm eight years old, rain shouldn't scare me.

But right now, it does.

Right now, it's raining, and a policeman is walking over to Henry, but he's looking at me and Robert as we stand a few feet away.

I want to run to Henry and tell him that I'm scared, but I don't. I stay next to my brother and try to concentrate on his hand on my shoulder. I try, but he's squeezing my shoulder a little too hard, and it's starting to hurt.

I'm about to say something, but the policeman says my parents' names.

"I'm here in regard to Thomas and Catherine."

"What about them? They're not home at the moment." Henry sounds almost mad, but I don't know why.

The policeman looks at Henry, but then moves his eyes over to me and Robert again. He almost looks sad, like he wants to cry, but why?

"I'm sorry," he says, looking between the three of us. "There was a car accident. Both Thomas and Catherine didn't make it."

I don't need to be a grown-up to know what "didn't make it" means.

I know what those words mean as soon as they are said.

I know my parents aren't coming home.

Bad things happen when it rains.

I don't know what it is, but something shakes me awake, causing my eyes to pop open as if there was a terrifying monster behind my closed eyelids, and I needed to look into the light. But there's no light to look into, just the typical darkness.

It takes a few seconds to find myself again and to bring my breathing back to normal. My eyes stay open the entire time, because if I close them again, the nightmare might drag me back in.

Nightmare or memory?

At this stage in life, I don't know the difference between the two anymore. They both feel equally terrifying.

A deep breath flows through my body.

Months.

It has been months since a nightmare, or a memory of that fateful night, has hit me so hard. I think back to when the last one I had was, and all I can remember is that it was around my mother's birthday. Which was over seven months ago.

For a solid minute, I try to think about what might have triggered tonight's sleep distress, but nothing comes to mind.

It's not my father's birthday.

Or the anniversary of their death.

There's nothing significant about today's date, so why did the memories decide to hit me like a truck filled with a ton of bricks?

No matter how much time has passed, the death of my parents still haunts me, and there is no amount of therapy that will change that. Not even the most expensive kind.

A soft snoring sounds from somewhere next to me, and I instantly jerk toward it. I sleep alone, so the only snoring that should be sounding through the room is mine, and, well, I'm wide awake.

My eyes squint through the darkness and focus on a lump a few inches away from me, covered in all the blankets I'm sure are in the house. I don't need to move the covers off the lump to know that the ten-year-old made it to my bed sometime between putting him to bed and now.

A sigh escapes me.

It has also been months since he last snuck in here in the middle of the night, and I can't help but wonder if the same thing that triggered my nightmare triggered his.

Not wanting to wake the kid, I shift slightly and reach for my phone on the nightstand.

Five in the morning. Might as well get up, because there's no chance I'm falling back asleep now, especially not when the nightmare is still haunting me, and I know that a snorlax is sleeping next to me.

We really need to make a doctor's appointment to get his snoring checked out. There's no way those noises coming out of his small body are normal. I'll have Henry call later today to make an appointment.

As I get out of bed, the lump tosses and thrashes, and I take a minute to calm him down and get him settled again before heading downstairs to start the fucking day.

If someone had asked me ten years ago if I would willingly get out of bed at five in the morning to start my day instead of ending it, I would have laughed in their face, but here I am.

As I make my way down to the kitchen, the house has

this quietness to it that is sort of comforting and creepy at the same time.

The house being silent used to be a normal thing, since it was only Henry and me here most of the time, but when the kids arrived, it became a space of never-ending noise. To some, it would have been a nuisance, but to me, it's like fucking music. It's what the place needed after nearly fourteen years, and I'm not going to keep it from happening. Part of me wishes I could bring all that sound back right about now.

But times are different, no matter how much I wish they weren't.

With the kids on my mind, I quickly turn my phone on as I reach the stairs to the first floor and do the one thing I've been doing for the last ten years. Quickly search for my brother.

When nothing new comes up, same as yesterday, and the day before, and the days, weeks, months, and years before that, I slide the device into the pocket of my pajama pants.

Disappointment runs through my body, just like it always does when I look for Robert and nothing comes up, but when I get to the kitchen, I try to bury it as best as I can. I'm not the only occupant of this house awake this early in the morning, something that I'm not surprised to see.

Henry, the house caretaker and the man who raised me after the death of my parents, my pseudofather, sits at the kitchen island, a cup of coffee in his hand.

"You're up earlier than usual," I voice, walking over to

the coffee pot that smells like it has been brewing for a bit now.

Henry doesn't even jump at the sound of my voice. He just lifts his coffee cup at me in a way of greeting.

"I have a feeling today is going to be a bit chaotic, so I figured I'd get an early start, get things settled just in case they go off the wire."

His words stop me mid-pour, why would today of all days be a chaotic one?

Then I remember.

That has to be why the nightmares returned. There's no other explanation.

"I forgot about my meeting with Gerald today," I say as I pour the remainder of my coffee.

How I was able to forget that small piece of information is beyond me.

I've been waiting for Gerald to call me into his office for a "serious meeting" for almost two years now. When he finally scheduled one for today, it felt like all my efforts were finally paying off.

Gerald Goldman is one of Lane Enterprises' oldest employees and, what some people would describe him as, the rock of my family's company. Not only is he the oldest employee and longest serving, he is also the man that the Board of Directors made CEO almost a decade ago.

Did he know anything about running the company? Fuck no. Sure, some of his business acquisitions were phenomenal, but nothing he did warranted making him the head of the company.

The only reason the old man was given the job was

because I had finally expressed interest. My life had changed drastically for what felt like the millionth time in my life, and I needed to get my shit together, so I did what Henry had been telling me to do for years. Try and help build up the company in a way only a Lane could.

Did I expect to be named CEO right away just because I had finally come to my senses? No, but I also didn't think the board would hate me so damn much and give someone a permanent executive seat, one that had been filled intermittently by countless people, just because they didn't want me to walk in and claim the title.

That isn't something I could have done anyway, since it was stated in my father's will that neither of his sons could be named CEO before the age of thirty. It was something the idiot board would have known if they had actually done their homework, but they have their heads so far up their asses with overinflated egos that they don't do the proper research that is needed.

How the fuck they run a company of this magnitude is beyond me.

At least they won't be running it for much longer. Thank fuck for that.

"I'm surprised. You know, since this is something you've been planning for the last two years."

There's nothing stopping the smirk from forming on my face.

"Henry, I would never plan for a man to come to his senses, call me into a meeting, and announce he is leaving a position he has held for almost ten years," I say before taking a sip of my coffee and facing him head on, sarcasm heavy in my tone. I'm sure my smirk is still very well defined, even with a mug covering half of it. "I simply made a few suggestions to our friend Gerald, ones he hopefully took to heart and made the decision to retire on his own."

And they really were suggestions—strongly-worded ones, but suggestions nonetheless.

As long as there was someone occupying the seat, I knew I was always going to be a step further from what I wanted. So, I've been doing what I have to do to get Gerald out of his position.

Henry shakes his head at me before responding. "I'm surprised nobody has caught on to your little game, but apparently, I'm the only one who finds it odd for a thirty-two-year-old man to become friends with an almost-eighty-year-old."

"Nobody has found it surprising because they know I spend most of my free time with you."

"Are you calling me as old as Gerald, Mr. Lane? That man is a walking casket," Henry scoffs, sounding offended by the whole thing.

I shake my head. "You're old, old man. I think it's time to get used to it."

"I would take those words back if I were you. Just because you're in your thirties doesn't mean I'm not allowed to punish you anymore." He gives me the same eye roll I get from the teenagers who occupy the house. I guess I know where they get it from. "Gerald isn't able to run or play football with a ten-year-old, now, can he? How about learning to ice skate or shoot a puck because one of the kids wants to play ice hockey? The poor bastard is prone to breaking a hip coming down the stairs. I still have my coordination intact, thank you very much."

Jesus. This is not the tangent that I was expecting at five in the morning.

I wonder if I tell the man that the reason he can still do those things and Gerald can't is because of his military background and the fact that he still occasionally works out. Gerald just sits behind a desk.

"You seem offended," I throw out, my smirk growing.

"I'm no such thing. I'm simply pointing out a few facts."

"Of course you are." I finish my coffee before giving him my full attention. "Speaking of the ten-year-old, can you make Drake a doctor's appointment? His snoring doesn't seem normal."

The subject of Gerald and Henry being offended is instantly dropped at the mention of Drake.

"I'll call as soon as they open. Were you able to hear him from down the hall?"

I shake my head. "No. He ended up making it to my room sometime last night, and I heard the snoring when I woke up."

Right away, I notice the concern on Henry's face when I mention that Drake, my ten-year-old nephew, came to my room.

"Do you think the nightmares are back?"

I let out a sigh, wishing I had an answer. I won't know until I talk to Drake, and that's if he even tells me. Every time I ask him, he closes up and tells me he doesn't remember his dreams.

"If they are, that would make two of us."

My nightmares are understandable. I experienced a lot as a kid. With my parents dying and my brother walking out of my life a month later, my abandonment issues know how to make the dark stuff come out. But when it comes to Drake and his nightmares, I continue to scratch my head, as they come with more questions than they do answers.

When he came to live with me, he was too young to possibly remember anything he might have witnessed or experienced. He was just a baby. But I guess nightmares come at every age, because he had just turned one when I experienced his first nightmare, and it scared the living shit out of me. So much so that I rushed him to the emergency room because of how much and how badly he was screaming. Thankfully nothing was wrong with him physically, but the nightmares have persisted throughout the years.

Maybe his issues are similar to mine.

He was abandoned, after all.

Ten years ago, at the ripe age of twenty-two, I became the sole guardian of four kids I had no idea existed.

My older brother, Robert, the very one who, at the age of sixteen, decided to leave me behind to never see or talk to again, showed up one day on the doorstep of our childhood home with his four kids in tow.

He was in crisis. Something had happened back in Mexico, where he and his family called home, and he needed to get the kids out before things got bad.

"It's to protect them."

"If they stay there, Bennett, something could happen, and I won't be able to live with myself if it does."

"I promise, it won't be a permanent thing. I will be back. It will just be until things settle down."

"Please. Do this for them if not for me. Do this for them. I'm begging you, brother. Please."

At the time, it had been fourteen years since I last saw my brother. He had walked out one night about a month after our parents died, and he had never looked back, no matter how hard I wish he had. I didn't know the man standing in front of me. I wanted to be mad at him for thinking it was okay to come back to the home he left so out of the blue, but the kids, even though I didn't know a single thing about them, had me pushing the anger down.

I did try to make him see reason. I did try to make him stay. But as much as I fought with him to not leave his kids like he left me, other things took precedence for him, apparently, and he left anyway, leaving me to take care of his four kids.

Ten-year-old Elliot, seven-year-old Samantha, four-year-old Grayson, and ten-month-old Drake.

I didn't know the first thing about taking care of kids. Hell, that very morning Henry was giving me a lecture about how I needed to stop partying and drinking and at the very least try with the company that was left to me by my parents.

If I couldn't get my shit together, how the hell was I going to make sure four kids stayed alive? They didn't even know me. I was a literal stranger to them, and yet I was all they had at the moment.

It was a hard fucking road, but with Henry's help, I did it. And when my brother broke his promise about coming back, taking care of the kids became top priority.

I may not have been a dad, but I was going to act like a damn good one since the one the kids knew never came back for them. To this fucking day, I don't know where my brother is. I have all the resources in the damn world, and I can't find the one person I need to find. For all I know, he's dead, but until I have confirmation of that, I'm going to keep looking.

That day not only changed me—it changed the kids too. I didn't have to know who they were before to know that their dad leaving them here with me impacted their lives in ways they may never be able to talk about. Still, I have tried to give them the best life I could, and I think I've succeeded.

For the most part.

There have definitely been times where I was told I was hated by one of them.

"The nightmares are back, sir?" Henry's question takes me out of my own head.

"Just tonight. But I wouldn't call it nightmares, more like memories that can't seem to be forgotten."

"Sir," Henry starts, letting out a sigh. "What you went through as a child is not a normal thing. That is something you will never forget, no matter how hard you try or how much therapy you attend. It simply gets easier over time," Henry states, getting up from his seat and walking to the sink to dump out the remainder of his coffee.

I take a second to run through his words.

He's right.

Of course he's right. He always is.

But just because he's right doesn't mean I'm going to stop trying to keep the nightmares from coming. Or losing hours of the day to the dark memories seeping in.

Hopefully, the dream I had tonight is the only one for a while.

"Is there anything else you need from me this morning besides getting Mr. Drake a doctor's appointment?" Henry asks, changing the subject.

I give him a nod. "Can you deposit money into Elliot's account?" Maybe then he will actually answer one of my phone calls or come home. "And make sure Sammie and Grayson have everything they need at school."

There's a list of other things that need to get done in my head, but those are the most pressing ones.

"I'll get everything done as soon as I get Mr. Drake off to school."

"Thank you, Henry."

"Of course, sir. If there is anything else, just let me know. I will be at the office just in time for the board meeting this afternoon."

I grind my teeth at the mention of the board meeting. This is just your run-of-the-mill board meeting, where we talk about the quarterly numbers and future projections. The only reason I'm attending is because I inherited a seat on my eighteenth birthday. I hate attending them; they're boring as fuck.

The only board meeting I will look forward to is the one where Gerald announces his retirement.

The day the acting CEO is going to announce his retirement and officially stepping down from the company, all board members and executives will make their way to our downtown office for the official announcement, not only to see Gerald off and wish him well, but to also hear who Gerald picks to fill his seat before the board votes on his replacement.

And I'm hopeful that the last part is going to be pointed at me.

Not only because I deserve it, but I also did spend the last two years trying to convince Gerald that it would be a great idea to retire.

If Gerald wanted to go golfing after his children and grandchildren turned him down on more than one occasion? I took him golfing at the best courses the country had to offer.

He wanted to take his wife to a new restaurant that opened up down in Boca? I handed over my private jet and paid for their weekend away.

He wanted to talk business and ask me my opinion on certain acquisitions? I was his man.

In a short period of time, I not only became the man's confidant when it came to business but also his friend he sees almost like a son.

Was it sadistic of me to befriend an eighty-year-old man so I could take his job? Yes, yes, it was, and I will be the first to admit that I am, in fact, an asshole for it, but what Gerald doesn't know won't hurt him.

Besides, there were a lot more genuine moments

between us. Not everything was a lie. I'm not that fucking cruel.

But if I wanted to make sure the title of CEO landed on my head, I had to put in the work to get it done.

I have no doubt in my mind that Gerald will name me his replacement. What I do have doubts about is whether the board would vote me in.

There are a total of eighteen votes, and when that vote comes, according to our bylaws, I need ten to get the seat.

Off the top of my head, I know I have six solid votes, but that leaves four uncounted for.

Those four can make and break everything.

But what the board doesn't know is that I will stop at nothing to be named CEO.

This is my family's company. It's fucking time that all the power returns to where it belongs, in the hands of a Lane, where it will stay.

One way or another, I will be CEO. And if I have to put someone in the ground to do it, so be it.

I don't mind getting my hands dirty.

4

BENNETT

I look out the floor-to-ceiling window and marvel at the skyline of the city. This view is one I've seen more times than I can count, one I have marveled at since I was a kid, and one I will never get tired of seeing.

For years, I hated this view. I hated catching a glimpse of it—of thinking about it—because all it did was bring up memories I didn't want to think about.

Memories of my father and the time when this office was his. Memories of him working as my mother sat on the couch reading, me and my brother sitting at the small conference table doing homework as we waited for him to be finished.

For years, I didn't even want to step foot into this room, but things changed. Now, all I want to do is look at this view, at the Chicago skyline, every chance I get. Now I want to make this office mine and be okay with letting myself get lost in all the memories, both light and dark, that I have. No matter how torturous it is going to be. No matter if it brings up all the damn nightmares and makes me afraid to look into the darkness.

But in order to do that, in order for me to live with the nightmares willingly, I have to get rid of the current occupant, and from the way things are going, it doesn't look like that's going to be happening anytime soon.

I'm currently in my meeting with Gerald, and for the majority of it, all we've done is have lunch and talk about his wife and her new love for tennis. It has been almost two damn hours, with no mention of retirement or even stepping down just a tiny bit.

If the old bastard doesn't say something soon, I may have to bring in reinforcements to make it happen—and I'd rather make it come sooner rather than later. Just the thought of it has me itching to reach for my phone.

"Stop the daydreaming, kid, and help me with these potential new hires," Gerald says from the conference table.

The second this office becomes mine, I'm getting rid of that damn table.

Since I'm doing everything in my power to stay on this man's good side, though, I move my eyes away from the Chicago skyline and turn to face Gerald Goldman.

Henry might be right on the whole Gerald-is-on-his-way-to-a-casket thing. For as long as I can remember, the man has been in his eighties.

"New hires? I didn't think we were in the market for new people," I say as I take a seat across the aging Gerald.

"We aren't. Not executives or senior employees, at least.

This is for junior- and lower-level employees. Apparently, we have an influx of assistants quitting."

I can think of a few reasons why.

I may not hold Gerald's title, but I still very much know what the hell is going on within the company with my name on it.

Assistants are dropping left and right because their working environment is toxic as fuck. Don't get me wrong, there are some executives and senior employees who know how to treat the people there to make their life easier, but there are a handful of individuals who ruin it for everyone else—Gerald and some of our board members included.

I've heard stories of yelling, of making people cry, of sexual harassment. I fucking hate it, more so since the actions of these people reflect on me. If my father was still here—hell, even my grandfather—they would have gotten rid of the toxic cloud that has surrounded our company in a damn heartbeat.

As much as I want to do it, though, I can't. Not yet, at least. I may work here, but I don't have the power to fire Gerald or the others.

"Maybe we should be looking at why they're quitting and not just replacing them," I throw out, reaching for the first file.

Standard. Degree in law and applying to be a junior assistant for our marketing department? That would be a no. I'm not going to hire someone for marketing when their potential would be beneficial somewhere else. I take note of the name to send to my lawyer in case he's looking for associates and move on to the next one.

"People just don't want to work, Bennett. We give them everything they could ask for here, and yet they still quit two months in."

I hold in my scoff.

Everything they could ask for? That sentiment would have been true twenty-five years ago, but not now. They want a good working environment, and that is definitely not something they're getting here.

I don't say anything, though, because even though my name is on Gerald's check, my opinion on change isn't welcomed. So I just keep silent and continue with the task at hand.

For the next hour or so, Gerald and I look through the files of potential employees. I know for a fact there's a more productive way of doing this shit that doesn't take all damn day, but Gerald is old school and likes to do things the slowest fucking way possible.

I have no fucking idea how he runs this company.

Yeah, you do.

I've been in his back pocket acting like a puppet master.

And I will continue to be the puppet master until Gerald hands over his title.

"None of these candidates are worth hiring," Gerald lets out, practically throwing the file in his hand across the table.

I pick up the paperwork that landed in front of me and check it out. Right away, the name at the very top catches my attention.

Elizabeth Vincent.

For some reason, her name sounds regal, like she comes from money and has no reason to be calling the dingy address she lives at home.

Looking over her application, I see she holds a business degree but has no experience working in the corporate world.

Someone like her would be eaten alive working for Gerald. If we were to give her this assistant position she applied for, there is no doubt she would be added to the list of employees who quit in two months' time.

Ms. Vincent would be better suited to working somewhere else, but for some reason, I find myself wanting to offer her a position here. She may not have any experience, but she could be trainable.

I could use someone like her, someone with a bit of knowledge, especially after the disaster that was my last assistant. She could not only become an asset but a powerhouse as well.

"This one is promising," I state, finally closing the file and handing it back to Gerald.

He looks it over once more before closing it as quickly as he opened it. "Then we'll hire her if you think she can be useful to you."

I nod and make a mental note to have Linda offer her the position. If I don't claim her as mine, someone else might, and they'd destroy her.

Gerald speaks before I'm able to respond. "Just don't come to me complaining when she ends up quitting after two months."

I resist the urge to roll my eyes. There may have been a

time I'd been harsh or an asshole, but never like Gerald and some of our other senior employees.

I've never made anyone cry.

"I won't," I say to him. "I still think we should look deeper into why people are quitting."

"When you become CEO, you can look deeper into it," Gerald says nonchalantly.

Is this it?

Is this what I've been waiting for? It better fucking be.

"Like that's ever going to happen." I say the words, but they are just for show. It will happen, even with all the obstacles in my way. I just need damn Gerald to say the same words.

Even though I'm anticipating his next words, they still take me by surprise.

"It will happen. When I retire, I'm going to name you as my preferred successor," Gerald says, looking me straight in the eye, not wavering a single inch.

"And when will that be?" I ask, trying to downplay this conversation, downplay that I've been waiting for this moment for years now.

"In two months."

If I could, I would be grinning from ear to ear, but I keep my face as stoic as possible. "You're retiring?" The question that he expected me to speak leaves my mouth after a few seconds.

Gerald gives me a nod. "I am. I will be announcing it in a few weeks. I just wanted to tell you first."

Fucking hell. Finally. Step one is complete.

"I appreciate that, but are you sure about naming me as

your replacement? I can think of a few other people who would be better suited for the job." I'm talking out of my ass. There's nobody better suited for the job.

"I'm absolutely sure. You're young and know the company better than anyone else. Besides, this is what your father would have wanted. You at the helm and no one else."

Putting the file in my hand to the side, I hold out my hand to show my gratitude to Gerald.

"Thank you, sir. I can't tell you how much this means to me. I promise I will do you proud." It's a bunch of bullshit. If I'm doing anyone proud, it's my parents.

"You are very welcome. If anything, I have you to thank. If it wasn't for you, I wouldn't have figured out that you are right. There are other things more important in this world than work." For a second, Gerald goes silent, as if lost in thought. After a few seconds, he comes back and gives me a smile. "Now, don't go telling anyone about my plans. I don't want anyone putting things in either of our heads and telling you that you are not capable of running this company when you are."

I can think of a few people that would do just that.

"I won't, sir. Promise." My face may not show it, but there's a sadistic grin forming in my mind.

This is the official confirmation.

Thank fuck.

I'm one step closer to getting my hands on everything I want.

All I need is for the board to vote me in as CEO, and then I'll really be the damn king of Chicago.

5

———————

ELLA

Refresh.

Refresh.

Refresh.

I wonder if you hit refresh more than a hundred times on a single page if the function stops working after a while. Like is there some internal chip inside my computer saying that the chick on this website is going crazy, so let's stop working all together?

Plausible.

But I doubt this singular website is out to get me. It's definitely refreshing; it's just that what I want to appear on the screen isn't appearing as fast as I want.

Or you didn't get the job.

The stupid thought makes it into my mind, and it stays there for a solid ten seconds before I shake my head and blow the thought away.

Even though it's a huge possibility, I'm not going to think negatively until I officially have an answer.

Positive thoughts.

So many damn positive thoughts.

I let out a sigh and try to center myself as best as I can.

It has been a total of three weeks since the night I applied for the assistant position at Lane Enterprises. Truthfully, I had put my application on the back burner and concentrated on checking in with the other fourteen applications I put in that night. I never thought I was going to hear back, because why would I? I have no experience; they have no reason to call me in for an interview.

That was my mindset for three whole days, but on the fourth day, that changed drastically.

Why? I got an email from whoever was in charge of hiring with an interview offer.

I think my jaw hit the floor when I saw the notification staring back at me.

Me.

A freshly-graduated twenty-five-year-old with an MBA in her back pocket and no corporate experience whatso-ever got an interview at the one company she thought was a fever dream.

Jaw fucking dropped.

I couldn't believe it.

I still can't believe it, and I've already gone through the very long interview process. The fact that I even got one blows my mind, and my mind continues to be blown as I wait for a response from said interview. The lady who interviewed me, Linda, said an email should land in my inbox today.

I've been hitting refresh since five in the morning, and now, two hours later, no email has arrived.

Refresh.

No new messages.

Fucking perfect. Today is going to be a very long day.

Somewhere in the distance, an alarm goes off, and I let my head drop back. I was so entertained with refreshing my email, I completely forgot about getting, at the very least, a granola bar ready for my sister.

Great. This job is already a distraction. It's probably going to be a pain in the ass if I get it.

When.

When I get it, because I will be getting this job. Lane Enterprises would be stupid not to hire me.

You're stupid for obsessing so much about this job.

I need to shut my mind up from saying stupid shit.

With a groan, I place my laptop on the bed next to me and throw the covers off my body.

Time to get the day started.

As the second alarm of the morning goes off down the hall, I quickly get dressed in a pair of leggings and a T-shirt that probably has been in my closet since middle school before heading out to the kitchen.

The second I open the fridge, I let out a sigh. Grocery shopping is going to be at the top of the list for today because the amount of food we have is comical.

The same can be said about the amount of money I currently have in my bank account. Now that the major bills are paid, the amount I saw three weeks ago almost feels like damn pennies.

This just keeps getting more and more depressing, and it's not even eight in the morning yet.

Putting thoughts of my empty fridge and bank account out of my head, I start making egg sandwiches from the food we do have. As I toast the bread and scramble the eggs, I start going through what I need to get done this week and what needs to be paid. Not only is getting a job at the top of the list, right next to getting groceries, I also need to call the building super to check the dryer and the shower since both have been out of commission for the past three days. Rent is paid for this month, but electricity, internet, and cellphones are all due Friday.

Just the thought makes my eye twitch.

Looks like I'll be doing food delivery on top of my sixteen hours at the restaurant until I'm able to secure something better. If I get super desperate, I can always become a dancer or something. Put those two years of barre to good use.

I'm wrapping the egg sandwiches in foil when I hear footsteps coming down the hall. I look up just in time to see my little sister coming into the kitchen, looking like she wants to do anything but go to school.

"You look like you were electrocuted," I say out loud, not able to take my eyes off her hair. Her naturally wavy, dirty blond hair looks like it's in desperate need of a brush and a conditioning treatment. Her clothes are also all wrinkled, as if she pulled them from the deepest pits of her closet.

"My hair straightener decided to crap out not even halfway through doing my hair, and the clothes I washed yesterday still haven't dried yet, so I had to go looking for a shirt that wasn't ripped."

I guess calling the super just went to the top of the list. I add buying a new straightener to the bottom because I need it too if I continue to interview for jobs.

"I'm sorry, Char. I'll call the super as soon as he gets in. I should have called him sooner to come fix the dryer."

My sister, who is just sixteen years old, looks up at me with a small smile. "Don't apologize. I should be the one saying sorry. I shouldn't have made it seem like it was your fault. It's not. You have enough stuff on your plate as it is. You don't need a whiny teenager telling you how much the dryer sucks ass."

I throw her a smile and an eye roll. "You're not a whiny teenager."

"That's not what grandma used to say."

A part of me breaks when I hear that, but I don't let it show, because if I do, it's going to make Charlie feel even worse.

A part of me breaks when I hear that, but I don't let it show, because if I do, it's going to make Charlie feel even worse. I don't have a whole lot of memories of our shared grandmother; I never spent a whole lot of time with her. I do remember that the woman was a bitch in a half. It was as if every single fairy-tale villain was put into a pot and out came out her. She used to call me names, and I only spent a few hours with her. I can't imagine what she might have told Charlie, who spent years with her. There's no doubt in my mind that she spewed hateful things at my little sister and actually meant them, probably traumatizing Charlie even more.

I give my sister an eye roll.

"Yeah, well, that lady didn't know shit, so I wouldn't take anything she said to heart." I should believe what I preach, because there is shit that woman said that still haunts me at night.

"I'll do that if you do the same," my sister throws back, as if she could read my mind.

And sometimes, I think she can, especially with everything that we've been through.

Charlie and I didn't have the greatest upbringing. To say it was dull and unadventurous would be a disservice. Those two things would mean we actually had a childhood, a sad one, but still one we would talk about occasionally.

No, the upbringing we had can only be described as cold and cruel. More so for me, and if Charlie hadn't come to live with me, she probably would have had the same fate.

I spent my fair share of my life in foster care and group homes, and Charlie spent eleven years of her life being raised by a pair of individuals who would take their frustrations out on her.

I thank whatever god is up there for informing me I had a little sister when I was sixteen and that I was able to find her at eighteen. I had just left a group home, and for some reason, I decided it was a good idea to reach out to my mother. I didn't find her, but I did find out that Charlie was living with our grandmother. And her situation wasn't as picture perfect as I had hoped.

As soon as I found out about the situation my sister was in, somehow I was able to convince all parties to give me what I wanted. I was twenty; she was eleven. Bringing Charlie to live with me is something I'm still paying for—and possibly always will—but one I will never regret.

She's here with you now. That is all that matters.

Still, I have to push down the ball of emotions forming in my throat and act as if my mind didn't go into a dark place just because we mentioned our grandmother.

I slide a wrapped egg sandwich over to my sister. "Here. Eat this so you can get going. You don't want to be late for school."

I get a nod, and thankfully, not a single fight as the egg sandwich gets unwrapped and eaten. I follow suit, and for a few minutes, we eat our sandwiches in silence.

Charlie is the one to break it.

"Speaking of school," she starts, as if we had spent the last few minutes talking about her classes and not eating. "I got an email this morning."

At least one of us did.

"What kind of email?" I ask instead of letting my brain talk for me.

My curiosity is piqued. I'm not the only one who has been waiting for a very important email to hit her inbox.

"The kind that says my application to Saint Christopher's Prep Academy has been accepted."

I don't know what goes wide first, my eyes or my mouth.

"Like accepted *accepted*?" I sound like I'm in disbelief, and in a way, I am.

We've been trying to get Charlie into that school from day one of her coming to live with me. It's one of the best in the city, if not the state, and the waitlist is a decade long. Charlie's application was submitted close to a year ago, and since she's in her second year of high school, I for sure thought we would never see the day.

"Like accepted *accepted*," Charlie lets out, absolutely beaming at her words.

It only takes me two seconds to register what she said before we are jumping up and down, screaming, and celebrating.

"Omigod. Omigod. *Omigod!*"

I'm sure the neighbors can hear us, but we don't give a shit.

This is big news.

"I just wish I could accept it," Charlie lets out once all the giggling has stopped and I have my arms tightly around her.

Her words have me pulling back and giving her a good look. I'm sure if I looked in a mirror right now, my eyebrows would be bunched in confusion.

"Why wouldn't you accept it?" I ask her, trying to find something in her face that will give me an answer.

"Because it's expensive. We can't afford it."

Dread swims through my body as the words leave my little sister's mouth.

I'm failing.

Bringing her to live with me five years ago was so I

could give her a better chance at life, to give her the opportunities our grandmother and parents were so determined to take from her.

But even though I have been giving her a better life, we are still struggling. We still live paycheck to paycheck. I still worry about the necessities.

I've tried to hide our struggles from her—she doesn't need to worry about that—but I've failed in doing it right.

I look into the hazel eyes we both got from our mother and see sadness flowing through them. It breaks my heart.

She's right; we can't afford to send her to Saint Christopher's, but I'll be damned if I don't give her that opportunity.

I give my sister the most loving look I can muster. "Do you want to go?"

Her eyes narrow, as if she's trying to figure out what I'm getting at. "Of course I do. You know that."

"Then you're going," I state matter-of-factly.

"But Ella—"

"No, buts." I place my hands on either side of her face. "You are not turning down an opportunity like this."

She shakes her head. "There's no way we're going to be able to pay for it."

"You let me worry about that, okay? You just worry about finishing high school and getting into the best college you can." If I have to take on three or four jobs again to give my sister this, I will. I will not let her life go down the drain just because I don't have my shit together.

If I don't hear back from Lane Enterprises, then I will look elsewhere. A few of my friends were talking about how a new club just opened. I think the name was Perversa, and they were looking for dancers. I can do that.

You are willing to sell your body for money?

For my sister, I would. For her, I would do anything.

But maybe I don't have to go that far. Schools like Saint Christopher's must have financial aid available or scholarships Charlie can apply to. That school isn't just for the rich kids. Normal kids go there too. Once we get Charlie's enrollment settled, I will look into it.

Tears start to form in my sister's eyes as she digests what I just said. "Are you sure? It's not only tuition—it's also uniforms and books and room and board on campus." Her voice shakes a little, like she wants to be happy but can't find it in herself.

Fuck that.

She should be happy, always.

I give her the brightest smile I can muster. "Yes, I'm sure. Send me the email, and I'll see what we need to get you enrolled. We'll figure it all out."

Her arms make it around my neck, and she knocks all the air out of me. "Thank you. Thank you. Thank you, Ella. I promise to do good and get good grades and get a job to pay for everything."

I hug her back just as tightly and shake my head when I pull back. "Nope. No job. You go to school, and that's it. Well, you play sports and join the drama club or whatever other club you want, but that's it."

I get an eyebrow raise, but I just raise one back.

For a solid minute, my sister and I have a silent stand-off, challenging the other. Like always, though, I win.

Charlie rolls her eyes and gives in. "Fine, but the second you need me to get a job, I will."

"If it ever comes down to that, you will be the first one to know."

My sister stares at me for another solid minute before a smile spreads across her face and she starts bouncing again. She bounces for a solid two minutes before she stops and slaps a wet kiss against my cheek.

"I love you. You are the best big sister ever."

"I know. You've told me a time or two. But you make it easy being the best little sister ever," I say back, my smile copying hers. "Now get out of here and get to school. We'll talk more when you get home about Saint Christopher's."

There's a bounce to her step as she leaves the kitchen to grab her book bag, and that bounce is still there when she heads out the front door.

She looks so damn happy. I wish I could be that happy with her, but the second the door to our apartment closes, a wave of worry washes over me. I just told my sister she's going to a private school that I'm sure costs more than anything I will ever own, and we don't even have food in our fridge to last us until the end of the week.

Stupid.

Stupid.

Stupid.

I don't even have a full-time job, for crying out loud; I have no stable income to even secure rent for the next three months, and yet I told her yes to a school that costs a fortune, and I won't be going back on my word.

She will be going to that school, and I will do anything and everything to keep her there.

Dancing is starting to look better and better by the second, I'm not going to lie. I should look at the job boards again to see if anything new has been listed before I start picking out my stripper shoes.

Maybe the email from Lane Enterprises has finally hit my inbox.

Maybe, but I highly doubt it.

Letting out a sigh, I clean up the messy kitchen, make a list of groceries that won't make my bank account weep, and finally call the super to check out our dryer and shower. Once all that is said and done, I head back to my room and throw myself on my bed.

I shouldn't have gone back to school, even if it was an online program. I could have saved that money to pay for Saint Christopher's instead of wasting it on a master's degree that apparently isn't enough to get a job in the real world. But I wanted to be selfish for once and do something for me. Now, it's biting me in the ass.

Stop with the pity party and do something to better the situation.

Half the time, my brain thinks of the stupidest shit, but right now, it's right on the mark.

With a groan, I sit up and grab my laptop. The screen is frozen where I left it. If I didn't want to check if Charlie forwarded me the email from Saint Christopher's while she rode the bus, I would leave the screen as is and not even touch the computer for a whole week.

Not wanting to think about it more than I already have,

I hit refresh for what could be the two-hundredth time today and watch as the screen populates.

One second passes. Then two.

Five seconds after I hit the refresh button, the screen shows my inbox again, but this time, instead of saying no new messages, two messages pop up at the top of the screen.

One from Charlie with the forwarded acceptance email.

And another from the hiring department at Lane Enterprises.

No fucking way.

I feel my eyes bulge, and it feels as if I stopped breathing. That feeling intensifies when my eyes scan over the subject line.

A straight-to-the point subject line.

Welcome to the team.

Holy shit.

I got the job.

I got the fucking job!

My fingers can't move fast enough as I click on the email and read through the contents of it a total of four times.

It's an official offer.

Lane Enterprises sent me, Ella Vincent, an official offer to work at their company.

I must be dreaming.

To make sure I'm not, I pinch my thigh, and when the pain radiates, I know I'm wide awake.

"Holy crap. I did it."

Instead of jumping for joy like I did with Charlie, I let the few tears stinging my eyes fall.

I needed this. I didn't want to admit it, but I really needed this job. Sure, it seems like it's entry-level, but the pay is good, and the benefits are even better, and if I want Charlie to continue to stay with me, I needed something like this to come to me.

Now, it has.

I got the job.

But now, I have to make sure I'm the best damn assistant I can be, because I cannot afford to lose it.

6

BENNETT

"Can I go to work with you today instead of school?" The question comes from the stool next to me as I finish up my breakfast.

Today is one of those rare mornings when I don't leave the house before seven in the morning in hopes I'm able to catch an investor over in Europe before they finish up their workday. I try to have these late mornings as often as I can, especially since Drake is the only one of his siblings living at home full-time. Now that the CEO title is close to being on my head, I'm trying to get in as many late mornings as I can before the job consumes me.

I turn slightly to look over at my nephew as he slurps up the remainder of his cereal.

"Why the hell would you want to go to work with me?" I say, and as soon as the question leaves my mouth, the ten-year-old turns to look at me like he caught me stealing one of Henry's cookies from the baking sheet.

"That's five dollars in the swear account, please," Drake almost sings.

I roll my eyes and take out my phone to transfer five dollars into one of the many savings accounts I have for the kids that was so infamously labeled as the swear account a few days after they arrived on my doorstep.

You would think after ten years, I would have figured out not to swear when the kids are around, but apparently not. I still get caught, and, depending on the words, a certain dollar amount gets deposited into the account.

I'm positive that by the time Drake reaches college, there will be a few million in the swear account.

After moving the money over, I show the kid so he can verify I did indeed deposit money. When he gives me a nod, I can't help but roll my eyes again.

And to think, I used to find this cute.

"Now answer the question. Why do you want to go to work with me?"

Out of all the kids, Drake is the one who likes school the most. He never willingly wants to miss a day of school, and it has to be in-person school with teachers and other students around him. I've learned from the countless trips I have taken him on during the school year that he hates having to learn virtually or with a tutor one-on-one. So the fact that he wants to skip school to go into the office for the day is surprising. It wouldn't be the first time he has gone to work with me, but it would be the first time he has done so while school was going on.

The kid gives me a shrug and concentrates on the remainder of his cereal a little too hard.

"I don't know. I just think it would be fun."

Fun.

There have only been a handful of times where he has called going to the office with me fun. When we had the World Series trophy in our building for a week after Chicago won their first championship in a hundred years a few years back. When an actor from one of his favorite superhero movies stopped by the office to talk about investing in one of our products. And the last one was when there was a snowstorm that got so bad, we had to camp out in my small office for the night.

Today has none of those things, so it would be anything but fun. Something has to be up.

"Fun, huh? You want to sit in my office all day while I have meetings?" The question earns me a little shrug. Something is really up. Putting my fork down, I turn to face Drake. I will get to the bottom of this. "What's going on, Bub? You never want to miss school, not if nothing fun is going on."

Drake's shoulders continue to slump as he starts to play with his cereal.

My mind goes to the worst-case scenario.

"Is someone bothering you at school? Is that why you don't want to go?" I get a shake of the head telling me no. "Okay, then what is it? You can tell me. You can always tell me what is going on."

I'm not his dad biologically, but I am the closest thing he has to a parent. So, I'm going to act like one, even if there are times when the kids hate it. If something is going on with them, I want and need to know. They know that they can depend on me no matter what.

I watch as the kid I raised plays with his cereal until he eventually sighs and looks up at me.

"It's Parents' Day at school today, and everyone's mom and dad is going to do arts and crafts with them and have lunch together. My parents aren't going to be there, so I want to go to work with you."

A part of me breaks when I hear him say his parents aren't going to be there—not because his parents left him, but because I know he's not talking about me. I may act like a parent, and legally, I'm his guardian, but I will always just be his uncle.

"Why didn't you tell me about Parents' Day? I can go with you. I won't go to work, and we can go do arts and crafts and eat nasty school food for lunch. It will be fun." I try to keep the hurt out of my voice as much as I possibly can.

I get a smile from Drake, but it doesn't reach his eyes. The smile nearly disappears when he shakes his head.

"Everyone is going to ask why my dad is there and not my mom, and I won't know what to say."

That small part of me fixes itself when he mentions the word dad.

"We can make something up, like she's in space or down in Antarctica with the penguins."

A sweet laugh rolls out of his body. "There aren't any penguins in Antarctica, Uncle Bennett. They are up in the North Pole."

"I don't know where you got that information from,

kid, but there are penguins in Antarctica." I start tickling him, and his laugh fills the whole damn kitchen. "I need to take you to a museum, because that expensive school of yours is not teaching you the right stuff."

His laugh continues to fill the space even as I stop with the tickle attack, my laugh combining with his.

"So what do you say? We go to this Parents' Day and tell them all about the penguins in Antarctica."

As much as I wish the situation with their parents was different, I can't change anything. It has been ten fucking years, and no matter how much I look for my brother, nothing will ever change the situation. My brother left them with me, and their mom—well, I don't know if she is dead or alive, and I don't give enough fucks to find out.

Drake is silent for a minute, probably thinking about my proposition. For a second or two, I think he is going to say yes, but the kid surprises me when he shakes his head.

"I still don't want to go, but instead of work, can we go to the museum?"

My schedule pops up in my head, and I run through everything that I have to do today and see if there is any wiggle room. There's a few meetings I can skip, but today is my first day with my new assistant, one I know nothing about. I need to get a feel for her, make sure she's not some plant sent out to get information on me or inept. Sure, I told Linda to hire her, but given that my last assistant was a damn mole, I'm not taking any chances.

"How about this? You skip school and spend the morning annoying Henry, and then after lunch, you two head to the office, and we will go to the museum from there. How does that sound?"

"It sounds awesome! I'm going to go call Grayson and Sam and tell them you're letting me skip school!" He runs off, abandoning his bowl of milk-flavored cereal.

There is no doubt in my mind that by the end of the week, I'm going to have two teenagers in my kitchen, eating everything they can think of, skipping school because I let Drake stay home today.

Better have Henry send out for some groceries.

The man in question apparently read my mind because he walks into the kitchen looking at me like he has some questions.

"Mr. Drake just ran past me, yelling something about not going to school and going to a museum. Something about penguins." He raises his eyebrows at me, like he wants to reprimand me for my decision.

When it comes to parenting, Henry is definitely the strict grandpa who folds whenever one of the kids throws puppy dog eyes at him. He is a military man, after all, so he wants things to go a certain way. He was like that when he raised me, and he is like that with my brother's kids.

Me, on the other hand? I can be strict, but I also let the kids get away with a lot more than I should.

I get up from my seat, grabbing our plates and walking them over to the sink before answering Henry. "Did you know that today is Parents' Day at Drake's school?" I ask.

Henry looks as surprised as I felt.

"No, I did not." He pulls out his phone, probably to see

if the school sent an email about it. "Who the hell sends a notification of something like this the day of?"

I can't help but laugh, but the laughter quickly fades when I get a death glare.

"When they notified us isn't important. What is important is that Drake doesn't want to go. He doesn't know what to tell the other kids when they ask about his mom or why his dad is there and she isn't. He actually wanted to go to work with me instead, but I suggested he just stay here, and after lunch, you two can come by the office and we will go to the museum."

Henry mulls it over, and I start to wonder if he is going to go on his whole spiel about structure and education.

"Right. Well, I'm sure Mr. Drake will learn more from a museum than from a classroom today. I will make sure to get tickets for this afternoon."

"Thank you, Henry."

Noting the time, I start to gather my things to head to the office.

Can't keep my new assistant waiting, now, can I?

Ella

I never thought I would see this day.

I'm looking in the mirror while wearing business

professional attire with a full face of expired makeup, my hair actually looking nice, ready for my first day at a company.

When I decided to go back to school, I thought about this day, when I would wake up and make a name for myself in the business world. I thought that if the day did ever come, it would be far, far in the future, but it's here.

It's fucking mind-blowing.

Not only was I able to get a second degree, but I got a job at Lane Enterprises. Do I know exactly what I'll be doing? No. Which is fine—I will learn on the job.

Hopefully.

I'm keeping my fingers crossed that I don't get fired on day one.

And why would they fire me?

Well, I've never been anyone's assistant. I can barely handle organizing my own life; what makes me think I can do that for someone else?

I'm secretly hoping there's training involved, even if it wasn't stated in my welcome email.

Assistants get trained, right? Let's hope they do. If not, then my nerves will really get the best of me, and then I will be saying goodbye to this job.

Not wanting to let my nervousness win this morning and mess up anything about my appearance, I decide that it's time to get a move on with my day. I can't stay in this room forever, no matter how much I want to.

You can do this. Today is your day, and you are going to do great.

Great. Today, I will do great.

The pep talk helps enough, and after giving my reflection a smile, I turn and finally head out to the kitchen.

It's a lot earlier than when I've been starting my day lately, which means I won't see Charlie off when she goes to school or make sure she eats breakfast. Still, starting my day earlier means that I'll not only be able to keep a roof over our heads and our fridge stocked but also pay for Charlie to go to Saint Christopher's.

After I got my offer letter, I didn't hesitate in accepting. I wrote Linda back within ten minutes, thanking her profusely for giving me the job—even more so after I saw the salary and the signing bonus that was attached to it.

Apparently, the old men who run that company pay their employees well, no matter how low their position. When I saw the number, I understood why people wanted to work there so much.

What I make at this job is going to be more than I have made in all my other jobs combined. Not only does it pay well, but the signing bonus is enough to help with half of Charlie's first year at Saint Christopher's. I just have to come up with the other half.

So as soon as Linda got back to me with all the final paperwork and my official start date, I pulled out the email Charlie had received and accepted her admission. More paperwork was requested of me for a damn private school than what I needed to submit for my new job. But it was done, and Charlie is set to start in two weeks; all we need to do is buy her a uniform and pay what we can with my signing bonus.

After pouring my travel mug full of tea, I leave some

cash for Charlie on the counter so she can buy something to eat on her way to school and head out the door.

I don't realize it until I'm on my second bus, but there is so much excitement rolling through my body. I know people usually would be scared or nervous about their first day at a new job, and even though I *am* feeling those things, excitement overpowers them.

This is the first page of a new chapter in my life.

The last couple of years have been hard, but it's finally looking up, and that is definitely something to be excited about. I should celebrate this new step in life with some wine, maybe some chocolate. I'll stop by the store on my way home and see what I can get my hands on.

For the remainder of my commute, three buses in total, I drink my tea and do something I haven't done in a long while: let my mind wander to all the doors this new job can open.

I don't usually let myself hope for things because life is cruel and can take everything away in a split second, but with this job, I can let myself hope, even if it's a little bit. With this paycheck, not only would rent and food and Charlie's school be taken care of, but with extra money under my name, I could pay off my debt a lot quicker.

That thought causes a lump of emotions to form in my throat, and not the good kind.

My debt isn't the normal type of debt people my age get into. There is no credit card or school debt. No, my debt isn't the normal kind. Mine is tied to my sister, and if I don't pay it off, I will lose her, and she will be right back to living a life she doesn't deserve with people who don't love her, who only want to use her for their personal gain. I'll be damned if I ever let that happen.

My mind drifts to a dark place, one where Charlie is crying in a corner, a figure looming over her.

Never. She will never go through anything that traumatic.

When the bus driver announces the next stop, I push the lump forming in my throat down and try to compose myself as best as I possibly can.

Get back to that excitement bubble from earlier. Don't let the darkness take over.

I can do that.

After a few deep breaths, I'm close to being back in the headspace I was in when I left the apartment. Not one hundred percent there, but close enough that I can put a smile on my face and actually mean it.

When the bus comes to a full stop, I'm in a better mental state, and it gets slightly better the closer I walk to the Lane building in downtown Chicago.

By the time I arrive, I feel like I did when I woke up this morning—so much excitement rolling through my body that I have to take a second to take it all in.

This is actually happening.

Sure, it's just an assistant position, something anyone could do, but it's a step in a good direction. An amazing direction. A direction I know for a fact many of my classmates would kill for. Makes me wonder just how many people in my class I beat out for this position. Surely there was someone more qualified for this job than me.

Who cares? I got the job, not them.

That's the mindset I try to stay in, but the more I look up at the building and take it all in, the more I feel the nerves, the more I feel like puking in the flowerpots by the doors.

You got this. You will not puke in the flowerpots.

"You got this."

I got this. I really, truly do. I just need to move my feet and walk into the building.

My mind may be ready for this new adventure, but apparently, my body is not.

"Just start walking. One foot in front of the other, and you will be inside the building."

"Never heard anyone giving themselves a pep talk to walk into a building before," a deep voice says from somewhere behind me, startling me.

With my heart beating a million beats a minute, I turn toward the voice, and for a second, I lose all train of thought.

Standing not even three feet away from me, close enough to touch, is one of the most gorgeous men I have ever seen. A gorgeous man I'd spent more time than I care to admit looking at through pictures of online.

Bennett Lane.

His dark brown hair is perfectly styled. His eyes look like they would look blue in some lights, possibly a version of green in others. A well-put-together face, scruff that covers his jaw.

My mind is going crazy with one singular question: why is this man, whose pictures don't do him justice, standing so close to me or even talking to me? Why did he approach me?

As much as I want to ask those very questions, I can't force myself to actually speak. I feel my mouth open, but not a single word comes out.

I don't know how long I continue to gape at this gorgeous man, but I do.

Great. My first day at a new job, and I'm already making a fool out of myself.

7

ELLA

There are a few ways I thought my first morning at Lane Enterprises would go. Running into a member of the family the company was named after before I even set foot into the building was not something I had at the top.

Bennett Lane is sex on a damn stick.

He's sex on a stick, and here I am, gawking at him as if he were butt naked in front of me.

It's with that thought that I snap out of the weird stupor he put me in.

"I'm sorry," I stutter out, completely confused about what I'm apologizing for.

Bennett—or does he go by Mr. Lane?—smirks down at me. I may be imagining it, but he definitely feels closer to me than he did a second ago.

His height takes me a bit by surprise. He has to be over six foot something, because I'm five-six and wearing a small heel, and I still have to look up at him.

"What exactly are you apologizing for?"

That's the same question I'm asking myself. I try to come up with an answer before I make a bigger idiot of myself, but it seems like I'm failing.

Way to go, Ella.

"Sorry," I say again, but I find myself quickly shaking my head because why am I apologizing again?. "You startled me a bit when you spoke."

The way this man looks at me has me wishing for a black hole to open and suck me through or peel off all my clothes. I can't quite figure out which one.

"So what you're saying is that I should be the one apologizing?" The smirk this man wears is affecting me in ways it shouldn't.

I may know this man's name and who his family is, but apart from that, Bennett Lane is a complete stranger. Sure, he is a handsome stranger, but still a stranger nonetheless. His hot little smirk shouldn't have me wanting to cross my legs to keep a certain part of me from throbbing.

I don't realize that I'm taking way too long to answer the man's comment before he continues, throwing me off with his next few words.

"I'm sorry. I shouldn't have approached you without any warning."

I can't help but give him a confused look. Is he apologizing because he really means it, or is he just apologizing to keep this whole bit going?

Who knows; the tone of his voice isn't giving anything away, but that doesn't matter. What matters is that having this man's attention on me has a blush creeping up my neck and covering my face. There is no reason I should be blushing right now.

I try to shake off my embarrassment before I continue, my voice barely audible. "Don't worry about it. I was being a little weird. Most people don't talk to themselves, let alone try and convince themselves to walk into a building. It's my first day, and the nerves decided to hit hard the second I walked up."

I don't know why I chose this time to start rambling. I'm just killing it with the good impressions with this guy.

Speaking of which, he just continues to look down at me, his facial expression blank. You would think I would get at least a smile when I told him it was my first day.

Is he always like this?

Bennett continues to look down at me for a few more seconds before he speaks again. This time takes me by surprise again, but this time for a whole different reason.

"Which department are you working in?" he asks, sliding his hands into his pants pockets, all while taking a step back.

"Um." I scramble to grab my phone and look for the answer to his question. It takes me a full minute to pull up the email Linda sent me yesterday with all the instructions for today. You would think with how many times I read through the email, I would have it memorized by now.

"It doesn't say," I finally tell him as I read through the email for what feels like the hundredth time. "I was just told to come here, head up to the eighth floor, and report to Linda."

I look back at Bennett and give him a small smile, and surprisingly, I get one back. A small smile, but I'm taking it as a win.

"What's the position?" he asks with curiosity in his voice.

"Oh, I'm just coming on as an assistant. Nothing important."

For some reason, the smile of his starts to disappear as the seconds go by, making me think that this guy doesn't find assistants are important either.

But he doesn't come out right and say that. He just takes another second to look me up and down, almost like he's assessing me with those blue, almost green, eyes of his.

Not being able to take the scrutiny, I look away from him. I can already feel his judgment.

Instead of looking up at his face, I take in what he's wearing. A designer suit that fits his body beautifully. It probably costs more than my rent, and it's probably one of a few hundred made specifically for the man wearing it. It fits almost like a glove, molded specifically for his body.

"Can I give you a piece of advice?" he asks me, taking me out of my exploration of his form.

Without a second thought, completely embarrassed about my perusal, I look back up at his face. "Yes. Absolutely."

I should have told him no. He's probably going to tell me that working for a company like Lane Enterprises is going to destroy me, that I should probably reconsider and go look for a job somewhere else.

"Don't sell yourself short. It doesn't matter if you're working here as a security guard, a mail recipient, an executive, or an assistant. Your job is important. *You* are important."

It takes me a second to register what he says, and when I do, I'm at a loss for words. *Again.*

Here is someone who is a billionaire, someone important, especially when I look behind him and see what looks to be not one but two security guards standing close by, ready to pounce in case they need to. He probably has other important things to be doing, but here he is.

It takes me a second to collect my thoughts before I'm able to respond. "Do you say that to everyone, or just the individuals you find outside the building, trying to talk up the courage to walk inside?"

That makes him laugh, and oh my god does it do something to my insides.

This is not the time to get butterflies, Ella. Or for blushing. Or holding your thighs tighter. Control yourself.

"I try to say that to everyone."

"Gee, and here I thought I was special."

That earns me another laugh, but this one is a bit throatier and a lot fuller than the last one. Again, it does something to me.

Great. My first day on the job, and I already have a crush on someone who may not be my boss, but my boss's boss, and who I'm possibly going to see every day.

"You're definitely something." The words come out of his mouth, and it takes both of us by surprise.

I try to ignore the words altogether, but it becomes a

little difficult when hearing those words just heightens whatever I'm feeling even more.

But nonetheless, I push the words out of my mind and whatever I'm feeling down and just give him a small smile. "I should head in," I say, waving toward the front door of the building. "My workday is about to start, and I can't be late."

"How about I help with the nerves a bit and walk you up to Linda? Wouldn't want you to chicken out in the elevator."

This guy is full of surprises, isn't he?

If I were him, I would have concluded I was weird and let me walk into the building alone to never speak to me again.

"Why would you do that?" I find the question leaving my mouth without much thought, ignoring the elevator comment.

He gives me a shrug, his hands never leaving his pockets. "Because I want to, and it saves you from getting lost and me from the meeting I'm supposed to be attending."

A no-bullshit answer.

I should say no, that I can find my own way, especially since I'm sure that the meeting he has to attend is important. I mean, he is a Lane, after all; I'm sure all the meetings he attends are important.

Yet, I still find myself giving him a nod. "Okay. Lead the way, but if I'm late, I will be sure to tell Linda it was your fault."

He waves toward the entrance of the building, the smirk still very present. It doesn't go unnoticed that when he moves, the security guards behind him move too. Interesting.

"You won't be late, but if you are, have Linda call whoever you are reporting to and tell them it was my fault."

His fault. There's a cockiness to his voice that I like a little too much.

I don't respond. Instead, I keep quiet and try not to get overwhelmed with everything going on as we walk into the building.

There are so many people roaming around as they head to wherever they need to go to start their days. Everyone looks like they are dressed to the nines, so well put together in an expensive way. For a second, it makes me self-conscious about my thrifted outfit.

That self-consciousness continues when everyone within a few feet turns to look at me as they walk by.

Do I have something on my face?

It's not until we reach the security section of the lobby that I realize people aren't looking over at me, they are looking at who is walking me up to the eighth floor.

"Good morning, gentlemen," the butterflies-causing Bennett says to the security team checking everyone's bags and ID cards. "This is a new Lane employee." He waves in my direction. "She most likely doesn't have her credentials just yet, so you can put down that I'm vouching for her."

One of the security guys nods and starts typing something on his tablet before turning to look at me. "Can I get a name, Miss?"

"Ella Vincent. Or Elizabeth Vincent, if you want my full name."

When I say my name, it doesn't go unnoticed that Bennett tenses up ever so slightly. I probably imagined it, though, since he composes himself just as quickly.

My attention goes back to the security guy, who gives me a nod and waves us through without searching my bag or even having us walk through the metal detectors. Apparently, when you're Bennett Lane or walking in with him, you get special treatment or something.

Another thing I notice is that the deeper we get into the building, the more rigid Mr. Lane gets. He didn't smile much outside, but at the very least, he didn't have what looked like a permanent scowl on his face. It's like this place sucks the life out of him.

"Do you like working here?" I ask, keeping the real question I want to ask away from my mouth. What does he do here? The website had no mention of him working here, nor did one of the thousands of articles written about him. They mentioned he ran another company called Titan, but there was no mention of working at his family's company, which added to my surprise.

A weird look passes across his face, but only for a second before it disappears, replaced by a look of indifference. "Sure."

Sure? That's a shit answer if I've heard one.

"That's what someone on their first day should be hearing," I mutter sarcastically as an elevator dings and I get into the steel cart.

Bennett follows behind me and presses the button for floor eight before turning to me and facing me head on.

"Do I like what I do? Without a doubt. Do I like who I'm doing it for? Depends on the day."

Still not reassuring.

"So what you are saying is that there's a slight chance I'm going to hate whoever's assistant I become."

"I can reassure you, the person you are going to work for may be an asshole at times, but he will try to make sure you actually like coming into work. They aren't someone who wants to bring this company down." The look in his eyes when he says those words causes a shiver to roll through my body.

I'm about to question his comment, to ask him how he knows, but the elevator dings as it comes to a stop on the eighth floor, causing my question to go out the window when I realize I'm seconds away from reporting for my first day at work.

Things just got a lot more real.

As I walk off the elevator, I half expect for Bennett to stay in the elevator and go on his merry way, surely that meeting that he is late for is important, but again he surprises me and walks off, waving for me to follow him away from the elevator. He doesn't turn to look at or talk to me the whole time as he guides me past desks and people, or even when we reach a glass door with Linda's name on it.

"Linda, I have your new hire."

Linda, a beautiful woman who might be in her fifties, looks up at the sound of his voice. By the way her eyes bulge, I would say she is very surprised to see him standing in the doorway to her office.

"Bennett," she says, taking control of her facial expression and giving the guy a smile. "Out of all the people I expected to see this morning, you were not one of them."

"Is that your way of telling me I need to visit more?" Bennett says with the same ease in voice he had when we were downstairs.

"No, because you visiting me means more work," Linda tells him, getting up from her desk. She holds out a hand to me. "You must be Elizabeth. It's nice to meet you. I'm Linda."

I shake her hand without hesitation and give her a smile. "It's nice to meet you too. You can call me Ella."

She gives me a curt nod. "Ella it is."

I get a smile back, and for a few seconds, we stand in awkward silence. Me looking at her. Her looking at me. Both of us looking over at Bennett.

Linda is the one to break the silence. "I'm sure you have other important things to do today." The smile she wears looks sweet, but her words feel like they are anything but.

I turn to look over at Bennett and notice his face is back to being stoic.

"Unfortunately." He answers her before turning his attention back to me for the first time since the elevator. "Have a good first day, Miss Vincent."

Just like a few minutes ago, his words affect me. They shouldn't, but they do.

It's the way his voice speaks to my body; no matter how

gruff he sounds, it's like a song that is fine-tuned to everything flowing in me.

I don't notice that my eyes stay with Bennett as he makes his way out of Linda's office and down the hall until Linda clears her throat and grabs my attention. She gives me a small smile before nodding me deeper into her office.

"Do you know Bennett personally?" Linda asks once Bennett is out of sight. She waves for me to take a seat in one of the chairs in front of her desk.

I follow orders and give her a shake of my head. "I met him downstairs only a few minutes ago. He's…" What is the best way to describe my interaction with Bennett? "Interesting."

The word doesn't seem like enough, but I can't have Linda knowing I have a crush on the man after spending no more than ten minutes with him.

"Interesting is one way to describe him," she mutters as she takes a seat. When she looks back at me, her eyebrows are bunched. "So you don't know him whatsoever?"

"No, ma'am."

"He just decided to walk you up here for no reason?"

Her questioning is making me uncomfortable, so much so that I can't help but shift in my seat. "Is that out of character for him?"

Linda is silent for a few seconds before she says anything. "Yes. Yes, it is. More so because he was the one who hired you."

What the actual fuck? He hired me? *Me*? I'm sure that even though this is a low-status position, there had to be hundreds of applications. So out of all those applications, he chose *me*?

So many questions roam through my mind as Linda gives me a crash course on all my employment forms that I don't even pay attention to her.

As I sit here, listening to her speak, I can't help but wonder who Bennett Lane really is.

Why did he deem me so special?

8

———————

BENNETT

The second I walk out of Linda's office, I feel as if someone is watching me, just like I did the second I stepped onto this floor. As I head back to the elevator, I ignore all the eyes looking my way. You would think I was in a fucking monkey suit with how hard people stare in my direction. I know I barely make it out of my office most days, but it's ridiculous. If I were a different man, I would fire every single person on this floor just because their stares irritate me.

But I'm not that cruel.

Well, I am, but they don't need to know that.

As soon as I'm in the elevator and away from the infuriating stares, I pull out my phone and log into the company database. The urgency to learn everything I can about my new employee rolls through my body like a damn tidal wave.

Growing up, my parents and Henry would attend school conferences regarding my lack of attention when it came to certain subjects. It was something that extended well into high school. I wasn't as enthused about learning about English and history as I was about science or math, they would say. Those were my two favorite subjects, but to some of my teachers, that didn't matter; they wanted my attention no matter what.

Thankfully, my parents and Henry were on my side, and on more than one occasion, they informed the educators that it takes a lot for my attention to be captured. If they weren't getting it, then they were doing something wrong.

To this day, it still takes a lot for someone or something to capture my full attention. My concentration should be on the CEO position and that alone.

But all of that went to shit when I saw her.

From the angle of my car this morning, I was only able to see her back, but apparently, that was enough to have my eyes glued, taking in every inch of her as if she were mine for the taking.

Why she captured my attention, I have no idea, but she did, and as soon as my driver opened the car door for me, I started making my way to her. I had a meeting with a tech company in Australia, but they could wait. At that very moment, she was more important.

Whoever she was.

So, I walked over to her.

I was only going to catch a quick glimpse of her, see her face, and engrain it into my memory so I could find her later, but then I heard her speak. The words weren't for me, but when I heard her tone, I wanted them to be. I wanted every damn word that came out of her mouth to be for me and me alone.

I have no fucking clue what came over me when I laid eyes on this woman. I haven't had that visceral of a reaction to the opposite sex in half a decade, and yet, it's as if a firecracker has been lit up in me the second I saw her. More so when she let out a yelp as I spoke. I don't know why, but watching this woman get flushed and flustered was fucking adorable, and I don't usually find things adorable.

For a second, I wondered who she was and why I was so damn intrigued by her.

My intrigue for her grew when she turned to finally meet my gaze, her eyes going slightly wide and her mouth popping open just the slightest bit. From the back, I wanted to claim her as mine, but when I looked into those gray eyes and took in every single inch of her beauty, I wanted to ravage her and never let her go.

Damn, just thinking about it now makes my mouth water.

When I looked into her eyes, I knew I was going to fucking hell. Just a simple look was making my dick twitch. Her eyes were just as beautiful as every other part of her.

For a few minutes, I was enamored by her, and I didn't want the feeling to go away.

It should have, though. It should have when she told me today was her first day as an assistant. That should have been my first clue as to who she was, but I wanted to be naïve. I wanted to think we had hired other assistants to start today, that this was not the woman I told Linda to hire for myself. The few minutes I spoke to her, I wanted to believe this woman wasn't going to be my new employee, which would ultimately make her off-limits according to company policy. I wanted to be naïve, but then she said her name, and that plan went out the window.

You would think that the second I had confirmation that this woman was indeed my new assistant, the intrigue and my attention span would have disappeared, but no. The second I heard her name escape her lush lips, not a single fuck in the world was given. The woman intrigued me, and I didn't give a single shit that she was my new employee.

Am I going to do anything about this newfound attraction to my new employee? No, but that doesn't stop me from wanting to know every single last detail about her.

I have to know if she can be trusted. More so now that I find myself wanting to actually be Bennett when I'm around her and not just another cold-hearted asshole. If I'm going to be CEO, I need people in my corner who aren't going to stab me in the back and spill my dirty secrets to every person they meet.

Which is why I'm currently letting myself into the company database. I need to learn all that I can about this woman, and I need to do it before she comes up to my office and officially starts her first day.

I may not be the CEO, but I know every single thing that happens within every sector of this company. The board may think that by keeping me from being the head of the company, they take away my ability to know anything and everything they do, but they're wrong. With a few swipes of my fingers, I have access to everything this company buys, sells, and does. And the board is none the wiser.

That's what happens when the board and all the execs are a bunch of old nimrods who only care about their egos and filling their pockets, not bettering the company.

Every single technology upgrade this company has seen in the last ten years has been because of me. Hell, if I hadn't stepped up and given myself access to the company database to implement a cybersecurity system, we would've been hacked more times than they would have known to do with and lost millions in the process.

A bunch of good-for-nothing, old-ass idiots.

Soon, though. Soon, they will all be gone, and then this company will be mine, and I'll be able to do whatever needs to be done to keep the company at the very top. I don't need a bunch of old men telling me what the fuck I can and cannot do. I get enough of that from Henry.

With a few more swipes, I find Ella's employee file and skim through all the information she provided. There's nothing here that will tell me if she is trustworthy or not, which I expected, but I do take note that the references she provided aren't tied to the company whatsoever. That's a good thing.

As the elevator dings for the fortieth floor, I mentally write down the date of birth and address to send someone to look deeper into Miss Vincent and slide my phone back into my pants pocket before the elevator doors open.

Just like down on the eighth floor, the second I step

foot off the elevator, all eyes are on me. You would think that I have three heads.

Apparently, it doesn't matter how much time has passed since you started working in the same building; if you share a name with the company they work for, they will stare. Some individuals will even make fuck-me eyes at you in hopes that you would notice them, that you'd stop living up to your most-eligible bachelor title and marry them.

But what they don't know is that I'm not going to be marrying anyone.

Marriage isn't something I want. Not now. Not later in life. Not even with my parents as an example. There are important aspects to life that don't require a wife, and I already have children. I don't need anymore.

Especially if they come out just as mouthy as their cousins.

Putting the thought of a wife and marriage out of my mind, with all the annoying stares, I walk the remaining distance to my office.

You would think that with how much the board hates me, they would put me in an office the size of a closet, with no windows or air conditioning, but when you bring in as much money as I do, they can't really justify it. Especially with all the high-profile meetings I have any given week. I find it ironic that they give me a corner office, the one on the top floor with redwood doors and floor-to-ceiling windows, but they won't give me an executive title.

Doesn't matter, though; the title I want is going to be mine in no time.

As I approach my office, I go through everything I need to get done today, including the meeting I'm late for and sending Ella's information over to someone, but all those plans go out the window when I step inside and see that it's not empty.

Sitting behind my desk, in the chair specifically made for me, is Peter Hill, the chairman of the Lane Enterprises board of directors.

My number one enemy.

From day one, Mr. Hill has been trying everything in his power to make me not only leave the company but also sell my shares. He wants the company for himself, I just fucking know it, but he will never get his hands on it. Even if I'm dead.

Seeing his face in my space irritates me more than the damn stares.

But I hide all my irritation with a look of indifference. Can't have this fucker seeing all my cards.

"Peter. I must have missed the calendar notification that we were meeting this morning," I say in place of a greeting, stopping right in front of my desk.

The old fucker apparently doesn't have anything else to do, so he gives me a fucking smirk as he leans back in my chair.

"My assistant must have sent the email over to your old assistant and they forgot to update your calendar. You should really start looking for a replacement. You can't keep missing important information like this."

My teeth grind the whole time he speaks.

The only reason I don't have an assistant and was in

the business of hiring a new one is because the last one was a mole for Peter, and everything I did was reported back to him. I figured it out after a week, and it didn't take much for me to fire them.

Which is why I'm so inclined to find out everything I can about Ella Vincent. I can't have what happened with my old assistant happen again.

Before her resume landed in front of me, I was hesitant to bring anyone on to help. I was without an assistant for a solid month, and I was able to do a lot on my own. Henry helped somewhat, but after a while it got tiring, and Ms. Vincent's application came into my life at the perfect time. I just have to make sure that she is someone who doesn't want to bury me. Otherwise, she will be fired before she even starts.

Ignoring his assistant comment, because I know for a fact that this little visit is not something he had planned, I cross my arms across my chest and stare the asshole down.

"Is there something I can help you with, Pete? Or are you here trying to plant a listening device so you can pass off one of my acquisitions as yours?"

The smirk on his face completely disappears while his whole back goes straight when I call him Pete, a name I know he hates.

"I would never do such a thing," the man says through his teeth, but we both know it's a lie.

"You planted a fucking assistant. I wouldn't put it past you to plant a device." I give him a shrug and walk over to my coffee machine.

I may have already had my allotted two cups for the

morning, but seeing Peter is making it the type of day where I'm going to need a damn IV to survive.

"You have no fucking idea what you're talking about."

I give him another shrug as I pour a cup of coffee. Thank fuck I have an automatic timer; if only I had a bottle of scotch stashed here too.

"What can I do for you, Mr. Hill?" The question leaves my mouth as I turn back to face the bastard who has officially made his way from behind my desk.

"There is a rumor floating around, Mr. Lane."

"Oh yeah? And what would that be?"

"One that says that Goldman not only is going to call a meeting to announce his retirement, but that he already has someone in mind to serve as his replacement." The old fucker decides to come closer to me and let his disgusting cologne fill my airways, as if he has a point to be made.

"This is the first I'm hearing of it." Lie, lie, lie. "Good for Gerald. His wife has been waiting for his retirement." I take a sip of my coffee to hide my own smirk threatening to form. "I wonder who he's going to name his replacement."

"Cut the crap, son. I know the old bastard told you who he was going to choose. Now, who is it?"

Not wanting to smell the god-awful cologne much longer, I put distance between me and the smell as I walk over to my chair. I may have to get a new one to get rid of the stench. At least I'm concentrating on the smell and not the anger rolling through me at the fact that Peter Hill just called me son.

"You should leave the "son" title for your own kid," I mutter as I take a seat. "Hate to break it to you, Pete, but I have no idea who Goldman is picking as his replacement. And even if I did, why the fuck would I tell you?"

"I would watch your mouth, kid, or did you forget who you are talking to?"

I let out a scoff and give him the same eye roll my teenagers give me. "Did you?"

"Your name may be on this building, but you have no power, and as far as I'm concerned, it's going to stay that way."

"Is that why you came in here, Pete? To threaten me? To tell me that if Goldman names me as his replacement, I will never wear the title?"

The way the old bastard grins tells me my assumptions are correct.

Of course they are.

Peter may think he's slick, but he wears his cards on his fucking sleeve. I know his next move before he does.

"Your father said you were smart. I didn't believe him until now."

The anger rolling through me is growing stronger. It's taking everything in me to not punch Hill in the damn face. He could use a new nose job anyway.

But I just roll my eyes and let the sarcasm slip. "Gee. You would think that all the damn business and money I bring into this company would have been an indicator."

The bastard's face goes beet red. "Cut the shit. If I were you, I wouldn't play games. I don't give a shit if the old geezer names you CEO and you get every single vote in that boardroom. You will never wear that title, not as long as I'm still fucking breathing. It's not meant for you."

I can't help but roll my eyes. "Let me guess: it's meant for you?"

The smirk that forms on his face would tell me all I needed to know if I wasn't able to read Peter Hill like a damn movie. "I've kept this company alive," he sneers. "I've made it what it is." Like fucking hell he did. "Not Goldman, and definitely not you. I worked fucking hard for it. It wouldn't be handed to me just because my daddy died. So if he names you, I will do everything in my power to make sure it never goes through. Do you fucking hear me?"

It wouldn't be handed to me just because my daddy died.

For the majority of my life, I've heard those words. Every time I hear them, I want to scream at the person speaking them until they understand that my parents' death didn't hand me a single thing besides being an orphan. Sure, I received an inheritance, but I've worked fucking hard to get where I am, and their deaths have nothing to do with it.

But Peter and everyone like him will never understand that. To them, I will always be the rich kid who uses his daddy's money to get what he wants, and that's fine. It will just make taking what they desire the most all that sweeter.

"Loud and fucking clear." My response to dear old Peter comes out as almost a growl.

Peter can threaten me all he wants. Nothing is going to stop me from getting the title of CEO, and that includes him. He will be destroyed before that happens.

"Good. Now, if you excuse me, I have important matters to attend to."

He throws a grin in my direction, and as soon as he's out of my office, I don't hesitate to open the top drawer of my desk and take out the scanning device.

I wasn't joking when I asked Peter if he was here to plant a listening device. A conniving man like him would do just that. Too bad I will always be one step ahead of him.

I take my phone out and start dialing a number that I've known since I was a teenager—the one number I call when I need something done. This call was initially to get information on Ella Vincent, but now that Peter Hill has paid me a visit, my reasoning has changed slightly.

The phone rings a total of three times before he answers.

"Whatever it is must be good if the prince himself is giving me a call on a Monday morning." Dante Rosetti's voice sounds through the other end of the phone.

When it comes to friends, I have very few. Getting thrown into fatherhood at twenty-two and raising four kids who aren't technically mine seems to scare people my age away. Some people, though, will stick by your side and open their doors to you whenever you need. The person on the other end of this call is the latter.

I met Dante in high school when I was a junior, and he was coming in as a freshman. We both come from prominent Chicago families, something we bonded over during computer science class, but where my family was known for its money and charity work, Dante's was known for something else.

Mafia.

That should have been something to sway me away from a friendship with him, but I didn't. If anything, being friends with Dante was something I actively sought. From the age of sixteen, I knew that being friends with someone like Dante was going to be beneficial for the both of us, and I was right.

I look down at the time on my watch and see that it's close to ten in the morning. "Good enough for you to answer. I would have figured with the club, you would still be in bed."

"Yeah, well, when your wife is craving pancakes, you get out of bed and get her pancakes and all the syrup in the world."

For the first time since I stepped foot into my office this morning, I actually smile. It may be a tiny one, but it's a smile nonetheless.

"Look at you, the most pussy-whipped man known to man. Angelina is a lucky woman."

Dante has been married to the daughter of his family's consigliere for a few months now, and he is still very much in the honeymoon stage.

Dante lets out a grunt on the other end. "One of these days, you are going to marry a girl and fly her across the world just because she wants something specific to eat, and when that day comes, I'm going to call you the most pussy-whipped motherfucker known to man."

I actually let out a laugh. "That day is never going to come."

"It will, and I will be waiting." If I didn't know any better, I would think my friend is a little annoyed, but he quickly changes the subject before I'm able to call him out on it. "Anyway, I know you didn't call me to talk about how whipped I am, so what's going on?"

Time for business.

"I need you to do two things." As I say the words, the scanning device beeps, notifying me that no listening devices have been found. Hill may not have planted them this time, but I have no doubt that he will if he ever gets the chance, especially now that I've planted the thought in his head.

"What are they?"

"I need you to dig into Peter Hill. I need the deep shit, the stuff I can't find on my side. He's a board member who would rather see me dead than CEO of this company. I know he's into something dirty; I need you to find out what."

The bastard has always been slimy and off-putting. There is no doubt in my mind that he has his hands in something corrupt, possibly has for years. I just have to find out what.

For years, I've been looking into the bastard, and every single time, I've come up empty. Whatever he's in, he is good at hiding it, which is why I need Dante's help. I may have connections, but he can dig into dark things in ways I can only dream of.

"You know, some people would say you are into some dirty things yourself."

An involuntary growl leaves my mouth. "What I do isn't on my company's dime."

"But you use your company's resources."

"I don't hear you complain when those resources have helped you or landed in your hands."

"You never let me complain," he says, pausing for a few seconds before he continues. "I'll look into Peter Hill and see what I can find. It's a common as fuck name, though, so if you have any more information on him, I'm going to need it."

"I'll send you what I have," I say, waking up my computer and typing out an email with all the information I know about Peter Hill.

"Great. Now, what's the second thing?"

Right. The second thing.

"This one is less dingy."

I shouldn't do this. I shouldn't look into the woman who is bound to walk through my door any minute now. I shouldn't want to invade her privacy because someone else invaded mine. I shouldn't look into her, but I want to.

I need to.

She captured my attention. She intrigued me. I need to know everything about her.

When I speak next, there is no hesitation. "Her name is Ella Vincent, and she just started working for Lane Enterprises. I need to know the basics about her."

"Okay?" Dante pauses, as if he is waiting for more, but there isn't any. "And who is Ella Vincent to you?"

I stay silent for a minute, trying to figure out the answer. It takes me longer than necessary to come up with a response, especially when the woman in question steps foot in my doorway.

Did she hear me say her name?

Her facial expression doesn't give anything away, but it does show nervousness, but there is a tinge of curiosity. It's buried deep, but it's there. I can see it.

Without taking my eyes off my new assistant, I answer Dante.

"I don't know yet. When I find out, I will let you know."

Ella Vincent may be my new assistant, but something deep inside me screams that she is going to become more than that. What exactly?

I guess I will find out eventually.

9

ELLA

As soon as I step into the office, I feel out of my element.

The nerves flowing through my body when I walked up to the building almost two hours ago were complete child's play compared to the ones swarming me at this moment. Not only do I feel like throwing up, I feel like I'm swimming in sweat.

This is not the reaction that I thought I would be having when Linda directed me to Bennett's office. I met the guy already; we even joked around a bit as he gave me advice. I have no reason to be freaking out about being his assistant, yet I am.

It's just first-day jitters.

I truly want to believe those words, but given the amount of sweat building up under my boobs, this feels like a lot more. If I had to guess, it has to do with the fact that Bennett Lane looks a lot more intimidating in this small space than he did downstairs.

As he finishes up his call, he radiates this cold energy

that terrifies me in a way, like if I say or do the wrong thing, I will be fired without a second thought.

Maybe who I met downstairs was just a mask, and the person sitting a few feet away from me is his true form. Or are they both masks, and I have yet to see the real person? Will I ever see the real person?

Well, I guess only time will tell, since I'm now going to be spending a lot of time with Mr. Lane.

A throat clearing takes me out of my thoughts.

It takes me a second to put together that I've been standing in the doorway for longer than needed, just staring at my new boss.

I'm just full of great first impressions this morning, aren't I?

Before I say anything to my new boss, I shake my head a bit to center myself as best as I can and not let the nerves win. It takes me a few throat clears, but eventually I'm able to find my voice and speak.

"Hi." The word leaves my mouth as I finally step away from the office doorway. "Linda said to report to you, Mr. Lane. All my paperwork is taken care of, and she said I'm ready to start my first day."

Bennett doesn't say anything. He just twirls his phone in his hand and looks at me as if he is trying to figure me out. He probably thinks I'm an odd one, and in this moment, I would agree with him.

After a few more seconds of him just looking over at me, his eyes never leaving mine, the phone twirling stops, and he looks away and waves toward the chair in front of his desk. "Take a seat, Miss Vincent."

Why do I feel like I just walked into the principal's office?

I follow orders and take a seat, clutching my bag as tightly as possible, waiting for the worst to come my way. He's going to fire me, I just know it. Not even two hours into my first day, and I already lost it.

The thought has tears forming in my eyes, something that doesn't go unnoticed.

Concern coats Bennett's eyes and voice. "Are you okay?"

"Please don't fire me."

"What?"

I take a deep breath, but no matter how many deep breaths I take, I still end up rambling. "I know I have no experience being someone's assistant, and that I might have come off as a bit weird downstairs, but I promise I will be amazing at this job. I will do everything you ask and be the best assistant you've ever had. Just please, don't fire me."

My rambling leaves Bennett speechless, and he opens and closes his mouth a few times, but nothing comes out. Eventually, he is able to get out of the shock I put him in.

"Is there a reason why you think I'm firing you? You haven't even started."

A blush creeps up my face in embarrassment. "It's a gut feeling, and well, you didn't look all that happy when you saw me in the doorway."

A sigh rolls through the room. "I'm not going to fire you."

"You're not?"

He gives me a head shake. "I have no reason to."

The words "not yet" hang in the air at the end of his statement. He doesn't have a reason to fire me right now, but that doesn't mean that couldn't change.

Either way, my shoulders relax a tiny bit. There are still nerves rolling through my body, but that doesn't stop me from releasing the biggest sigh of relief.

My job is safe. For now.

Bennett throws a small smile in my direction, and like earlier, my body likes it a little bit too much.

"You were really that worried?"

I give him a nod and return his small smile. "I really need this job."

For a solid minute, a pensive look comes across Bennett's face, like he is trying to wrap his head around those five little words. Eventually, he lets out a sigh and leans back in his chair. "Before we get into the nitty gritty of your job duties and what I expect of you, can I ask you a question?"

"Um, sure. Ask away."

"You said you have no experience being someone's assistant, so why apply for the position?"

I think about how to answer that question. Though Bennett was friendly enough to me downstairs, I don't know if I want to give him my complete life story right now.

He doesn't know what it's like to hold four jobs. He doesn't know what it's like to not have enough money to keep the fridge stocked, to wish you could give your little sister everything in the world with only five dollars in your bank account. A person like Bennett Lane will never understand what a job like this could do for a person like me.

I doubt this man wants to hear my sorry life story anyway, so I give him just the truth.

"I have my little sister living with me, and she just recently got into a really good private school that I can't really afford waiting tables. So, I decided to put my business degree to good use and get a well-paying job to help pay for her tuition."

My new boss gives me a nod, as if he understands. "What school did she get into?"

A part of me lights up that he asked me a personal question, which is completely stupid. He's not asking that question to get to know me. He's asking it to make conversation. But whenever I get to talk about Charlie, I smile.

"Saint Christopher's Prep Academy. She is set to start in two weeks."

"That's a great high school. Is she living on campus?"

My shoulders fall a bit at his question. The whole living on campus was something I thought about long and hard when it came to accepting Charlie's admission. As much as I wanted her to have the full experience, that was one expense I had to say no to.

The news of her not living on campus came while we were on a call with one of the administrators talking about what Charlie could expect from attending the prestigious school, when the woman on the other side of the line asked if they could expect for my sister to live on campus.

For a few seconds, Charlie wore one of the brightest

grins I have ever seen. She was so excited about the possibility of living on campus and having independence. But then she looked over at me, and that excitement was gone. It broke my heart to let her down, but her living on campus wasn't going to be possible. With my new job, we were going to be able to afford her tuition, but room and board was out of the question big time. It wasn't just about money, though. There is also a safety issue in the back of my mind, even five years later.

I give Bennett a head shake. "No. We aren't able to afford it this year."

An expression crosses Bennett's face, one that looks almost like compassion, but it quickly disappears, replaced by a small smile.

"How old is your sister?"

"Sixteen."

"I have a niece and nephew around that age at Saint Christopher's. Maybe they will meet and become friends." He sounds optimistic.

"Maybe."

I don't have the balls to tell him I doubt it will ever happen. We are talking about two kids related to him; they are probably just as rich as he is, and they probably don't want to hang out with a girl who lives on the southside.

For a long minute, we leave the conversation at that. Neither one of us continues to talk about the kids in our lives or even change the subject. We just sit in our respective chairs, looking at each other as if we are both trying to figure each other out and failing.

Without wanting to, I get lost in his blue-green eyes.

The sun doesn't shine directly in them like it did earlier, so they don't sparkle as much, but the color is still very much breathtaking. If this were anybody else, I would get lost in that color for as long as I could.

But I can't. Because the owner of those gorgeous blue-green eyes is my boss, and nothing can happen between us.

My crush on Bennett may only be a few hours old, but it needs to get squashed immediately. I can't be the assistant who has a thing for her boss.

The silence is eventually broken by Bennett.

"Look, Miss Vincent…"

"Please, call me Ella."

He pauses for a second, as if he really has to think about calling me by my first name.

"Or Elizabeth is fine. Anything but Miss Vincent," I add quickly, not wanting to make him uncomfortable if he wants to stay professional.

A curt nod comes my way. "Elizabeth." The way he says my name not only has butterflies forming in my stomach but also liking my name a lot more than I did when I woke up this morning. "You're not getting fired, but I wouldn't blame you if there comes a time when you'll want to quit."

"Why would I quit? You told me downstairs that the person I will be working with may be an asshole at times but will actually make me like coming to work. Does that not apply anymore?"

A smirk forms on his lips, and I have to kick myself for liking it.

"It still applies." My eyes may be deceiving me,

because I swear I hear him let out a little chuckle before he composes himself. "But not every day is going to be easy. There's going to be days you won't get to leave this building until well after midnight. Days where I say something and you are going to want to wring my neck. Days that will make you cry. Things are going to be shifting in the next couple of weeks, and I want to make sure you are prepared for everything to come. If you aren't, then, like I said, I wouldn't blame you for wanting to quit."

Does he see me as naïve? Does he think I see this job as the easiest thing in the world, that I don't know that there are going to be days when I don't even want to step foot into this building?

I know it's going to be hard. I know there will be a handful of days where I won't want to talk to him or anyone else who works for this company. I know that with a company of this magnitude, I'm going to be working longer days than I did waiting tables or delivering food. I know all of that, and even then, I will try my hardest to make this job work.

Because I need it.

For me.

For Charlie.

I need this job, and not even my boss is going to keep me from at least trying.

My shoulders square themselves. "I promise you, Mr. Lane, I can handle anything that comes my way. Like I said, I need this job, and I will do anything to keep it."

Long nights. Tears. Anger.

I will take it all as long as I'm getting paid and giving Charlie the life she deserves.

Nothing else matters.

I try to convey that I'm here to stay to my boss as best I can, and we have yet another stare-off. The only difference between this one and the one we had a few minutes ago is that I'm not getting lost in his eyes and feeling butterflies in his stomach as his eyes take me in. This stare-off is all about business.

Like the last time, Bennett is the one to break the silence between us.

"All right then." The way he leans back in his chair shouldn't be sexy, but it is. "I'll teach you the ropes, and I will mold you into the best assistant you can be. I just need one small thing from you."

"Anything."

"If I'm calling you Elizabeth, you will call me Bennett."

The easy smile he gives me tells me that the crush I formed for this man two hours ago isn't going to go anywhere anytime soon. Especially if I keep witnessing smiles like that.

I push all thoughts about his smile out of my mind as best I can and give the man sitting in front of me a nod. "Bennett when it's just the two of us, but any other time, it will be Mr. Lane."

"I can get down with that." He stands from his chair, shedding his suit jacket in the process. I applaud myself for not staring as he rolls up his shirt sleeves. "Let's get down to business."

10

BENNETT

It's when I'm leaving the office to meet up with Henry and Drake down in the lobby that I finally check my phone.

Some notifications aren't important, like the one from Drake's school notifying me that my nephew wasn't in school today or the one from the Australian tech company thanking me for meeting with them this morning.

There is one notification, though, that trumps all the others.

One from Dante with the subject line *Elizabeth Vincent*.

I didn't think that I would be getting the information I requested so fast, but I guess when the devil is tasked with something, he does everything in his power to get it done.

Not a single ounce of hesitation runs through me as I open up his email.

Everything I need to know about Ella Vincent is staring back at me. Some things, I knew. Date of birth. Social Security number. Address and where she got her high school education. But what Dante sent over gives me a deeper look at the woman currently up in my office.

Some of the information starting back at me is so deep, I wonder how Dante got his hands on it. Like the fact that Ella has been in more foster care homes than I could ever imagine and the bank account and credit card in her name.

I scroll through the email and take mental note of all the information it provides. The names of every single school she has ever attended, every place she has ever lived, every job she has ever held.

From the age of twenty, the woman has held a steady stream of jobs, more than anyone else her age. It's impressive but also angering. She was trying to get by, and in the process, she was drowning in work.

I continue to read through everything, including the information about her known associates, which thankfully don't include anyone under the Lane Enterprises umbrella, until I reach the bottom and find the information regarding a sixteen-year-old girl.

Charlotte Sinclair.

Not Vincent like her older sister. They must have a different dad.

I scroll through the sister's information, but there isn't much there. There is enough information to make her identifiable, though. Perfect.

After taking a second to save the information in the appropriate place, I shoot off a thank you to Dante and continue my way down to the lobby.

As the elevator climbs down, my mind goes back to Ella.

The woman captured my attention this morning, enough to get Dante to look into her. But the second she was in my personal space for more than five minutes, she not only had my mind's full attention, but my body's. Every time I got a whiff of her perfume or her hand grazed mine as I passed her a file, my dick twitched. It took everything I had in me not to wrap my arms around her waist and sit her on my lap as I showed her how to use our communications system.

The woman is clouding my mind, and I need to find a way to get out of it. With her being my employee now, I can't keep having these types of thoughts, especially in a workplace environment.

As the elevator stops on the first floor, I decide I need to keep my distance from Ella. She may have captured my attention, but it has to stop there. I can't act on my attraction to her. Nothing can come from my knowledge or how she makes my dick twitch without even touching me.

It's for the best. I can't have a woman get in the way of something I worked so hard for.

I got what I needed anyway. Ella isn't attached to anyone who may want to bring me down, so she is trustworthy. Now, she just has to work her way up, having one hundred percent of my trust. Just because her report came back clean doesn't mean I trust her yet. Things can arise.

Walking through the lobby, my mind shifts from my new assistant to the kid running full force in my direction. Sometime in the next couple of years, Drake is going to stop getting excited whenever he sees me. He's going to become the typical teenager and not want to hang out with his uncle like he does now. He'll be just like his siblings.

It's life, but just because it's life doesn't mean I like the idea.

"Can we get ice cream?"

I ruffle his hair, just as dark as mine, before responding. "Only if you ate all of your lunch and you listened to Henry."

"I did." He looks up at me with the biggest puppy dog eyes.

My eyebrow raises a bit, not believing him, so I turn to Henry for confirmation.

The old man gives me a nod. "He even cleaned his room."

"Your brothers have to learn from you," I say, looking back down at Drake.

The kid laughs like it's the funniest thing in the whole world. "That will never happen."

One day, it will, and Drake is going to be surprised beyond belief.

"Let's go. You have school tomorrow, and we can't spend all night at the museum."

Thankfully, he doesn't argue, and he starts walking toward the main door.

As we are about to leave the building, I feel as if there are eyes on me, so I turn to see who's staring at me now.

To my surprise, I find Ella coming off the elevator with a small smile on her face as she watches me. She must have caught me, because her eyes go from looking over at

Drake to looking me in the eyes. For a split second, she looks slightly embarrassed that she was caught, but the embarrassment is gone as quickly as it appeared, replaced with a real smile while she sends a wave in my direction.

That's when I realized that pushing away my attraction for this woman is going to be harder than I thought. Just a small damn wave, and I want to be as pussy-whipped as Dante is.

I wave back and make my way out of the building before I do something absolutely insane, like cross the lobby just to be near her.

Fucking hell.

What the actual fuck happened to me this morning? I meet a woman, and only a few hours later, she's all I can think about? I think my therapist is going to be getting a call, because this isn't me. It has never been, and I'm sure as hell never going to be.

I'm able to push any thought of Ella out of my mind for the majority of the drive to the museum, but when Drake mentions his call with his siblings and them coming for the weekend like I predicted, I'm reminded of her again. More so, I'm reminded of the idea I had when Ella was telling me about her sister.

"Henry," I call from the backseat of the Rolls Royce.

"Yes, sir?"

"Has the Lane Foundation filled all their Saint Christopher's scholarships for the year?"

The look he gives me through the rearview mirror tells me he knows I'm up to something. Handling the foundation is usually something I don't do.

That foundation was my mother's baby, right next to her two sons and her art gallery, so when it came to running it, I handed everything over to Henry. I couldn't do it. I still can't. Sure, I will attend a charity function here and there, but I can't run my mother's baby.

Which is ironic since I'm on the verge of being murderous if Gerald doesn't make his retirement announcement soon to give me my father's baby.

"No, sir. Not yet. There are still scholarships available."

"Good. I have a candidate who needs to be put up for consideration."

I've officially been Bennett Lane's assistant for a whole two weeks, and I truly don't know how to feel.

I'm excited about the job, don't get me wrong, and I actually like it a lot more than I thought I was going to, but I didn't think that handling someone's life was going to be so draining.

He was right when he told me there were going to be days where I'm going to want to quit, and two full weeks in, I've already had three days where I wanted to cry.

Not because of Bennett, though. Not fully, anyway.

As far as bosses go, he's one of the best ones I've had, and I've had more than my fair share of nasty bosses. Bennett is definitely a hard-ass at times, meticulous about how he likes to file things, and on more than one occasion, I've rolled my eyes at his demands, like his ridiculous lunch order, but he is easy to work with and for.

The tears threaten to come because some of the executives at this company can be brutal. In the two weeks, I've attended a few meetings with Bennett to take notes, and whenever a senior employee is in attendance, I'm getting brought down at any given moment.

I can't get someone's coffee order right? I'm incompetent.

I can't find a document fast enough? I'm a waste of time and space.

If I ask a question about something I don't understand? I should never have been hired.

Bennett has defended me each and every time, even got into screaming matches with the person voicing the jabs, but no matter how much he defended me, hearing those things hurt. Every time an insult came my way, I wanted to bow my head and cry.

I didn't, though. I didn't walk away. I took every single insult and continued to do my work the way Bennett told me.

Though every time I see Peter Hill, the senior executive who apparently hates Bennett and hates me in association, I cower a little, waiting for him to bring me down once more.

I hate that I do it.

Maybe with time, I will grow enough of a backbone to not let his words get to me. Hopefully, it will happen soon. I'm keeping my fingers crossed.

For now, it's the start of week three of this new job, and it's already starting out a bit crazy.

As I was riding my third train in the morning to get to work, I got a bank notification that a deposit had hit my bank account. I usually wouldn't question a deposit—I'm all for more money in my bank account—but when the amount that hits my account is the same as what I paid for Charlie's first semester at Saint Christopher's—my signing bonus—panic flowed through my body.

I tried to call the school as soon as I saw the notification to figure out what the hell happened, but of course, my phone decided that was the perfect time to not have service. I did think about going to the school directly, but then I would be late for work. Even though Bennett is affable with a lot of things, I doubt this would be one of them.

So I ran to the office, and the second I landed in my desk chair, I grabbed my office phone and called my sister's school.

As I try to catch my breath, I look over at the time and see I have ten minutes before my day officially starts. Good.

Thankfully, my call is answered right away, and within seconds, I'm directed to the financial department, where I tell them the situation.

It takes longer to get a response than it took to get someone to answer the phone.

"All right, Miss Vincent. I looked over Charlotte's account, and it looks like the reason your money was returned was because the balance was overpaid."

My eyebrows don't hesitate shooting up. "Overpaid? How? I only made that one payment."

"Hmm, let me check."

How can her balance be overpaid? There wasn't enough money in my account for the balance to be overpaid. And if it was overpaid, why wasn't the payment applied to the next semester?

"It looks like the scholarship Charlotte received has gone into effect."

Scholarship? I try to remember Charlie telling me she applied to one, but nothing comes to mind. Did she apply to one without telling me? But why?

My response comes out a bit confused. "I'm sorry, I wasn't aware she had applied for a scholarship."

"Yes, it looks like it was one from the Lane Foundation."

No way I heard her correctly. "Did you say the Lane Foundation?"

"Yes. The foundation offers scholarships to some of the students every school year, and it looks like Charlotte was one of the lucky recipients."

I truly want to believe my sister was indeed lucky in getting this scholarship, but given who my boss is, I can't. I highly doubt this is part of my employment benefits.

I'm trying really hard not to freak out, but it's getting hard. In order to keep myself calm, I try to get as much information as I can.

As the words come out of my mouth, I feel as if ants are crawling all over me. "Would you be able to tell me what the balance would be for next year so I can prepare?"

The lady sounds confused as to why I would even ask a question like that. "There isn't a balance for next year."

"I'm sorry?"

"The scholarship not only covered this year's tuition

but the next two years as well. Actually, not only tuition, but room and board too."

I don't know whether to scream or cry. Everything is covered, but at what cost? I'm already in debt and owe one person when it comes to Charlie. With this, I'm going to drown and never come up for air.

You're jumping to conclusions. It's possible Bennett had nothing to do with this.

It's hard not to jump to conclusions.

I hear the lady on the other end shuffling around paperwork, telling me I've probably taken up too much of her time and that she has other things to do.

I let out a sigh and put a smile on my face, even though she can't see it. "Thank you so much for your time. I greatly appreciate you helping me with all of this."

With that, the call ends, and for a few minutes after, I stare into space, trying to digest the last few minutes.

Charlie not only got a scholarship, but one that pays for everything until she graduates. Everything is covered. I don't have to worry about her losing her spot because I can't make payments on time. I'm excited, but at the same time, I'm pissed off at the possibility of her only getting that scholarship because of who I work for.

Don't look a gift horse in the mouth.

It's hard not to.

As soon as Bennett gets in, I'm going to ask him about it, because this isn't something to just avoid.

For the next thirty minutes or so, I concentrate on other things—making sure the coffee machine is running, updating Bennett's schedule, cleaning up the notes I took at a meeting he had on Friday, and scheduling a meeting with a Japanese car company he apparently has been working with since his early twenties.

Every day, I learn something new about Mr. Lane, and yet he still seems like the biggest mystery in the world.

My morning tasks are enough to distract me. All that goes away, though, the second I hear the elevator ding and footsteps approaching the corner office. I don't have to look up to know it's Bennett.

In the short amount of time I've worked here, I've become somewhat attuned to the sounds Bennett makes, the way his feet hit the floor when he walks is very much one of them. I noticed that when he wears certain shoes, his steps are more pronounced, like today, which tells me that he is wearing a pair of red bottoms.

Before this job, I've never seen a pair of those expensive shoes off a screen, and now, I see them almost every single day.

When I look up from what I'm doing, I'm met with a sight I don't think I will ever get tired of seeing: Bennett Lane in a suit that is made to fit him perfectly. My mouth waters a bit at the sight, and I have to reprimand myself for it. The man is still very much my boss, no matter where he is on the hotness scale.

"Good morning, Elizabeth," he says as he passes my desk and sends a nod in my way.

Nobody calls me Elizabeth. Not my friends, not the little family I still talk to, not a single person in my life. Yet he does, and I like it way too much.

You're the one who told him to call you that.

Yes, but at the time, I didn't know how much hearing those syllables come out of his mouth like that would affect me.

"Good morning," I answer, grabbing my notebook and following him into his office.

As I walk into his office, my eyes stay on him as he puts something on his desk before walking over to the coffee machine in the corner.

Black, one sugar. Sometimes a splash of milk.

I don't realize I missed him asking a question until he says my name a little louder.

"I'm sorry." I shake my head to bring myself back to the task at hand. "Did you say something?"

Bennett gives me a smirk, and I try really hard not to stare at it for an extended period of time.

"I asked what was on the agenda for today." He takes a sip of his coffee, but his eyes never leave me.

A small blush crawls up my neck, but I try to hide it as I look down at the schedule I wrote down before he got here.

"I have you meeting with the head of the tech department this morning at ten. He emailed last night that he wanted to run a design by you. Then you have a meeting with the Japanese car company at six this evening."

It's not until I say who the meetings are with out loud that I realize that even if I've been working here for a couple of weeks, I still don't know what Bennett actually does. His business cards and email say he is a senior employee who helps with acquisitions, but tech and automotive seem so far away from each other. There's no way he has a hand in designing computers *and* cars.

Does he?

"And in between?" Bennett's question takes me out of the spiral of questions about him I was getting lost in.

"Um." I look down at my notes. "I have you going over the information sent from Tokyo and us discussing your travel plans for next month. You had on your schedule that you were going to California, but there weren't any specifics attached, so I didn't know where to book the hotel or if I should rent you a car."

Bennett gives me a nod. "Go ahead and clear your schedule so you can attend both of today's meetings with me. Don't worry about a hotel or car for the California trip. It's a personal trip, and all those things are taken care of."

"Oh. Okay."

"Look over the design the tech department sent over and gather your thoughts. I will send you all the information for Japan so you have a better idea as to what the meeting will be about."

I give him a nod. From the very beginning, not only has he been defending me, but he has also included me in everything. He doesn't make me feel like I'm just another employee or beneath him; he makes me feel his equal. Something more than just an assistant who handles his emails and calendar.

"Anything else?" he asks as he makes his way over to his desk.

I look down at my notes, but I already told him everything I have written down. The only thing that comes to mind to bring up is Charlie's scholarship.

But I don't think I can make the question leave my mouth.

If he did have something to do with it, I'll probably come off as ungrateful. What if he rescinds the scholarship?

I try to talk myself out of not asking him about it, but the need to do it is too strong.

"Actually," I start, closing the distance between us ever so slightly. Why? I don't know. "Can I ask you a question not relating to work?"

Bennett looks over at me, his eyebrows bunching up just the slightest bit. "Yes. Of course."

I don't know why, but I feel nervous. "I told you my sister got into Saint Christopher's, that she was living at home because we couldn't afford for her to live on campus."

"You did."

Just ask the damn question.

"This morning, I got a notification that the money I used to pay for her first semester landed back in my account. So I called the school to see if there was a problem, and they told me the money was refunded because my sister had gotten a scholarship. One from the Lane Foundation that covers everything until she graduates. You didn't have anything to do with that, did you?"

The way he just slides his hands into the pockets of his slacks and looks me dead in the eye tells me everything I need to know.

"The foundation gives out scholarships to hundreds of kids every year."

"But do they give scholarships out to kids who don't apply?"

I get a shrug. "I don't know. I'm not the one in charge of the foundation."

Bullshit.

Tired of the lack of answers, I ask him point-blank. "Did you give my sister that scholarship?"

"Yes."

"Why?"

He doesn't answer right away. He just continues to look at me, his face unreadable. Eventually, he lets out a sigh and answers my question.

"Because I wanted to help you out. You said you needed this job. I don't know what your financial situation looks like, but when you take a job so you can pay for your sibling's school, I'm going to take that as you need money. So, I decided to help in any way I could, which included talking to the head of the foundation and finding out there were still scholarships available. I just suggested your sister for one."

"How did you even find out her name?"

Charlie and I don't share the same last name, and it's for a good reason.

"You added her to your medical benefits."

I did? I try to think back to when I filled out my benefit form and if I included Charlie, but I can't remember. In the time she has lived with me, I have never included her in those types of forms because I'm not able to. If I added her to my benefits, it was a huge mistake on my end.

I take a second to collect myself before I say anything else, but my words come out sounding angry.

"Why would you want to help? I've only worked here for two weeks. I'm practically a stranger."

The distance between us closes some more, and I don't notice until I'm within a foot of him, close enough to touch. I should take a step back, but I don't. Anger is rolling through me right now, and I'm standing my ground.

Apparently, I'm not the only one annoyed by all this. The way Bennett's nostrils flare show his annoyance prominently.

"Who cares?"

"I care! Why would you do that?"

Our chests are almost touching, and neither one of us is taking a step back.

"Because I wanted to, okay? I saw the worry in your eyes, saw how hard you were trying to hide that you were struggling. I wanted it to go away. So I did the one thing I could think of that wasn't giving you a one hundred percent raise—which I would do, by the way, if the board would give me what I fucking wanted. I wanted to help my employee. I see nothing wrong with that, and you shouldn't either."

I don't know what comes over me.

Maybe it's the proximity of his body to mine.

Maybe it's that he said he wanted to take my struggles away, as if they were his to bear.

Maybe it's that he did something so big for Charlie.

I don't know what, but something comes over me as I slide my hand around his neck and bring his face down just enough for me to slam my lips against his.

The second our lips touch, it's as if my mind clears, and the fact that he paid for Charlie's school no longer matters.

His lips are soft against mine, and that is all that matters. It's all I can think about until a hand lands against my waist, and I swear I can feel his touch burn me through my clothing.

That should have been my sign to pull away, but I don't come to my senses and realize what I'm doing until one of us makes a sound. Who? I don't know, because I start to spiral.

I'm kissing Bennett, *my boss*. I pull away and put as much distance between us as I possibly can.

"Omigod. I'm so sorry," I let out as soon as there is a good five feet between us.

Why the hell was I thinking?

You were thanking him for his generosity.

I could have used my damn words!

My eyes meet Bennett's, and for a second, I forget how to speak. His eyes are slightly wide, and from the looks of it, he is just as stunned by my actions as I am, but there is something else rolling through his blue-green eyes that I can't pinpoint.

Is it anger?

Is it lust?

A combination of the two? I don't know, but right now, with all the embarrassment flowing through my body, I don't want to find out.

"I'm so sorry," I repeat, because that seems like the only thing I can say right now.

Bennett shakes his head, but I don't know if he is doing it at me and the situation, or to possibly clear his head.

"It's okay."

"It's not okay. I just kissed you. I kissed my boss at our place of work."

I feel like I'm having an out-of-body experience.

Why did I do something so damn stupid?

Oh my god. I'm going to get fired.

Kissing your boss is a fireable offense, isn't it? I should have read my employee manual more thoroughly.

"Ella, it's fine."

My heart beats so damn loudly, I'm sure Bennett can hear it from where he stands.

"Please don't fire me." The words escape without me even thinking about it, but I guess my mind is spiraling so much, it's trying to find ways to keep the best job I've ever had.

A look of confusion crosses Bennett's face. "I'm not going to fire you."

"But I kissed you."

"I know, and it's fine. We can act like it never happened and move on. It was just a simple mistake."

Act like it never happened.

Those words shouldn't sting, but for some reason, they do—even more when you add the words *simple mistake*. But Bennett is right: it was a simple mistake, and we need to forget that it ever happened.

So, I push my feelings down and give him a nod.

"Right. A simple mistake that never happened." The words sound wrong, but they are the only ones that can be said at the moment. "I'm still sorry for kissing you. I don't know what came over me."

Something that looks a lot like sympathy crosses Bennett's face. Great. He pities me.

"Like I said, it's okay. We both got caught up in the moment."

Both of us? Does that mean he didn't want to pull away either?

No. He probably doesn't want me to feel guilty about it, so he is taking some of the blame.

A small smile forms on my lips. "Right. Caught up."

He gives me a small smile back, one I've become accustomed to seeing. Bennett doesn't smile much, but I enjoy seeing it nonetheless.

We stand there, five feet apart, just looking at each other, neither one of us moving an inch to head back to our desks. We just stand in our respective spots, a lot of awkward tension between us.

Apparently, both of us are so damn lost looking at each other that we don't notice that someone has come into the office until there is a knock against the door.

The second I'm out of the Bennett Lane cloud and I turn, I feel a lot more embarrassed than when I kissed Bennett.

Why?

Well, having the CEO of the company walk in while you are having a weird, tension-filled stare down with your boss will do that.

How long has he been standing there? Did he see the kiss?

All I can think of doing is staring at Mr. Goldman as his eyes move between me and Bennett.

Thankfully, my boss is composed enough to fill the silence. I'm sure that silence was only for a few seconds, but it felt like a damn eternity.

"Gerald, what can I do for you this morning?"

The man in question throws a smile in my direction, and I try my hardest to send one back, but I'm sure it looks strained.

"I hope I'm not interrupting anything, but I wanted to inform you of the news." Again, Gerald smiles, but this time, it's bigger, like he is a kid on Christmas morning. "I'm calling a board meeting. I'm announcing my retirement and calling for a vote."

My eyes move from Mr. Goldman to Bennett for some clarification, but Bennett looks a little too stunned to speak, so I insert myself.

"I'm sorry, but calling a vote? What does that mean?"

Gerald smiles and doesn't take his eyes off the man I just kissed.

"It means that if everything goes how I think it will, come next week, the new CEO of Lane Enterprises will be Bennett Lane."

12

BENNETT

I walk down the long hallway to my parents' room, and when I reach it, I stand in the open doorway watching them as they move through the room, getting ready.

My dad is the one to notice me first.

He gives me a smile that slows the rolling in my stomach but doesn't stop it.

"Hey, buddy," he says, waving me in as he puts on his cuff links. "Are you okay?"

I give him a nod, not wanting to tell him about what I'm feeling in my stomach.

"Where are you going?" I ask, like I don't already know. This party must be special, because my dad only puts on his cuff links when it's special.

"Your mom and I are going to a small gathering at a friend's house. They just sold their company, and they want to celebrate," my dad answers, giving me a small smile.

"But it's raining." I'm not usually one to whine, but the rain is making me uneasy.

My dad gives me a smile and forgets about his links as he crouches down to my eye level. "I know, bud, but don't worry. Mom and I will be back in a few hours, and when we are , we can talk about our trip for next week. We can plan all the rides we want to get on."

I feel a smile form on my face.

For weeks, I had been asking Dad if we could go to the place with all the rides in California like we did last year. I kept telling him I was finally tall enough to ride with him and Robert, and every single time, he would tell me he would look at his schedule.

I didn't think he was ever going to say yes.

Until last week, when he came home and gave me a laser toy gun and told me I was going to need it when we headed out to California.

One more week.

"Can we plan to do only the fast rides?" I ask, almost jumping up and down.

"Only the fast rides? You don't want to do the slow ones with me? I thought for sure you'd want to at least do the carousel." My mom's voice sounds out, and when I look up and away from my dad, I see her walking back into the room as she puts on her earrings.

I think my mom is the most beautiful girl in the world. She doesn't need earrings to make her even prettier.

"That ride is for babies, Mom," I say to her, and right away, she smiles at me.

"You're still my baby. I'm requesting that you at least ride the carousel with me once," she tells me, messing up my hair.

My legs burn as I let this treadmill take everything I have. The memory that woke me over two hours ago has been in my head on repeat. No matter how hard I run or how badly I want the nightmare to go away, it's still present.

Our family never went on that trip to California.

My parents died that night, and the next time I saw them was as their caskets were being lowered into the ground.

Out of all the memories that could have come back to haunt me, the memory of my parents happy and smiling was not one I was expecting. I would have taken their funeral over seeing them smiling any day, but of course, my subconscious doesn't work that way.

Of course my mind decided to hit me with one of the most painful memories today of all days.

Gerald is announcing his retirement and me as his replacement.

This is the day I've been waiting for for years, but only two hours into it, and I already want it to be over. I should be fucking excited about the fact that my father's company is going to finally be mine. I should be out celebrating and drinking from the most expensive bottle of scotch I can get my hands on, but instead, I'm dreading it.

And it all has to do with my parents.

My father should be the one handing me this title, not some old bastard who didn't deserve it in the first place.

It's not only my parents I've been thinking about though; my brother has also been at the top of my mind.

Robert, just like my parents, is a topic I try not to think about all that often, mostly because thinking about him pisses me off beyond belief, but when the kids bring him up, I try to be as neutral as possible. Some days are harder than others.

If he hadn't left a month after the funeral or even stayed when he brought the kids to Chicago ten years ago, he could be the one named CEO today, not me.

There are a lot of could haves and could bes playing in my head, and they are messing me up just as much as the handful of nightmares I've had this week. It doesn't help that this morning during my daily search for him, something new popped up.

I've been searching for Robert for ten years, and in that time, nothing out of the ordinary has come up, but today of all days, something does.

A phone number.

Not the number he had when he was sixteen, and not one he had while he lived in Mexico, but a new one with a Florida area code.

It's taking everything in me not to call it and see if it's truly him, but I can't find it in me to do it.

If I do call and it is him, what do I say? Come back?

That his kids miss him and need him? They've gone ten years without him and their mother; I'm sure they miss them, but they don't need either of them. I made fucking sure of that.

The burning in my legs intensifies, which tells me I forgot where I was for a second and pushed myself harder than intended.

Not wanting to end up in the hospital with broken bones on this important day, I turn off the treadmill and get off.

Feeling my body want to give up with exhaustion, I slide down to the floor and try to control my breathing, to think about something other than the family I once had.

If today goes how I think it will, I will be CEO. I'm not worried about not getting it.

From the second Gerald told me that he was going to be retiring, I've been working double time to get the votes I need. I have all ten accounted for.

Did a vote or two come with a price? Absolutely, but it's one I'm willing to pay to get what I want. The other party just has to stick with their side of the agreement, and I will open my wallet however wide they want.

The thing I'm worried about is the board throwing me a damn curveball.

Dante is still working on getting me information on Hill. The information he has gotten me so far doesn't tell me anything I don't already know. But he says to give him time, so I am.

As soon as my breathing is controlled, I get up from the floor and head up to the kitchen. It's not even six in the morning, but I need to get the day started. It's going to be a long, mentally challenging one for sure.

Approaching the kitchen, I hear the house alarm chime, notifying me that someone opened the front door.

My back straightens up right away as I head to the foyer to see who the fuck is coming into my house at this hour because I know for a fact that nobody is leaving it.

Drake is still asleep.

I hear Henry in the kitchen, and Grayson and Samantha are back at school after being home for a few days. It's sure as hell not my security team, because they know not to come into the house before seven.

The closer I walk over to the front of the house, the more I think to myself that I need to move one of my guns closer to the door, but that thought disappears when I make out the figure that just walked in.

"You were supposed to get here last night," I say to my twenty-year-old nephew, who is currently dumping a duffel bag on the floor that looks like it's filled with a year's worth of clothes.

Seven months, actually.

Elliot turns, and instead of giving me a wave or even a greeting, he throws a shrug in my direction.

"My flight got canceled, and the only way to get here was to take a flight to London and get the last flight out to Chicago. You should be happy I made it at all."

I blame the fact that I haven't had coffee yet for my eyeroll.

"If you would have taken the plane I sent, you wouldn't have had an issue."

"Maybe I wanted to struggle."

A sigh escapes me.

When it comes to our relationship, describing it as strained doesn't even cover it. I try to be a parental figure to him, but there are only ten years between us, so him seeing me as a parent is difficult. Since the day we met, he has tried to defy me every chance he gets. If it wasn't for Henry, Elliot wouldn't have had any discipline.

Now that he's twenty, that big brother thing is ever so present, and I hate it. Thank fuck Grayson, Sam, and Drake listen to me at least.

Not wanting to get into it so early in the day, I change the subject.

"Henry's in the kitchen making breakfast if you're hungry." I nod toward the kitchen.

Surprisingly, he follows me out of the foyer. "I'm starving."

As he walks into the kitchen, I take note that Elliot is not a little kid anymore. He's almost as tall as I am and looks a lot more like a man than the last time I saw him. I guess when you are backpacking through Europe and Asia, that happens.

The second Elliot walks into the kitchen, he has Henry's attention.

"Mr. Elliot."

He doesn't hesitate to wrap the old man in a hug.

Where the fuck was my hug?

You didn't even greet the kid.

Whatever.

Elliot claps Henry on the back. "It's good to see you, old man."

"How was the flight? You should have told me you were coming in at this hour. I would have gone and picked you up."

"The flight was fine. I slept the whole way. And I didn't tell you because I didn't want to put you out. I figured you had your hands full with things here anyway."

It's subtle, but I know when someone is throwing a dig at me.

I ignore it and listen to them as they talk about Elliot's backpacking adventures. Henry has heard all these stories since Elliot actually answers his calls and talks to him at least once a week, but he is taking in every single word as if it were the first time he'd heard them. The way he smiles at my nephew makes me think that if my dad was still here, he would have the same smile on his face.

"So, does someone want to tell me why the board meeting is so important that I had to fly in?" Elliot asks as we sit at the kitchen table, eating our breakfast.

Eli looks over at both me and Henry, waiting for one of us to give him an answer.

Since the age of eighteen, Elliot has been part of the Lane Enterprises board of directors. Since we don't have any confirmation whether Robert is dead or alive, the seat that would have gone to him on his eighteenth birthday went to his son, and when the other three kids come of age, they will get a seat as well. They also own a percentage of the company. Where I hold forty percent ownership and Henry holds five, they hold ten percent each. The other fifteen percent is either public or distributed to members of the board.

So when Gerald announced he was calling a board meeting, everyone who holds a seat has to be present, which meant Elliot had to cut his stay in Laos short.

Except neither Henry nor I told him what the board meeting was about. We just told him that he needed to be present.

I put my fork down and answer his question.

"Goldman is announcing his retirement, and with that, his replacement. The board is going to be voting on his pick."

He gives me a nod, a small smirk playing on his face. "And is that replacement you?"

"According to him, yeah, it is. Is that going to be a problem for you?"

There's a bite to my tone—one I didn't mean to let slip, but I couldn't help it. The nightmares and memories and Elliot looking like he would rather be anywhere else but home are all messing with my head.

It takes a second for Elliot to answer, but he finally does, and he surprises me.

"No. No problem. I know how hard you've been working to get to this point. It might not have been done all morally, but you put in the work. I've seen it. Everyone at the company has seen it. They would be stupid not to vote you in. Besides, I'm sure it's something Grandma and Grandpa would have wanted for you. So you have my vote."

It's been a while since I heard him say that many words to me. I have to take a second to digest everything he said. "Thank you. You have no idea how much I appreciate it."

He throws me a nod and goes back to eating without saying another word.

The remainder of breakfast is almost silent, with a few things said here and there. When all of us are done, Elliot and I help Henry clear the table before we go through a run-through as to how the day will play out.

"Mr. Lane, I sent a car over to Ms. Vincent's residence like you requested. She should be here in about an hour and will ride with you to the office. I will wake Mr. Drake and make sure he is at school on time before doing some work for the foundation and heading to the office later this afternoon for the board meeting. Are there any changes for me?"

I shake my head. "No, Henry. Thank you."

"Who's Ms. Vincent?" Elliot chimes in, another smirk playing on his face. It's crazy how much he looks like his dad when he does that.

"Mr. Lane's new assistant."

"Assistant? And she is coming here? You never let any of your assistants come near the property, let alone the house."

I grind my teeth, because he's right.

In all the years I've had assistants working with me, I've never let them come to the manor. The penthouse in downtown Chicago, sure, but never to the house where the kids live. It has been a boundary for years.

Yet, I'm removing that boundary for my brown-haired, doe-eyed assistant.

My mind goes to the kiss we shared earlier this week. It was short and definitely not planned, but I haven't stopped thinking about her mouth since she slammed it against mine.

Every time I pass by her desk, I want to lean over and get another taste of her. I've found myself looking at her mouth a little too much, checking her out as much as I possibly can. There is this pull to her that doesn't seem to go away, no matter how hard I try.

I keep telling myself I can't have her, yet she is all I can think about outside of the nightmares and memories sneaking in. I'm sure the second I become CEO, it will go away, because I will have more pressing things to occupy my mind, but I have a feeling that whatever attraction I have for my assistant will still be there no matter what title I hold.

"According to Dante and what I've witnessed, she can be trusted."

Elliot's smirk grows into a full-blown grin. "You had Dante look into her?"

My teeth grind.

Out of all the kids, Elliot knows a bit about some of my "friends" and what they may have their hands on. Not because I wanted him to know but because something came about around the time he turned eighteen where I had to tell him I had connections in dark places.

"Yes, because I needed to know if she could be trusted."

His grin grows even more. "You like her."

"I don't know what the fuck you're talking about."

"Yeah, you do. You only have Dante look into people when it's something serious. Knowing if someone is trustworthy is serious, but I would bet all the money in my wallet right now that you find this woman attractive and you wanted to know everything about her. Is she hot?"

If it was acceptable to punch my nephew, I would do it right now.

"Don't you have something to do? Like sleep? You did fly commercial, after all. I'm sure you're tired. You don't get much sleep in those tiny-ass seats."

"I'm going to take that change of subject as a yes. Now, what is Ms. Vincent's name?"

Annoyance runs through my body. I think I liked it more when he didn't say full sentences to me.

"I'm done with you." I grab my phone and start making my way upstairs to get ready for the day.

Elliot laughs, and I hear it all the way up to the second floor.

Not going to lie, going back and forth with him felt nice. That hasn't happened in years, and it wasn't until this moment that I realized I missed it a whole lot. I hope Elliot stays in Chicago for longer than just today, but I feel like that's just wishful thinking.

After checking to see that Drake is still asleep, I take a shower before changing into the suit Henry put out last night. An all-black, slim-fitting Armani suit seems appropriate for a day like today, but as I slide it on and look at my reflection in the mirror, something seems off. This is a suit I've worn a hundred times, but today, it feels like something is missing.

It doesn't take me long to figure it out.

The dream.

There was a reason I had that particular memory pop into my head today of all days.

After taking a deep breath, I walk to the closet and open the watch drawer. Inside sits a small cuff links box that I open maybe once a year when I want to drown myself in memories.

I'm not one for cufflinks, so wearing them today will be something Henry will notice.

Opening the box, I quickly scan the contents until I find the pair I'm looking for. The pair my father wore the night he died were buried with him, but because I wanted a piece of him, I had them reconstructed a few years back.

I remember every single detail of the ones he wore, so they are the exact same.

My hands shake as I put them on, but the second that they are both attached, the suit feels complete.

I guess no matter what I do or how old I get, I will always need a piece of my parents with me.

Not wanting to think about it anymore, I put the box back in its place and head downstairs.

As soon as I step onto the first floor, I feel Henry's eyes scanning my appearance, and I see the moment he notices the cuff links.

A sad smile forms on his face, but he doesn't say anything about the links.

"Are you ready for today, sir?"

I throw a curt nod in his direction and grab the briefcase he's holding out.

"I've been ready for this for years, Henry. It's time for that CEO title to be mine."

13

———

ELLA

"Was that your brother?" I ask as the car pulls away from the Lane property and heads back into the city.

If you had asked me, it seemed like a big waste of time to send a car to pick me up, drive me to the Lane house an hour outside of Chicago to pick up Bennett, and then head back into the city. But, according to Bennett, it was necessary. How? I have no idea. But hey, he's paying me from the second I step out of my apartment building, so you won't hear me complain.

"Who?" Bennett asks from the seat next to me, not looking up from his phone.

"The guy who looks like he could almost be your twin."

That causes Bennett to look up from his phone and give me a confused look. "Elliot doesn't look like me."

A small snort comes out of me. "Add some facial hair on him, put him in a suit, and maybe style his hair, and he is the spitting image of you."

When the car pulled up to the house, I half expected to

see Bennett, maybe a housekeeper, opening the door, but I was pleasantly surprised when I saw two other men waiting with smiles on their faces.

Bennett thinks about my assessment for a few seconds before he shakes his head and goes back to looking down at his phone.

"He's my nephew. My brother's kid."

That makes sense.

"Is your brother going to be joining us for the board meeting?" The question comes out without a second thought, and when Bennett's shoulders tense up, I regret it.

I watch as he drops his phone on his lap and turns to look out the window.

He answers a full two minutes later. "No. My brother hasn't stepped foot in Chicago for ten years, and I doubt he is going to do it any time soon."

I've been around Bennett a lot these last three weeks, and in that time, I know when something has hit a nerve and he is trying his hardest to keep his anger in check. This is one of those times.

Feeling embarrassed, I drop my head slightly and apologize. "I'm sorry. I shouldn't have asked. Curiosity got the best of me."

It takes a minute, but Bennett finally turns back to face me.

"Don't apologize. You didn't know." A weird look crosses his face, but then it quickly disappears. "My brother...is a sore subject. Especially on a day like today."

My curiosity tries to get the best of me, but this is the

one time I don't let it. I already made him upset with my last question; I don't want to do that again.

The silence between us lasts for a few minutes.

"You want to ask why, don't you?" he says, breaking the silence.

I let out a sigh. I guess I have to learn how to school my facial expressions.

"I do, but I'm not going to."

"Why not?"

A small smile forms on my face. "Because I respect you, and if you say it's a sore subject, then I have no right asking about it."

He studies me, his eyes moving across my face as if memorizing it. My brain is telling me to shy away, but I don't. I want him to keep looking at me like this, because even if it's for a split second, it makes me feel like he wants me.

And I hate myself for even thinking that.

A man like Bennett Lane could never want me. He's one of the most eligible bachelors in the world, who can have any woman he wants. There is no way he would settle for someone like me.

"How much do you know about my family?" he asks, his question not one I expected from him.

"Only what I learned when I applied for this job."

"Which is?"

"Not much. Just that your parents died when you were young and that your brother hasn't been very public about his life."

And it's true. That's all I know about his family. I've

heard a few whispers about the Lanes, but I don't stay to listen. It feels wrong learning about the family when I'm working for one of its members.

A small scoff leaves Bennett. "I guess that's one way to describe my brother." It sounds like there's anger in his voice.

"How would you describe it?"

We were supposed to use this drive to talk about the board meeting and a few other things we need to get done, but I have a feeling we won't be doing that.

Bennett turns to look back out the window, and he stays like that for a few minutes. I just sit there watching him, waiting for anything he might say.

I start to think I won't be hearing anything at all when he speaks.

"My brother isn't hiding from the public. Well, maybe he is, but not in the way the internet told you. Nobody has seen him in ten years. Not me, not his kids. He fell off the face of the earth, just like he did when he was sixteen."

A lump forms in my throat. "Did he..."

"Die? I have no fucking clue. I've spent years trying to find some confirmation that he's dead or alive, and to this day, I have yet to find anything. To find him."

The lump gets even bigger as my heart swells for him. I see the hurt in his eyes, hear it in his voice, and it takes everything in me not to shed a tear for him.

"What happened when he was sixteen?" I find myself asking. I should just let the conversation drop, but I find myself enthralled by everything Bennett says.

"A month after my parents died, he just got up and left.

He told me he was going to come back, that he was just going to take some time to figure things out. I didn't see him again until fourteen years later, when he showed up on my doorstep with his four kids, asking me to watch them while he got things settled. And, well, he never came back. He abandoned me when I was eight, and then he abandoned his kids the same way."

If my heart wasn't broken before, it definitely is now.

In a matter of weeks, Bennett lost his parents and then had his brother walk out of his life, not once, but twice. That's a lot of trauma for one person to handle, and from the sounds of it, he's still dealing with it.

I guess for some of us, it's harder to let go of things than it is for others.

Wanting to be there for him in some way, I push all my emotions down and place my hand on top of his, giving it a squeeze.

His eyes move from me to our hands. I know what he's probably thinking. I shouldn't be touching him, but he doesn't do anything to move me away, and neither do I. For some reason, having our hands touch like this feels right. Being close to him feels right.

"I know these words probably won't sound like they have sentiment, and that I'm just saying them because it's the acceptable thing to say, but I'm really sorry you experienced something like that. I know what losing someone you love feels like. I know what goes through your head when someone who is supposed to be there leaves when you need them the most, and it's the worst thing in the world. I hated it, and I'm sure you did too. It sucks, and I'm so damn sorry it happened."

I don't realize that I'm crying until Bennett wipes away a few tears running down my face. This is as close as we've been since I kissed him.

If only I could get closer.

But we already said that the kiss we shared was a mistake. We can't keep making them.

"You had a tough childhood." It's a statement, not a question, his hand not dropping from my face.

I give him a nod. "Yeah, you can say that."

Bennett must understand, because he gives me a nod as he pulls his hand away and straightens up in his seat.

As soon as there's distance between us, I miss him. I miss his touch, his scent burning my nose.

Before I decide to do something stupid, like kiss him again, I wipe the remaining tears away and change the subject.

"Tell me what I can expect from today's board meeting."

From the second Mr. Goldman told Bennett he was calling a board meeting, things have been going like any other week. I would have figured with news like that, Bennett would be on edge or at least shadowing Mr. Goldman or something, but no. Sure, there were times this week where he was stoic, but he has come out of every meeting with a bounce in his step, which is not something I'm used to seeing.

I realized rather quickly that the news he was going to be CEO was not news to him. He has probably known for a while. He might not have been worried about this new position, at least not from what I could see, but I was, because if he got promoted? Did it mean that he would be getting a new assistant?

I asked him that very question two days ago, and he reassured me that my job was safe, which calmed me down a bit, but I still have tons of questions.

According to Bennett, I'm his assistant, and I have to be there. Why? Who the fuck knows, but I'm going to be there, and I don't want to go in unprepared.

"It will just be like every other meeting that you've sat in on. Goldman is going to lead it and go on about how much the company means to him, right before announcing he is going to retire."

I nod. "Then he is going to announce you as his replacement and the board is going to vote on whether they agree to give you the title or not?"

"Yes."

"Are you nervous about the vote?"

Bennett shakes his head. "No. I need ten votes. I have no doubt in my mind that I will get them."

"But are you nervous?"

I didn't want to say anything, but when I switched the subject to the board meeting, the man sharing the back seat with me started getting a bit fidgety. Either he's nervous about the meeting or being this close to me freaks him out.

A deep sigh escapes his body. "No. I'm not nervous but." He pauses to think about it. "I know the board. They don't want me to have this title, so they are going to do everything in their power to keep me out of that seat. I just don't know what, and not knowing is driving me insane."

Right away, my mind goes to Peter Hill. He hates Bennett. I really hope I'm wrong, but I think he's scheming. I hope Peter doesn't interfere. Even though I've only been working at Lane Enterprises for a short period of time, I know Bennett would be a great CEO. He already does so much for the company, but the higher-ups don't even care. From what I've seen, he's the best choice, and I just hope that nobody takes it away from him.

I cross my legs and square my shoulders, as if I am ready to walk through a battle. "If they do try to take that title away from you, we will just have to find a way to stop them."

Bennett turns to me with what looks like fire in his eyes and a grin on his face. This is a new look I never want to go away.

"Those are mighty words, Miss Vincent."

I shrug. "Well, if people want to play with fire, they should know the consequences that come with it: getting burned and the chance that there won't be anything to stop the flames from overtaking them."

THE DAY PASSES a lot slower than I thought it would. All people can talk about is the board meeting. According to the chatter in the cafeteria, nobody knows why Gerald

Goldman would call a meeting; apparently, he only informed me and Bennett.

From what I'm hearing, some people are guessing right, but others are just throwing the most random things out there, like Gerald is leaving Lane Enterprises to go to another company. Someone else said they think Gerald is opening his own winery in Italy.

The most eye-popping one, though, is that Thomas Lane himself is coming back from the dead and kicking Gerald out as CEO. Apparently, this person thinks the Lanes faked their own deaths and are choosing now to come back. Who even thinks that?

If I were a less civilized person, I would have walked out of my stall and punched the lady in the mouth for thinking such a thing. She no doubt took something before coming into work, because that idea is absolutely bonkers.

I look at the time on the corner of my computer screen and let out a sigh of relief. The board meeting is thirty minutes away. Thank God. I don't know how much longer I can sit at the edge of my seat. Bennett may not be nervous about the vote, but I am.

What if it doesn't go his way? Will he quit? Will he continue working here while the board looks for another replacement?

I also can't take the amount of pacing happening in his office right now. He's been going back and forth between the coffee maker and the door for the last hour, and it's driving me insane. For a guy who says he's not nervous, he is shit at hiding it. I think about going in there, but then I might do something stupid, like kiss him again to distract him.

So, to keep myself from walking into the office, I try to keep myself busy until it's time to head up to the conference room.

I'm in the process of sending a text to Charlie, telling her I'll be late and to use some of the money I left this morning for dinner, when I hear footsteps approaching me. When I look up, I'm a little surprised when I see a little boy in a suit standing in front of my desk.

He beams with a smile as he gives me a wave. "Hi."

His smile elicits one of my own, and I wave back. "Hi. Are you lost?" I ask, looking behind him for an adult.

The little boy laughs. "No, my uncle works here."

I study the little boy, and he looks familiar. I've seen him before, and now, as I take in his face, his familiarity is more than seeing him down in the lobby. It's almost as if he's the younger version of the man currently pacing in the room next to me.

"Who's your uncle?" I ask for confirmation.

"Bennett Lane," he announces, his smile growing bigger. "I'm Drake."

He holds out a hand for me to shake, and I can't help but chuckle a little as I slide my hand against his.

"It's nice to meet you, Drake. I'm Ella, your uncle's assistant. Did you come here by yourself?"

The little boy shakes his head. "Henry and Elliot are coming up. I just beat them to the elevator. They're too slow."

"Are they now?"

As if on cue, the two men walk toward my desk. Henry looks annoyed, and Elliot looks amused.

"Mr. Drake, what did I say about running?" Henry reprimands, but the little boy just gives him a shrug.

"I was excited."

Henry shakes his head and is about to say something to me when he is interrupted by Bennett's twin.

"Hi, I'm Elliot. We didn't get to meet back at the house. You must be Ms. Vincent."

This guy can't be much younger than me, so him calling me Ms. Vincent has me scrunching my nose.

"Call me Ella, and it's nice to meet you too. If you guys want to go in and see Bennett, you can, but I should warn you, he's been busy pacing a hole into the floor."

Just then, the door to Bennett's office opens, revealing the man himself.

"Uncle Bennett, look! We're matching." Drake's voice breaks the silence as both Bennett and I look over at him, who is indeed matching his uncle.

Omigod. That is the most adorable thing in the world. Before the night is over, I need to take a picture and get it printed so I can put it in Bennett's office.

"That you are," Bennett says as he gives the little boy a smile, one that reaches his eyes and makes him even hotter.

No, he is the most gorgeous man ever, and I'm going to hell for thinking it.

The Lane men talk for a few minutes as I kick myself for thinking my boss is hot. I'm still lost in thoughts of his smile that I almost miss when Bennett calls out my name.

"What?" I ask, shaking myself out of the daze.

"Are you ready to head upstairs?" Bennett asks, his eyebrows bunching up in the process.

I frantically grab my notebook, pen, and phone before getting up. "Yes. I'm ready."

Bennett situates Drake in his office, and once that is taken care of, he, Henry, Elliot, and I head up to the top floor.

"This room is as stuffy as I remember," Elliot mutters.

The three men head to the huge conference table in the middle of the room and take a seat while I head over to the windows where three other assistants sit.

There are so many people in this room I have never seen before. I guess that should tell me the importance of the CEO calling a board meeting.

Gerald Goldman stands at the head of the table, a smile on his face.

"Thank you everyone for coming tonight. I know this was a bit late, but I appreciate the effort." Mumbles fill the room before the attention goes back to Gerald, who takes a second to collect himself. "Many of you may know why we are here tonight. I called this meeting to officially announce that I have decided to retire."

Claps sound out, and more than a handful of people get up to either give Gerald a handshake or a hug, congratulating him on his retirement, including Bennett.

Once everyone has had their chance to thank Gerald for putting in the work at Lane Enterprises, everyone sits back down and waits for the current CEO to continue speaking.

"Since I'm retiring, not only do I have to announce who I'm proposing as my replacement, but a vote to put the change into motion needs to happen. Why not just do it all in one go?"

Gerald scans the room, meeting the eyes of every single board member.

From the corner of my eye, I see someone moving. I turn to see Peter Hill place his elbows on the table. The asshole thinks it's going to be him. Of course he does. It finally clicks as to why Peter hates Bennett so much: he sees him as a threat.

So when Gerald doesn't speak right away, of course he is the one to speak up about it.

"We don't have all night, Gerald. Who are you choosing as your replacement?"

A look of anger passes across Gerald's face when Peter speaks, but Gerald composes himself and gives the room a bright smile.

Peter is practically foaming at the mouth, and I see Henry place a hand on Bennett's shoulder. If I were sitting next to him, I would be holding his hand.

"There was nothing hard about my decision. I know my choice will always do well by this company."

"Who is it?"

I swear, Peter is on the verge of jumping out of his seat and celebrating a victory that is never going to come.

Gerald looks around once more, and the bright smile from before overtakes the room.

"I'm proposing Bennett Lane to replace me."

There's silence for a few seconds before the room fills

with claps and cheers. Like with Gerald, people walk over to Bennett to give him their congratulations, as if the vote already came and went. Everyone congratulates Bennett—everyone but Peter.

My eyes stay on my boss for a minute or two, and I love that there is actual happiness flowing through his eyes. I want to see that happiness every day.

My marveling is cut short, though, when I notice Peter get up from his seat, a sadistic grin on his lips.

This man is up to something.

"This is absolute bullshit. He can't be named CEO," Peter snarls, slamming his fist against the conference room table, grabbing everyone's attention.

It's Bennett who confronts him.

"And why the fuck not?" he lets out, the happiness in his eyes completely gone.

The grin on Peter's face grows even more. "The bylaws are clear: the CEO must be married."

14

BENNETT

I knew it.

I fucking knew Hill was going to pull something. I knew something was coming, but this is far from what I expected.

A marriage clause? That's one of the stupidest pieces of shit I have ever heard.

Anger rolls through my body as I look at the grin on Peter's face. The fucker is enjoying this. From the looks of it, I'm not the only one who's pissed off; Gerald is too.

"What the fuck are you on, Pete? I've read the company bylaws top to bottom. There is no marriage clause."

Sure, I read them years ago, but I'm positive I would have remembered something that fucking absurd.

Without even thinking, I search for Ella. She was by the window when Gerald was speaking, but when I look over, she's not there. No, she's standing a few feet away from me, looking up at me with a single question in her eyes.

Not even a month working together, and we already know how to have silent conversations and know what the other wants.

I send a nod her way, and right away, she starts typing on her phone, trying to find this damn clause.

Peter moves to stand at the head of the table next to Gerald. From the looks of it, Gerald isn't all that happy with Mr. Hill either.

"Looks like you didn't read deep enough, because it's there, and it specifically states that in order to hold the title of CEO, the candidate must meet all the requirements, including being married at the time the title is handed over."

I try to think back to when I read the bylaws. So much pops into my head—everything except for that. Did I skip over it? Did I miss it completely? Why the fuck can't I remember that damn clause?

Given the look on Henry's face, I'm not the only one that can't remember either. He read those guidelines more times than I did. If there was something in there about a damn marriage clause, he would have pointed it out.

My plan to get this company into my hands was meticulous. I did everything that I had to do from the second I turned thirty, and if I had to get married to get what the fuck I wanted, I would have done it way before Gerald told me he was going to retire.

"This fucker is pulling shit out of his ass," Elliot spews, narrowing his eyes toward Peter.

"I would watch your mouth, kid. You're only here because of your daddy."

I don't have to look over at my nephew to know that there is anger in his eyes and that I need to place a hand on his shoulder to stop him from storming across the room and beating the ever-living shit out of Peter.

"Calm down," I mutter into Elliot's ear.

Peter is already causing a scene; we don't need to create another one.

Everyone else starts inserting themselves into the conversation, some saying we should just hold the vote and forget about the clause while others side with Peter.

As everyone argues about what we should or shouldn't do, I search for Ella. Right away, she looks over at me, as if she sensed I was looking for her. I don't even have to ask her what she found. Her facial expression tells me everything I need to know.

There is, in fact, a marriage clause.

I was so close to becoming CEO, and in a matter of seconds, it was fucking gone.

Fucking hell.

"Everyone quiet down!" Gerald yells, bringing the arguing to an end.

"Has anyone checked? Is there indeed a damn clause that prevents Mr. Lane from taking my place?" Henry voices, his shoulders squaring as if he were still in the military and is about to go into battle.

Ella lets out a sigh, and her shoulders drop. "Yes, sir."

"When was it dated, Ms. Vincent?" Henry asks.

Ella looks like she's about to cry as she answers him. "Three years ago, sir."

Three years ago.

Before I started putting my plan into fruition to convince Gerald to retire.

A year before my parents' will said I was able to become CEO.

And a year before Elliot earned his seat on the board.

This was planned. It had to be. The bylaws have been the same for the past fifty years; there was no reason to change them, not unless there was someone you wanted to keep out of the office on the top floor.

"I don't remember ever voting on something like that," I state through clenched teeth. Changes to bylaws have to be voted on, and I sure as hell wouldn't have said yes to something like this. More so because it affects me.

"Neither do I," Henry states from next to me.

Peter's smirk gets deeper. "Interesting. It might have been during a proxy vote when you were out of town."

Motherfucker.

He knew.

This fucker knew I would be vying for Gerald's seat the second I turned thirty. He fucking knew and decided to interfere years before it happened.

I knew this fucker had something up his sleeve; I just didn't think that it would be this.

"Well." Peter claps, gathering everyone's attention,. "Since Gerald's choice of CEO doesn't meet the requirements, should we reconvene in two weeks with another plan?"

Everyone around the room starts to mumble in agreement. Before I know it, words are flowing out of my mouth.

"There is no reason to reconvene. The vote will happen

tonight," I announce, stopping everyone in their tracks as they start leaving the room.

"You don't meet the requirements to become the head of this company. There is no reason to hold a vote," Peter snarls, frustration written all over his face.

"I may not meet the requirements now, but I will next week." The words flow so easily out of my mouth that even I believe them.

"What the fuck are you talking about?"

"I'm talking about the fact that I'm getting married next Saturday." Gasps ring out across the conference room.

I don't take my eyes off Peter as I say the words, but from my peripherals, I see both Elliot and Henry stiffen.

"Like hell you are."

I throw him a shrug, trying to remain as emotionless as I possibly can. "I'll be sure to send you a copy of our marriage license."

Peter goes red, but I can't really tell if it's from anger or embarrassment.

"Who the fuck are you marrying? The last time I checked, you were single." I will bet a good million that Peter stalks social media and all the news outlets to find my personal information.

"Given who I am, I kept things private, for her sake. But if you must know, I've been with my girlfriend for over a year, and I proposed in January. This wedding has been planned for months, but if I had known you were going to pull this shit, I would have walked down the aisle sooner."

I'm a bit shocked at how easy the lies flow out of me, how believable they sound.

"I don't fucking believe you," Peter snarls.

"Then don't, but it's true. If you want, we can hold off the vote until then. I'll bring the proof that I'm indeed married, and then we let the board decide if I should be CEO. How does that sound?"

There's a cockiness to my voice that shouldn't be there, especially when all I'm doing is spewing lies.

How the actual fuck am I going to pull this off?

The vein in Peter's neck looks like it's going to explode with all the anger rolling through him.

I did say that I would do anything to get Gerald's title; I just didn't think I would go this far.

Gerald lets out a sigh before throwing a nod in my direction. "We will hold off on voting for two weeks. Give you time to settle down from the craziness and catch your breath before you go on your honeymoon."

Peter lets out a scoff and rolls his eyes before addressing the man who is still technically his boss. "You seriously can't be believing this bullshit?"

Gerald is the one getting angry now, and it's the most glorious thing ever. "I do believe it. Want to know why? Because I was one of the few people who knew he was engaged."

Holy shit.

I don't know what shocks me the most: the fact that the lie came out so easily or that Gerald is going along with it.

Why would he do that?

I can only think of one reason: he truly believes I would be a good replacement.

Damn. I misjudged Gerald. The old bastard has a few

tricks up his sleeve. My respect for the man has definitely gone up.

"Does anyone else want to challenge my decisions?" Nobody dares speak. "Great. It's settled."

With that, people start to disperse, some angrier than others, until it's only Gerald, Henry, Elliot, Ella, and me left.

The calm after the storm is full of tension.

Elliot is the one to break it.

"Damn. If I knew board meetings were going to be this entertaining, I would attend them more often."

The comment earns him a slap on the back of the head from Henry.

Ignoring my nephew, I turn to Gerald.

"I'm guessing this marriage clause took you by surprise as well." Given how pissed off he looked and the way he lied, he couldn't have known about this change.

"Yes. I remember Hill suggesting we make changes to the bylaws but never signing off on them."

I let out a snort. There is no doubt in my mind that Mr. Hill probably forged Gerald's signature to get what he wanted. The asshole did something I would have never done.

"But why marriage? Out of all the clauses you could add, why the hell would you add a marriage clause? Bennett might not have been in a relationship three years ago, but things could have changed." Elliot looks around the room for an answer.

My mind goes to an interview I did a few years back

when I was asked if I was going to settle down. My answer? No, never.

Hill probably saw it and put shit into motion.

"Because it's the one thing he knew I would never do. He used it to his advantage."

Gerald lets out a heavy sigh. "I'm sorry, kid. I hope you can follow through with that idea of yours because I truly don't want to give this role to Peter."

With a nod in our direction, Gerald leaves the room, closing the door behind him.

"So what? We're in the mail-order bride business now?"

I roll my eyes, but my mind can't help but go in that direction. This damn clause is putting me in a bind, and it's causing my mind to spiral.

"There will be no such thing. There are other options," Henry states, trying to be optimistic.

"There isn't." I bow my head in defeat. "It's either get married or give up being CEO. There's no in-between."

Elliot comes up next to me, and for a second, I know what Ella was saying this morning. He does look like me. "So I'll ask again: what now?"

What now? I'm not sure, but I do know one thing.

"I'm not going to give up becoming CEO." I've worked so hard to get this title; I'm not going to give up just because of a stupid clause.

"So you're going to hire a random chick off the street and pay her to marry you?"

A noise from the other side of the room takes my attention away from Elliot and goes straight to Ella. She let out a scoff, as if she couldn't believe that was even a suggestion, but right now, it's all we have.

What if that wasn't the only choice, though? What if there was someone else I could approach with a proposition that will give us both what we want? What we need?

Someone like Ella?

Someone exactly like Ella.

She isn't a stranger, and I already have an attraction to her I'm unable to explain. The kiss we shared earlier this week still replays in my head.

It wouldn't be unheard of for someone to marry their assistant.

The woman in question meets my gaze.

A small blush crawls up to her face as words leave her plush mouth. "Why are you looking at me like that?"

"Because you're the answer to all of this."

15

ELLA

"Answer? What do you mean *I'm the answer*?"

No way is he suggesting what I think he's suggesting. I'm all for helping out my boss, but this is going to be a hard no.

Bennett doesn't answer; he just continues to look at me like I'm a prized possession or something.

"If you are suggesting that I marry you for a stupid title, the answer is no."

"Ella."

I start shaking my head before he can say anything else. "No, I'm not going to marry you."

"It would be beneficial for both of us."

A snort leaves me, and I can't help but roll my eyes. "Beneficial. You get a CEO title, and I get what? Your damn last name?"

"No," he lets out in a matter-of-fact tone.

"Then how is it going to be beneficial?"

"You'd get whatever you want. Money, property, anything."

My eyes go wide at the same time that my mouth pops open.

He'd give me anything I wanted if I married him? Who offers that?

A billionaire, that's who.

The room goes silent as Bennett and I have the most intense stare-off we've ever had. It's not until someone clears their throat that we look to where Henry and Elliot stand.

"We will let you discuss this...situation privately. We have to get Mr. Drake home."

Henry grabs Elliot's arm and pulls him out of the office. Bennett's nephew goes reluctantly, but at least he leaves. Now, I can have a screaming match with his uncle.

"Are you out of your mind?" I ask, though it comes out more like a whisper instead of the yell I thought was brewing inside me.

Bennett lets out a sigh and takes a seat in the nearest chair, dropping his head into his hands.

"Possibly. At this point, I almost feel desperate."

"Why, though?"

"Why what?"

I walk over to the conference table, leaving a few feet between us but not taking a seat. "Why is becoming CEO so important? Why the desperation?"

When the question leaves my mouth, Bennett looks almost stunned, like I'm the first person to ever ask him.

It takes him a whole two minutes to come up with an answer.

"The company deserves to be run by a Lane."

I agree, but that's the most bullshit answer I've ever heard.

"Is that why you want to do it? Because it's what the company *deserves*?"

"Yes."

"That's a bullshit answer, and you know it."

Bennett's jaw tics, and I can see the anger in his eyes. Good. I'm not going to agree to anything until I know the full story. I'm not going to jump into a meaningless marriage just because my boss asks.

"It's not." Bennett stands up from his chair and closes the distance between us, looking down at me as if to tell me to back down. Not going to happen.

"It is. Why the fuck do you want to be CEO so badly?"

"Why are you asking?"

"Because if you want me to sign my life over to you, I need to know why the fuck you want this so badly that you're willing to marry the first woman you see."

He doesn't say anything. He just continues to stare me down, but I stand my ground.

After a minute, when he still doesn't say anything, I let out a sigh and turn toward the door to leave. I'm not going to get an answer. There's no point in waiting for one.

I'm a foot away from the door when he finally says something.

"You want the absolute truth?" His voice comes out in a whisper, something I've never heard from Bennett.

I turn to face him. "Yes."

The man standing a few feet away from me is not the same man I've been working with these last few weeks. This man is wearing his emotions on his sleeves, trying to keep himself together. The man I've been working for doesn't show an ounce of emotion, is always stoic.

"Then you'll get it, but you have to promise me something."

"And what would that be?"

"That you won't judge me for what I'm about to say. You want the truth, I'll give it to you, but just because I'm handing it over doesn't mean you'll like it."

There is no hesitation in me, no second thought as I throw a nod in his direction. Nothing he could say is going to make me look at him differently, that much I know.

"There are two reasons; one you will think is endearing, and the other, well, you might hate."

"You don't know that."

"Oh, but I do, sweet Ella."

A shiver runs through my body at the term of endearment. I shouldn't like it as much as I do, but everything this man does and says affects me in ways I would never want to admit out loud.

"What are the reasons?" I ask softly.

His eyes don't move from mine as he speaks. "What I told you a minute ago wasn't complete bullshit. The company deserves to be run by a Lane, and if things were different, it would have been. If my father hadn't died, he would be here right now, giving this company his all. But he did die, and his oldest son isn't here, so now, giving this company what it deserves falls to me."

My heart stutters a bit. Bennett may not hear it, but I do. There is so much heartbreak in his voice that all I want to do is wrap my arms around him and never let him go. My brain is telling me to do it, but I stay rooted in place.

"And I know what you might be thinking," he continues before I'm able to say anything. "But it's not out of obligation. Nobody is obligating me to take on this role. I don't feel obligated to wear the title just because my parents are dead or because my brother isn't here. I want to do this. I want to build this company to surpass my father's dreams. I want to make my parents proud and see from wherever the fuck they are that at least one of their sons is doing okay. I want them to be proud that their son took meaning in their work and made it his own."

He was right. I *am* finding the first reason endearing and heartbreaking. Here he is, this larger-than-life man with everything he'd ever want in the whole world, just wanting to make his parents proud.

For a few seconds, I picture the person in front of me the same age as Drake and wonder if he was that excited to see his dad when he came to the office, if he wore matching suits just for the fun of it.

A tear rolls down my face, but I catch it before more follow.

"What's the second reason?" I ask, wanting to stop any more emotions from taking over.

"You're not going to like it."

"Try me."

His face changes. In a matter of seconds, the little boy who lost his parents is gone, and in his place is a man I don't recognize. A smirk forms on his face, and it's not one I love seeing. This smirk is different from the others. This smirk almost scares me.

"I want the power. I want the power that comes with the title. I want the respect. I want the ability to ruin the lives of the people who have wanted to ruin mine. I want people to answer to me, not the other way around."

A shiver runs through my body in a different way than it did a few minutes earlier.

He wants power, and if he is propositioning me with marriage, I know he will stop at nothing to get it.

But as much as I want to think it's egotistical, I understand it. I understand why he would want something like that, why he would want the respect and the authority. Having that type of power makes you a different person, and I can see Bennett using it in a way that would not only benefit him but others as well.

"Power is a good thing to have," I let out, trying to figure out why I don't hate the reason like he said I would.

Bennett comes closer, almost crowding me. "Not the type of power I want. What I want, what I crave, shouldn't be at anyone's disposal. I don't want to just run Lane Enterprises—I want to take over the damn city. When I'm done with Chicago, I'll move on to different parts of the world."

I swallow audibly, not sure what to do or say.

Run, Ella. Run now and don't look back.

I would. I truly would if it wasn't a smidge beneficial for me.

It's the type of power that would stop me from looking over my shoulder, the type of power that would protect me and Charlie if anyone came looking for us. The type of power that can pay off my debts. He did say I could ask for whatever I wanted. I could ask for the money.

"Tell me what you're thinking, sweet Ella."

There's that nickname again, and I can't help but feel a throbbing between my legs.

I take a second to compose myself.

"I'm thinking...that I should say no to your offer."

"But?"

"But I don't want to."

"Then say yes."

I want to take Bennett up on his offer, even if the vows we take will be the most disingenuous things I've ever said. He will get his title, and in return, there's a possibility I could get something I've been wanting for years.

Safety.

It may be a lie getting me there, but I'm okay with that.

I guess Bennett was right—this little idea of his is beneficial for both of us. He gets the title and whatever power comes with it, and I get to be *free.*

The more I think about it, the more I'm leaning toward the answer I least expected to give.

Not an ounce of hesitation coats my voice when I answer my boss.

"Yes."

"Yes?"

I nod. "Yes. I will marry you."

"Let's come up with some rules, then."

16

"Rules?" The question leaves my mouth in a bit of disbelief. You need rules for a fake marriage?

"Yes. We need to put some in place to make this work."

"Make this work..." I run the words through my head a few times. "I guess I just figured that we would get married, you'll become CEO, and then we'll get a divorce a month later, so rules wouldn't apply."

Saying that plan out loud makes me realize that won't work. People would see right through it, and Bennett seems to agree.

"No. The board members will never take that. If we divorce before the ink is dry, being CEO will be out of reach. The marriage has to last for a while."

My palms start to sweat a little bit. "How long is a while?"

"At least two years."

My eyes bug out. Two years? I can barely handle my

attraction for this man for a day; how am I going to handle two years?

"Two years is a lot, don't you think?"

I need to protect my heart. Sure, what I feel for Bennett is a crush, one that continues to grow with every passing day, but two years is a long time, and a lot can happen. A lot of feelings can change. I don't want to leave this with a broken heart that may not ever be prepared.

Bennett gives me a smile that almost looks sad. "Do you have a better timeline?"

I don't even have to think about it. We both know that I don't.

"Okay, two years." My nods are slow, trying to digest that I'm spending two years of my life with this man.

Two years. It will pass quickly. Two years will be nothing.

Right. It will be nothing.

Apparently, I'm so stuck in my head that Bennett thinks I might pass out because he guides me to the conference table and orders me to take a seat.

"Are you okay?" he asks, concern very distinct in his voice.

"Yeah," I say, looking up at him, a smile that doesn't reach my eyes on my lips. "I'm just trying to process every-thing." I definitely didn't think my first board meeting would go like this.

"Before we nail anything down, I want to apologize."

The way he says the words takes me more by surprise than the words themselves. It's a complete contrast to the man who was telling me he craves power.

"Why are you apologizing?" I ask, looking into his eyes and seeing a bit of fear in them.

"Because this is a big ask, not only with the marriage aspect of things but also with the time dedicated to this. I'm basically asking you to sign away your life to me for two years."

Interesting how he doesn't say that he would be signing his life away to me. He's making it sound as if, for the next two years, I will be his property and his property alone. Wouldn't the same sentiment apply to me? Maybe it's his way of telling me he can fuck around during our two years of marriage, but I can't.

I try hard to push down all the weird emotions spurred by the thought of Bennett fooling around behind my back and concentrate on the present.

"This is something I'm agreeing to. There is no reason for you to apologize." My words come out with a bit of a bite to them, and if Bennett notices, he chooses to ignore it.

While he doesn't say anything about my tone, he grabs the notebook I brought with me. His eyes peer into mine, and for a second, I forget about what we're about to talk about.

Every time Bennett looks over at me, I find myself trying to find all the different shades of blue and green in his eyes when I should be concentrating on the rules we are putting together.

Public displays of affection in public and some small displays while we are in the office. Hand holding whenever possible. Traveling with him at least eighty percent of the time to make it seem like I can't spend more than two days away from him. Dates at least twice a week in a public space.

Sounds doable.

Doable, but there's no doubt in my mind that my heart is going to hate me at the end of the two years.

"Would I be able to tell my sister about this 'arrangement'? I won't be able to lie to her for two whole years," I say as Bennett writes something down about a family vacation in the next six months.

Apparently, that's what I'm marrying into: a family that takes family vacations.

In my whole life, I've never taken one, and now I'm going to be a part of one in six months.

Bennett gives me a nod at my request. "Yes. She's very much one of the need-to-know people. My older kids would eat me alive if I held something like this from them, and given that they live with me, it would be hard not to explain."

My eyebrows shoot up a little bit. "Kids?"

He could be talking about his brother's children, but I could be wrong. Maybe he has a kid he hasn't mentioned.

"Sorry, I meant my niece and nephews." I'm rewarded with a smile I put away for safekeeping.

"Is there anyone else you'd like to tell?" he asks once his beautiful smile finally fades.

I shake my head. "No. Charlie is all I have."

A look of pity crosses over Bennett's face, one I've seen before, and it stays on his face longer than I'd like. He looks like he wants to say something, but he holds back and gives me a small smile.

My past has become something I hold close to my heart, but if I'm going to be married to Bennett, there are a few things that can't stay hidden. He's going to have questions, and I will have to give him answers.

"You can ask, you know," I say, looking down at my hands, not wanting to see any more pity directed at me.

"Ask what?" The question leaves his lips as if I didn't see him hesitating just a few seconds ago.

"Why Charlie is all I have?"

I put the question out there, and I watch Bennett go through a string of emotions before he settles on curiosity and leans back in his chair. He had discarded his suit jacket a few minutes after we sat down, so the movement has the sleeves of his button-down rolling up.

"You don't have to tell me."

He's right. I don't, but for some reason, I find myself wanting to.

"We're going to be married. Isn't one of the things that makes a marriage work—not hiding things from the other?"

He's silent for a few seconds. "I guess it is."

For a second, both of us just sit and process the fact that this is legit. We are really getting married, and there is no backing away now.

I take a deep breath before I say anything.

"My childhood wasn't the very best, at least not the parts I remember. My mom had me her last year in high school. My bio dad was a rich kid who apparently had a future ahead of him, so his parents paid my mom to 'take care of the situation.' She took the money, but instead of getting rid of the pregnancy, she had me. She thought my bio dad would grow a heart and give her more money to help raise me. Newsflash: that didn't happen."

My mind goes to when I was five and a random man came to our door, yelling at my mom. He kept telling her he wanted nothing to do with her and to stop looking for him. It took me a few years to figure out that the yelling man who made Mama cry was my dad. I never saw him again.

"When I was a little, she developed a drug habit, one that made her forget she had a kid at home. When I was about six, she left me by myself for three days. She always told me to never go outside unless she was home, but I had finished all the food we had left, so I thought it was a good idea to go next door and ask the neighbor for some. To this day, I don't know if that was a good idea, because that neighbor called child protective services, and within two weeks, I was in a foster care home in Nevada.

"Neither my mom nor her mother came for me. Neither did my father or his family, so I became a ward of the state, and that's where I stayed until I was moved to a group home here in Chicago when I was thirteen."

I don't know what I hated more: going from one foster home to another or getting shipped out to a different state because nobody wanted to take in a teenager.

I wasn't a bad kid. I wasn't mouthy, and I followed all the rules, but even when you are doing everything you're supposed to do, it doesn't mean foster care is a joy-filled ride. Sure, there were families I loved being with, and I got the feeling they loved me, but even then, that wasn't enough to lead to a permanent home. More so when I got older.

The group home I spent five years in was just an extension of high school. You would think that being in similar situations would bring people closer together, but no. For five years, I was surrounded by catty bitches who didn't know how to keep their hands off my stuff.

Not wanting to go down a very deep and very depressing rabbit hole, I bring my story to an end so I don't cry in front of my boss—err, my future *husband*.

"Anyway," I say after clearing my throat. "I cut ties with my family, and it's just me and Charlie now."

I cross my fingers under the table, away from Bennett's eyes, and hope he doesn't notice I didn't mention how Charlie came into my life.

My future husband stays quiet for a few long seconds, as if digesting everything, before he gives me a smile, one filled with sympathy.

"I'm sorry you had to go through that."

I give him a shrug. "It's okay. It's something I've dealt with already."

Liar. I still very much have deep-rooted abandonment issues, but I never let them see the light of day.

We go silent for a few seconds, not knowing how to move on from the dark turn this took. Not wanting to get lost staring at Bennett again, I break the silence.

"Okay, so we have our list of need-to-know people. What else do we need to figure out?"

Not a single beat is missed. "Living arrangements."

"Excuse me?" The question comes out a little too loud and way too surprised.

We're getting married; did I think we were going to leave separately? Well, maybe.

"We have to live together to make this believable."

"Right. Believable."

If I want to ask him for the money I need, then I have to make sure this marriage comes off as real, no matter how fake it may be.

Besides, I already agreed to PDA. I can handle living with the man for two years.

As I try not to spiral, we decide Charlie and I will move into the Lane compound sometime next week. I offered to pay rent, but he turned it down before the words were fully out.

I should have been mad, but a part of me is relieved at the agreement because it means that for the first time in my adult life, I don't have to worry about paying rent. I'll have to find a new place to live after our time is up, but that is something I'll think about when the time comes.

After figuring out how we are going to live, we move on to the type of wedding *I* want. My *fiancé* was very specific about that.

Even though this isn't real, he still wants me to have the wedding I want. Not a single expense matters.

Given how I grew up, I never really thought about what my wedding would look like. Sure, there has been a time or two where I've scrolled through social media and really liked a dress or a ring, but it never went past that.

So why is it that, as I sit here, I want to tell Bennett I

want a big wedding? I may not have the friends and family to fill the seats, but I still want to feel like a princess. I still want to see myself in a big puffy dress, possibly even wear a tiara, get my makeup and hair done, and just be the center of attention for a day. I want all the flowers and all the candles. I want the wedding any girl would think of.

But I can't find it in myself to ask for it. He's already done so much for me and is going to do a lot more from the sounds of it. I can't seem to find it in me to ask.

Which is why I suggest a small wedding, one that doesn't have the big puffy dress and all the flowers in the world. A small wedding that is just us and our families.

Thankfully, we don't have to look far for a venue or even a caterer because Bennett offers the Lane compound and all the chefs he has on staff.

Once the wedding is planned and the rules are set, there is only one thing left to discuss: what I get out of all this.

"You don't know what you're offering," I let out when Bennett reminds me he's willing to give me anything and everything I want for helping him.

""But I do. Give me your price, Elizabeth, and it will be yours."

Ask him.

Ask him, and you will no longer have to look over your shoulder every day or be wary of who you open the door to.

The words form on the tip of my tongue, but I can't make them come out.

I open my mouth a few times, trying to find my voice, but no matter how hard I try, nothing comes out.

Bennett is patient with me, not pushing me to say anything until I'm ready.

It takes me three whole minutes to come up with a sentence that won't break me down.

"Can you promise me you won't ask any questions? That you won't judge? That you will just keep your end of the deal and that is that?"

He doesn't even hesitate. "I promise."

Here goes nothing.

"I want..." I shake my head. "No, I need to come out of this marriage with a million dollars."

Shame runs through my body, so much so that I can't even look at Bennett. I find it a bit ironic, really. He was able to hold his head high with his request, but I can't even look him in the eye for mine.

I expected him to think about it, to tell me that it was a lot of money, but once again, the man takes me by surprise.

"Okay."

One simple word to take care of all my worries.

"Really?" I ask in disbelief. Nobody in their right mind would agree to this, not even a billionaire, but I guess when you're desperate, you would agree to anything.

"Yes. I told you, if you agree to this, you could have anything you want. If you need the money, I will give it to you."

Just like that.

This time, I can't find words, but for a different kind of reason.

Charlie is going to be safe, and there won't be any more fear of anyone coming to take her away from me.

"Thank you." I reach out and place a hand over his.

He looks down at my hand but doesn't do anything to move it off him.

"No need to thank me. Besides, I should be the one thanking you. Not anyone would have agreed to this."

"Well, I guess you made a good choice in a wife."

"Yeah, I guess I did."

Something passes between us as we both look into each other's eyes. It's not lust, or even something that may resemble love with time. It's more like acceptance. We are really doing this. We are going to be man and wife.

Before the moment gets too deep, Bennett looks away, pushing his chair away from the table, leaving me to look up at him. From this angle, he looks as if nothing can touch him. It's as if, for a moment, he's the king of everything before him.

He holds out a hand and gives me a rare smile, one I put in my mental vault for safekeeping.

"Do we have a deal?"

This is it. I walked into this conference room, hoping I still had a job after my boss became CEO, and now I'm going to leave it as his future wife.

Standing up, I place my hand in his, ignoring the way my body shivers as our skin touches as I shake it, putting our plan into motion.

"We have a deal. Let's get married."

"Let's get married, Mrs. Lane."

17

BENNETT

I look at my notifications and let out a sigh. I thought I was going to have more time, but given the text message that just arrived in the family group chat, that time is up, and I'm going to get my ass chewed out by a seventeen-year-old girl.

SAMANTHA

What the HELL is this?!

THERE's no point in clicking on the link; I know where it leads: a news article that states that I'm getting married.

I knew news was going to start from the second everyone left the board meeting last Friday; I'm just a bit surprised it took them this long to get it out into the world.

The press probably needed concrete evidence I was

indeed getting married, and since Ella and I went to get our marriage license yesterday after work, they got it.

Even though having news articles talk about my upcoming nuptials is something I expected, I still send the article over to Henry in a separate message thread and tell him to get rid of it.

From what I can tell, Ella is hiding something. What, exactly, I haven't found out yet; even Dante is having a hard time with it. Whatever it is, though, is enough to make her skittish, so if I can protect her from whatever it is, then I will.

How husbandly of you.

Another message comes through, taking me away from my thoughts.

ELLIOT

It looks like our dear uncle finally decided to give us an aunt.

SAMANTHA

Since when? Who is she and why the hell did I have to find out through a damn tabloid?!

I CAN HEAR her wrath all the way from here. Out of all the kids, Samantha is the most protective of me. Every time I brought someone around, she would always do her best to ice her out, which is why I knew I had to tell her and Grayson the truth. I just haven't gotten to it.

Hopefully, once she meets Ella, she'll warm up to her. I don't know if I would be able to make it two years with her mad-dogging my wife every chance she gets.

Did I just think of Ella as my wife?

Great. I'm not even married and I already have my brain thinking that this marriage is real.

GRAYSON

I have so many questions, but…is she hot???

I ROLL my eyes and decide to interrupt them before the messages get out of hand.

BENNETT

I'll explain tonight. Grayson, Samantha, I'm sending over a car. Be ready by three.

I LOOK at my screen for about a minute, waiting to see if they start back up again, but all I get are okays from the two teenagers as the chat quiets down. I really should have called them at home when Ella and I agreed to this, but I didn't know how to admit that I essentially hired my assistant to be my wife.

I still don't, but at least I have a better understanding of the situation than I did last week.

Was it stupid for me to ask the woman who has been in my head for over a month now to be my wife so I could become CEO? Yeah, it was.

The fact that she even agreed still astonishes me.

From the sounds of it, she needs me just as much as I need her.

She could have asked for anything in the world, and she only asked for a million dollars. I would have given her a hundred million if it would have made her agree.

Why would she only want a million? Maybe she's looking to buy a house or she thinks that a million would set her up for life. I want to believe it's one of those two things, but the way she wouldn't even look at me tells me there's more to it.

She may have started to become comfortable around me at the office, but this situation is different, and she has yet to give me all her trust. I saw it in the way she didn't go into all the details of her childhood, and I felt it when she asked for the money.

Who knows if I will ever earn it, but it wouldn't hurt to try. Maybe once she moves in, it will be easier.

I decided to work from home to get things done today, Ella having the day off.

That to-do list isn't really happening, though, because every few minutes, I'm getting distracted with thoughts of her. All morning, I've been trying to finish a proposal for our applied science department, but instead, I'm thinking of ways to make Ella's life a little easier. After another fifteen minutes, I give up on the proposal and start working on things for her.

And that's how I spend most of the afternoon: thinking about all things Ella, including setting up an appointment for a jeweler so that we can pick out our wedding rings.

I hesitated with that.

Marriage may not have been something I planned on doing, but if I ever did, I always thought I would propose with one of my mother's rings. Her wedding ring would be perfect for Ella. Hell, a lot of my mother's jewelry would be perfect for Ella, but it's too much. This is only for two years; I can't risk losing something that meaningful. For now, all my mother's pieces will go to the kids, and hopefully, they are able to appreciate them when the time comes.

"Mr. Lane," Henry announces as he walks into my home office, taking my concentration away from the lookbook of suits on my computer.

"Yes?" I ask, looking up at the old man holding out a glass of water, which I take.

"Miss Samantha and Mr. Grayson just arrived, and I will say that Miss Lane doesn't look all that happy."

I chug down my water, trying to give myself more time before I have to deal with my teenage niece. In times like these, I think of my mother and wonder if I would be this scared of her if she were still here.

"Maybe Ella will become a good role model for her, calm down some of the anger," I say, handing the glass back to Henry.

"One could hope, sir."

A second later, the front door opens, and I hear footsteps approaching my office.

I let out a sigh. "Make sure Drake is occupied; I'll handle the teenagers."

"Of course."

As Henry leaves the room, Grayson and Samantha appear, Elliot right behind them. I watch as they greet Henry in a way grandkids would greet their favorite grandfather.

Once the kids are in the room and Henry is gone, all the warm and fuzzy greetings disappear, replaced by stares and stances that are defensive and full of questions.

"Before any questions, close the door," I order Grayson, my fifteen-year-old nephew who desperately needs a haircut. His dirty blond hair looks like a damn mop.

I'll have to call a barber before the wedding tomorrow.

"Why are we closing the door?" Samantha asks, standing her ground as her brothers take a seat on the couch.

"Because there are little ears around, and we know for a fact that he can't keep a secret."

The fact that he came to me this morning and told me that Elliot took him to get ice cream at midnight after I'm sure his brother told him to keep a secret is telling enough.

"Drake doesn't know you're getting married?" Sam asks, raising her eyebrows in the process.

"He knows, and he knows we are going to have new people living here, but I'm keeping the why from him."

"Do we get to know?" Grayson asks, and I try to ignore that he looks a lot like his dad right now.

"I'm surprised Elliot didn't tell you already."

Elliot shrugs. "I just thought it would make more sense coming from you."

I pinch the bridge of my nose. Sometimes, I wish I didn't have to deal with this shit.

I take a second to collect myself and explain why I'm getting married. I don't go into much detail, like how long this marriage will last and what she will be gaining from this, but I do tell them about the vote. They both ask questions, and in the end, Grayson looks just as confused as he did when he walked in here earlier, but Sam actually looks like she understands.

"What's her name?" Gray asks, trying to get all the information he can.

"Ella."

He nods like he likes the sound of her name. "How old is she?"

This is where I should lie, but I still find myself answering truthfully.

"Twenty-five."

All three mouths fall open in disbelief.

"Dude, she's only five years older than me?" Elliot lets out, a tinge of disgust in his voice.

Yup. I should have definitely lied.

"Doesn't that make you a cradle robber?" Gray says, scratching his head.

I should have definitely kept Ella's age to myself. "No. I'm not a cradle robber."

"But she's way younger than you," Sam throws out,

having sat down next to her brothers about twenty minutes ago.

"Only by seven years," I say through clenched teeth. Why am I even arguing about this? "Her age doesn't matter. What matters is that she and her sister are moving in tonight, and we are getting married tomorrow. This marriage will be real. I don't give a shit how you feel about it; you will respect her and her sister and treat them as part of this family. Do you understand?"

All three of them nod.

"Good. Anything else do you want to know?"

They look at each other, and for a second, it seems like they are having a silent conversation.

Eventually, it's who Grayson speaks. "How old is the sister?"

Please let it be that he is asking that question out of curiosity and not because his hormones are going rampant.

"Sixteen. You might have already met her. Her name is Charlie, and she started at Saint Christopher's a few weeks ago."

Grayson eyebrows shoot up, and Sam looks like she's trying to run through faces at Saint Christopher's to find the one I might be talking about.

"Wait, Charlotte?"

"Yes. I'm guessing you've met.

"We have a few classes together, but I haven't met her yet. She's been keeping to herself."

I would too. If I got thrown into a new school without

knowing a single person, I wouldn't want to interact with anyone.

"Well, as of tomorrow, she's going to be family, so treat her as such." Sam gives me a nod before I turn to her brothers. "And that means not hitting on her. Think of her as your cousin, sister, whatever it takes."

"Damn. Do you seriously not have any confidence in us? That would be like flirting with Sammie, and just the thought of it makes me gag."

"Then keep thinking it."

A knock sounds, and I turn in time to see Henry poke his head in.

"Sir, sorry to interrupt, but Ms. Vincent's car has arrived."

"Thank you, Henry."

I guess this is it.

My life is changing yet again.

All because I want to hold the title that my father once held. There's no going back now.

The next two years of my life are about to begin.

18

ELLA

"*This* is where we are going to be living for the next two years?" Charlie lets out in awe as the car Bennett sent to pick us up drives through the gate to the Lane property.

"Apparently so."

As the car drives up the long driveway lined with trees, I see the house in a newer light than I did when I first came here last week.

The last time, I was able to admire the property. Now as we drive up, I pick on the little things I didn't notice last time. Like that all the trees have "children at play" signs attached to them, or even that there's a swing set close to the house, bikes and toys scattered everywhere. Things that make this huge-ass property actually feel like a home.

But will it feel like *my* home?

God, I sure hope so. I don't want to spend the next two years being miserable.

The car pulls up to the house, and for a solid thirty

seconds, both Charlie and I just sit there, staring at the house in awe.

Was the house this massive last week?

It had to have been, but I wasn't paying attention. I was concentrating a little too hard at how good Bennett looked in an all-black suit to take notice how big the house was.

"This house is huge," Charlie says, her face nearly plastered against the window.

"This is going to be the biggest house I will ever live in," I say with the same awe.

That awe increases when the driver opens the door and holds out a hand for me to step out.

I guess this is my life now. I live in a massive mansion and have people open the door for me every time I get out of a car.

I'm so much in my head, I don't notice Bennett walking to meet the car a few feet away until Charlie says something.

"Oh my god. You didn't tell me I was going to know two of them," she whisper-yells in my ear.

"Huh?"

"I know two of his kids. They go to school with me."

Right. I forgot about that small detail.

Hopefully they aren't complete assholes and don't make Charlie's life a living hell both at home and at school.

But I don't say that to my sister.

"He mentioned it once, but I completely forgot to tell you. They aren't bad kids, are they?" I try to keep my voice low to make sure Bennett doesn't hear me.

Charlie shakes her head. "Not from what I've seen."

That's good, I guess.

You can't judge them without getting to know them.

Do I want to get to know them? I'm only going to be here for two years, and then I'm gone. If I get to know them, all of us could be hurting when it's time for me to leave. I don't think I would be able to do that.

But it's something that would be important to Bennett.

Looks like I'll be doing things that make him happy for the next two years, and for some reason, I'm okay with that. Really okay with that.

I need to get my mind straight and not get lost in this damn marriage.

"Should we go inside?" I try to smile over at Charlie, but it comes out strained.

"Why do you look like you're going to puke?" My sister takes a step back while she examines me like I'm about to cover her with everything in my stomach.

And honestly, I feel like it's a possibility.

For once, I actually tell her what I'm feeling instead of hiding it. "Because I'm freaking out. What if this is a bad idea? What if we both end up hating this?"

"Both as in you and me? Or both as in you and Bennett?"

"All the above?"

Charlie takes my hand and gives it a hard squeeze, acting like the best little sister she is.

"We can leave. It may be awkward, but we can take the driver and steal the car and go back to our apartment."

I can't help but smile at her and squeeze her hand back.

"Tempting, but I think I need to pull my big girl pants on and walk inside."

"Whatever you say. I'm totally down to drive a hundred-thousand-dollar car."

I let out a laugh, something I really needed, and for the first time today, I relax. I've been on pins and needles from the second I woke up this morning. I couldn't even relax as I was getting my nails and hair done or even during my waxing appointment, something my sister convinced me to do, so laughing at a moment like this feels good.

"Let's go."

With my sister's hand in mine, we walk the few feet separating us from Bennett and his family. All of them look so perfect, so put together, even with Bennett wearing jeans and a T-shirt. All the while, me and Charlie looked like we just got home from the gym.

We don't belong here.

You're doing this to make sure Charlie stays with you. You are doing this for her.

I'm doing this for Charlie.

"Hi." I send a small wave in their direction, feeling a bit awkward.

"Hi," Bennett greets back, an awkward smile on his face.

I don't know how long we stand there, awkward tension surrounding us, waiting for the other to say or do something to break the tension. Thankfully, it's broken when one of the teenagers says something.

"You two need to do something about your communication skills because they suck ass," the boy I haven't met says out loud.

"Seriously? We're supposed to believe you are madly in love?" Charlie throws in.

A blush creeps up my face as I look up to see four pairs of eyes looking between the two of us, as if we were a circus act.

Bennett clears his throat, his own blush covering his face, and tries to act less awkward, but I can see it on his face that he's struggling.

"Um, Elizabeth, this is my niece, Samantha, and my nephew, Grayson." He waves to the two kids I have yet to meet. Is it weird calling two people who are maybe ten years younger than me kids? Does that make me sound old?

I put the old thought away and send a wave and a smile over to Bennett's niece and nephew. "It's nice to meet you. This is my sister, Charlie."

Everyone greets each other, and within seconds, we're back to standing around in awkwardness.

This is going so well.

"I can't with this," Samantha says before facing Charlie. "Do you want a tour or something? Maybe food? Let these two figure out whatever's going on with them."

"Um." Charlie looks over at me, as if she is asking me if it's okay if she goes.

I want to tell her not to go, to stay with me and help me deal with the awkwardness, but I can't do that to her. Not only is this my life for the next two years, it's hers, too. She should be friends with these people and feel like she's at home.

Which is why I let go of her hand.

"Go. I'll find you later."

She gives me a smile before she follows Elliot, Samantha, and Grayson into the massive house.

Once the four of them are in the house, it's just Bennett and me left on our own.

"We didn't really think this through, did we?" he says, looking down at me as he plays with his hands a bit.

I give him a smile. "No, but we will figure it out."

"Right." He throws a smile back before he looks away. "Is a moving truck coming later with your stuff?"

A snort escapes me before I can even think about it. I compose myself before speaking. "No. No moving truck. We didn't have a whole lot of stuff, so we were able to fit everything into a few suitcases."

When I told Charlie about this whole situation, we decided almost nothing from our apartment was going to come with us and what we were going to put into storage or sell.

It didn't take that long for us to figure out that there weren't a lot of things within the walls of our small apartment with sentimental value. There were a few small things, but the majority of the stuff we had accumulated was meaningless, so it made getting rid of things easier.

In the end, we ended up with only two large suitcases each that we were able to fit into the car that picked us up, and that was it. It's sad, really, that after so many years, all we have was able to fit into four suitcases.

"I'll have someone bring them upstairs for you." I give him a smile before he continues. "Let me show you around before dinner."

"Sounds good. Lead the way."

Like a sad little puppy, I follow Bennett through the property, listening to every word he says, getting lost in the small little touches between us, marveling at almost everything he points out. The place is massive, and there is no doubt in my mind I will be getting lost until I find my footing.

The house has bedrooms the size of the apartment I just gave up, gorgeous bathrooms, and massive closets that look like they could be filled with whole department stores worth of clothes. There's a movie theater, a whole kitchen that any cook or baker would dream of having, game rooms, and a garage probably bigger than a football field and filled with so many different cars. There's even a massive pool in the back that has a waterslide attached to it.

The library, though, may be my favorite.

That is, until Bennett shows me my bedroom.

The second I walk in, I'm in awe. Everything about it is perfect, from the colors on the wasll to the four-poster bed in the middle. There are white hydrangeas on the bedside table that almost match the walls, and a bay window that overlooks the expansiveness of the property.

As a little girl, I always dreamed of having a room like this, but I knew I was never going to get it. Yet, here I am, standing in it.

"The closet and bathroom are over here," Bennett tells me, waving me over to a massive door I didn't even notice.

I follow him through the doorway and let out a small gasp when I see a massive room filled with everything any girl would dream of.

Dresses of every kind.

Purses for every occasion.

Heels in every color and height, sitting next to every article of clothing you could imagine. Men's clothes are in the corner, suits organized by color.

Everything is so organized, ready to be worn.

"What is all of this?" I ask after finding my voice. I take in every aspect, trying to figure out who all of this belongs to.

"A gift from me to you," Bennett says, and right away, my eyes leave the clothes and go to him.

"What do you mean?"

My future husband walks over to where I am, leaving only about a foot of distance between us. "It means that all of this is yours—to wear, to keep, to do whatever you want with it. You can think of it as a wedding gift."

I'm at a loss for words. He got me clothes? There have to be pieces in here worth thousands, and I get to call them mine?

"You filled a whole closet for me?" I ask in disbelief.

Why would he do something like this?

"I did. Well, a personal shopper did. I figure that since you're going to marry a Lane, you should have a closet of one."

Butterflies flutter in my belly, and the more I take what

Bennett gives me, the more the fluttering increases. He got me a whole *closet*.

"I didn't get you a wedding gift." Well, I didn't know I needed to get one, and now I feel bad.

"That's something you don't need to worry about." Yeah, too late. Now, all I can think about is how I could get him a new tie, maybe one that matches his eyes. "Anyway, the bathroom is through that door, and on the other side of that is my room."

"We're not sleeping in the same room?" I don't know why I sound disappointed. Of course we are not sharing a room. Just because we are getting married doesn't mean sharing a bed would be a good idea.

A sweet smile spreads across his face that is new to me. "Not unless you want to."

My face doesn't hesitate in going red right away. "No, w-we can sleep in separate rooms."

Did it get hot in here suddenly?

The distance between us gets smaller, and Bennett places a hand on my shoulder. "Calm down, Ella. I was kidding."

"Right. I knew that."

Another sweet smile appears. "I just figured it would be easier. For the both of us. To be in separate rooms, but still close. Drake doesn't know the truth, so having your room on the other side of the house wouldn't be a good idea."

"Thank you for thinking about that." Because I sure as hell didn't.

Bennett shows me his room, which I notice is a lot

smaller than mine. He must have given me the master bedroom, but why?

I don't get to ask; I just continue to follow him as he leads me out to the same hallway that gives me access to my room. We are close to each other but still far apart to not do anything stupid—like consummate our marriage.

Bennett finishes up the remainder of our tour before leading me over to his home office, where he tells me I have free range over anything I want, including the credit card and bank card he hands me with my name on it.

I'm in shock as he tells me that if I ever want to drive myself, I can take whatever car I want from the garage. The shock continues when he tells me that also applies to flying. If I ever want to fly somewhere to let him or Henry know, and they will get the jet ready. The same goes for Charlie. Whatever she wants, she gets.

"You are doing too much," I say, looking down at the credit card he just handed over.

"For what you're doing for me, it's not nearly enough."

Something passes through us, something I can't explain. This very thing has happened once before, and I brushed it off, but experiencing it now feels like an electrical current. It feels right.

"Either way, thank you. For everything. I promise that once the two years are up, everything will be in place."

"Don't worry about it," he says, walking over to the drink cart in the corner and quickly moving the conversation to a different subject. "So from the way Charlie is making herself at home, she took the news of our impending marriage well?"

I watch as he pours a glass of dark liquid and offers me one.

Might as well. It might help with the nerves that have yet to go away.

I throw a nod in his direction and answer his question. "Surprisingly, yes. I for sure expected her to lecture me about marrying someone I barely know, but she didn't. She was actually excited when I told her. She said it was like a rom-com playing out in real life."

Bennett walks over, handing me a glass of amber liquid, and takes a seat next to me. "That's somewhat better than the reaction Sam and Grayson gave me," he says before taking a drink from the glass.

I follow suit but instantly regret it. I guess scotch or whiskey or whatever this is is not for me.

Once the horrible taste is nearly gone from my mouth, I speak. "Was it bad?"

"No. From the looks of it, Grayson didn't really care, but I know he was surprised. Sam, on the other hand...she definitely was a little hurt that she found out about the wedding through a magazine. She was okay with the decision, though."

I know how Sam feels.

When I saw the article this morning, I was a little shocked. I didn't think a simple wedding would be such big news, but then I remembered whose wedding it was. Bennett is one of the most eligible bachelors in the world; of course his wedding is going to be big news. I just didn't think people would be so interested in the woman he's marrying. For a half hour or so, I got scared someone was going to be looking into my past and finding something they shouldn't, but the article and any mention of who Bennett was going to be marrying were scraped from the internet.

It didn't take me long to put it together: my future husband probably had something to do with that.

Future. After tomorrow, there will be no future about it. Bennett will be my husband in all senses of the word. I guess it's time to get used to it.

"Hopefully she is still okay with it after tomorrow," I say, but I don't really know who I'm talking about, me or Samantha.

"She'll be fine," Bennett says, taking another drink before turning to give me his full attention. "What about you? Will you be okay?"

I think about it for a second, and surprisingly, the answer is one I didn't expect. "Yes. Yes, I'm okay with it."

And...I am.

I'm really okay with marrying Bennett. I didn't think I was, and I've been having my doubts since we came up with this plan, but as I sit here, I realize all the doubts are gone. This is transactional, nothing else.

"Good." He brings his glass over and taps it against mine. "You're ready to conquer the world by my side?"

By his side.

I like the sound of that.

"Let's make you CEO, Mr. Lane."

"Fuck, do I like the sound of that."

19

BENNETT

This day was never supposed to happen. I was never supposed to get married and have my worst fear become a reality.

Yet, here I am, standing under an arch put together by a florist, an officiant standing three feet away as my bride comes walking toward me in an off-white gown that fits her gorgeously.

This day was never supposed to come, yet I find myself wanting to go back in time so I can make this all right and give Ella the wedding she deserves.

I saw her face in the conference room that night. I know she didn't want a small, intimate wedding, yet she asked for one, and now, as she approaches me, nobody walking at her side, I want to go back and make her ask for a big wedding, for a wedding she fucking deserves.

Ella should be wearing the dress of her dreams, not one she picked out just because, with her favorite flowers surrounding her as she walks down the aisle with her sister at her side to the man of her dreams. A man who would move the heavens for her. A man who isn't marrying her just because he wants something from her. A man who loves her wholeheartedly and isn't in love with the feeling that corruption and deception brings. Ella deserves a life where she is happy every day and smiling that beautiful smile while letting out her gorgeous laugh.

She deserves everything and more, and here I am, taking everything away from her.

It's only for two years.

For two years, she will be all mine, in every single legal sense of the word, but then the two years will come, and she will leave and find the person she is meant to be with.

Because no matter how much my brain wants it, she won't be mine. Not truly. She will share my last name and have access to my bank accounts, but that's it. That's where our connection will end.

I will never be the man she loves.

The officiant has us say our vows out loud, and as we do, I can't help but think if he knows how corrupt they are, how the words he has us repeat don't mean a single thing. Not really.

As I slide a diamond ring onto my new wife's finger, one she picked out this morning, I think about my parents. They would have loved Ella. They would have treated her as a daughter and Charlie as a granddaughter, but they would have been disappointed in me for choosing to marry this girl solely for a title. They would have hated everything this marriage is going to stand for.

And as Ella slides a black band onto my finger, I

conclude I would have been okay with their disappoint-ment. Because it gets me what I want, and as my parents, they should have known I would have stopped at nothing to get what I wanted. If it wasn't marrying Ella, it would have been putting Peter Hill in the ground.

I have no shame in admitting that I would have killed the bastard with my own two hands and hid his body so it would have never been found.

It's such a shame it never came to that, but I have no regrets with my decision.

I may not be the man Ella deserves, but I plan on being the best man I can be for her.

"With the power vested in me, by the grace of God and the state of Illinois, I pronounce you husband and wife. Bennett, you may kiss your bride."

There is no hesitation as I close the distance between me and my wife and take her face between my hands. She looks up at me with those beautiful eyes of hers, and for a second, it's as if this is supposed to happen. It's as if this is truly our wedding, and we are both excited about our future together. She wants me to kiss her just as much as I want to kiss her.

So, I do.

I kiss my bride in the way I've wanted since our last kiss: with urgency and need.

It takes her by surprise, but only for a second, and then she is kissing me right back.

When we pull apart a minute later, she has a look in her eyes that I won't be forgetting anytime soon. One filled with lust.

"I present to you all, Mr. and Mrs. Lane."

The kids and Henry cheer and congratulate us, and for a few minutes, it feels like an actual wedding, rather than one filled with lies.

But the feeling quickly goes away, and in its place is one filled with vigor.

It's time to get that CEO title and everything I've ever wanted.

ELLA

It's interesting how life works sometimes.

Two months ago, I was looking at my bank account, dreading the day all the bills would hit, and the money I had would dwindle. I needed to look for a better job with better hours and was hoping I would find a way to pay for my sister's school.

Now, cut to today, and everything is taken care of. And it's all thanks to a certain billionaire I now share a last name with.

It's a little mind-blowing.

And something I'm still very much getting used to, even a week in. I have a feeling that even with the two years this arrangement is going to last, I won't be able to wrap my head around it.

Another thing I won't be able to wrap my head around is how easily Bennett moves money around.

Within two days of us saying our vows, the money he promised me landed in my bank account. How he got my bank account information is beyond me, but he did. When I brought it up to him, he brushed it off and acted like it wasn't that big of a deal.

It is very much a big deal.

This was one million dollars, but even when I threatened to send it back or to not touch it until two years from now, he just rolled his eyes and walked away.

So now, I'm staring at my bank account showing more zeros than I know what to do with, debating whether it should stay in my bank account for the next two years or if I should just use it for what I need it for now.

The logical decision would be the latter. That way, I can walk away from everything that terrifies me, but if I send the money all in one shot, it's going to look suspicious. To the person on the receiving end, it's going to seem like I either came into money or I have more money to give, and they could come and ask for more.

I know I could send the money the same way I've been sending it for the last five years, but I want to be done with this.

Sending the money altogether is the way to go. I just have to find the courage to do it. This is a lot of money to be playing with.

My finger hovers over the transfer button for a solid minute, trying to talk myself into making the transfer, but no matter what pep talk I give myself, I can't seem to push it.

"Just do it," I say it out loud, but even voicing the words doesn't help.

"What are you trying to talk yourself into doing this

time?" The question rings out, and, much like the first time I heard his voice, I jump and let out a yelp.

With my hand on my chest, I turn to find Bennett standing in the doorway that separates the closet and my bedroom.

In the week we've been married, this has started to become a thing. I'll get ready for the day and forget to close the closet door behind me, which prompts Bennett to check in on me every morning as he's tying his tie or sliding on his belt.

Who am I kidding? I don't forget to close the door. After I left it open the morning after our wedding and caught a glimpse of a shirtless Bennett, I've kept the door open every morning.

Today, though...today, I should have closed it if I didn't want him to ask questions.

"Stop doing that," I let out after catching my breath.

A lazy smile forms on his face. That smile might have made its way to the top of my list.

"Sorry. You just looked a little stressed." He slides his belt through the last loop, and for a second, I lose my train of thought.

I quickly regain it, though, and shut my laptop before he sees what I was doing.

"I-I was just checking your schedule and making sure everything is in line for today." I stutter a few of my words, but I'm able to get the rest out without problem.

But still, Bennett notices. "You're checking my schedule before we even get in the car."

Another habit that has sprung up this week: getting ready for our day on our drive to work.

"It's an important day. I wanted to make sure everything was in line."

I feel a bead of sweat forming at my temple and threatening to fall. Lying to your husband makes it feel like you're in the hot seat.

At the very least, I'm not lying through my teeth. Today is an important day; the board is voting on whether to name Bennett as the CEO, so checking the schedule makes sense.

"Right," Bennett says, his eyebrows bunching up in the process. He still doesn't believe me, but he takes it nonetheless.

When he turns to walk away, I let out a sigh of relief. I know I shouldn't be lying to Bennett and that I should tell him what I would be using the money for, but I'm not completely ready for that. Maybe one day, I will be, but not today.

"Elizabeth," Bennett calls out, bringing my attention back to him.

"Yes?"

He takes a second before he says anything. "If anything was wrong, you'd tell me. Right?"

His words take me by surprise. Since the wedding, we've been mostly keeping to ourselves. The moments when we have acted like a couple have been far and few between.

I answer him truthfully, though. "Yes. I'd tell you."

And I would. There are certain things I can't keep from

Bennett—at least, not for long—so if they ever arise, I will tell him. That much I know.

I get a nod from my husband, and he goes back to his room to finish up getting ready.

When he is out of sight, I open my laptop back up again and finish what I was doing.

Sending the transfer.

I put in the information, and as soon as I click the button, the money is gone, and my debt is paid.

I did it.

Charlie isn't going anywhere.

And if anything trouble comes up, I will do what I promised Bennett.

I would tell him if anything was wrong.

THE ATMOSPHERE in the conference room is a lot different than it was two weeks ago.

During the last meeting, the room was filled with joy and people smiling. Today, almost everyone looks like they have a stick so far up their asses, it's affecting their faces. Nobody is talking at full volume; just mumbling here and there, as if they're keeping secrets.

The more I look around the room, the more I notice a divide. On one side of the conference room, there are the people who stand with Mr. Goldman. On the other are those against it, Peter Hill front and center.

Seeing him today, the cockiness all over his face, puts a sour feeling in my stomach that I do not like. I don't have to speak to the guy to know he thinks everything and everyone is on his side. And from the looks of things, they just might be.

Bennett had told me he needed ten total votes to be named CEO. Counting the heads in the room, and where everyone is standing, he might have lost one to Peter.

The sourness in my stomach intensifies.

As I look around the room, my eyes catch Bennett's, and I send a small wave and smile his way. He had gone to lunch with a possible client and only got back to the office about five minutes before, so we didn't walk in here together.

"You okay?" he asks, looking down at me with concern in his eyes as he joins me by the window.

I give him a nod. "Yeah, I was just taking everything in."

Tell him about the head count.

"This will be a lot quicker than last time. After we're done, we can go to dinner or something to celebrate."

I try to ignore the fact that my husband-slash-boss just asked me to dinner and stay on topic.

"I don't think that dinner is going to be a celebratory one," I whisper, my eyes dancing around the room.

"What?" Bennett asks, coming closer to me.

Our bodies are basically pressed together as I tell him what I noticed. "It looks like Mr. Hill gained a vote and you lost one."

Bennett turns away from me as he counts heads. His jaw tics as he finishes, and his body goes rigid.

He knows it, and I know it.

He's going to lose, and the wedding was for nothing.

When Bennett turns back to me, his face doesn't have as much anger swimming through it as I expected.

"It's fine."

"Fine? You lost the vote. It's not fine." If he doesn't get this, will he ask for the money back? My palms start to sweat; the money is no longer in my account.

A piece of hair falls in front of my face, and I stop breathing when Bennett reaches out and tucks the strand behind my ear. Since the wedding, I've experienced small touches from him, here and there, but nothing as intimate as this.

Well, except for the kiss on our wedding day. I swear, I can still feel it every night as I go to sleep.

Our eyes catch as his thumb glides down my cheek, and the way his eyes gleam makes me feel like my knees are going to buckle under me.

It only lasts a few seconds, but to me, it lasted a lifetime.

When he finally pulls away, I can't help but smile when I catch sight of his wedding ring.

I didn't think that he was going to wear it, yet there it is. It has only been a week, but I haven't seen him without it.

"Everything is going to work out. I promise."

I want to believe him, but I have my doubts. Still, that doesn't stop me from giving him a nod.

With one more smile in my direction, he walks away, and I go back to my place by the window as Gerald enters the room.

"All right. We know what we are all here for. There is no need to make this longer than it needs to be. We will get a head count and then move on with the vote. Does that sound good to everyone?"

Everyone in the room nods, and from there, one of his assistants doesn't waste any time taking a head count of all the board members.

I don't have to follow the assistant's counts to know that all twenty members of the board are accounted for. Bennett made sure of it.

"Twenty members are present," Gerald's assistant tells her boss before sitting down a few chairs away from me.

Gerald nods and turns back to the conference table.

"Let the vote to appoint Bennett Lane as CEO begin. A reminder that Bennett and I cannot vote, so it will come down to eighteen of you," he announces and turns to the individual on his right.

The man in a navy suit stands from his seat and addresses the conference table. "I vote yes."

I let out a breath. One vote down, hopefully nine more to go.

As soon as the man sits, the pattern continues, with the person next to him standing and giving his vote.

No.

It's crazy how hearing two letters together like that can make your eye twitch.

The vote continues around the table. When it gets to Elliot, it's seven yeses and nine nos.

Elliot stands up with a cocky smirk on his face and looks at Peter. "I vote yes."

Peter lets out a scoff as Elliot sits and Henry stands.

"I vote yes as well."

My fingers wrap around my phone so tightly, I feel like I'm going to break it. The vote is officially tied. Bennett was so sure he was going to get the vote that he didn't tell me what to expect if he didn't.

What now?

Do we all go home and then vote again in two weeks, fingers crossed that someone flips back to Bennett's side?

"Well, it looks like we have a tie," Gerald lets out, looking a bit disgruntled while Peter looks happy as a fucking clam.

"We should reconvene in two weeks. Surely by then, we will be able to make a decision." Peter stands from his chair, buttoning his suit jacket like he owns the damn place.

"We don't need to reconvene," Bennett announces, sounding almost bored.

Is he rethinking all of this?

Peter looks angry when he responds. "And why the hell not?"

For a few seconds, it feels like everyone is on the edge of their seats waiting for a response from Bennett.

"Because not everyone voted."

What the hell is he talking about? Everyone who was supposed to vote did. Am I missing something?

"Son, I think you need to go back to school and take a math class. Nobody is missing."

Bennett is facing me, so I see the smirk spread as he gets up from his seat. "But there is."

I look around and find Gerald, Henry, and Elliot all wearing the same smirk Bennett has, which tells me I should be terrified with whatever these four have planned.

"How? Everyone was accounted for."

Bennett's smirk deepens. "Before Thomas and Catherine Lane died, they were voting members. When they passed, those two seats went to the person stated in their will. Since my brother and I already had our seats accounted for, those two seats went to others."

"Who?" Peter spits out, getting desperate.

"As per their will, my father's seat went to Henry Carmichael, and my mother's seat went to her son's wife. Since there is no evidence that her eldest son ever got married, that seat falls to the wife of her youngest son."

My eyes go wide. Is he saying what I think he's saying?

There's no way...is there?

My eyes stay with Bennett as he reaches into his suit jacket and pulls out some paperwork.

"As of last Saturday, Catherine Lane's seat was filled by Elizabeth Vincent."

Papers land on the table, and Peter doesn't even hesitate reaching for them.

As the asswipe reads them over, I look over at Bennett, who's already looking at me.

One look at him, and I know. He knew about this. He knew that once we got married, his mother's seat would be mine. That's why he told me everything would work out—because he had this up his sleeve.

The papers that Peter was holding slam back onto the table, taking away my attention from my husband.

"So you met a clause with a clause, big fucking deal. Your wife isn't here and isn't able to give her vote, so we have to reconvene."

Bennett's eyes move back to mine, causing a shiver to run down my spine.

"Oh, but she is here."

All eyes in the room look over to me, and all I want to do is sink into my chair and hide. But I don't cower. I don't sink into my chair and let embarrassment take over.

No, I school my facial expression and square my shoulders, as if preparing for battle. And in a way, I am, given the expression Peter is throwing in my direction.

"Your assistant. You married your fucking assistant?" the man in question throws out through clenched teeth, as if it disgusts him.

Bennett slams his hands against the conference table, his face looking almost malicious. "I married the woman I love who happens to be my assistant. Watch yourself, because if you disrespect my wife again, I will do everything in my power to end you."

The silence that fills the room is bone-chilling.

Peter just looks at Bennett like he wants to jump over the chairs between them and murder him.

Gerald is the one to break the silence.

"Mrs. Lane, would you please cast your vote?" he says to me, giving me a nod.

Another hand slams against the table, this time is from Peter. "This is absolute bullshit."

"But it's not, Mr. Hill," Gerald starts, looking over at the disgruntled man. "It's in the paperwork. Catherine Lane's voting seat is to go to her first daughter-in-law, and that is Elizabeth. She is here, she is present, and she has the right to give her vote. Now, do us all a favor and sit the fuck down."

In my time working for Gerald, I've never seen him talk to someone the way he just spoke to Peter. It's quite impressive.

I get a nod to proceed, and after taking a deep breath, I do what everyone else did before me. I stand from my chair and give my vote.

"I vote yes."

Ten votes.

It's official.

Gerald's loud voice fills the room. "Congratulations, Mr. Lane. You are officially the new CEO of Lane Enterprises."

Since I have a few things to take care of now that I have a new title attached to my head, I decide to go back to my office instead of calling it a day like everyone else.

Because I'm still surrounded by my colleagues, a few looking like they want to throw a tantrum at the fact that I'm now their boss, I decide to keep my celebrations to myself until I reach my office.

I do let a smile slip when Peter storms past me as if his ass was on fire and needs to go find a hose to put it out. Newsflash, he won't find one. That fire is going to be lit until I fucking die.

"I need to get out of this monkey suit," Elliot announces as he, Henry, Ella, and I approach the elevator.

"You three head home. I have a few things to take care of. I'll call the car when I'm ready," I say as we get into the elevator and push the buttons for my floor and the lobby.

Both Henry and Elliot nod, but Ella doesn't say anything. She just looks at me with those eyes that make me want to dive into her head and see what she is thinking.

When the elevator arrives on my floor, that's when she speaks.

"I'll stay, if that's okay."

Something is on her mind, and she wants to talk about it, that much I know for sure. I may have only known this woman for a few weeks, but I'm already learning all her tells—like the way she plays with her fingers when she's nervous or how she stutters when she's lying.

This morning was a prime example of that. Not only did she stutter, she also slammed her laptop closed, as if she didn't want to get caught doing something. My new bride is hiding something, I just don't know what.

I give her a nod. "More than okay."

She gives me a smile and makes her way out of the elevator, with me following closely behind. Part of me hopes she's staying to tell me, but given what just happened, she may have questions, and I'm more than willing to answer them.

The second we're in the safety of my office, I close the door behind us and lock it. I don't need anyone barging in on our conversation.

As soon as the door is closed, that's when it fully hits me.

I'm officially the CEO of Lane Enterprises.

All my damn work has finally paid off. I can't express how fucking good it feels. For the first time in a long time, I feel this joy inside of me I can't explain.

Apparently, Ella feels the same way, because the smile

on her face is so bright, it could light up the whole damn building. Her smile is so infectious, I want to take a picture just so I can look at it whenever I want.

"Why didn't you tell me about your mother's board seat?" she asks, her smile still big and bright.

A part of me thinks I'm corrupting my wife beyond repair, but given her smile, she's more than okay with that.

I send a shrug her way and get rid of my suit jacket. "I didn't think I was going to need it, but when you told me the vote was going to be tied, I pulled it out. It was a Hail Mary just in case shit went south."

When I first read my parents' will at eighteen, I never thought that my mother leaving her voting seat to her future daughter-in-law would have been beneficial to me, especially since in my search for my brother, a Mexican marriage certificate popped up, one that was dated a few months before Elliot was born, I came to find out a few years after the fact.

I knew it was legit because the same name was on all the kids' birth certificates: Marisela Serrano. In my head, if Robert came back, the seat would go to her, and that would be the end of it.

That is, until I looked into it more. I had my suspicions that Peter was going to flip someone, so I went back to my mother's will and asked a lawyer for some advice.

As it turns out, since my brother and his wife can't be found and we don't have proof that they're alive, the seat would fall to my wife.

And thank fuck it did.

Without Ella, I wouldn't have been able to get what I

wanted. She doesn't know this, but I will forever be in her debt.

"Were you ever going to tell me that small detail?" Her smile disappears, and by the way she bites her lip, I know what she's truly asking: if I'm going to keep secrets from her.

There are a few things I will keep from her, but this is not one of them.

I roll up my sleeves and close the distance between us.

"Yes," I answer truthfully. "I was going to tell you. It's part of my wedding gift."

"How romantic. A closet full of clothes and a board seat. What more can a girl ask for?" Her sarcasm bleeds through, and I can't help but smile at her.

"She can ask for a lot of things, and since she helped me get what I wanted, she would get it."

A small blush creeps up her neck, and I wonder what other parts look like in that shade of pink.

"You would have figured out a way to get it done. You didn't need me." I don't know if she notices, but her body inches closer to mine when she speaks.

It's because of the closeness that I let myself do what I've wanted since my lips met hers on our wedding day, since my finger glided down her skin in the conference room: I touch her.

I place my hand under her chin to tilt her eyes up to meet mine, and surprisingly, she leans into my touch, bringing her mouth all that much closer. It's unknowingly, but she still does it.

"No, I did need you. There's a reason why your résumé

landed in front of me. It was the universe's way of telling me you needed to be in my life; otherwise, I wasn't going to get what I wanted."

Ella lets out a small snort, but her eyes gleam with excitement. "Now that you got what you wanted, are you going to be thanking the universe?"

Her hand circles around my arm, and for a second, I think she's going to push me away, but no. She wraps her hand around my forearm and holds me in place.

A smirk forms on my face. "I think I'll do more than just thank the universe."

"Oh? And what would that be?"

"Thanking my wife."

Her eyes fall to my mouth, and when they look back up, they're full of curiosity.

"And how will you thank her?" She steps even closer to me, leaving maybe two inches of space between us.

My hand finally drops from under her chin, and I place it against her hip. "In whatever way pleases her."

"What if she says she wants a kiss?" The question comes out in a whisper, as if she was scared to say it any louder out of fear that I was going to deny her.

Never.

I wouldn't have denied her the first day I met her, and I won't deny her now.

My other hand slides onto her hip, and with both hands, I bring her body closer to mine, leaving no room between us. I lower my face to hers, taking in the scent of her perfume. "Then I would say her wish is my command."

There's no hesitation, no thinking about my next move or that I shouldn't be doing this.

There's nothing but me and this woman.

Just me and her and our mouths slamming together.

Much like the other two kisses we've shared, there's nothing slow or sweet about the way my mouth takes hers. Everything is hungry and desperate.

As if she is the last woman I will ever kiss.

As if she is mine and always will be.

I've been fucking dying to have this woman in my hands, pressed against my body, and now that she is, I never want to let her go.

I swipe my tongue along her bottom lip, and when she opens for me, her sweetness takes over, and all I want is more of her. A sweet moan escapes her when my hands move away from her hips and around to her ass, then another one as I unwillingly pull away from her mouth and trail my lips down her neck.

"We shouldn't be doing this," she breathes, yet her body is melting against mine.

I almost growl along her throat. "Why not?"

"Because you're my boss."

I pull away slightly and look down at her. "Right now, I'm your husband, but if you want to stop, we will."

A second goes by, then two, and I'm about to count to three when her hand goes to the back of my head as she brings my face back down to hers.

Fucking hell, this woman.

As she swipes her tongue against mine, I grab her ass and lift her until her legs wrap around my waist. Without taking my mouth off her, I walk us over to my desk and deposit her on the very edge.

I need more of Ella. Kissing her isn't enough right now, and if I'm being honest with myself, now that I'm getting a full taste of her, it may never be.

Moving my hands from her ass to her thighs, I take in the little whimpers she lets out when my skin meets hers as I slowly push up her dress.

Before last week, Ella hadn't worn a single dress to work, which I was fine with—her ass looked amazing in her slacks—but now that she has a whole closet at her disposal, I've been rewarded with seeing her in dresses these past few days.

Every day, I've pictured this very scene: her on my desk, her skirt pushed up around her waist, her legs wrapped around me, ready for me to take.

Now, that visual is coming to life.

My fingers dig into her thighs, and a moan leaves Ella's mouth. *Fuck.*

I need more.

So much fucking more.

Moving my hand just slightly, I let my fingers glide over the fabric of her panties. Her heat meets my fingers, and I let out a groan of my own when I feel the wetness against my fingertips.

She's drenched for me.

"I didn't peg you as a satin type of girl," I growl into her neck once I finally pull my mouth from hers.

"I'm not. These are new. Bought them a few days ago."

I glide my knuckle over her, debating if I should rip the

fabric off her body to get to where I want or slide it down her legs.

"Did you buy them with my credit card?" I place my mouth over the sensitive skin just under her ear.

"Does it matter?" Her voice is almost breathless, and I fucking love that it's because of me.

I run my tongue from the hollow of her neck back to the spot under her ear. "Yes. It matters."

A shiver runs through her body. "Why?"

I can't help but smirk against her skin. "Because if you bought them with your own money, I'll slide them off you. If you bought them with mine, then I'll rip them off you and buy you a new pair."

Her sigh tells me everything I need to know.

"Yes, I used your credit card."

"Good."

Not a second is wasted as I pull my mouth away from her neck and fall to my knees. I drag my nose along her exposed skin, taking every inch of her. If this is the only time I have her, then I'm going to make the most of it.

I spread her legs a bit wider and drag her closer to my face.

Her scent overpowers my nose just how I want it.

I let my hand glide over her pussy, touching Ella as softly as possible before I wrap my fingers around the fabric and pull.

Ella lets out a gasp, and I get the feeling she'll come undone with just the simplest touch.

"I've been starving for you, sweet Ella. From the second that I saw you, I wanted to mark you as mine."

"Bennett," Ella breathes out, but all words cease when my tongue meets her bare pussy.

Like our kiss earlier, there is nothing sweet or slow about the way I eat Ella's pussy. I'm a starving man, and I won't stop until she's writhing under me, satisfied and screaming my name.

My fingers draw circles against her clit as I tease her entrance with my tongue. Her legs tighten around my head, and I can't help but hum at how good she tastes.

"Oh, god."

I move my head just slightly, enough to nip at her inner thigh. "You like your pussy played with, don't you, Elizabeth? You're soaking wet for me."

"Yes."

I hum at her response and move my mouth to her clit, sucking as if it were my favorite candy.

"You're so fucking perfect." My hand moves under her ass, and I hold her to me. I let my fingers tease her entrance, and I'm rewarded by her legs shaking uncontrollably against my head.

"Come on my face, Elizabeth. Cover my tongue with all you have."

"I—" Her words disappear from her lips, and in their place comes one of the sweetest moans I have ever heard as she explodes.

For a second, I'm pissed—I should have waited until I was in my new office to eat out my wife, because then, every time I see my desk, I'd be rewarded with this fucking gorgeous memory. If this isn't just a one-time thing, I may have to recreate it on my new desk.

As Ella comes down from her high, I continue to kiss and lick at her pussy with more sweetness than before. I savor every last drop of her.

I lick up her release before kissing my way up her body. She is still fully clothed, but that doesn't stop me from placing kisses as if she were completely nude.

"That was one hell of a thank you," she lets out with a lazy smile, running her fingers through my hair, pushing it back from my forehead.

"It was warranted."

Her smile starts to fade, which tells me what I just did to her is setting in and she's about to freak out. We may be married, but anything sexual was not part of the rules. We didn't determine if this was a step we were going to take, and frankly, I never really thought we would.

Yes, my wife is one of the most beautiful women I have ever seen, but I thought I would spend the next two years fantasizing about her body, not actually experiencing it.

My mind tells me to step back, but instead, I grab one of her legs, wrap it around my waist, and thrust my hard cock against her heat. I don't care that I'm fully clothed and that her pussy is rubbing against the fabric of my slacks. In this moment, she is mine, and I'm showing her just how fucking hard she gets me.

A moan falls from her lips, causing a smile to break out over mine. I lean down to give her one more kiss before giving her the space she needs.

"Wait," she says, reaching out for me and dragging me back into her.

Maybe I was wrong; maybe she wasn't starting to regret this.

She looks up at me as she toys with my belt. "I want to say thank you too."

Fucking hell.

If my cock wasn't rock solid, it is now.

I place a finger under her chin and look into her eyes. "You can thank me all you want," I say, rubbing my thumb over her lips. "But not here."

"Then where? Back home?"

I smirk down at her. "I was thinking more along the lines of our honeymoon."

For a second, her eyes go wide with worry and surprise, but it's quickly replaced by excitement.

When this whole marriage of convenience was brought up, a honeymoon was mentioned by Gerald. I hadn't put much thought into it; I just needed to get married, and that was it. There was no need for trivial things like taking Ella away for a whole week.

But after spending time with Ella outside of the office, getting to know her a little better, I thought maybe it would be a good idea to go somewhere touristy. Go together but still give her space.

I hadn't brought it up to her yet, since it was still an idea, but now a new idea has sprung, and all I need is for her to say yes, and I will set it all up.

"That is, if you want to go on one," I throw out, leaving the option up to her. She may not believe me, but for the next two years, what she says or wants goes. I'll just follow along.

She wants to go on a tropical vacation? I'll take her.

She wants to go after someone who has wronged her and put them in the ground? I'll pull the trigger.

After these two years, there's no chance in hell I will ever marry again, but that doesn't mean I won't at least try and be a good husband. I may fail, but fuck it.

Ella gives me an excited nod. "I want one."

From what Henry told me when I got home, rumors have started to circulate about Lane Enterprises having a new CEO. Nothing has been confirmed yet, but that isn't stopping people from trying to get in contact with me.

I had turned off my phone before stepping foot in the conference room earlier today, and I didn't think about turning it on until after Ella and I were on the way home from the office.

Looking down at the screen, I expect an incoming call to be from someone I know, but when I see the number, everything in me goes cold, and I stop dead in my tracks. It's a number I don't have saved, but it's one I've memorized.

The Florida number that came up a few weeks ago in my search for Robert.

This has to be a fucking joke.

Someone had to have planted the number for me to find and is now deciding to play a sick prank on me.

But what if it's not a joke?

One way to find out.

Before answering, I look over my shoulder and find Ella instantly.

When we got to the house, excitement rolled through her about going on our honeymoon. She told me on the drive here that she has never gone on a vacation not within driving distance, so as soon as we got everything situated, she ran upstairs and started pulling out clothes.

She has been at it for a good hour, throwing things around, trying to find the perfect outfit. I haven't even told her where we're going, but she doesn't care.

With her preoccupied, I close the door separating my room from the bathroom and answer the call. A shiver runs through my body as I bring the phone to my ear, and I answer with a bite, "Who is this?"

I can hear movement and people talking on the other side, but for a solid minute, nobody speaks directly into the phone.

"How did you get this number?"

No answer, and thirty seconds later, the line goes dead.

I don't hesitate calling right back, but it goes to a generic voicemail, nothing identifiable about it.

I try one more time but get the same result.

Anger rolls through my body, and the urge to throw my phone across the room and let it shatter is strong, but I keep myself together enough to dial a different number.

"Shouldn't you be in marital bliss with your new wife?" Dante's voice comes through. From the music in the background, I know he's at Perversa.

"I'm going to send you a number, and I need to know everything tied to it."

Right away, Dante is on alert. "Does this have to do with Hill?"

I fucking hope not. "No."

"Your wife?"

"My brother."

The silence is deafening, as if the fact that this is tied to Robert shocked Dante as much as it shocked me.

"Send it over to me, but I'm also calling a favor."

"What would that be?"

"Are you CEO?"

"Yes."

"Good, because it has to do with my *famiglia*."

He's not talking about him and his wife or even any cousins or uncles that he may have left. He's talking about his other family.

The Mafia.

"Whatever you want. Just get this done."

22

———————

ELLA

Nervousness ransacks my body.

My palms are sweating, I'm stuttering my words, and I swear, I've forgotten more things in the last twenty minutes than I have my whole life.

I can only think of one thing that could be causing it: going on this honeymoon with Bennett.

Any newly married person would love having their new husband's undivided attention for a whole week. If I were anybody else, and Bennett and I actually had a real relationship, I would be one of those people. There wouldn't be nerves running through me, I wouldn't have the urge to tell my husband to just forget about the trip and head back to his house. No, I would be over the moon that I would be spending seven uninterrupted days with my new husband.

Instead, I'm sitting on a private plane, biting my nails off, wishing I would have told Bennett no instead of yes.

All because I don't know where we stand after yesterday.

Spending time with him is fine. It was bound to happen. We work and live together. Sure, we usually have the buffer of Lane employees and the kids, but we can handle being alone for an extended period.

I don't know how to do one full week of just me and him, though, not when I have a feeling he regrets our little sexcapade.

We're three hours into our flight, and I'm so close to telling him to turn the plane around, all because I've been in my head this whole time with Bennett being somewhere else.

From the second we left the house, Bennett has been on his phone, only switching over to his laptop when we got on the jet. Apparently, when you become CEO, there are a lot of things you need to do to make it official. From what I can tell, he has been signing paperwork and talking to lawyers the whole flight. I volunteered to work with him, help him out, but he waved me away and told me to relax.

So I've been sitting here, watching whatever TV show or movie I've been able to find on the many screens this plane has to offer, trying to relax but instead overthinking everything.

And by everything, I mean what happened in Bennett's office yesterday.

Not only did we kiss, but he made me feel so damn good with that tongue of his. I didn't want to stop. I wanted to continue, to not come up for air until we absolutely had to.

Having Bennett Lane between my legs was something I've dreamed about a few times since I met him, but I never thought it would happen. Then it did, and I've been thinking about it ever since.

The way his mouth felt on my skin. The way his tongue licked me up as if I were a melting ice cream cone. The way he was so damn hard that when he thrusted against me, I thought I was going to see stars.

He made me feel what others haven't, and I want to repeat it as often as I possibly can.

When he mentioned the honeymoon, I was scared for a second, but then I thought about what we would be doing. We weren't going to hide the attraction we had for each other anymore; we'd explore whatever was pulling us together. Hell, I even thought he was going to land in my bed last night after the way he looked at me in his office, but he never came.

He said goodnight and closed his door, and I didn't lay eyes on him until this morning.

All night, I couldn't help but wonder if what happened in his office was truly a spur-of-the moment thing, or if it meant something to him.

I try to push that thought away, to be excited about this trip, but instead of excitement, the nerves take over. What if something else happens between us, and instead of bringing us closer, it puts even more space between us?

Is that something I even want, though? To get closer to Bennett?

It would be nice to leave this marriage at least as friends. Who knows? Maybe once the two years are up, we won't even get divorced.

Yeah, right. I need to get a grip. We are only a week into this marriage; I can't start thinking that far into the future. That wasn't a part of the deal.

Two years, and that's it. Nothing more.

Besides, Bennett doesn't even want to be married. Who knows why, but he doesn't, and I'm not going to force him into anything outside of the two years.

"You look like you're thinking a little too hard over there," Bennett says, taking my attention away from my thoughts.

I turn my body slightly to look over at him and find him typing something on his laptop. A part of me wants to answer with a snarky comment, but instead, I decide to give him a bit of truth.

"I'm just trying to get my nerves down a bit." I say, and surprisingly, he takes his eyes off his screen.

His eyebrows bunch up before he speaks. "What are you nervous about?"

I decide to be truthful again. "What we're going to do on this trip."

This time, he shuts his laptop, and he gives me his full attention. "What do you mean?"

I give him a shrug. "Exactly that. What do we do? Do we act like a married couple actually on their honeymoon? Do we just hang out and hope we become friends once we go home? Do we act like strangers and both go off and do our own thing? What do we do?"

There is more that wants to come out of my mouth, like asking if he regrets what happened yesterday, but I hold that particular question back. I really do need to get a grip. One orgasm, and I've become the clingiest person in the world.

Who cares what we do while we are on this trip? I'm on my first vacation, that is all that should matter.

A sigh leaves Bennett, and he stands, coming over and taking a seat on the couch I have designated as mine for this flight. He doesn't say anything at first; he just sits there and looks forward.

"What do you want to do?" he asks after about a minute. When his eyes meet mine, I see a bit of the sweet side of Bennett, the one from when his niece and nephews are around. I've also seen him bring it out with Charlie this week, and it melts my heart every time.

"Would wanting to get to know you a little better be on the table?"

The man gives me a smile, something that I've noticed he doesn't give to many people. "Yes. It would definitely be on the table, and it is, but tell me something," he says, moving so his front is facing me. I give him a nod to continue. "Was there something else you wanted to ask?"

I swear, he knows how to read me a little too well.

Now I'm the one sighing. There's no reason to lie.

My head lands on the back of the couch. "Yes."

"What?"

I take a second to gather some courage. "If you regretted what happened between us yesterday."

There is silence, and without warning, a laugh fills the cabin. It's not just a chuckle or a small laugh you give to a little kid—it's a full-blown laugh.

In the time I've known Bennett, he has never laughed like this. I don't know whether to pull out my phone and record it, laugh with him, or cower into myself because he is laughing at me.

"Great. You're laughing at me," I mutter, already feeling my face get red for all the wrong reasons.

Bennett's laugh dies down a bit, but there's still a very prominent smile on his face when he speaks again. "I'm not laughing at you."

"Seems like you are."

He shifts again, this time coming closer, his arm landing on the back of the couch.

With that move, his scent encapsulates me. It's this cloud of citrus, wood, and fresh air, all wrapped up together. Smelling it takes me back to the first time I kissed him. In this moment, I don't want to pull away. I want to close the distance between us and burrow my face into his chest so I can engrain the scent into my mind.

His fingers land in my hair, and he starts twirling a few strands as he speaks. "I wasn't laughing at you. I was laughing because regretting something like that is fucking ridiculous."

Goose bumps form all over my body.

"But you closed yourself off last night."

It was careless of me to expect he would have come to my room last night. It was careless to even think things between us were going to change just because he stuck his tongue in my pussy. I should have thought better. I should have been okay with sleeping alone, because now that I'm hearing the words come out of my mouth, I really do sound like the clingiest person in the world.

Bennett lets out a sigh, all laughter and smiles gone. "I didn't regret what happened between us. Actually, I very much want to continue what happened in my office. Last night wasn't about you or regret."

"Oh."

If it wasn't about me or regretting what we did, then what was it about? The question forms on the tip of my tongue, but I don't let it out. Looking at his facial expression, the answer is going to be personal, and I don't know if we're at that stage yet.

I'm okay with not knowing everything about this man, just like I'm okay with him not knowing everything about me.

But apparently, Bennett feels differently.

"How much do you want to get to know me?"

I want to know everything, but that seems like a little too much, so I give him the response that I would give him if he ever asked me that question. "However much you are willing to tell me."

There is silence. The only things that could be heard are the roar of the plane and the flight attendant doing something with glasses at the front.

I don't know how long we sit there, but it's enough time for the movie playing on the screen to end and for a new one to start.

When Bennett speaks, I'm on the edge of my seat.

"You know my brother is gone. Left his kids with me and Henry, and to this day, he has yet to come back." I nod. "I might have mentioned looking for him in passing or as a throwaway comment, but I don't think I've told you the extent of it."

I shift and place a hand over the one resting on his knee. "You don't have to."

No part of me wants to push him to give me information. If he wants to tell me, he can, but it has to come from him, not because he feels obligated.

He looks down at our hands. "I want to tell you."

A lump forms in my throat. Who would have thought that a week after the wedding, we would be having this heavy of a conversation?

I don't say anything, but I know he can read my face and see the encouragement for him to continue.

"I use whatever resources that are at my disposal to look for him. Because Lane Enterprises is in security and high tech, it's not hard to access things only available to the police or government agencies. I only ever use that tool when it comes to my brother; otherwise, I use other ways to get information."

The way he says it sends a shiver down my spine, like there is something dark that comes with it. It makes sense, though. Bennett is a billionaire; of course he has something like this at his disposal.

"For the past couple of years, I haven't been able to find anything new. At the beginning, a new address would come up occasionally, but every time I would send someone to investigate, it either turned out to be an empty lot or he was long gone. Same thing with phone numbers. If one ever appeared, it would be disconnected by the time I got to tracking it down or calling it. I think it had been four or five years since the last address or number appeared."

Something takes me by surprise. "Had?"

Bennett gives me a nod. "The day of the first board meeting, a number popped up."

That's the day he told me about his brother, how he hasn't seen him in ten years. It's a creepy coincidence.

"Did you call it?"

He shakes his head. "I wanted to, but it took everything in me not to do it. For all I knew, it was just a dead end. It was probably someone with the same name."

"You didn't want to be disappointed."

"No, but that didn't stop me from committing the number to memory."

"Is that what you did last night? Call the number?"

He scoffs at my question. "No. The number called me."

A chill runs through my whole body. I take my thought back. There's no way in hell this is a coincidence. A number pops up the day he's announced as Gerald's replacement, and then he gets a call from the same number the day the title is officially his? Someone is behind this and is trying to get deep under Bennett's skin, but the question is who?

"Did you answer?" My question comes out almost in a whisper.

Anger rolls through his face. "I did, but whoever was on the other end wasn't in a talking mood."

Without even thinking about it, my hand wraps around him, and I give him a reassuring squeeze. "I'm sorry."

And I am. I couldn't imagine looking for someone all these years, being so close to getting your answers, only to encounter a dead end.

"Don't be. I'm going to find out who was on the other side of that call. Whoever it is wants something, and I'm not going to stop until I find out what."

"What would you do?"

His jaw tics, and for a second, I think he's not going to tell me, but he surprises me yet again.

"Whatever I need."

The way his eyes go dark tells me everything I need to know. This man will stop at nothing. I have a feeling that if he needed to, he would kill to get the answers he wants. The man got married to get ahold of his family's company for crying out loud. I'm sure a bit of blood on his custom-made suits wouldn't deter him.

Knowing that the man I married could possibly kill someone to get something he wanted should be terrifying. It should be reason enough to tell him to turn this plane around and to stay as far away from me as possible. Instead, my heart opens for him a little more, because if I were in his position, I would do the same. In a way, I have.

I intertwine my fingers with his and decide not to run.

"And whatever you decide to do, if you need someone at your side, I'll be there."

His eyes fill with wonder as he squeezes my hand. "I appreciate that. I hope you know the same goes for you."

I smile and try to make a joke. "Even after our two years are up?"

"Even after our two years are up," he answers with all the seriousness in the world

Hearing those words and seeing how serious he is makes my heart swell. Bennett Lane is going to be a part of my life after all of this is over, and I couldn't be happier.

I don't know why, but I get the sudden urge to kiss the man—not only because he opened up to me, but because he made a promise not many people have given me.

After about ten seconds of trying to talk myself out of doing it, I say fuck it and lean in to place a small kiss against Bennett's lips. This marriage may be fake, but there is something happening between us, and I will be damned if I keep myself from kissing my husband. For the next two years, my lips belong to him and only him.

"What was that for?" he asks, giving me a small grin as I pull away.

"For opening up to me, and because I wanted to."

His smile grows even bigger before he leans in and gives me a kiss of his own.

When he pulls away, his smile is still there. "About your other questions, the whole how are we going to act. What do you say to just acting like this? Having fun and doing things because we want to. There's no need to put on a show. We can just get to know each other."

I nod, bringing my body closer to his. "I'd like that."

"Good. Now, let's give you the best honeymoon, Mrs. Lane."

Mrs. Lane.

I've been called that once or twice since the wedding, but it feels different coming from Bennett.

And I freaking love it.

Come time for our divorce, my heart is going to be shattered. I just know it.

23

BENNETT

I'm going to be honest. When it came to this honeymoon, I expected one thing and one thing only: Ella landing in my bed and my cock sliding into her warm pussy.

That's where my mind was when I mentioned the honeymoon and where it was on the drive back home, where it was when I was booking the trip for the next morning—a tropical getaway where it was just the two of us, a bed, and someone to bring us food when needed.

That was my expectation before my phone rang. The second I answered that call, my mind went in an entirely different direction. As soon as I was done talking to Dante, the call and that damn number were all I could think about. I was in my own head for the rest of the night and well through the morning. For nearly the entire plane ride, I hid behind my screens, pretending to be working when, in reality, I was trying to do my own digging.

Not once did I think my distance would affect Ella.

She didn't say it did, but I can see it in her eyes and

body language. She was afraid I regretted our little moment of exploration. She probably had it in her mind that I was just using her and didn't give two shits about how she felt, which was far from the truth.

I decided to put the call and anything to do with my brother out of my mind for the remainder of the trip. Ella deserved to make good memories, and I'd be damned if I took that away from her.

The second we landed in Costa Rica, the expectation of sliding into Ella's pussy every waking moment was no longer top priority.

Her having the time of her life was, along with getting to know more about her.

And that's exactly what's been happening. For the past six days, we've done everything that didn't involve a bed. ATV riding through a rainforest and trying to find waterfalls. Visiting thermal waters. Taking a boat out on the ocean to catch the sunrise. Zip-lining. According to Ella, though, her favorite activity of them all was feeding the baby chimps and sloths.

In the time I've known her, I haven't seen her smile this much, haven't heard her laugh so freely, or truly act her age.

This trip has shown me a new version of Ella I don't think I want to let go of.

Even more so as I learn little things about her.

Like her dislike for snakes, her love for vanilla ice cream with chocolate chips, and her deep friendship with Bloody Marys.

It has been nice seeing her enjoy herself so much, but she's not the only one having fun.

It wasn't until halfway through this trip that I remembered how fucking good it felt to de-stress. For years, my mind has been set on one thing and one thing only: becoming CEO.

Whenever the kids brought up wanting to go on a trip, I would take them, but I would work ninety percent of the time. I haven't truly gone anywhere just to forget all the outside noise. Not since I was twenty-two at least. Not since I wanted to go to the farthest possible place in the world and just forget about everything. The nightmares, the memories, the feeling of wanting to drown.

For the first time in a long time, I know what it feels like to actually act my age, and it feels so damn good.

And it's all thanks to my wife.

As she watches the sun set from our balcony overlooking the ocean, I take her in. She looks happy. Would she be this happy if I hadn't propositioned her with this marriage? I want to think she would be.

Since we already had dinner brought up to our villa here in Playa Conchal, I grab some of the ice cream I had the front desk bring up on our second day and make her a bowl just how she likes it: extra chocolate chips sprinkled on top.

The smile that she gives me as she takes it from me goes straight to my dick. "Look at that. He's learning, ladies and gentlemen."

"Cut the crap, or I won't add ice cream and mini chocolate chips to the weekly grocery list."

She lets out a gasp. "You wouldn't dare."

"Try me."

Her eyes narrow before a smirk forms on her face, and she throws a shrug in my direction. "It's okay; I'll just tell Henry to add them myself. He already loves me, and you're just jealous."

I laugh. "I wouldn't call it jealousy."

"Then what would you call it?" Her eyebrow raises in the sexiest way.

I find eyebrows sexy now? When it comes to Ella, yes.

"Competition."

"What is there to compete about? I'm Henry's favorite and you know it." She sticks out her tongue at me.

Now it's time for me to narrow my eyes. "You're his favorite right now. I've been his favorite since I was born."

"Please. If anyone has been Henry's favorite since birth, it's Drake."

I open my mouth to throw out a rebuttal, but it gets stuck in my throat. She does have a point. The kids all have Henry wrapped around their pinkies, but Drake has him wrapped around both of his.

"I stumped you, didn't I?" Her smile is so damn proud and bright, I can't even be mad at her for pulling the Drake card.

"That you did."

She places her ice cream bowl on the table between our chairs and raises up her hands. "I win."

Another laugh escapes me. "And what exactly do you win?"

She purses her lips and taps her finger against them, as

if she truly has to think about it. "A game of never have I ever?"

I snort. "You want to play a drinking game?"

"It doesn't have to be a drinking game. You can drink whatever you want, and I'll just eat my ice cream."

All I can picture are her lips wrapping around the spoon, but the spoon quickly turns into something else. *My dick.*

Before I let that thought escalate, I get up from the chair to grab whatever alcohol I could find. Besides Ella's Bloody Marys, there hasn't been a whole lot of drinking on this vacation.

That's something I'm surprised about, since I tend to have at least one glass of scotch every day. This trip is doing something to me, and I like it a lot more than I should.

After grabbing a bottle of champagne left by the hotel as a wedding gift, I head back outside and pop it open.

Ella smirks when she sees what I'm drinking. "I thought you said that was a cheap bottle."

"Yeah, well, it's the only alcohol we have in the room."

She grabs her bowl and holds out a spoonful of somewhat melted cream. "You can have some of my ice cream."

Tempting, but I shake my head. If I eat ice cream right now, I'll want it to be off her body or from her mouth, not from a spoon.

I chide myself a bit at the thought. Apart from the kiss on the plane ride here, Ella and I haven't done anything else. No kissing. No handholding. Besides sharing a bed, we have done absolutely nothing.

Granted, today is the first day we've been back to the room before sunset.

"Your loss," Ella throws out before sliding the spoon into her mouth.

If only she could slide something else into her mouth.

Okay, I need to get a handle on all the sexual thoughts.

I take a seat and look over at her. "Do you want to start?"

She contemplates before answering with a nod, and I'm internally cringing at the headache the champagne is going to induce.

"Never have I ever..." She brings the spoon to her mouth and starts tapping it against her lips. Watching her has me readjusting. I seriously need to stop thinking about things going into her mouth. "Owned a car that was worth more than fifty thousand dollars."

Oh, I see how we're playing this.

I roll my eyes and take a sip of champagne. My throat constricts at the taste. If we ever come back here, I'll pay for them to change it out. This is fucking disgusting.

"Your face looks ridiculous right now," Ella says through a giggle. The sound makes the champagne slightly better, but not much.

"It's fine," I say, trying not to gag. "I've never..." Why the fuck is this so hard? "Spent a night in jail."

I came close once for arguing with an officer after getting pulled over, which is a stupid fucking reason. Connections were on my side though when a police lieutenant drove by and had the police officers release me. I didn't know until after that the lieutenant was the same individual that came to the house the night my parents died and notified us.

I kick the memory out of my head when I see Ella scoop up some ice cream and bring it to her mouth.

"No fucking way."

Dante's report had nothing about an arrest.

Her face goes red. "I was sixteen, and it was only for one night. It wasn't even my fault."

Her grumbles are cute.

"Whose fault was it?" I try to hold in a laugh, but it's getting hard.

With her face still very much red, she lets out a sigh. "Teenage hormones. There was this guy in the group home I was in who I had a crush on. He was like a wannabe rebel."

I let out a snort. "Wannabe rebel?"

"Like he wanted to be a bad boy, but the dude was too much of a goody-two-shoes to actually pull it off."

I place a hand over my mouth to hold in my laugh. "Sounds like an awesome dude."

"Whatever. Do you want to hear the story or not?" There's a bite to her tone that's sexy as fuck.

I hold up my hands. "I'm listening."

An eye roll comes my direction. "Anyway, it was after dinner, and we wanted some snacks, so we went to the corner store to get some. When we were there, my crush had the bright idea to just walk out without paying, and since I wanted to impress him, I was all for it. Little did I know, the store owner had cameras everywhere and caught us. And since the asshole was a wannabe, he dropped all the snacks on the floor and told the owner it was my idea. The owner called the cops, we both spent a night at the police station, and in the morning, the head of the group home came to pick us up. The charges were dropped, and that's that. The end. My turn."

As much as I appreciate her wanting to drop the subject, she's not getting off that easily. I need more details. "Did anything ever happen between you and the guy?"

Ella shrugs. "Nothing. A few weeks later, he aged out of the group home into his own apartment. I saw him a few years ago when he came into the restaurant I was working at, but that's it."

"No rekindled crush?"

I'm not going to lie, Ella with narrowed eyes is also sexy as fuck. "No. The crush disappeared the second he put the blame on me. It was *his* stupid idea."

I let out a small laugh, which makes Ella relax a little bit as she laughs with me.

"His loss. I doubt he'd be able to handle you giving him a death glare every time you remembered what he did."

Another chuckle leaves her. "No, he wouldn't. Is it my turn now?" I give her a nod. "I've never been to a strip club."

"Never?" I ask, bringing the bottle to my lips. This second drink is worse than the first.

Ella shakes her head. "I've never been curious enough to step foot in one."

Right away, an idea springs into my head. "We may have to use one of our weekly dates to take you to one."

"You want to take me to a club where naked women are going to grind all over you?"

She sounds jealous with a tinge of anger in her voice, but she has no reason to be jealous. This marriage may have an end date, and we may not be in a relationship, but that doesn't mean I would do anything to embarrass her. I'll be fucking damned if I let another woman touch me while I'm married. I wouldn't do that to Ella. There are plenty of reasons why I don't want to truly be married, but commitment and monogamy aren't part of that.

"There are different clubs where people don't grind on you," I throw out, one club already coming to mind.

She gives me a speculative look. "Really?"

"Yeah, my friend owes one. It's called Perversa. It's more performances in private rooms than lap dances and throwing money around."

Her face screws up when I mention the club's name. "I've heard of Perversa. I was actually thinking about applying there before I got hired at Lane Enterprises."

I don't know why, but knowing she was thinking about working at Perversa angers me. Dante takes care of his employees, going above and beyond for them, protecting them with top-of-the-line security, and even giving them a place to live. I know if Ella had gotten the job, Dante would have looked after her. What angers me is the fact that she would have been dancing for random people, showing off her body that should be for my eyes only.

You're getting angry over something that never happened.
Right.

I guess it's safe to say my wife drives me crazy, even if this marriage is a sham.

"If you want, I'll take you, show you what it's all about. Give you the whole member experience."

Given the look she gave me earlier, the way she beams at my suggestion takes me by surprise.

"That sounds like fun."

I nod. "I'll arrange it when we get home."

I'm rewarded with a smile, and then we go back to the game. For the next twenty minutes, we throw never-have-I-evers at each other. This may have started out as just a drinking game to pass the time, but it has turned into a nice way of getting to know Ella in a natural way, not because I had a Mafia boss look her up.

There are things I would have never known from a background check, like what she just said about her sexual experience.

"I'm sorry, can you repeat that?" I ask, feeling a little bewildered. If I had taken a drink, I would have spit it out as soon as she spoke.

With a full blush on her chest and face, Ella repeats her never have I ever.

"I've never done anything kinky during sex."

"Like?"

Her blush gets deeper, and for a second, I think she's going to cower, but she doesn't.

"Like wax play."

That's very specific. I was half expecting her to say something like getting tied up or blindfolded. Wax play wasn't even in the top ten of possibilities.

Then, the image of Ella tied to a bed, a blindfold over her eyes and wax over her pussy and nipples, pops into my head. My dick goes hard imagining it, and the more I see, the more I'm hungry for it.

I clear my throat before responding. "Have you been curious about wax play, or is it just the first thing that came to mind?"

Have I ever experimented with wax play before? No, but I would be up to trying it.

Ella looks down at her bowl as she responds. "It's a very new curiosity."

I don't even think before I speak. "How new?"

My wife bites down on her bottom lip and looks at me through her lashes. "I started thinking about it last week."

I have to do some readjusting before I respond. "What brought it on?"

My voice sounds strained, and by the blush covering Ella's body, she knows why.

"Do you really want to know?" Her eyes travel to my groin, a hint of sparkle in them.

I answer way too quickly. "Yes."

She doesn't even take a pause before answering. "I know it wasn't necessary, since this marriage is a sham and all, but I still wanted to get pampered before the wedding, feel like a real bride, you know? So I did what every bride does the day before their wedding: get pampered. Hair, nails, waxing. I've only ever waxed my eyebrows, but since it was a big day, I decided to get a Brazilian—not because I thought we were going to have sex or anything, but because I wanted to feel good. So I got it done, and as I was laying there, I couldn't help but think how the wax felt nice, especially." She pauses for a second. "Down there. From there, the curiosity grew, and I looked some things up."

A story about getting pampered shouldn't be a fucking turn-on, but my dick thinks it is. Especially when it hears about wax going anywhere near Ella's pussy.

Fuck, this woman is turning me into a teenager again.

"What did you look up?" I ask, curiosity getting the best of me, but when she responds, I wish I'd kept my mouth shut.

I see her swallow. "Where to buy the sex-safe wax. You know, the kind they use in porn."

She's torturing me, I fucking know it.

I try to be as natural as I can with this conversation, but the more she speaks, the more chance I'll have to get up and take care of business.

"And did you like what you saw?" My voice cracks as I speak. She really is turning me into a teenager.

It doesn't go unnoticed that she presses her legs together a little bit tighter. "I did."

What the fuck do I do with that information? Say *okay, great, let's order some wax and we can explore it together*?

I need to get my head on straight, but right now, in this very moment, I have no idea how.

"If it's something that really interests you, you should explore it," I throw out, because my mind is being taken over by my dick and all I can think is *let me pour wax all over you and fuck you until you can't remember your name.*

"Would you want to explore with me?" Her voice is soft, almost like a purr.

Don't fucking purr right now, baby. I can't fucking take it.

Fuck, I need to start thinking like the thirty-two-year-old man I am.

It takes me a moment to answer her question, because all I want to say is *yes, yes, yes!*

"If you wanted me to, then yes, I would want to explore wax play with you."

Ella doesn't say anything right away. Instead, she sits in her chair as a smirk forms on her face.

My eyes stay on her as she stands, closing the space between us to stand right in front of me. Her eyes travel down to my groin, where my cock is begging for attention.

"I want to do that with you, but I think before we do that, we should do something else."

"And what would that be?"

A groan nearly escapes me as Ella kneels in front of me, her body between my legs, her hands landing on my thighs.

"Explore each other."

All my resolve goes out the damn window.

"What my wife wants, she gets."

"You're so sweet about it."

I look down at her with a smirk. "You don't want sweet?" She gives me a head shake. "What do you want?"

There's no hesitation in her answer. "The man who told Peter Hill to never speak to his wife that way again."

There's a slight chance I'm corrupting this woman, but I don't give a shit.

I open my legs further, bringing a certain part of me closer to her face.

"Then be a good wife and suck your husband's cock."

24

ELLA

I don't know how our little game of *never have I ever* turned into something sexual, but I'm not mad at it. I've been waiting for this very moment since we got to Costa Rica, and up until now, it had yet to come.

A woman can only take so much of seeing the man she's attracted to shirtless, wearing nothing but a towel, soaking wet as he comes out of the water. It's been a very interesting week for the spot between my legs, with my hand or the showerhead attacking it every time I have an ounce of time alone.

But now, after one simple game of trying to get to know each other better, I'm on my knees in front of Bennett.

His words are still ringing in my ears, and everything inside me is tingling.

With a smile on my face, I don't waste any time following orders. I bite down on my bottom lip and reach for the waistband of Bennett's shorts. I love seeing the man in a suit, but there's something about him wearing casual clothing that really does it for me. I wish I could see him like this more often.

As I pull his shorts down enough for me to release his cock, I feel Bennett's eyes on me. I don't have to look up to know his stare is intense, devouring everything about me.

His cock springs free, and I can't help but run my tongue along my lips.

There is nothing average about Bennett Lane—not in his work life or his home life, and definitely not his cock.

The man is gifted, and I can't wait any longer to have him in my mouth.

And from the curse he just let out, he can't either.

"You look like a fucking angel, Elizabeth, sitting on your knees like that," Bennett lets out as I run my tongue across the underside of his cock.

I keep my eyes locked with his as I take him in my mouth, giving his head a good suck.

"Do that again."

I do a few more times before moving my mouth down his shaft, covering him in my saliva, before I bring my mouth back up and take him as deep as I can.

Bennett lets out a groan as I wrap my mouth around him, my hands still very much on his thighs, massaging as I bob my head.

"Such a fucking sweet mouth. You like sucking on my cock, don't you?"

I answer with a hum as I continue to work him, taking my hands off his legs and wrapping both around his length.

With every sound from his lips, I want to reach down

and play with myself. So, when one of his hands lands on the side of my face, guiding my mouth, I slide my fingers down.

I'm wet and silky, and all I can think about is how good Bennett would feel sliding into me. He feels so good in my mouth; he would no doubt feel good there too.

"Fuck. Are you touching yourself?" he grunts out, his hand moving to the back of my head to hold me in place.

I simply nod as I feel him in the back of my throat.

"Who knew someone so sweet-looking as you could do such dirty things. Let me have a taste. I've been craving it since we left my office."

I oblige, bringing my hand up for him to suck my fingers clean. As he lets out a hum at my arousal, I slide his cock from my mouth and slide my tongue from the tip down to the base, marking every single inch of him.

A slight pain radiates from my fingers, a sharpness that can only come from one thing: Bennett's teeth.

"Did you just bite me?" I ask, pulling my mouth away just enough to speak.

The smirk on his face looks dangerous, and all I want to do is kiss it off. "In a few minutes, that won't be the only biting that you are going to be getting."

Flutters swarm my whole body, and excitement rolls deep in my bones. "Didn't your parents or Henry ever teach you about teasing and how it's not nice to say something that you don't mean?"

Both of his hands land on my face, a sadistic yet lust-filled look in his eyes that has arousal sliding down my leg.

"I mean every word that comes out of my mouth. Now

slide my cock down that pretty throat of yours one last time."

My mouth waters even more as I follow orders to do exactly what he wants.

I wrap my lips around his cock and slide down until he's the only thing I can feel, taste, and smell. I feel him at the back of my throat, and I hold him there for a few seconds, enjoying the feel. My eyes water, starting to sting, but when I look up at Bennett and he caresses my face in the gentlest way, I don't feel the pain.

"Fuck. You're so damn beautiful."

Since I can't smile, I try to convey with my eyes just how much I love his praise. From the way he smirks at me, he takes note of it.

Bennett's hand pushes my head down for a few seconds before he lets me go, and his cock slides out of my mouth with a pop.

I'm in the process of catching my breath when it's taken away again as Bennett crunches down, picks me up, and throws me over his shoulder.

"You know, I could have walked," I say as I hang against his back.

Throwing me over his shoulder must have been a spur-of-the moment decision, because his shorts are hanging halfway down his ass.

Even this man's ass is gorgeous.

"What would be the fun in that?" he lets out as he walks into the villa and deposits me onto the bed.

He has a point.

I'm about to request that he carry me around like a

caveman everywhere we go, but the words get stuck in my mouth when he starts kissing his way up my leg.

Thank God I changed into a dress after dinner. Less fabric to worry about.

I watch in awe as he kisses his way up my body, as if he's the first man I've been with who has wanted to take their time with me. Feeling his lips on my skin, how his fingers dig into my body, it sure as hell makes it feel that way. I've been with a handful of people in my life, and not one of them has made me feel what I'm feeling with Bennett.

The fact that I'm feeling more with a man who is legally my husband but I'm not truly with is telling. Bennett and I are diving headfirst into things when we should be putting space between us. This ends in two years, and at the rate we're going, when the divorce comes, it's going to hit harder than anything I will ever experience.

I'm going to hate it. I'm going to hate myself for agreeing to this because it will ultimately rip out my heart. But it's okay. I will be okay. As long as I have memories like this one to hold onto, I will get through the heartbreak.

Because there will be heartbreak.

A few weeks into this marriage, only a few months of knowing this man, and he already has a place in my heart, and he doesn't even know it.

As Bennett's mouth makes it to my inner thigh and he situates himself between my legs, I can't help but to give myself a mental kick in the ass. If someone was put in this position and offered a million dollars for two years of marriage, they would have kept their heart out of this. They would have gone these two years without falling for their husband or falling into bed with him. But I did the opposite, and it probably stems from one thing: my abandonment issues.

I fall fast and hard, hoping the other person doesn't leave me. Knowing that, I should have walked away.

It's too late now, though. I'm in it and don't want to leave.

When I feel Bennett lick me through the lace of my panties, all thoughts about abandonment issues and regrets fly out the window, and I'm brought back to the moment.

"Oh my god," I let out, feeling like I'm having an out-of-body experience.

"I've been wanting this since I first tasted you." His tongue flattens out against me, and when he rubs the lace against my clit, one of my moans fills the room.

There's no hesitation as he rips a second pair of my panties and plants his mouth on my pussy. The way he eats me is as if he wants to savor each and every drop. It's fucking amazing.

My legs tighten around Bennett's head, and my hands make themselves at home in his hair. I want to pull him closer and push him away at the same time.

"So damn responsive. I wonder what you would do if I did this."

One of his fingers slides into my pussy before he slides it back and then inserts two fingers into me.

"Do that again," I pant, never wanting it to end.

"Your pussy takes my fingers so beautifully. I wonder if it will be the same with my cock."

"Yes!"

He hums against me, the vibration moving through my whole body. "Come on my tongue and hand, and then I'll slide my cock into this delicious pussy and make you come again."

"Bennett, please." A moan escapes me as his fingers slide out of me again, his tongue continuing to toy with my clit.

A chuckle leaves his lips. "Are you begging for my cock or for me to make you come?"

I pull his hair a little harder. "Both."

He lets out a noise that sounds like a growl, and for a second, he doesn't do anything other than lick me in the most methodical way, as if savoring me, but then he switches it up. His mouth becomes more forceful, and his fingers slide into me, as if on a mission to throw me over the edge.

Everything that he is doing feels so damn good, and my body is having a hard time keeping up.

My legs start to shake uncontrollably, and I pull at Bennett's hair so hard, I'm scared I'm pulling hair out. Still, he doesn't tell me to stop. The only thing on his mind is me and giving me one of the best orgasms ever.

His fingers pump into me as his teeth meet my clit, and I'm so close to the edge—but that's not what takes me over. It's the way he hums against me that does it.

As my orgasm hits, I pant out his name as if it is the only word I know how to say.

Bennett continues to work his magic, as if he hadn't just made me explode. His methods are aggressive, but they work to get me where he wants me. Orgasm number two hits, and I swear, I black out. I try to speak, but nothing comes out.

Kisses land on the top of my pussy and travel up until Bennett is hovering over me with a smirk on his face, as if he just won the biggest trophy in the world.

"Think you can give me one more?" he asks as he leans down and places his mouth against my pulse point.

I shake my head. "I don't think I can handle it."

If two orgasms almost made me black out, what would a third one do?

"I think you can." The cockiness is prominent in his voice, and as much as I want to roll my eyes, I don't. All actions and words are forgotten when Bennett slides off me and starts taking off his clothes.

I've seen a lot of Bennett without a whole lot of clothes on during this trip, and I will have fantasies of this man until the day I die, but this throws all those fantasies out the window.

As Bennett undresses, his eyes stay with mine. I try to keep his gaze, but it becomes hard when he takes off his shirt. My eyes slide down his body, taking in every single inch. When he starts sliding off his shorts, my mouth waters and my center screams in enjoyment.

I lied. Casual Bennett isn't my favorite—completely nude Bennett is.

As my eyes roam his body, I sit up and take off my dress, throwing it to the foot of the bed at his feet. He snatches it midair and brings up the fabric up to his nose, taking in a breath. I can hardly breathe. There is nothing special about the body wash or perfume I wear, nothing over the top or expensive, yet Bennett is taking it in as if it were the best thing he has ever smelled.

My belly tingles, but when he drops the dress and his eyes rake over my body, those tingles turn into something else, something a lot stronger. It's as if the attraction I have for this man is sweating through every single one of my pores and calling him to me.

With our eyes never moving away from each other, Bennett grabs me by my ankles, dragging me over to the edge of the bed. My legs open voluntarily, and his cock lines up so perfectly with my entrance. I wrap my hand around his cock and slip it through my lips, coating the length of him with my arousal.

When I slide the head into my entrance, he lets out the most delicious groan I have ever heard.

"We're going to need a condom," he grits out as I slide the head of his cock back out of me.

I just give him a nod, and ten seconds later, he returns with a condom in his hand and starts sliding it on. Watching Bennett give his dick a few tugs is one of the sexiest things in the world.

Once we have protection in place, Bennett situates himself back between my legs, and with his eyes on me, he guides himself inside me.

My mouth pops open as he slides deeper. At one point, I don't think I'll be able to take any more of him, but he proves me wrong.

I'm able to take every inch of him.

He stretches me perfectly, and all I want to do is keep him there forever.

"Fucking hell. You feel so damn good." The way the words leave Bennett's lips has my arousal skyrocketing.

Bennett starts to move, and I lose all ability to think about anything but him. He has taken over every single one of my senses, and it's the best feeling in the world.

My legs are wrapped around Bennett's waist, not leaving any space between us. He pounds into me, and I feel him everywhere. Praises fill my ear, and each one pushes me closer to the edge than I was a second ago.

Three months ago, when I applied for the assistant position, this wasn't even a possibility or a thought, but now it's all that I can think of, and I don't want to give it up.

Pleas for him to make me come fill the room, and there is no hesitation from Bennett. He follows orders as if it were his favorite job in the world.

It doesn't take long for both of us to hit the edge together, waiting to jump.

I slide my hand between us, touching where we meet. As my fingers slide against his shaft, Bennett whispers in my ear, "This is the best fucking pussy I've ever had. It's like you were made for me, Elizabeth. Come on my cock, baby. I want to feel you squeeze me."

That's what does it.

I'm thrown over the edge of the cliff and glide into the clouds below me. I'm screaming out Bennett's name, which triggers his own release. His grunts and moans are music to my ears.

For a long minute, Bennett hovers over me, almost placing his weight on me, and it feels amazing. I never want him to leave. But eventually, he pushes off to get rid of the condom, returning with a towel to clean me up.

Somehow, the aftercare feels more intimate than all the other things we've done tonight. It feels really nice being taken care of like this, rather than being treated like another slash on the bedpost.

Once I'm clean to Bennett's standards, he climbs into bed and takes me in his arms.

I never would have thought a man like Bennett would be a cuddler, but I'm glad I'm wrong. The second his arms are wrapped around me, I feel at peace, safe, and weirdly enough like I'm home.

If I wasn't attached before, I am now. That should be a sign to pull away from this and from Bennett, but I don't. This is where I want to be, and nothing is going to make me pull away.

Absolutely nothing.

BENNETT

When I was twenty, I experimented with a few things. The world was at my disposal. I had money that no twenty-year-old should have, and I had unresolved shit I didn't want to think about. So, for a small period in my life, I turned to drugs. It wasn't the brightest decision in my life, but it got me through the day.

I thought I would never feel those highs again.

I was so fucking wrong.

Those highs are nothing compared to the one I'm currently experiencing.

I expected the next two years to just be a means to an end. In my head, I would be grateful to Ella for doing this, for marrying me to help me get what I wanted, but that was it. I didn't think anything would come out of it. I thought that, at most, we would be friends. No emotions. No feelings. No labels. `

But the woman is a damn bulldozer and knocked all

those thoughts out the damn window without thinking twice.

I should have expected it, since she's the one woman who was able to do what others haven't. I should have known from day one that she was going to be more than just an assistant. More than just a fantasy. More than anything my mind could conjure.

It has been three months since we got back from our honeymoon, and in those three months, a lot has changed.

Not only has my role as CEO officially been cemented and I officially moved into my father's office, but things with me and Ella are also different.

Before the wedding, we had come up with a set of rules we would abide by during our two years of marriage. We put lines in place, rules, but shit changes, and now I crave to cross each and every one of those lines.

The rules are forgotten, and there are days both of us forget we are only married for convenience, not love.

We've been acting like an actual married couple, something that took everyone by surprise. I don't know what Henry and the kids thought would come from this, but I doubt it included catching Ella and me making out in the kitchen before breakfast or right after dinner.

But from what I've noticed, everyone is embracing it.

Henry says he hates having two more people to cater to, but from the way he smiles whenever Ella or Charlie enter the room, I know that isn't true. When it came to embracing things, I knew Henry would be easy.

My worries were mostly with the kids.

In the last ten years, I've never brought someone into their lives like this. I've never had a girlfriend long enough for them to spend time with them, so I thought there would be issues with having Ella and Charlie living with us.

But they proved me wrong.

All four kids have welcomed Ella and Charlie and made them feel like they are part of the family, so much so that it's hard to remember how things were before we got married.

For the kids and for me.

I went from sleeping alone and occasionally getting woken up by a snoring ten-year-old to sharing a bed with a beautiful woman I don't want to let go of.

We spend most of our days together at the office and then come home to spend even more time together. Since the honeymoon, we have spent maybe three full days apart, and I don't see that changing anytime soon.

I crave being near her. I want to see her and have her within arm's reach. If I go out of town, she's coming with me. If I have a meeting I need to attend, she is sitting in the chair on my right.

Three months, and I don't want her to leave my side.

It's the fucking unhealthiest thing, but I don't give a shit. If I have two years with this woman, I'm going to take advantage of it.

Two years won't be enough.

No, it won't, but that's all I'm going to get.

The thought that I could ask for more time with Ella

pops into my head, but right now may not be the best time to think about something like that.

Especially since we are currently at a hockey game with all the kids and Henry, having a *family night out*, as Drake dubbed it.

"I can't believe you bought a hockey team for him," Ella says from next to me in one of the boxes at the hockey arena.

It's opening night for Chicago's own hockey team, the Dark Knights, and Grayson just finished telling Ella how I bought the hockey team for him when he was eight.

"It wasn't really for him. The old team owner was in a bind, so I decided to step in and take on the burden. It just so happened that I had a nephew whose favorite sport was hockey, with dreams of being a professional hockey player one day."

Hopefully, said nephew could play for the team I own one day. It's nepotism at its finest, but I've seen Grayson play. He's going to make a name for himself on his own. It doesn't matter if he plays for his uncle's team or not.

Ella looks at me, dumbfounded. "If his favorite sport was baseball, would you have bought a team too?"

I don't even have to think about it, because the answer is a hard yes.

Just like with Ella, anything the kids want, they get. It may be in obscure ways, but they still get what they want. Instead of telling Ella that, though, I give her a shrug.

"Oh my god. What other random things have you bought the kids?"

Before I can respond, Sam inserts herself. "For my

sixteenth birthday, he got me a 1964 Shelby and a brand-new Aston Martin."

Ella quickly turns to my niece. "Aren't both those cars worth like a hundred grand each?"

Sam gives her a nod. "The Aston Martin is a good two hundred grand alone."

"You got a teenage girl a two-hundred-thousand-dollar car?" she asks, sounding bewildered.

Instead of answering, I turn to look at Sam and Grayson, narrowing my eyes at both.

They mouth "sorry" and turn their attention back to the game on the ice.

Instead of doing the same, I look back at Ella, who looks like she has a lecture ready to go on the tip of her tongue.

"I did," I answer, holding up my hands in defense. "But to be fair, I'm a rich kid who doesn't know what a reasonable car for a teenager is. So I just got her a car I would want."

"That's a crazy way to spend money."

"Sure." I wonder what she would say if she found out that the ring she's wearing cost more than sixty grand.

"How does spending that much money not bother you?" she asks, almost in a whisper.

I know where she is coming from. If I had a childhood like Ella's, I would feel the same way about money. But we didn't have similar childhoods. Money has always been around, and there's a lot of it, so spending it on things like a professional hockey team or cars doesn't seem like a lot.

"I guess when you have the amount of money I do, buying things like that seem trivial."

With the way she scrunches up her nose, I know that what I said was wrong.

"Must be nice," she grumbles, turning her attention back to the game, but I know she is still very much thinking about the whole money thing.

"If you had that type of money, what would you do with it?" I ask, both out of curiosity and to make her less mad at me.

The question has her facial expression shifting away from frustration.

Her answer comes a lot quicker than I thought it would, like she has thought about this.

"I'd help foster kids." She turns to me and gives me a small smile. "I know it sounds cliché, but I'd dedicate my time to helping them. Create programs to help the kids who age out so they aren't just thrown out into the world on their own. Establish group homes that are safe spaces where a child might actually choose to go. I'd spend money providing foster parents more education on mental health and how to better help those with special needs. I'd also use some of the money to find better ways to screen foster parents, make sure everyone who applies to be one is doing it for the right reason and not because they are in it for the money."

I run through all of her ideas, and I like every single one of them. To pull something like that off, you need a lot of funding, possibly a well-known backer.

The more that I think about it, the more an idea springs into mind.

"What if you did have the money?" I ask, already drafting up opportunities in my head.

Ella lets out a small chuckle. "What are you going to do, give me the money?"

"In a way."

She turns to look back at me just as the Knights take the puck from the other team and drive it across the ice.

"What are you suggesting?"

"The Lane Foundation. They have a lot of the resources you would need to pull off something like this, plus the money. We can bring you in, and you can start wherever you need. It won't happen right away, but I think with some time, you can really do great things."

As I think about it more, Ella would be perfect for the foundation. I know Henry has been wanting to step down for a while now, and Ella would be a great replacement.

The foundation already donates money to different foster care programs, but it's not enough. With Ella at the helm, I think the foundation could do great things.

"You really think I could do something like that?" she asks, her eyes full of wonder.

I'm honest with her. "Yeah, I really think you can. The foundation could really use someone like you."

And they can. Henry has done a great job for almost fifteen years, but there are a few things that need a female's touch, and if my mother was still here, she would think Ella would be perfect for the job.

The roar of the crowd puts our attention back on the game, but as the cheering calms down, Ella turns back to me.

"Maybe we can talk more about this at home? Get Henry's opinion on this. I don't want to step on any toes."

I give her a smile while I reach for her hand and bring it up to my lips. "Whatever you want."

My wife beams and leans over to place a kiss against my lips. It's quick and easy, just enough to get me through the rest of the night until we're back home and I have her in my bed, whimpering under me.

We go back to watching the rest of the game with the kids. By the end, the Knights lose the game three to one, but at the very least, we got some bonding time with everyone.

"Why is the team called the Dark Knights? Why not use a color or something?" Ella asks as we make our way out of the arena to the car.

"Because of Batman," Elliot answers, as if that is enough explanation.

"Excuse me?" she asks, looking at Elliot and me for more details. "What does a hockey team have to do with a comic book character?"

"Everything," Grayson and Drake say at the same time as they make their way to the car.

"It was Grayson's favorite character when he was younger, and then it became Drake's. When I bought the team and the opportunity to change the name came up, I let them pick, and that's what they landed on."

"And because Uncle Bennett is Batman!" Drake yells out right before jumping into the car.

Ella lets out a laugh. "I didn't know you were a vigilante. Do you have a mask and a cape hidden somewhere I don't know about? Do you sneak out at night to fight crime?"

I roll my eyes. "None of the above."

"Then why does the kid think you're Batman?"

"Apparently, being a billionaire with a bunch of kids who aren't his running around, with a big house and a lot of cars, makes you seem like the Caped Crusader."

A finger lands against Ella's lips. "I mean, I can see it. You *are* dark and broody. Maybe we should get you a mask and see how it looks on you."

I can see her mind working with the idea. I better put a stop to it before she actually buys one.

"I'm not a mask guy."

"Oh, come on—it will be fun." She walks in front of me, and before she is able to get far enough away, I wrap my arm around her waist and bring her back to my front.

"You buy the mask, and I get to use the wax I have in my nightstand."

"You bought it?" she whispers.

I press my lips against her ear. "I did, and I would rather use that than a stupid mask."

She lets out a hum and grips my hand so tight, it almost hurts, but in a good way.

"Then let's forget about the mask and just concentrate on the wax."

"That's my girl." I take her lobe between my teeth,

thankful she has her hair down so nobody could see. "Let's go home."

With an extra pep in her step, she closes the distance to the car. Since we came here straight from the office, Henry and the kids climb into their own car while Ella and I get into another. I'm about to suggest for the driver to take us to my penthouse only a few blocks away so Ella and I could have a night without being quiet, but a phone starts to ring.

Since becoming CEO, it has been nonstop hours for both of us. Something is always happening on the other side of the world that needs someone's attention.

My screen is blank, so whoever is calling is calling Ella.

When I turn to see who's calling at this hour, I find Ella with a ramrod straight back and shoulders so damn tight, she may need a massage to relax them.

"Who's calling?" I ask, reaching for the phone, but she moves it out of the way.

"Nobody," she says, her voice a whisper. Her face almost seems ashen as she looks down at the screen. "It's just an unknown number."

"Are you going to answer it?"

She locks the screen, ultimately ignoring the call.

Finally, she looks up at me with a hint of fear in her eyes. "No. It's late. Whoever it is can leave a message and I'll call them back later."

My teeth grind. It's not like her to ignore a call, no matter the time. She always answers a call, whether it's personal or business.

"Are you okay?" I ask, because there has to be something behind this.

She gives me a tight smile. "Yes. I'm fine. The call just took me by surprise. There's nothing to worry about."

I don't buy it, not for a fucking second.

But I don't question it. She promised me that if anything was wrong, she would tell me.

I'm hoping she keeps that promise.

26

ELLA

My leg bounces as I watch my cell phone ring. The same South Carolina number has been calling for the past two weeks, and every time it pops up on my screen, I feel like I'm going to have a nervous breakdown.

Seeing a number across my screen shouldn't scare me so much, but I know this number. This number has been in the back of my head for five years now. I thought I was never going to see it again, that now that my debt was paid off, I didn't have to worry about it anymore.

Yet, here it is, taunting me, putting fear in me that I thought I was never going to feel ever again.

When the number first came up, I thought I was seeing things. I thought maybe I was remembering the number wrong; there was no way the number I never wanted to see again was on my screen in front of me. But the more I looked at it, the more realization hit.

He found me. He found us, and now he's calling to take everything away.

I wanted to tell Bennett as we drove home that night. I wanted to confess everything, including where the million dollars he gave me went and why, but I was too scared to do it. I didn't know how to form the words so it didn't end in judgment.

If I told him, he would have questions I'm not ready to answer. I told him everything was fine, but in reality, nothing is.

The phone stops ringing for about a minute before it starts back up again.

He's getting more eager, and I get the feeling that if I don't answer soon, he's going to change tactics and possibly come to Chicago. I can't have that happening, not if I want to keep Charlie safe and not tell Bennett.

I reach for the phone with all the determination to answer it, but I can't seem to make my fingers hit the button. So I watch it ring until it stops, and once it goes to voicemail, I throw the device into my drawer and try not to think about it.

But every time it vibrates, it becomes harder and harder.

For the majority of my time, I try to concentrate on this proposal I'm working on for the foundation, the one I told Bennett about at the hockey game, but everything feels like it's jumbled up. Nothing is making sense, and the more I continue to work on it, the more frustrated I get.

My mind is occupied, and not with the things I need to do.

I haven't even officially started the new part of my job,

and I'm already failing at it, all because I can't find it in me to answer a call.

Maybe once I do answer the call, everything will get better. Maybe the person calling me is only doing so because they want to tell me they got the money and our debt is all squared away. The chances are slim, but it could happen.

I hate the feeling that these stupid calls induce. I hate that I have to look over my shoulder everywhere I go, even with the security detail I received once I married Bennett. The only way it will all go away is if I answer the damn phone and face my demons.

As much as it pains me, I reach for the drawer and pull out my phone. I look at all the missed calls I have from that one number and suddenly feel the urge to cry.

I can do this.

I can make the call.

Taking a deep breath, I look into Bennett's new office. He moved in the day we got back from our honeymoon. It's spacious and fit for a king. It fits him perfectly, like it was made for him, just like the CEO title. If he were here, I would tell him just that, but he isn't.

The man is at lunch with the Commissioner of the Chicago Police Department, something about working on gun reform.

It's both good and bad that he's gone. Good because I can make this call and not have him asking me any questions, but bad because in a short period of time, he has become my safe haven, someone I've depended on to bring me back when I felt lost. I could really use him right now, but I know it's best that he isn't here.

After about a five-minute mental pep talk and a few deep breaths, I wake my phone up and dial the number that has been haunting my life for as long as I can remember.

As it rings, I'm hoping the call doesn't get answered, that it will just go to voicemail, and I won't have to hear the voice I've hated since I was eighteen years old.

But luck isn't on my side, and the call gets answered after three rings.

"About damn time you fucking answer the phone, you incompetent twat. Do you have any fucking idea how many times I've called you?" The voice makes me shiver, and not in a good way.

I square my shoulders, as if I'm about to step foot into battle, and bring out the bitch inside me.

"I've been busy. What do you want, Josiah?"

Josiah Sinclair is my mother's fourth husband and Charlie's father. I hated him when I first met him when I was eighteen, and I hate him even more now.

"I got all your damn money. Let me guess, you sold your pussy to that billionaire husband of yours to pay me off."

I want to cry at how close to the money he is.

"How did you know I was married?" I want to be naïve and think he hasn't seen one of the many magazines or newspaper articles talking about how the most eligible bachelor in the world is officially off the market. The press has been hounding us, plastering our pictures all over the place since I went to a charity gala with Bennett two months ago.

But of course, luck isn't on my side yet again.

"How do you think? Your picture is all over the damn place, baby girl. Did you think I was going to miss something like that?"

I had hoped.

"Fine. You saw the pictures and you got the money, so what the hell do you want?"

I can hear his answer before he says anything.

"Whatcha think? My price went up."

Anger runs through my whole damn body. "Like hell it has. I paid you the million I promised. My side of the deal is set."

A laugh rings out from the other side, and the sound makes me want to puke. "You forgot all about the interest, baby girl."

"Interest? What fucking interest? We did not agree to any interest. You agreed to a million. You got a million."

"Yeah, well, I want another million. Two hundred grand for each year it took you to pay off what you owe me, and I want it by the end of the month."

Another million by the end of the month. I can't pay that.

"No. I can't do that. I can't give you more money. Be happy with the money you got."

"Then it looks like Charlie is coming to live with me. Newspapers say that you're in Chicago. I don't mind taking a drive up there and going to collect what's mine. How does next week sound?"

Bile moves up my throat, and I try my hardest to keep it down, but I'm failing.

He can't take Charlie. If he does, he will destroy her.

The girl currently enjoying life with her new family and having the best high school experience will be gone if she goes back to live with that monster. Who she is now will be a ghost of the past that will haunt me forever. She will be absolutely destroyed if, after we worked so hard to get where we are, she has to go back to living with Josiah in that hellhole.

I can't do that to her.

I can't take a life she loves so much away from her and put her back in a place that might kill her.

Tears start to roll down my face at the thought of my sister no longer being here, of her no longer laughing and smiling. I can't lose her like that.

I have to do it.

I have to find a way to get that money and pay Josiah and hope he doesn't ask for anymore. But how?

You are married to a billionaire. You have access to his bank accounts.

No. I won't steal from him. That's not a line I will ever cross. He has trusted me so much in the time we've known each other; I will not betray him by taking money from him in secret.

But there is a way to get that money from him that doesn't include writing myself a check and letting Josiah and his greediness come between us: going to him. I should tell him absolutely everything and then keep my fingers crossed he will help.

That is my only solution, and I think Josiah was hoping for that.

As much as I don't want to, that is what I have to do.

Swallowing my pride, I finally give Josiah the response he's looking for.

"I'll try to get you the money before the end of the month."

"There is no try, baby girl. You will if you want me to keep my side of the deal and not take back what's mine."

I hate his voice so much, I wish I could reach through the phone and punch the living shit out of him.

"Okay. I will."

"Much better."

The line goes dead, and I'm no longer able to hold back the bile climbing up my throat. I grab my trash can and let out everything I have.

When everything is purged, I slump back in my chair and cry.

Tonight, when I get home, I will tell Bennett about the past he doesn't know about.

It's going to hurt, but I have to do it. It's the only way to keep Charlie safe.

27

BENNETT

The second I walk into the penthouse apartment, I let out a sigh of relief.

The meeting with the commissioner took a lot longer than I wanted it to, and all I want to do is fucking de-stress with a good drink. I was supposed to go back to the office after lunch, but because Commissioner Nolan can talk forever, I had Ella cancel everything else on my schedule for the day.

I would've gone to the houser, but Ella had sent a message about two hours ago about how she wanted to talk about something, so I decided it was best for both of us to spend the night here, away from prying ears if needed.

Not that there are a whole lot of ears at the house now, with Grayson, Sam, and Charlie all living at Saint Christopher's for the new school year and Elliot out in Vancouver doing God knows what. The only ears would be Drake, but now he gets to have a night with just Henry, which he has been begging me for for a while. I guess Henry lets him watch the old spy movies I always say no to.

Which is fine. I'm all for having some alone time with Ella. In the last two weeks, it feels like we haven't been alone together, even when we spend most of our time in each other's presence.

Throwing my phone and money clip on the entry table, I walk further into the apartment, looking for my wife.

"Ella?" I call out after not finding her in the living area.

"In here!" she yells, and it sounds like she's coming from the kitchen.

As I walk down the long hallway, I take off my jacket and my shoes, not wanting to feel like a damn monkey in my own house.

Walking into the kitchen, I find Ella sitting at the island with what looks like a cup of tea in her hands.

Tea before dinner? That's new.

"Hey." I approach her, and when she turns to look at me, I lean down to place a kiss on her lips, something I haven't done since we've returned from Costa Rica. Except this time, she pulls away from me before our lips even touch. Odd as fuck.

"Hi," Ella lets out, her eyes not looking up at mine.

"Everything okay?" The question rolls off my tongue easily, since I've been asking it every day for two weeks now. Something is going on with her, and she has yet to open up to me. I'm grasping at straws as to what it could be, and it's driving me insane.

As she opens her mouth, I expect the same answer she

has given me for the last two weeks, but she takes me by surprise.

"No. There's something we need to talk about."

Fucking finally.

"What's going on?" I place my hands on the counter, ready for whatever she is about to say.

She looks down at my hands, curling her lips inward, debating what to say.

"Think we could go to the living room?" She places her mug on the counter, and when she looks up at me, I see a hint of fear in her eyes.

Is she afraid of telling me what is going on or afraid of how I will react?

I wave her toward the living room and follow behind. Ella plays with her hands for a solid minute before waving me to sit on the couch while she remains standing.

I follow silent orders and take a seat facing her.

She doesn't start talking as when I sit down, though. She continues to play with her hands for another minute. To build up the courage, I guess.

After some more time passes, she finally opens her mouth and speaks.

"I'm going to tell you something, but you have to promise me you aren't going to react until I finish."

My jaw tics a bit. "I will try."

She nods and takes a deep breath. "When I told you about my past, I didn't tell you everything."

I knew that, but that's not what I say. "Okay. What didn't you tell me?"

Another deep breath leaves her body, and her shoulders slump a bit. "About Charlie and how she came to live with me."

In Dante's report, there was minimal information on Charlie—only her name, birthday, and where she went to school. I didn't bother to look for more.

""I'm listening," I say, nodding at her to continue.

She takes another minute before she opens the floodgates.

"I learned about Charlie when I was sixteen. For seven years of my life, I didn't know I had a little sister. If I had, I would have tried my hardest to stay with my mom. I didn't find out about her until one of the group home leaders asked me if I wanted to go to the store and buy a Christmas present for my sister to send to her. Apparently, there was a section in my file that talked about how my mother had another child, and they thought I knew about her."

A tear rolls down her face, her pain ever so present in her voice. I want to wrap my arms around her, but if I do that, I don't know if she will continue. So, I stay seated.

"I asked the group leader if he could tell me things about her, and he did. He didn't know much, but he knew enough. Her name. Her age. That she lived in a small town in South Carolina, but that was it. He didn't know if she was still under my mom's custody or if she was living with someone else. I spent so many days and nights thinking about her. If she looked like me. If she knew who I was. If she even knew she had a sister out there somewhere. I had so many questions but nobody to answer them. So, I started looking into her."

Curiosity gets the best of me. "Looked into her how?"

"You can find anything on Google if you have enough information. With the address and the last name, I was able to find who lived at the address and look them up on social media."

You can find anything on Google.

If only that was really true. You're only able to find what people want you to find. Otherwise, the search for my brother would have ended years ago.

"And did you find them on social media?" It's a stupid question—of course she did.

She gives me a soft nod. "I did."

"Did anything come of it?"

"Not like I had hoped."

"What did you hope for?"

Ella lets the tears run down her face, but she doesn't make a move to wipe them away. Instead, she takes another deep breath and comes to sit on the couch next to me.

When she speaks next, she turns to face the floor-to-ceiling windows behind us and stares out at the Chicago skyline.

"For whoever was taking care of my sister to be a good person. I had hoped that once they found out about me, because I know for a fact my mom didn't tell them, they would take me in or, at the very least, let me get to know my sister, even if it was from afar."

"But that didn't happen."

My heart breaks when she turns, and I see all the pain swimming in her eyes.

"No. My social worker tried, but Charlie's family didn't

want anything to do with me. They had enough on their plate, according to them, and couldn't take on another kid, let alone a teenager. So I dropped it, and for the next two years, I stalked her dad's social media in hopes I would catch a glimpse of her. The second I turned eighteen, I took the first opportunity that came my way and went to South Carolina."

When I first saw her résumé, I noticed that she listed a community college from South Carolina on there. I also noticed that while she was at said school for almost two years, she never finished and came back to Chicago.

"What happened once you got down there?"

"On my first day down there, I looked up the address I had memorized when I was sixteen."

Another tear falls down her cheek, and this time, I reach over and wipe it away.

She gives me a small smile before she continues down the path of her memories.

"The house looked well-manicured and in what looked like a nice neighborhood. There were kids playing outside, people walking their dogs, and for a few minutes, I was happy my sister had the life every kid deserved."

"But she didn't, did she?"

Ella shakes her head, more tears rolling down her face.

"The exterior was picture perfect, but the inside wasn't. The door opened, and I saw all the lies. As it turns out, Charlie and I had similar upbringings. The only differ-ence was that I spent the majority of my time with bad people in foster homes, and she spent it with bad people in her childhood home. I found out her father was a drunk with anger issues and would take out his anger on her. Because of that, Charlie was living with our maternal grandmother, who I had no idea had moved to South Carolina."

She pauses. Her eyes dance along the skyline behind us as the sun sets. The colors of the sunset fill the room and surround both me and Ella. The glow of the sunset makes her look ethereal. Her eyes almost dance with all the colors swimming in them. She looks absolutely beautiful, even with all the pain running through her.

"You would think living with your grandmother would be a saving grace, but that woman was vile, had been since I was a little girl, from what I remembered. She would always get mad at something my mom did and take it out on me. Verbally, physically. She did the same thing to Charlie, except my sister had it worse for a lot longer.

"The first time I saw Charlie, she was so small. To a normal person, she would look like a normal kid, but to someone who had been surrounded by malnourished kids all their lives, I saw the signs. I wanted to help her so badly, but she didn't know who I was, and my grandmother had shut me out and didn't want anything to do with me. For almost a whole year, I couldn't do anything."

"What *did* you do?"

It takes her a few seconds to answer.

"It took time, but I found out that my grandmother was getting state benefits for Charlie. She applied to every single program at her disposal and took advantage of it. Lied on the paperwork, everything. She was living the high life, using the money for her own necessities, while her granddaughter was starving and didn't have any clothes that fit. So, I reported her to the state."

"Where the fuck were her parents?" The question slips out from all the anger rolling through me.

In the time Ella and I have been married, I've gotten to know Charlie. The girl has the biggest heart and has become as much of a niece to me as Sam. Hearing that she went through so much shit growing up pisses me off. I'm starting to see red, and the only way to make it go away is to go to South Carolina and put someone in the ground.

"Her dad lived a few blocks over, but he didn't want anything to do with raising her, so he pawned her off to our mom. My mom cared more about having a good time than raising a child, so my sister landed with our grandmother."

"What happened after you reported her?" I ask, trying to get control of my voice.

Ella lets out a sigh, and her shoulders deflate. "They sent Charlie to live with her dad, which was just as bad as dear ol' grandma."

Tears start rolling down her face, harder now.

"For two years, I kept my eyes on Charlie, going as far as getting a job at her school to make sure she was okay. But with every passing day, I could see she wasn't. I tried so hard to protect her, to save her, but nothing worked. My sister deserved a lot more than the life she was living, but neither her dad nor grandma cared. They pushed me away, called me every name in the book, even threatened to kill me if I didn't go away. So, after spending so many days watching the little girl I didn't really know but who owned my heart become a ghost of who she was and getting told no, I finally snapped."

I don't need to be touching Ella to know her body just went cold.

"What did you do, Ella?"

A sob escapes her lips, and when I reach over to pull her into my arms, she pushes me away.

My hands drop, and I wait for her to speak.

"I went over one night and asked her dad if we could talk. Surprisingly, he let me in. Charlie was in her room, so we were able to talk freely in the living room. I remember there being beer cans and liquor bottles everywhere, and there was this smell that had me gagging. I asked him what it would take. What did I need to do for him to let Charlie come live with me? As soon as the question left my mouth, he got angry and charged at me. He started hitting me and yelling, saying how I couldn't take his kid away from him. Turned out, he was also getting money from the state, and if he lost custody of Charlie, he would lose that too."

That's why in the search for information on Ella, both mine and Dante's, there weren't any legal documents tying her to her sister.

"I remember laying on the grimy carpet as he kicked me in the ribs, how I kept telling myself I needed to come up with something to make him stop. So I screamed the biggest number I could think of. I told him I would pay him that if he gave me Charlie. He could keep custody and take my money, but I got Charlie. He accepted. So I paid him everything I had in my bank account, which wasn't much, grabbed Charlie, and left."

She promised him money.

What kind of low life accepts money for a child?

My mind goes back to when I hired Ella. I got a lot of information on her, including her bank accounts, but out of all the things I checked, I didn't check her bank activity. Maybe if I had, I would have found out about this sooner and taken care of the problem.

"How much did you promise him?" I say, looking my wife in the eye, hoping she would be truthful with me.

"You'll get mad," she whispers, her eyes red from all the crying.

That's my answer right there, but I need to hear her say the words.

"Baby, I won't. Just tell me how much you promised him."

With a trembling lower lip, she tells me. "One million."

When she first threw out the number in negotiations, it seemed odd that she would request so little money. She could ask for any amount, and she only asked for a million. I just chalked it up to her thinking that with one million, she would set for life. But I guess I was wrong.

"The money you requested for this marriage..."

Ella finishes my thought. "Was to pay Josiah."

"When did you do it? When did you pay him off?"

"The morning you got voted in as CEO."

I knew something was off with her that day. I should have pressed harder. I should have stayed there until she told me what was wrong, but we didn't have the relationship back then that we do now. Back then, she was simply my assistant whom I married to fulfill a clause.

Now, she's more than that. Now, she drives the nightmares away.

Anger rolls through me, and not because she used the money I gave her to pay off Charlie's dad. No, it's because she thought she couldn't come to me with this sooner.

"And now that you've paid him off, he wants more money?"

That's the only logical reason I could think of for Ella to open up to me about this now. The fucker probably found out who she's married to and decided to cash in.

"He was the one calling me the night of the hockey game and has been for the past two weeks. Today, I finally caved and answered. Get him more money, or he takes Charlie."

I'm going to hunt down this fucker and kill him myself.

"How much?"

Ella cowers a bit before she answers. "Another million."

I grind my teeth. This asshole, Josiah, will get the money, but I know people like him. Once they have their hands in something, they won't stop until they get more. The fucker is going to take the money, and in a few weeks or months, he's going to threaten Ella once again. It's going to become a cycle for him. I have to stop it before it goes any further.

"Send me the bank information, and I will take care of it."

Ella bows her head, and I see the tears running down her face. I tuck a finger under her chin and bring her face up so I can see into her beautiful, tear-filled eyes.

"What's wrong?"

"I told you all of this because I wanted your help, and now that you're giving it, it feels wrong. Like I'm using you. Using your money to benefit me." A sob escapes her, and this time when I bring her closer to me, she lets me.

As she sobs into my chest, I speak into her hair. "Did you forget?"

"What?"

"That you can ask for anything and I will give it to you. For the rest of this marriage, use me. Use my money. I don't give a shit."

She pushes me away and stands from the couch. "You should give a shit. I could be filled with all the damn sob stories in the world just so you would give me money."

"You're not," I say from my place on the couch.

"How do you know that?"

"Because if you were, you would have not only asked for money when we were discussing this arrangement—you would've been asking for more money from the very beginning. You asking for money now isn't you using me. It's you coming to me for help and me giving it to you."

"You shouldn't. Josiah is just going to keep coming back and asking for money. That should be my burden to bear, not yours."

I stand from the couch and go over to her. I leave no space as I take her face between my hands.

"For as long as you have my last name, any burden of yours is mine. I don't give a shit what it is; I will take care of it."

Her lower lip wobbles. "But you don't need to."

"But I want to. You and Charlie are family. You're Lanes.

For as long as this marriage is intact, it will stay that way. Both of you will be taken care of. Nobody is going to separate you. I'll make sure of it."

"How?"

By burning the man alive and not leaving until his screams stopped.

"I don't know yet, but I will handle it. I promise."

She gives me a small smile, one that doesn't have a whole lot of reach, before reaching up and placing a kiss on my lips.

"Thank you."

"Always."

28

BENNETT

It's well after midnight when I reach for my phone and dial the one person who can help me with this plan I have.

It has been a few hours since Ella opened up to me about Charlie's past and how her father is now asking for more money. After she calmed down a bit, we had dinner and watched a movie before she fell asleep on the couch. I brought her to bed about twenty minutes ago and stayed next to her until she was sound asleep.

As soon as I heard the little snores, I started setting a plan in motion.

Now I just need my call to be picked up.

"I know we're friends and everything, but I've heard from you more in the last four months than I have in the two years before." Dante's voice sounds out as I make it to the home office I have here at the penthouse.

"You can add it to my long list of favors I owe you," I say, closing the door behind me. I don't want Ella to wake up and hear this conversation.

"What's going on?" Dante gets right to the point, probably noticing the hardness in my voice.

"Do you have any connections in South Carolina?" As far as I know, Dante and his syndicate only work within Illinois state lines to not step on any toes, but I know he has connections all over the damn world, and I'm hoping South Carolina is one of them.

"There's a motorcycle club down there that owes me a few favors."

"I'm going to need you to cash in some of those."

I swear the bastard singsongs his next response. "And why would I want to do that? Those favors look so pretty where I have them."

"Because this has to do with my wife, and I will stop at nothing to get it done." The anger I'm feeling about this whole thing is seeping through.

I swear, I can hear Dante nod from the other side of the phone. "You need information?"

"No. I need a fucking body."

"Jesus," Dante mutters. "That's going to cost you more than just a favor."

"I don't give a shit. Add it to my tab. I'm willing to pay anything to get this done."

I still owe him a meeting for looking into the number that popped up under Robert. So far, every lead has ended up a dead end. According to what he found, the number is attached to a burner phone bought at a gas station in Miami. Conveniently, the gas station lost all footage from the day the phone was purchased, and since then, anything with the phone has been dead.

No more calls.

No leads.

Fucking nothing.

"Are you sure you want to do that? It could mean you becoming a weapons dealer."

I figured that was why he wanted to call a meeting with me. For years, I've not only papered myself for this but the company.

When Dante took over the family business after his uncle died and he was the only Rosetti left in the family line, I told him that the second I became CEO, he could come to me with whatever he needed. Neither of us had any more family, so someone had to look out for the other. But my promise to him became a benefit to me.

If I want to rule Chicago, I need to know the good and the bad happening in the city. That includes knowing where the Italian mob is and does their business.

Which is why I've been working hard for years to build up an applied science department at Lane Enterprises, with Gerald's permission, to make sure everything was in line whenever the time came for Dante's request. Not only would we supply weaponry to the Mafia but also a small majority of our armed forces.

"Whatever you want. Just as long as you agree to this."

I'm desperate for this. If Dante doesn't agree to call in a favor with the MC, I will fly down to South Carolina in the morning and take care of shit myself.

My friend is silent for a long minute. "I'll get in contact with the MC's president, but I'm going to need you to tell me your plan. Nobody can be going in blind."

So I tell him my plan and everything I need done.

Around one o'clock, the plan is set in motion with an agreement with the MC.

By noon tomorrow, the threat of Charlie's dad will be gone, and hopefully, she and Ella will never have to look over their shoulders again.

There will not be any more money being asked for.

There won't be any more threats of taking Charlie away.

Everything will be gone.

And as long as I have a say, Ella will not lose her little sister, and they will both live the lives they deserve.

29

ELLA

As a kid, I always wanted a big family. For most of life, it was just me, and even though it was nice at times, especially when I wanted to be alone, I still wanted to be part of all the chaos that came with a big family.

Every time I went to a new foster home with a lot of kids, I always got excited. Every time I walked through a door and saw a bunch of kids running around, I thought that that would be it. That would be the home I was meant to be in.

But that never happened.

Either the parents were super nice and caring but the kids they had were mean, or it was the other way around.

As I got older, I made a promise to myself that when I was ready, I would give myself the family I always wanted. A handful of kids, a big house with enough space for Charlie, and a husband who loved me beyond measure. The promise was going to take some time, especially since before this arrangement with Bennett I had been single for a long time, and I didn't have the income to support that type of life, but it was going to happen. I was going to make sure of it.

When I first agreed to marry Bennett, I didn't think I would gain much from the transaction besides the million dollars to pay off Josiah and a place to live for two years without having to worry about rent. I didn't think anything else would come from it.

But something has: the family and life I always wanted.

Who knew all I needed to do was marry my billionaire boss, and all my dreams would come true?

It took me a while to get to this point, but now that I've been a Lane—in the legal sense for a few months now—I feel like both Charlie and I belong with this family.

All four of Bennett's kids have opened up to me, have made me feel as if I'm an asset in their lives instead of a burden. Even while they are at school or traveling the world, they have made me a part of their everyday life, going as far as including me in text threads with their uncle, and it has made me feel as if I'm actually their aunt instead of a stranger that they were forced to like. And the fact that all four of them have done the same to Charlie means the absolute world to me.

Bennett doesn't know this, but I look forward to the days that all of us are under the same roof. Every time, it brings a smile to my face.

Which is what I have on my face now, as most of us sit at the dining room table, ready to feast on this amazing breakfast Henry has prepared with the chefs who come on the weekends.

I went from having no food in my fridge to having chefs and a housekeeper. That is absolutely insane.

"When is Uncle Bennett coming home?" Drake asks as he dives mouth first into a stack of pancakes that Henry placed in front of him.

The kid may be small, but he can eat.

I look over at Henry to see if he's going to answer Drake, but all he does is give me a smile before taking a seat next to Grayson at the end of the table.

"He should be back later this afternoon," I answer.

Which is all the information I have. Bennett woke up early this morning, leaving me in his bed at the penthouse with a simple whisper that he would be back before dinner. He didn't say where he was going, and I had my questions, but he just said not to worry about it.

So that's what I've been trying to do.

"Cool. When he gets back, I need to ask him a question," Drake says around a whole mouthful of food.

I grab my own fork and take a quick bite before turning my attention back to him. "Oh yeah? What are you going to ask him?"

"If it would be okay if you go with me to the mother-son dance at my school later this year."

His answer takes me by surprise. I drop my fork, and a piece of pancake wedges itself in my throat. I try my hardest to cough it up. Tears start to run down my face as I feel a hand land on my back and give me a hard pat.

"Thank you," I say to Grayson on my left.

After wiping the tears away from my eyes, I give

everyone a smile before turning to look at Drake sitting across from me.

"Are you okay?" he asks, his little eyes full of worry.

I give him the best smile I can while trying to hide my panic about the whole situation.

"Yeah, sweetie. I'm fine." I'm still slightly out of breath, but I don't know if that is from the choking or from what Drake just said. "You want me to go to your mother-son dance?"

Drake and I have gotten really close these last few weeks. He's been my partner in crime in almost everything —from watching movies together to baking to him even showing me his computer game skills. From the second I get home from work until he goes to sleep, he is always in the same room as me. I knew we were getting close, but I never really thought he saw me as a mother figure.

That's big.

No, that is fucking huge, and just knowing that he wants me to go to this dance with him has a lump of emotion forming in my throat.

His little face lights up as he speaks. "Yeah, I want you to go."

My smile grows a bit more, but then when an intrusive thought pops into my head, the smile starts to disappear. I'm only in his life for a year and a half more. What's going to happen to other mother-son dances that I can't attend because I'm no longer part of this family?

That thought hurts, but I try to come up with an alternative. "Are you sure? Maybe Samantha would be the better choice to go with you?"

I look over at Sam, hoping to find her with a smile or something. Excited I suggested she go with her brother, but when I take in her face, I just see disappointment.

Is she disappointed Drake asked me instead of her? Or is she disappointed I'm turning down her brother?

When I turn back to the little boy in front of me, I think I have my answer.

"You don't want to go with me?" Drake lets out, his voice not as loud as it was before.

Tears form in my eyes when I see his bottom lip wobble.

Dammit.

I get up from my chair, crouching down next to him, taking his hand in mine.

"I do want to go. I just thought since we haven't known each other all that long, it would be better for your sister to go with you. But if you want me to go, then I will be honored. We can even get matching outfits and everything."

The way his face transforms melts my heart.

Little arms wrap around my neck, and Drake slams his body to mine so tightly, he falls off his chair and pushes the both of us to the ground.

Both his laugh and mine fill the room, and just hearing it has my heart soaring. Who knew I'd love hearing two Lane men laugh so much? Every time is like music to my ears and my heart.

After a few minutes of giving Drake the biggest bear hug, I let him go.

"Finish your food. Maybe after, we can go shopping for

our outfits," I say to him, ruffling his hair before pushing him toward his chair.

"Oh, can we go too?" Charlie throws out, pointing to her and Samantha with her piece of bacon. "My one good pair of jeans ripped, and I need new ones."

Before I took the job at Lane Enterprises, I would have told her we would have to wait. To give me her jeans so I could fix them to make them last just a tad bit longer. We couldn't afford it.

But now we can. Not only is Bennett handling all our expenses, something he wouldn't budge on, but now that I'm the assistant to the CEO, I got a hefty raise I haven't touched. We have money, plus Bennett's credit card that he tells me to use every single day, so I'm sure he wouldn't mind if I used it to buy Charlie some jeans and myself an outfit for the dance.

I give my sister a bright smile alongside the words I'm sure she never thought were going to come out of my mouth. "Yes, you two can come. We can't have you walking around with ripped jeans."

She gives me a bright smile back.

A ball of emotions rolls through me as I realize I haven't seen my sister this happy in a long time. She needed this change as much as I did, and she is thriving in it.

Before I get over sentimental about it, I turn to Grayson. "Do you want to go shopping too?"

He makes a face at my question. "I'd rather not. I'll stay behind with the old man and make sure he doesn't break a hip or anything," he responds and nods toward Henry, who is sitting to his left.

"Excuse you. Who was able to get five pucks past you yesterday?" Henry throws out, narrowing his eyes.

Grayson scoffs. "You were only able to do that because I let you."

"*Let me.*" Henry lets out a snort. "We'll see about that."

The two of them argue as the rest of us go back to finishing our breakfast.

As the two girls and Drake are upstairs getting ready to leave, Grayson in the game room, Henry and I stay behind, helping the kitchen staff clean up.

It's when I hand him a stack of plates that I notice he is giving me a funny look.

"Is something on your mind?" I ask with a smile on my face, trying to hide the weird nervousness I feel at the moment.

"Just a memory," he states, giving me a strained smile.

"And what memory would that be?"

Henry continues to clean as he speaks. "One from a few months ago. Mr. Drake had Parent's Day at school, and he begged Mr. Lane to take him to work instead of sending him off to class. He didn't want the kids to ask questions as to why his father was there but his mother wasn't. That day was such a contrast to what I witnessed earlier."

"Did he go to school that day?" I ask, the dish I have in my hands a little too hard.

"No. Mr. Lane let him have a day off and took him to a museum. The two of them had a whole afternoon learning about penguins."

A smile forms on my face as I think about Bennett and Drake nerding out over arctic birds, but it quickly disappears when I think of why they were at the museum.

"Henry, do you think me going to the mother-son dance with him is wrong?"

His head snaps in my direction. "On the contrary. I think it's a good idea for you to go. Mr. Drake could have done what he did all those months ago and asked not to go, but instead, he asked you to go with him. He sees you as someone important."

I run through his words in my head. "In the long run, isn't that a bad thing, though? Given that I'm only here for a year and a half more?"

I watch him as he runs through my questions. For a few seconds, he just stands there, as if he is trying to figure out the right thing to say.

"Mrs. Lane, I have a feeling that even though your arrangement with Mr. Lane is for a finite period, you are going to be a very important figure in this household for years to come.

"What makes you say that?"

He gives me a shrug. "Decades of taking care of this family. I know when someone important walks through the door."

His words have the hairs on the back of my neck standing up.

Important.

Henry, one of the most important people in this family, is calling me important. Does that mean there's a chance that, when the two years are up, I won't walk out with a broken heart? Because all the Lanes have wedged themselves in there deep, and I don't think they will ever be able to get out, Bennett most of all. I've fallen for my husband, and there is no turning back.

"May I ask you a question, Mrs. Lane?" Henry lets out when the dining room is close to being spotless. "How are Mr. Lane's nightmares? He hasn't mentioned anything in the last few weeks about having one, and I wanted to ask."

My eyebrows bunch up.

Nightmares? Bennett has nightmares?

We've been sharing a bed for four months now, and not once has the topic of nightmares come up.

"I wasn't aware he had nightmares." Has he had them, and I just haven't noticed? "Do they happen often?"

Henry throws a small smile my way. "Only on occasion, but from the looks of things, he must have done something to help with them."

I nod even though I'm still very much lost in my head. "Yeah, he must have."

Am I that something?

I want to hope I am.

"Since you will be going to the dance with Mr. Drake, I have something for you to inspire your shopping adventure," Henry lets out as he guides me out of the dining room.

For a second, all thoughts of Bennett's nightmares go away, and I concentrate on Henry.

"Oh?"

The older gentleman gives me a smile and nods in the direction of his section of the house. "Follow me."

He guides me through the lower level of the house until we reach his quarters, which are bigger than a decent-sized apartment.

I stay by the entrance as he goes to a room, re-emerging with a small box in his hands.

A small velvet jewelry box.

"I think a mother-son dance would be the perfect occasion for you to wear this."

He opens the box, and nestled inside is a beautiful gold bracelet with a line of five diamonds in the middle.

I take the box from him and take in every single detail of the piece of jewelry.

"Henry, this is gorgeous, but I can't possibly wear it. I could lose it."

"That's a risk that could happen with any piece. Besides, if I didn't have the utmost confidence in you, Mrs. Lane, I wouldn't have offered it. Please, take it."

I give him a smile of appreciation. The fact that he is letting me borrow this is big. This is his way of telling me how important I really am.

"Thank you, Henry. I will bring it back to you in one piece."

"No need. That is yours to keep. Think of it as a thank you, from me to you, for agreeing to go to this dance with Mr. Drake."

Tears form in my eyes. This family knows how to make someone feel special, don't they?

I raise up on my tiptoes and place a kiss against Henry's cheek.

"I will cherish it forever."

Right next to my wedding ring.

A FEW HOURS AFTER BREAKFAST, Samantha, Charlie, Drake, and I are walking through the mall, a few security guards trailing behind.

Surprisingly, we were able to find everything we were looking for. Charlie was able to get more than just a pair of jeans, and Drake and I were able to find our matching outfits for the dance.

Now, we're just walking around, going store to store, seeing if anything else catches our eyes, which doesn't happen until we find a toy store and Drake drags Charlie inside as Sam and I stand by the entrance. Since it's just the two of us, I decide to broach the subject of what happened at breakfast.

"Hey, I hope you're not mad at me for suggesting you go to the dance with your brother. I didn't want to step on any toes, so I just thought it would be better for you to take him."

Sam gives me a smile that doesn't reach her eyes. "I'm not mad. Him asking you just took me by surprise, is all. I'm glad he asked you."

"Are you sure? Because if you want to go, I'm completely fine with that."

She is shaking her head before I can even finish. "Go. It would mean a lot to him. None of us got to go to those things when we were his age. It would be nice for him to experience it."

Her comment wakes up a thought. I've always wanted to ask Bennett, but the time never presented itself. I know he hasn't heard anything from his brother, but what happened to their mom?

As much as I want to ask Sam about it now, it's not the place or time. For all I know, their mother is a sore subject and should never be spoken about.

I take her hand in mine and give it a good squeeze. "I promise to make it the best mother-son dance ever."

If I wasn't looking right at her, I would have missed it, but tears start to form in her eyes before she looks away. "Thank you, Ella."

I get the sense that she wants to say more, like there is something on the tip of her tongue she is dying to say, but she is keeping it in and just smiles as she walks into the toy store.

As I stand there, I start to think back to what Henry said—that I'm going to be an important figure for years to come.

I keep thinking of the two-year deadline with Bennett as the end, but it doesn't have to be. I can still be a part of the kids' lives in some way once all of this is over. As their ex-aunt, their friend, even a mother figure if they need it.

They may not be biologically related to me, but my life has taught me that family doesn't have to be blood. Your parents don't have to be related to you to be your parents. The Lanes may not be my blood, but that isn't going to stop me from treating them as if they are.

No matter what happens between me and Bennett.

And that's the headspace I'm in for the remainder of our shopping trip and as we drive back to the Lane Manor.

When we get back to the house and the kids run upstairs, Henry stops me and directs me to the study at the edge of the first floor.

"Mr. Lane would like to see you in his study," he states, his face empty of any emotion.

"Okay?" I say, the word coming out as a question.

Henry just gives me a nod and leaves me to walk into the home office alone.

As I open the large wooden door, I feel like I'm walking into the principal's office and I'm in trouble. Did Henry tell Bennett Drake asked me to go to the mother-son dance with him and he's mad?

There aren't a whole lot of possibilities as to why he would want to meet me in the study.

"Bennett?" I say as I walk into the room. My eyes travel around the room as I find him standing in front of his desk, his back to me.

"Close the door," he orders, not turning to even look up at me.

Goose bumps form on my arms as I do what he says and stay rooted in place, not wanting to overstep and close the distance between us.

"What's going on?" I ask after about a minute of standing in silence. Whatever is happening is messing with my nervous system and making my palms sweat.

Bennett turns to face me, and two things grab my

attention. The red scratch mark just below his left eye, and the folder he has in his hand.

Without thinking, I close the distance and start surveying him.

"What happened to your face?" I place a finger slightly on the scratch, and he flinches.

"It's nothing."

"It doesn't look like nothing."

He pulls my touch away from his face but doesn't let go of me. "Ella, I'm fine. The scratch doesn't matter. What I have in my hand does."

He holds up the folder in his other hand, and my eyes travel over to it. When he hands it to me, I'm hesitant to open it, but I do anyway.

The second I read the words at the top of the first page, a wave of confusion travels over me.

"A custody declaration?" I ask, looking up at Bennett for answers.

"Keep reading."

With uncertainty, I do as he says and read through the file.

It's paperwork that Josiah Sinclair has not only given me full custody of Charlie, but he has terminated his parental rights and made me her legal guardian.

Tears escape from my eyes as I put together what this means.

Josiah isn't going to come after us anymore.

I never thought that this would happen, yet I'm holding the evidence in my hands.

But how?

I look up at the only man who can give me the answer. "How did you do this?"

"Don't worry about it. Just accept that it's done and that you will never have to deal with Josiah ever again. Charlie is yours, and it will stay that way."

Tears run down my face, and he reaches over and wipes them away. This man has really made all my dreams come true.

There are three words I want to say to him, but I keep them inside. I'm not ready for those words to come out, even if my heart is screaming for them.

Instead, I say two other words I truly mean and will mean until the end of time.

"Thank you."

30

BENNETT

I knock on the door of the house with the perfectly manicured lawn, and I swear, I can hear the anger swimming through my body seeping through my fist as it meets the wood.

But a hard knock isn't enough to get the attention of whoever is in the house, so I decide to kick my foot against the wood instead, and as soon as I do, I hear footsteps on the other side.

As the door opens, I'm met with the stench of alcohol mixed with body odor and urine. I guess I know what this mother-fucker did with the million dollars he received three months ago. He wasted it on booze instead of bettering his life.

Pity.

"What the fuck do you want?" the drunk bastard, who I recognize as Josiah from a few mugshots, mutters, his words slurred as he leans against the doorjamb.

"You Josiah Sinclair?" I ask, even though I know the answer.

"Who the fuck is asking?" he spits out, his eyes narrowing at me.

I try to keep my anger controlled, but I know that if this bastard says the wrong word, I'm going to break.

"That doesn't matter. I'm here to get something from you."

"I don't have shit to give." The fucker pulls back the door to slam it in my face, but I stop it and push myself inside the house, causing the poor fucker to fall to the floor as a result.

"Oh, but you do." I squat down and make sure my eyes are at level with his. "You remember your daughter Charlie, right? Well, I'm here to make sure you never think about her or her sister again."

Spit lands against my face. "Like hell you are. That little bitch is going to make me rich, and you're not going to take that away from me."

I reach forward and wrap my hand around Josiah's neck, tightening the grip. He reaches his hand up, and one of his grimy nails makes contact with the skin under my eye. It stings, but not enough to let him go.

"You're not in control here, drunk fucker. I am. So this is how it's going to play out: you're going to sign over your parental rights and give Ella full custody of her sister."

Josiah claws at my hands, and I loosen my grip just a tiny bit to let him speak. "What's in it for me?"

Nothing. He will get nothing out of this. Not for the way he treated Charlie and not for the way he assaulted and took advantage of Ella. But of course, I keep that piece of information to myself.

"You'll get another million, and my friends over at the Shadow Assassins pay you a visit."

His face nearly goes white when I mention the motorcycle club. He has history with them, and from what Damian, the

MC president, told me, they are waiting for the right moment to take the bastard down.

Interesting how Josiah here is more fearful of a motorcycle club than losing his daughter.

"Okay. I'll do what you want," Josiah lets out, almost crying.

I loosen my grip on his throat and let his head hit the floor.

"Good."

It takes a fucking hour to get the fucker to fill out the forms I had drawn up a few days ago.

With all the paperwork in hand, I leave the house without another word to Josiah.

As I walk to my rental car parked across the street, I send a nod over to Damian, giving him the signal to send his men in.

He doesn't even hesitate to release the command, and within seconds, five members of the Shadow Assassins storm Josiah's house.

As I pull away, my phone starts to ring, and when I see who is calling me, my stomach churns. One piece of the past is taken care of, but it seems like one is still looming.

I answer the phone, and as soon as I hear the voice, I want to hunt it down.

"Hello, Bennett."

My body jerks awake as the memories from earlier claim my mind as their own. Memories and figments of my imagination. I knew what I did today was going to haunt me, but I didn't think it was going to play with my mind like it did. The phone rang with the same number as before, and I answered, and like the first time, nobody spoke on the other side.

Usually, when it comes to these types of nightmares, everything is the exact same. Nothing ever changes, yet tonight they did.

But why?

Another question: why that voice? Out of all the voices from my past that could haunt me, why that one?

"Hey." Ella's sweet voice sounds through my room, reminding me I'm not in bed alone. "Are you okay?"

Her hand slides up my back as I sit up, and I try to take comfort in that.

"Yeah, I'm fine," I say, turning to give her a smile, even though she can't see it in the darkness.

The bed shifts as she sits up with me, wrapping her arms around my stomach and resting her cheek against my back. Her hands move to my front and slide against my body.

My heart is still racing from the nightmare, but her caress is calming me down.

"Did you have a nightmare?"

I tell her the truth. "I did."

"Do you want to talk about it?"

I grab onto one of her hands and bring it up to my lips. "It's just my mind playing tricks on me. You should go back to bed."

Ella doesn't move.

After about a minute, she releases a breath.

"Henry asked me earlier if you had been having any nightmares lately," she lets out.

"And what did you tell him?"

"That I didn't even know you had them."

As much as I wanted to keep this little tidbit about myself a secret, I knew that, at some point, it was going to come out.

With Ella's hand still in mine, I shift so I'm able to lay down and bring her body down with me. As her head lays against my chest, her hand close to my heart, I open up to her.

"The nightmares started when I was a kid. It was about two months after my parents died and a month after Robert left. My mind started remembering all the details of the night we were told about my parents' accident, and ever since, I've never been able to make them go away, not fully. These last few years, they have only come on days of importance. Their birthdays, the anniversary of their deaths, when something important happens that they were supposed to be here for."

Ella scoots her body closer. "Do you only dream about the night they died?"

"The majority of the time. Sometimes, it's other memories that have stuck with me." All bad moments, but I don't tell her that.

Part of me wonders if I had stayed to watch what Damian and his club did to Josiah, if that moment would have stuck with me as much as my parents' deaths.

"What did you dream about tonight?"

Her question is a normal one, one I should be able to answer, but I can't have her knowing just how dark I'm willing to get to make sure she is taken care of and at my side. Because if she asked me right now, I would answer that I want her at my side forever, which is a dangerous thought to have. Every day, I get closer and closer to making Ella mine for real, but I can't. If I do, then there is a chance my biggest fear may come true.

So, I tell her a lie. "Just a bunch of memories jumbled together. Nothing for you to worry about."

She lets out a sweet hum that goes straight to my cock. What I wouldn't give to get lost in her right now.

Ella must be a mind reader, because the hand she has against my chest starts to travel down to dangerous territory.

"Maybe I can make you forget about the nightmare." Her hand lands on top of my boxer shorts, and she gives me a good grip.

"Oh yeah? And how are you planning on doing that?"

She lets out another hum, and I swear she knows just how weak that sound makes me. "With my mouth?"

Her lips land against my neck, and all I'm able to do is bring her closer to me.

"Maybe with my mouth on your cock?" Her hand grips me tightly through the fabric. "Maybe with your cock in my pussy?"

So many glorious images, and I need all of them to play out. Just thinking about my mouth on that bare pussy of hers has me as hard as a rock and my mouth salivating.

Not wanting to waste another second, my hands slide over to my wife's body, and I drag her on top of me.

"I'm going to need you to sit on my face," I growl as my lips meet hers. She tastes as sweet as the first time I had her, and I will never get tired of it.

Her tongue swipes against mine before she puts some space between us. "I can't sit on your face."

I growl for a different reason. "Sweet Ella, it wasn't a question." My hands travel down her body until they meet her ass and move her up my torso. "It's a damn order. I am your boss, after all. What I say goes. Now, sit that pretty pussy on my face and enjoy it."

"So damn commanding," she says with an eye roll, but the smirk she wears gives her away.

I'll show her commanding when, come Monday morning, I make her get on her knees in my office and gag on my cock while I'm on a conference call.

But I don't tell her that. Instead, I take her bottom lip between my teeth.

"Sit on my face already. Your back facing the headboard."

She follows orders this time after swiftly sliding off the silk sleep shorts I bought for her when we first got married.

With a look of uncertainty, Ella gets back on the bed and straddles my chest. The girl looks tense, like she has never done this before. My chest jolts at the thought of being the first.

"Scoot back, baby."

She does as I say, and the sight of her ass in my face is the best cure for any nightmare.

But she doesn't slide back enough, so I slide my hands around her thighs and bring her within an inch of my mouth. A yelp leaves her at the rapid movement, but it's quickly replaced by a moan when my mouth meets her bare pussy.

A hum leaves me as I slide my tongue through her folds. Her pussy is just as sweet as her mouth, and I will never get enough of it.

With my hands gripping her thighs, I move Ella's body so she's grinding herself against me, covering my face with her scent and taste.

I slide one of my hands forward to meet her clit, and the movement is just enough for Ella's body to fall forward and have her rest against my stomach.

Before pulling away ever so slightly, I take a bite of her ass.

"If you want to be a good wife, take my cock out and put it in your mouth."

She lets out a moan and runs her nails along the outline of my dick, causing my legs to shake just a bit.

"You should know by now that I'm always a good wife who follows orders." The words are sultry, and I'm sure if I were looking into her eyes right about now, they would be gleaming.

All thoughts leave my mind the second she pushes my boxers down and her mouth wraps around me.

For a few minutes, the room fills with moans, hums, slurps, and praises. As my tongue slides into Ella's entrance, I feel her getting closer to the brink of explosion. With the way her mouth and hands are working me, I'm getting close too, but I need her to come first before I paint her tongue.

"I fucking love the way you taste. It's going to be stuck

in my head forever," I say against her entrance, trying to ignore the way her tongue is swirling around the head of my cock.

"I feel the same way about your cock," she moans as I insert a finger into her tight pussy. "It stretches me perfectly."

I'm about to ask if it's her mouth or her pussy she's talking about, but the question disappears when I feel my head hit the back of her throat. She's too fucking good at that, and I can't take it anymore. I'm too close. She has to come first.

Though I'd rather stay in her mouth forever, I slide a hand up to her hair and pull her off my cock until all of her weight is on my face, and I feast as if I were a dying man.

Her arms stretch back until she is gripping the headboard, giving her body the perfect arch as I have the best meal of my life.

"Bennett, oh god. I'm right there."

I hum against her clit, not slowing my assault on her pussy.

Her thighs tighten around my head, and it's the best feeling in the world. She's there, I can feel it, and as soon as I rub her clit between my fingers, my tongue deep inside her, she screams out my name in the most beautiful way.

Her body goes slack against me as I lick up every single drop of her release. Eventually, she shifts, swinging her leg away from my face and freeing me from one of the best prisons I never want to escape from.

I don't let her get far. Within seconds, my hands are on

her body, and her back is to the mattress, and I'm hovering over her, with my cock perfectly aligned with her entrance. But I don't slide into the warmth of her body just yet.

"I fucking love how you scream my name. Makes me fucking delirious." My mouth slams onto hers as I let her get a taste of herself.

Needing to be inside her, I pull away, but she holds me in place by wrapping her legs around my waist.

"I need to grab a condom," I say against her mouth.

"No, I want to feel you. Every single inch of you."

I swear my cock twitches at her words. "Are you sure?"

She gives me a nod. "I'm sure. I want it. I want you."

"You fucking have me." For as long as she wants me, I am hers.

Shifting a bit, I slide into her warm heaven. My cock is wrapped so tightly in her pussy, I need to take a second to compose myself. I have to think about something other than coming inside of her and filling her up with everything I have.

Ella's hands run through my hair, making the moment more intense. There is sweetness, but there is also desperation.

The second I start sliding in and out of her, I'm living every dream I've ever wanted to live. This woman has driven the nightmares away, and the only thing I ever want to dream about is her and how she controls the chaos.

Our bodies slam together in perfect unison, and my cock is practically weeping for a release.

"Please tell me you're close, sweetheart. I don't know how much longer I can last."

"I'm there. Don't stop."

And I don't. I give her everything I have until we are panting messes and I'm dripping sweat.

I hike up one of her legs and change the angle. All it takes is one more thrust into her, and she is screaming her release. With my name on her lips, she explodes around my cock, and the image is going to be implanted in my mind for as long as I live.

The image before me is enough to drive me over the edge, and I release everything I have into my wife's pussy, giving her every last drop.

"Holy fuck," I grunt out, all my weight dropping on the beautiful woman underneath me.

I don't know how we stay like that, but eventually I get up to grab a washcloth to clean up our mess.

As the night moves to dawn, I don't sleep. Even after everything we did before she fell asleep in my arms, my mind is spiraling with thoughts and questions.

Thoughts about marriage and if I'm willing to work on my fears of abandonment and losing someone I love again to give this thing with Ella an honest shot.

Questions about if I'm even capable of doing that.

I was never supposed to get married, but now that I am, I don't want to let the woman I married go.

31

———————

ELLA

"The transition has gone well," Gerald says as he sits across from Bennett in his former office.

It has been six months since Bennett officially became CEO, and Gerald decided to come all the way from Boca to give his replacement his congratulations. He came in about five minutes ago and went straight into Bennett's office. I'm trying really hard not to eavesdrop, but it's becoming a hard task, especially with the door wide open. It's like they want me to hear.

"It has. It seems like everyone is accepting the change," Bennett answers, and I just know the man has the most stoic facial expression right now. Interesting how he will smile for me and the kids, but nobody else.

"Everyone? You're telling me Peter Hill has gotten off your back?"

I let out a snort that comes out a little too loudly, so I quickly try to cover it up before Bennett gets up from his chair and closes the door on me.

"Hill is very much still Hill, but he has calmed down a bit."

That's one way to put it.

He definitely has lowered his voice, but he still walks into every room with a permanent stick up his ass and looks down at Bennett every chance he gets.

It makes me think that he might be planning something, but if he was, he would have done something by now, right?

I sure hope so.

For now, though, I'm going to continue throwing nasty looks in his direction every time I see him and flipping him off behind his back.

"Hopefully, it stays that way," Gerald lets out.

"Let's hope," Bennett returns.

"And how's married life? Everything you thought it would be?"

As soon as the question leaves Gerald, I chide myself for listening. I will myself to get up from my chair and close the door because I shouldn't hear what Bennett answers, but I can't find it in me to do so.

So, as Bennett speaks, I feel a blush crawl up my face.

"It's more. I never expected to get married, never wanted to, but I guess it takes the right person to change your mind. Ella is perfect for me."

His words have butterflies fluttering all over my insides.

Bennett and I have grown a lot closer these last few months, but there are still so many uncertainties that surround us.

If he truly means the words he just said, maybe there is a chance we won't say goodbye and we can continue this without a timeframe. Because I feel the same way. This marriage has turned out to be more than I expected, and I would like to see where it could go—where Bennett and I could go. I'm hoping that when the time is right, we can sit down and discuss it, not just brush it under the rug.

"Marriage looks good on you. You look like a changed man from the one across from me earlier this year. You look happy," Gerald tells him, and I hear a smile in his voice.

"I am."

God, how I hope he is telling the truth. Because if he is, then maybe when the time comes, he won't want to walk away.

The subject quickly changes between Bennett and Gerald as they start talking about golf and how Gerald is enjoying life down in Florida. I try to keep up with what they're saying, but halfway into Gerald describing the different types of snakes he found in his yard, I lose interest and actually try to concentrate on doing my work.

When I first started this job, I had no idea how to run someone else's life. I was barely handling my own, but with time, I learned, and now I'm running a nearly perfect system. I'm still learning, but I have everything in place to help Bennett run this company just the way he wants it. Everything is organized and prepared and ready for when it's needed.

For the next thirty minutes or so, I work on inputting every meeting and trip Bennett has for the next month into our calendars, and once I'm done with that, I move on to the new portion of my job.

Helping with the foundation.

After Josiah signed over custody of Charlie to me, I was able to put my full concentration on my project proposal for the foundation and presented them my ideas a little over a month ago. The board didn't even take a second to think about bringing me on, and now I'm working on a program to expand education for future foster parents. There are going to be a lot of formalities, a lot of time dedicated to getting the program off the ground, but I'm determined to get it done.

I'm in the middle of looking through the state's resources for foster parents when Bennett and Gerald walk out of the office. The old CEO throws me a wave before walking away, leaving Bennett standing by my desk.

"Gerald wants to grab a drink," he states with a slight eye roll.

I can't help but to smile a bit. "Sounds like fun."

He fully rolls his eyes this time before tilting my chin up with his forefinger.

"I'll be back in an hour."

"I'll be here."

A smirk lands on his face before he leans down and gives me the most chaste kiss in the world.

As I watch his retreating figure, I can't help but smile a bit.

He really does look happy. Well, happier than he did when I first took this job.

With a smile on my face, I go back to work. I'm so

concentrated in what I'm doing, I don't look away until I hear the sound of heels clicking along the floor.

Lately, the only heels that sound on this side of the building and on this floor have been mine. If there are other heels coming this way, they don't sound like stilettos.

The woman approaching is gorgeous. Beautiful dark hair down to her waist, black slacks that elongate her legs, and a white blouse that looks perfect against her skin. And her eyes—her pretty brown eyes are directed right at me. This woman looks like she just came off a runway in Paris or something. Everything about her screams expensive.

The more I take her in, I get a thought that I never thought would pop up. That she looks exactly like the type of woman that Bennett Lane should have married—, elegant and beautiful and not his assistant, who still can't get rid of the clothes she thrifted before getting married.

I try my best to shake that out of my head and concentrate on the task at hand.

Who is she, and why is she here?

"Is there something that I can help you with?" I ask, ignoring my work and giving this woman my full attention.

As I stand, the woman doesn't say anything. She just looks me up and down, assessing me. From the look on her face, she doesn't like what she sees.

Well, I don't like her either.

"No, thank you." She turns up her nose at me and walks past my desk, directly into Bennett's office.

Who is this bitch, and who the fuck does she think she is? Nobody goes in there without permission.

Feeling irritated, I follow behind her. "I'm sorry, but you can't come in here."

"Yes, I can," the bitch answers, dropping her bag on the leather couch before digging into it and pulling out a box she twirls in her hands. "So, where is he?"

"Where is who?" The question comes out through my teeth.

The snotty bitch has the audacity to roll her eyes at me like I'm the problem.

"Bennett. Where is Bennett?" she asks, clearly annoyed.

I bring out the sweetest customer service voice I have as I respond. "Mr. Lane isn't in at the moment, but if you would like to wait for him, you are more than welcome to do so downstairs in the lobby. Or set up an appointment for another day."

I don't know who this woman is, but that doesn't stop me from running through Bennett's schedule in my head, trying to remember if he had a meeting at this time that the both of us completely missed.

The only thing he had was Gerald. Nobody else was scheduled to come in today, unless I missed it completely, but I don't think I did.

The woman rolls her eyes again before taking a seat on the couch. "I'll just wait for him here." She throws a smirk at me like she won.

Seeing the smirk makes me hate this bitch even more. If she stays any longer, I'm going to be grabbing her by the hair and dragging her and her expensive shoes out of here.

Who the fuck is she?

There is something familiar about her, but I know for a fact that I have never seen her before. I would have remembered interacting with her. I try to think if I have seen her in passing at an event or somewhere around the office before, but her face doesn't register. In a way, and this sounds absolutely crazy as it runs through my head, she reminds me of Samantha.

That has to be a coincidence, right?

""Unfortunately, you can't wait here," I say to her, throwing a smirk right back, trying anything to get her out of here. "Mr. Lane doesn't like having uninvited guests in his space when he's not present. Actually, he doesn't like any invited guest period. So I suggest that you get up and leave this office before I call security and have you escorted you out."

The way her face gets all smug makes me want to slap her straight across the face. "Yeah, that is not going to be happening."

"And why is that?"

"Because my name is on the building," she snarls, standing up from the couch and coming toe to toe with me.

A cold chill runs down my body.

Her name is on the building? *Her* name is on the *building*?

If her name is on the building, does that mean...

No.

There is no way.

There is no way that the woman in front of me is who I think she is.

But what if she is telling the truth?

What if she really is a Lane?

Security is tight here. Everyone who walks into the building has to be checked and on an approved list. So either security let her through because she really is who she says she is, or she snuck in.

I want to believe her, but something is telling me not to trust this woman or a single thing she says.

"I don't believe you." I cross my arms along my chest, trying to show strength and not that she rattled me.

"Believe it, honey. Now, be a peach and call Bennett. He would want to know I'm here." She snarls out the words, as if she were above me.

She's not.

I don't give a shit who she might be. I've dealt with a lot in my life, and I don't have to deal with this. This woman is a nobody, and if anyone is going to pull the Lane card, it's me.

What I say fucking goes.

"I'm not calling him. So if I were you, I would walk out this room. While you are it, leave this fucking building, and we won't have any problems."

To my surprise, the smirk on her face wipes away and she starts to back down. It may be all for show, but I don't care, just as long as she leaves.

With her eyes trained on mine, she places the box she was twirling in her hands on top of Bennett's desk.

It looks like she is putting on a show, but I'm done entertaining her.

She keeps her eyes on me as she starts making her way out of the room.

At least, I thought she was making her way out. When she walks past me, she stops.

"You have no idea who you are talking to, do you?" she snarls, coming close enough for me to smell her perfume.

I don't know what comes over me, but the words that come out of my mouth surprise even me.

"I couldn't care less who you are. All I see is a bitch who needs to be put in her place."

"You little whor—" The woman swings her hand back, getting ready to slap me across the face, when a voice stops her.

"Is everything okay in here?" a male voice asks, and I turn to see one of the security guards who usually mans this floor standing in the doorway. His hand is on his belt, ready to draw his weapon.

He must have heard us. Thank God.

"Everything is fine, Caleb," I say to the security guard before turning back to the woman. "Would you please escort our visitor out? She is not welcome here."

The woman snarls, and I see something deadly in her eyes.

"Whatever you need, Mrs. Lane." Caleb walks further into the room and grabs the woman by the arm.

It takes me a good five minutes after Caleb and the woman walk out of the office for me to find some of my bearings. The whole situation riled me up, and I came so close to calling Bennett.

There is no need for him to come back early. The situation has already been taken care of. There is no need to worry him. I'll just let him know what happened when he returns.

Needing to get some air, or at least splash some water on my face, I head to the restroom and try to control my breathing.

I don't know how long I spend in the restroom, but it was enough time for Bennett to come back. When I make it back to my desk, he is just walking into his office.

Instead of just bombarding him, I follow him into his office and plant a smile on my face.

"Did you two get a good drink in?" I ask, taking note of the box still on his desk and wondering what could be in there.

The woman was twirling it like it was just a regular old box, but she left it here for a reason, and I can't help but wonder why.

"Sure," Bennett lets out, taking off his suit jacket and making himself comfortable in his chair. "He wasn't here to get his old job back, so I guess you could call it good."

"Did you think that he was?" I ask, feeling my eyebrows bunch up.

Bennett shrugs. "No, but you never know. He might have gotten tired of retirement and wanted to get back to the grind."

"But he doesn't."

"No. Gerald is very happy living the rest of his years in humid as fuck Florida."

"Good, because I like seeing you in that chair." I throw him a nod and hopefully a smile that he doesn't question.

Apparently, it works, because a smirk forms on his face as his hand reaches out and pulls me onto his lap. "Do you now? Because I could think of a few things we can do with me in this chair."

Even though my mind is going crazy, a giggle still escapes me as his lips meet my neck. "We're at work."

"So? We'll close the door and have some fun." The way his hand travels up my thigh feels good, and I know I'm crazy to turn down this man, but my head is still all over the place, and it won't stop until I tell him about what happened earlier.

"Enticing, but the answer is still no."

A groan leaves him, but his mouth doesn't move away from my skin. "One of these days, I'm going to have you on your knees in here, begging for more."

Any other day, I would love the image his words paint, but I can't right now.

Instead of responding and snuggling deeper into Bennett's arms like I want to, I push myself off him and go over to the box sitting on the other side of the desk.

"What did you order?" he asks the second the box is in my hand.

"I didn't order anything. Some woman came in here acting like she owned the place and left this here."

Bennett's body tenses, and right away, he stands from his chair. "What woman?"

"I didn't get her name. I was trying my hardest to get her to leave, but she wouldn't budge. But she said she had a right to be here since her name was on the building."

So many emotions appear on Bennett's face. Confusion, realization, until he finally ends up on anger.

He takes the box from me and looks like he wants to tear it open but holds off. When he speaks, his voice is hard. "What did she look like?"

"Beautiful, with expensive clothing. She looked familiar."

His next few words come out through clenched teeth. "Familiar how?"

I throw my thought out from earlier. "She reminded me of Samantha, just with darker hair and complexion."

The second the words come out of my mouth, he rips open the box with so much anger, pieces of cardboard fly everywhere. As soon as he takes out the contents, his hands start to shake.

A beautiful watch lays against the palm of his hand.

"She left you a watch?" I ask, the question slipping through with some confusion.

Bennett's face distorts in disgust, and the next thing I know, he grabs the stapler from his desk and throws it against the wall.

A yelp escapes me, and I'm about to ask him what is going on, but he's already grabbing his phone, calling someone.

"I need the security tapes of everyone entering and leaving the building in the last two hours, and I need it now." His whole body shakes as he slams the phone back down onto the receiver.

"Bennett, what the hell is going on?" I ask, my hands sweating in the process.

The vein in his neck looks like it's about to pop as he responds.

"This watch," he starts, but he stops just as quickly, trying to find composure. "This watch was my father's. He gave it to Robert for his sixteenth birthday. The last time I saw it was on my brother ten years ago when he dropped off his kids. The only people who would have access to this are him or his wife."

A chill runs down my body.

I was right.

"That's who it was, wasn't it? The woman who was here was his wife?"

Bennett takes a second to collect himself, his eyes moving back down to the watch.

"If she reminded you of Samantha, then yes."

I try to piece everything together, but I can't figure out why he would have this visceral of a reaction to his brother's wife being here. "But why is that bad?"

"Because for all I know, that woman is fucking dead."

32

BENNETT

I look at the computer screen in front of me and grind my teeth for what feels like the hundredth time tonight.

Staring back at me, clear as day, is Marisela Serrano.

If I had put money on a dead person popping out of nowhere, my money would be on anyone but her. My brother, sure, but his wife? I should be more shocked that she is currently on my screen, but I'm not.

There is a reason she decided to make an appearance after all these years, and it wasn't to drop off my brother's watch. She's here for something. I know she is. Otherwise, she wouldn't have spent time playing games and would have contacted her children and contacted me directly, not just shown up at the office one random weekday.

You would think that your children you haven't seen in years would be your first damn priority, but for someone like Marisela, playing mind tricks is at the top of the list.

"You staring at the computer screen for hours isn't

going to give you the answers you're looking for," Dante says from where he sits across from me.

We're sitting in the study at the penthouse and have been for about three hours now, looking over the security footage from earlier today that has my sister-in-law front and center.

It has been six hours since Ella told me about Marisela being in my office and five since the Lane security team was able to get me every single tape I requested and talked to the security guard that escorted Marisela out. I made some calls, and Ella and I made our way to the penthouse.

When Dante arrived a few hours ago, we started to go through everything. Every piece of camera footage, every single angle. Everything that showed Marisela, we have overanalyzed. Nothing has given me the answers I want.

Why is she here? Why the fuck do it now?

But the question that keeps plaguing my mind is what my brother's watch has to do with any of this. Is she trying to send a message?

I have a feeling that the watch is just to get my attention. But why?

"I need to figure out why the fuck she is here," I say, moving my eyes away from the screen and meeting the stares of the Mafia boss sitting in front of me.

"And you will, but concentrating on how she got into the building without security noticing her isn't going to help with that."

I won't tell him as much, but he's right. I can't keep obsessing over how she got in. If anything, I should concentrate on what she did while she was in my building.

From what the footage is telling me, Marisela was inside for a total of twenty-five minutes. From what Ella says, she was in my office for five at the most, so what did she do during the rest of her time? The possibilities are endless.

As I think about it, something comes to mind, and I can't help but mentally kick myself in the ass. I'm looking at the wrong footage. If her coming and going isn't going to give me any answers, looking for her as she moves through the building probably would.

Not wanting to stew, I quickly pull up the footage from the elevator cameras and the ones in front of my office.

"There's no footage of her in an elevator going up, only coming down with the security guard."

"How is that possible?"

I'm asking myself the same question. Our security is top of the line; we don't have errors like this.

"Looks like she chose the one elevator that didn't have functioning security cameras all day." Even as I say the words, I don't believe them. Someone messed with the cameras before she arrived, I fucking know it.

Not wanting to stew too much on who might have messed with my security system, I move to the footage of my office. The cameras don't have a direct line into my office, but there is a direct line to Ella's desk.

I replay the footage from when Gerald and I leave the office to when security escorts Marisela out. Nothing catches my eye until I zoom in.

The second I do, my teeth start to grind again.

As the security guard walks out of my office with

Marisela's arm in his hand, the woman stretches over and swipes something from Ella's desk.

My jaw feels like it's going to break with how tight I'm holding it shut as I hit replay and slow down the footage. Sure enough, she swipes something from the desk. All I can tell is that it looks like a piece of paper, but I can't get a clear enough picture.

"She took a piece of paper from Ella's desk," I state, feeling fucking irritated that the more that comes out, the more questions I have, and I'm not anywhere near getting answers.

"It could be nothing," Dante tries to reason, but the second I throw him a glare, he backtracks. "Okay, best-case scenario, it's just a random piece of paper with no information. What about the worst case?"

I see red just thinking about it.

"It has a signature," I grumble, feeling like I'm seconds away from pulling out my own hair.

Dante sits back in his chair and thinks, his eyes as dark as mine feel. "Okay. Let's say it does have a signature. What can she do with it?"

If it was my signature, she could do a lot. Forge contracts, take money out of my bank accounts—anything that could come to mind for a person like her.

But if she has Ella's signature, she can't do much with it. Even though Ella is my wife and holds my last name, her signature doesn't hold as much power because that's how I set things up when this whole arrangement started. Marisela could still do things with it, mostly anything attached to the bank accounts Ella has access to, but that's it. If this were happening a month from now, though, everything would be in jeopardy.

I guess luck wasn't fully on Marisela's side.

"Write herself a check and drain a few bank accounts."

"If she does that, how much money are we talking?"

"Anywhere between five and ten million dollars."

Dante lets out an exasperated sigh. "Damn. You really went all in on this marriage, didn't you?"

Of course I fucking did, and I have no fucking regrets about it. Giving Ella access to those accounts was never something I gave a second thought to. Even though I had my doubts about her in the beginning, a part of me knew I was going to be able to trust her, which is why I was getting everything ready to give Ella access to everything I own and do. Now, thanks to Marisela, that has to be paused.

"What I gave my wife access to doesn't matter. What matters is what the fuck we're going to do about Marisela. She's here for a reason. You don't come out of hiding just because. Something has to trigger it."

Dante nods and looks like he is contemplating something. "Have you talked to the kids? Have they heard from her?"

I fucking hope not.

"The only one I have talked to is Elliot, and even then, I didn't mention anything about their mother. He didn't sound like he knew anything. I just told him I was sending a plane to bring him to Chicago and he better be on it."

He asked me a million times why, but something like his mother popping up after years of us thinking she was dead is not something you mention over the phone.

They need to know, though, and as soon as I get more information, I will tell them.

The door to the study opens, and Ella pops in her head. She had excused herself about an hour ago to eat dinner and check in with Henry.

"Sorry," she says, throwing a small smile in my direction. "I just spoke to Henry, and he said Elliot is on his way. He should be at the airport in about an hour."

I give her a nod. "Thank you."

Ella stays by the doorway, looking nervous. I watch as she opens that beautiful mouth of hers to speak a few times, but nothing comes out. After about a minute, she finds her voice.

"Can I ask a question?"

Both Dante and I give her a nod as she sits in the chair next to Dante.

"Is this woman..." She stops, as if she wants to rephrase what she's about to say. "Is Marisela a bad person? Why is her being here such a big deal? Apart from you thinking she was possibly dead."

It's times like these that I remember Ella still doesn't know the Lane family history. She is still very much new to all of this and doesn't know all the details.

Part of me knew the day she found everything out was going to come, but I wanted to believe that I could keep all the dirty secrets away from her. That my past would be just that, the past, but of course nothing ever stays there.

Letting out a sigh, I tell her everything I know.

"When the kids first came to live with me, he said that something was going on back where they lived in Mexico.

His father-in-law was stepping further into the political game, and because of some of his policies, his family became a target. The day he flew to Chicago, Marisela ended up going missing. From what I know, he flew back to find her and make sure her father and the rest of her family were safe."

I still remember seeing the fear in Robert's face that day. It was bone chilling. I begged him not to go. To stay here where he was safe. To stay here with his kids. To stay here for me.

Now that I'm married, I understand him leaving. If it were Ella, I would do the same, but that doesn't stop me from getting angry every time I think of it. My brother abandoned me twice, and both times he promised to come back. Never has that promise been held.

"How was he going to find her or protect her family?" Ella asks, taking me out of my haze.

"My brother enlisted in the military when he was eighteen, from what his records tell me. And when he was discharged, he moved to Mexico with Marisela and worked with the armed forces there to an extent."

Ella nods, trying to take in all the information. "I'm guessing since Marisela is here now, he found her?"

If only it was that fucking easy.

"As far as I know, he never found her. If he is still out there, there's a chance he doesn't even know she is alive."

"Is this the first time she has popped up?" she asks, her eyes bouncing between me and Dante.

I shake my head. "No, we found out she was alive about six years ago, before she went under again."

"How did you find out?"

Her question is simple, but the answer not so much. Because it touches things that I'm sure Ella never thought she would ever have a direct line to.

Dante looks over at me, as if to silently ask just how much we're going to tell her. With a simple nod, I answer him.

We're going to tell him everything.

"Have you heard of the Muertos Cartel?" Dante asks once he sees it's taking me a bit to form a response.

Ella looks over at him with wide eyes. "Yeah, but I don't know much about them."

Dante gives her a nod of understanding. "Six years ago, there was this big news story circulating about how the wife of the head of the cartel was killed."

A small chunk of realization hits Ella. "I think I remember that. She was shot coming out of a store or something, right?"

My friend gives her a tight smile for getting it correct. "That's right. For years, there have been a few rumors about why she was killed, but as of today, nothing has been confirmed. Some say it was a rival cartel that fired the shot to send a message. Others say that Ronaldo, the cartel head, had a mistress and promised said mistress everything. That he would leave his wife for her, but when she saw he wasn't keeping his promise, she took matters into her own hands. Rumors are that either the mistress fired the shot, or someone close to her did."

I watch Ella as she takes everything in, but I can see questions moving around in her eyes.

"And who do people say the mistress was?"

Dante looks over at me to answer.

"Marisela."

When I first heard the rumors, I didn't want to believe them. I didn't want to believe that my brother's wife would fake her own death to pop up as the mistress to a cartel head while her husband looked for her and I took care of her kids. But the more I learned about her, the more my perspective shifted.

"And you believe it?"

I give my wife a nod. "I do. Marisela had to be in something dark if nobody had heard from or seen her for four years. And her being intertwined with the cartel makes sense."

When I heard that Marisela popped up the first time, it came with a lot of questions. Where the hell was Robert?

I know for a fact that my brother went back to the home he and his wife built. What I don't know is what happened when he got there. There is something deep in me that tells me I already know what happened. He got caught in the crossfire while looking for Marisela. He is buried deep in the ground, and that's why I haven't been able to find him.

But I'm not going to accept that until I get confirmation—hard, solid proof that I see with my own fucking eyes.

"What happened to Marisela after the shooting?"

"She disappeared again. Her and her family basically fell off the face of the earth for about two years."

Ella's eyebrows bunch up in confusion. "Two years?

You mean they showed up again after two years? Did they come back for the kids?"

A bit of anger rolls through me as I remember how I became the kids' legal guardian.

My jaw tics as I speak. "Only she came back. According to her, she hadn't seen or heard from my brother in years and had no idea where he was, which I called bullshit."

She knows. I know she fucking knows, and if I ever get in the same room with her again, I will torture her until I find out.

"What happened when she showed up?"

I let out a sigh and relive a memory I tried so hard to bury.

"She went to the manor, and I took pity on her. I knew what it was like to not have my mother around, and I didn't want the kids to go through that any longer, so I let her in their lives. Which was one of the biggest mistakes I've ever made."

I see the question in Ella's eyes before she speaks it. "Why?"

"Because she didn't want anything to do with the kids. I don't know how much my brother told her about our family, but she knew we had money. So she came here, pretended to miss her children and wanted to give them a better life, but in reality, she was just here trying to figure out how to get her hands on the Lane family fortune. In a period of two weeks, she stole anything she could get her hands on. Turns out, my brother's wife is a greedy bitch only after two things: money and power. After I realized what she was doing—that she wasn't telling me the truth about Robert—I threatened her, and she signed over her parental rights."

I can still see the anger on Elliot's face when his mother told him that I was forcing her to leave. I was looking out for my family. He hated me for it, and to this day still holds some resentment toward me because of it.

He's realizing why I did it, though. It's taken a few years, but he's seeing that when it comes to him and his siblings, I would do anything to protect them. Including keeping them away from their mother.

She is as toxic as they come, and they don't need to be exposed to that.

"Why did you think she was dead?"

"Because much like my brother, she fell off the face of the earth when I made her leave. I had no confirmation that said otherwise."

"Why do you think she decided to pop up now, after all these years?" she asks, her eyes bouncing from me and Dante once more.

"That's the fucking question of the night," Dante mutters out.

"I don't know why she's here or why now, but she's here for a reason, and I will find out what it is."

Ella gives me a nod, like she is silently telling me she's with me on this. I wonder if she would still be with me if I told her that if it comes to it, I won't stop until Marisela is in the ground.

A phone rings somewhere in the penthouse, and Ella quickly goes to answer it, leaving Dante and me in the same place as before, with more questions than answers.

"What do you want to do? Be on the lookout and hope she pops up somewhere else?" Dante throws the suggestion out, and as much as I want to tell him we aren't going to be doing that, I can't.

We have no information to go off of. All we know is that Marisela is somewhere in the city. We don't know where she is going next, if she is working with someone, or if she will make another appearance anytime soon.

"That's the only thing we can do." I can't believe I'm just going to leave shit up to chance, but what more can I do? "I'll increase security. Here, the manor, the office. Hell, even at the kids' schools. She's going to pop out again if she wants something so desperately, and when she does, she's not going to have any place to run."

Dante nods in agreement. "I'll have men ready for whenever you need them."

"Thank you."

With that, I close all the security footage from today. I'm going to be obsessing over it for days to come, I know that for sure, but right now, I'm not going to be getting any information. I need to come back to it with a clear head.

As I walk Dante out of the study, I try to get everything that has happened today out of my head, even for a few hours, so I miss when Dante stops in his tracks until I run into him.

"Did Ella go somewhere?"

It takes me a second to register Dante's question, and as soon as I do, I go on high alert.

My eyes scan the area, and right away, I notice that the

door separating the foyer and the elevator to the garage is wide open.

Lately, Ella has gotten into the habit of telling me she is going to do something. If she was stepping away from her desk, grabbing something from the car, she has been telling me. So for her to leave the apartment without letting me know is raising questions when it shouldn't.

"Ella!" I call out and wait for a response, but nothing comes.

I don't have to call out again to know she isn't here.

"You don't think…?" Dante starts, leaving his question up in the air.

My nails dig into my palms, drawing blood. "I don't have to think. I fucking know."

Marisela was fucking here. I fucking know it.

How the fuck she got through my security team is beyond me, but she did and possibly has Ella. If she lays a fucking hand on her, I won't hesitate. Marisela will end up in the ground.

I don't give a shit if she's my brother's wife or the mother of his children.

She will fucking pay.

33

ELLA

From the second I noticed that it was my work phone ringing and not my personal phone, I should have known that something was off. Everyone I work with knows not to call me this late in the day unless it's an emergency and they need to get in touch with Bennett. Otherwise, they could email me.

Yet, I still answered the call from a number I didn't recognize.

Not a single word from the other side was said, but now I know the call was only to serve as a distraction. A diversion for someone to enter the penthouse, place a cloth over my mouth, and drag me out of there.

I tried to scream, but nothing came out. I tried to thrash against the person holding me, hoping I was strong enough to sway them and possibly hit something to get Bennett or Dante's attention, but I couldn't. It was like the second the cloth was placed over my mouth, my body gave out. I could still hear and see, but nothing else.

There was a point in my life where I thought Josiah coming after me and taking away Charlie would be my worst fear come true, but as I sit in the back of a car, men on either side of me, I realize that fear is nothing compared to this.

Tears roll down my face the further we make it out of the city. I might die tonight, and there is a chance nobody is ever going to find me. I don't have my phone or anything that identifies me. I'm all alone with these strangers who decided to take me.

As we continue to drive, I try to clear my head as best I can so I can catch if they do or say anything, but whatever they drugged me with is hitting me hard. Everything is either jumbled together or a complete whisper, and I can't make it out.

I don't know how long the effects of this is going to last, but I hope they end soon.

The only thing I can make out is that the men who took me are working for someone and they speak a different language, but because of the drugs, I can't figure out which one.

My eyes feel like they are drooping, so I try my hardest to keep them open as long as I can by keeping my gaze on the clock on the dashboard. For the most part, it helps, but eventually, I can't fight it anymore, and I let my eyes drop. The next time my eyes open, it's eighteen minutes later, and we are pulling into what looks like an abandoned office building.

As the doors to the car open, I try to do the math in my head.

When I first got in the car, the clock read twelve minutes past the hour, and looking at the time now, whoever took me only drove for fifty-two minutes. That means there is a chance we may not be in the city anymore, but we are still close.

Maybe I can run. Maybe once the drugs fade, I can run.

My body gets jerked to the side, and I get dragged out of the car by the two men.

"Walk," one of them growls in my ear and pushes me forward, but all I do is fall to the ground, getting the wind knocked out of me.

I try to push myself up, but my arms have no strength to even move an inch. I keep trying, though, but eventually, the two men grow tired of my attempts. One of them picks me up and throws me over his shoulder.

As they start walking into the building, I hear more voices, both male and female, but this new position is making me more disoriented, and I can't make out a single thing they're saying. I think they are speaking English, but nothing that comes out of their mouths makes any sense.

My eyes close again, and the next time they open, I'm strapped to a chair. My head is still foggy, but it starts to clear. Not a whole lot, but enough for me to make out words and different voices. Voices that sound familiar for some reason.

"You fucking morons. You weren't supposed to grab her. You were supposed to grab her fucking husband. What the fuck are we going to do with her? She is fucking useless."

I know that voice. It's male, and I know it. How do I know that voice?

"She's not completely useless. I can think of a few things she can do for me."

Something slides against my cheek, causing me to look up, and when I do, I'm met with a familiar face. The one that reminds me of Samantha.

Marisela.

I try to say her name, but nothing comes out.

It's not until the owner of the male voice comes into view that a small whimper leaves me.

Peter Hill.

"We both agreed we'd go after him. He was more important than the little slut he married. Having her here messes up everything."

I watch as Marisela rolls her eyes, and a smirk forms on her face. "Then I guess we just have to get rid of both of them."

All the blood in my body drains down to my feet. As I hear her words, the only thing I could think to do is run my finger along my wedding ring and make sure I can still feel the bracelet around my wrist. They are the only things keeping me calm.

As I run my finger against the ring, I can't help but wish Bennett was here so I could tell him two things.

That marrying him was the best decision I ever made and that I love him.

Bennett Lane owns my whole damn heart, and thanks to Peter and Marisela, I will never get to tell him.

34

BENNETT

Panic runs through my body, but I don't show it.

As much as I want to take the nearest weapon and storm out of this apartment to go find my wife, spilling all the blood I can along the way, I continue to stand where I am and try not to let the madness in my head take over.

But it's hard.

With each passing second, more and more intrusive thoughts are snaking in.

Thoughts like I never should have stepped into this arrangement with Ella. Thoughts like I should have figured out another way to become CEO. Because now, not only has someone taken her, I'm also at risk of losing her. There's a chance I lose someone that I care about.

Someone I fucking love.

I should have known from day one that this was where I was going to end up, but somehow, through all my stubbornness, I was able to convince myself that two years with this woman was going to be enough.

It wasn't enough when we went on our honeymoon and will never be enough fifty years from now. And now, there is a chance I might lose her altogether.

The longer she's gone, the more my anger rises. This is why I didn't want to ever get married. Even though my parents had a good marriage, I didn't want to go through the pain I would have felt if I ever lost that person, because losing them would have been inevitable. I've already lost three people I was never supposed to lose—why not add one more to the list and make my abandonment issue unrepairable?

If I'm able to get Ella back alive, I will either end our agreement early so she never has to go through this ever again or never leave her fucking side. I will be within arm's reach until the day I fucking die.

As I look out at the Chicago skyline, the voices of my security team and the Mafia men who infiltrated the space envelop me, but I don't pay attention to a single thing they're saying.

They are looking everywhere for Ella and have been since the second they were notified of her disappearance, and I should be partaking in the search. I should be at the forefront of finding anything that may lead to her, but I can't concentrate.

It was Marisela. I know it was, but why? Why take Ella? Why wait until we were home to do it?

They were in the same room just a few hours ago. Why not take her then? It would have been fucking easier. How the fuck did they know we were here?

There are so many questions that need answers.

"Mr. Bennett." Henry's voice takes me out of my head.

When I turn, my pseudofather is walking into the living room with Drake's hand in his, the girls and Grayson behind him. For a second, I take them all in. The kids are scared, but so is Henry. I notice the panic and the fear he is trying to hide, but I have known this man all my life; he can never hide anything from me.

I walk over to them, and as soon as I'm within reach, Drake breaks away from Henry and wraps his little arms around me. I haven't told them why they needed to come here, but by how tight Drake is holding on to me, he knows something isn't right. I wrap my arms around him too and try to get my bearings.

"Missed you today, bud," I say into his mop of hair, hoping to fucking God that my voice doesn't show the desperation I feel.

"What's going on?" His voice is soft when he pulls away from me, his eyes dancing all over the room, at all the people here with us.

It's a lot for me. I can't imagine how it is for him. I shouldn't have had Henry bring them here. They shouldn't be witnessing any of this.

But I needed to know they were all safe, and the only way to know that is if they are with me. For all I know, Marisela was also planning on hitting the manor or the school and taking one of the kids.

So until I find her and Ella, the kids are going to be wherever I am.

Placing a hand on Drake's shoulder, I guide him out of the living room and nod for the other kids to follow me out. As we walk down the hall, I try to think of what to tell them, but the hallway isn't long enough, and by the time we reach the bedrooms, I have nothing.

So I throw out the first thing I think of.

"Drake, bud, why don't you go pick out a movie? We're all going to be sleeping here tonight, and I thought it would be fun to have a movie night."

The kid looks up at me with eyes full of scrutiny. He knows something is wrong, that I'm keeping him out of the loop, but thankfully, he doesn't fight me on it and walks into the movie theater room.

As soon as he is out of hearing distance, I turn to face the three teenagers. No matter how hard I try, I won't be able to hide anything from them, so I might as well tell them what is going on.

"I need you four to stay here, okay? Keep an eye on your brother, and under no circumstance do you leave that room unless I tell you to, got it?"

Grayson is the one to break the silence. "Are you going to tell us what's going on?"

"Ella is missing." Bile creeps up my throat as I say the words.

Right away, panic coats Charlie's face as tears run down her cheeks. "What? No, you're lying. I just spoke to her like three hours ago."

She starts to walk past me with determination, but I wrap an arm around her waist and bring her back.

"Let me go. We have to go look for her." She slams her fist against my chest, trying to push me away but failing.

"Charlotte, listen to me." She shakes her head

profusely, trying to get out of my grasp, but eventually she realizes I'm not going to let her go. When she calms down, I speak again. "We are going to find your sister, okay? You have to trust me. She will come home to us. Those men in the living room? They are doing everything in their power to find her tonight. I know you want to help, but I can't put you in danger, so I need you three to go to the theater with Drake, where you are safe, and stay there. Once we find her, I will come get you. Can you do that for me?"

Tears run down her face as she nods.

For a second, she reminds me of Ella. Is this how scared she was when she ran from Josiah's house with a younger Charlie? I fucking hope not.

I place a kiss against her temple and let her go.

All three kids walk into the theater, and I let out a sigh of relief. Four members of my family are safe. But I'm not going to be able to breathe until all of them are under my fucking roof.

Leaving the kids, I head back to the living room and see Elliot has finally arrived, getting information from Dante.

I don't have to hear what he is telling him; I can see it all over his face. He knows his mother is back.

"Do we really think she took Ella?" Elliot asks moments after getting up to speed.

There's a small hint of optimism in his voice. Even though he hasn't seen his mother in years, he doesn't want to believe that she is capable of doing this. He has a small bit of hope that she isn't involved. I wish I could give him that, but all the signs point back to her.

"I don't want to, but given that she showed up at the office earlier today and now Ella is gone, I have to think that it's her."

He gives a nod, and for a long minute, I don't see him for the twenty-year-old he is. I see the ten-year-old kid who showed up on my doorstep all those years ago, his sister's hand in his, looking terrified as he watched his father leave.

Out of all the kids, Elliot is the one who holds the most on his shoulders. He feels a responsibility that someone his age shouldn't, and now that Marisela is here, I can see him get angry at himself for not being enough for her. She is here, in the same city as them, and they aren't her priority.

Me and him have had our differences, especially when it comes to his mother, but that will never stop me from making sure that she never hurts him again.

I place a hand on his shoulder and try to convey everything with not a whole lot of words before moving back to the task at hand: finding Ella.

Even with dark thoughts still plaguing my mind, I spend the next twenty minutes going through everything the security team and Dante's men have found.

Two men dressed in black made their way up the elevator to the penthouse from the garage about five minutes before they took Ella. Apparently, her phone ringing was a diversion. They figured calling a cell phone would cause enough noise that nobody would hear the elevator ding or the front door opening.

And the fucking kicker? One of Dante's men found

Ella's phone on the floor in the kitchen and took note of the number. It was the same number that has been messing with my mind for months. The same number that popped up under Robert's name. The same number that called me.

It must belong to Marisela. That's the only logical explanation.

The men who took Ella have been hanging out around the building for a week, according to my head of security, acting as window cleaners, but instead of working, they were canvassing the area and getting to know security patterns.

Since the penthouse is only used on occasion, the two window cleaners were overlocked.

"Were they canvassing the house?" I ask through clenched teeth. The house is a fucking fortress, but something could have slipped through the cracks.

"No, sir. Not as far as we know. We ran their faces through the security system at the manor, and nothing came up."

That should give me relief, but it doesn't.

"Did they follow us from the office?" I ask, trying to make sense of all of this.

"We checked traffic cameras, and there is no sign of that."

"Then how the fuck did they know we would be here?"

Was it by chance? They couldn't get to the house, so they decided to just scope out the penthouse until we showed up? It doesn't make any fucking sense.

They knew we were here, but how?

"They must have gotten lucky."

As soon as I hear the words, I think about strangling him, then firing him for such stupidity.

Thankfully, Henry speaks and stops me from storming across the room and murdering someone.

"Mr. Rosetti mentioned something about a watch that Ms. Serrano left in your office." It doesn't go unnoticed that even though we know Marisela is a Lane, he doesn't attach it to her. "What watch is he talking about?" he asks, his face full of contemplation.

I let out a sigh and answer him. "The one Dad gave Robert for his sixteenth birthday." There is no need to describe the watch. Henry was the one who got it ready for him.

Henry's eyes go wide at my words, though.

"What?" It takes him a second to speak. "Do you have the watch with you?"

I give him a nod and take out the device from my pocket where it has been all night.

Handing it over, Henry looks at it for a second before he lets out a sigh and looks up at me with regretful eyes.

"This is how she knew you were here," he says, placing the watch on the coffee table between us.

"What are you talking about?"

Henry lets out a sigh. "That watch has a tracking device, sir. Your father put it in there before he gave it to your brother. Even though he trusted him, he still wanted to know where he was as a safety measure. It's just under the dial, small enough to go undetected."

I feel like I'm having an out-of-body experience.

A tracking device.

If what Henry is saying is true and the watch has a tracking device, does that mean I had Robert's location all of this time?

"He took this watch with him the night he left," I voice out loud. "You're telling me you had access to my brother's whereabouts all this time, and you are just now informing me?"

Anger rolls through me. Out of all the people in my life, I never expected Henry to betray me like this.

I've spent years looking for Robert, and Henry knew that. All he had to do was tell me about the tracking device, and I would be able to find him, but he kept it to himself.

"I cannot express how sorry I am for not informing you of this sooner, sir, but at the time, there was no need. The device stopped working after three years or so, and nothing had come up since then. The fact that it even works now is a new development."

Marisela must have had the watch and found the tracker. Bringing the watch to the office was genius; she knew that I would keep anything tied to my brother with me at all times.

Fucking conniving bitch.

I'm reeling from all this information when Henry speaks again.

"The watch isn't the only thing that has a tracking device."

"What else has one?" I find myself asking a little bit too aggressively.

He looks me straight in the eye as he answers. "The bracelet I gave Mrs. Lane a few weeks ago. One of the diamonds is a tracker."

The bracelet comes to mind right away. It was my mother's, and when Ella showed it to me, I was a little stunned.

When it came to my mother's jewelry, I handed it over to Henry because I didn't want to lose any of it or give it to the wrong person. There are a few pieces I already set aside for certain occasions, but other than that, Henry can do what he wishes with them. The fact that he gave Ella something was monumental. It means he sees her as more than just the woman I married to get CEO. He sees her as part of his family.

"So we can find Ella?" Elliot asks, everyone looking at Henry for an answer.

"If she has the bracelet on, then yes."

For first time all damn night, I feel fucking hope that I won't find my wife dead somewhere.

All eyes turn to me.

"She hasn't taken it off since you gave it to her."

As soon as the words leave my mouth, Henry gets to work with our security team to start tracking the bracelet, and Dante and his men start filing out so they are ready to go when we have a location.

The next five minutes end up being torture in more ways than I can comprehend.

"Sir," a voice calls out. "We found her."

Sweet Ella, I'm coming to get you, and I won't ever let you go.

35

BENNETT

"You don't have to go in there, you know. We'll take care of everything and get her out of there in one piece," Dante says as one of his men parks the dark SUV across the street from an office building pinging Ella's location.

It's an office building an hour outside the city. There is nothing distinct about it, except for the fact that it looks like it has been deserted for years.

I take in every inch of the place that I can see through the darkness of the night sky as Dante's words run through my mind.

He's right—I don't have to go in there. Hell, I didn't even have to come to the location; I could have had my men take care of everything and had them bring Ella home to me.

But I couldn't sit around and just wait for her to walk through the door.

I couldn't risk leaving her life in someone else's hands. She's my wife, and I'd do anything for her—do anything to have her in my arms again. And if that means walking into an unknown situation that could possibly land me in a hole right next to my parents, then so fucking be it.

"I'm going in there."

"Of course you are." He lets out a sigh as he shifts in his seat, pulling out a handgun from his waistband. "Do you need a crash course on how to shoot a gun, or do you remember?"

I roll my fucking eyes and take the gun.

After the kids came to love me and I found out about their mother's possible extracurricular activities, I took all necessary precautions to keep them safe. That included military and arms training. If the rumors were right and the cartel was going to retaliate, I was going to be prepared.

If we had been at the manor instead of the penthouse, I would have come ready to storm the damn building.

"Don't fucking insult me right now," I say, checking the gun to see if it's loaded.

"Had to ask," he lets out before turning back to look out the window. "There's one man standing by the door. We'll take him out and storm in. Do you have any reservations whatsoever?"

I know my friend, and he is asking me, if it comes down to it, if I'm okay with Marisela taking a bullet tonight.

"No. We do what needs to be done to get Ella out of there."

He nods and opens his door, his men following suit.

It's time to get my wife back, and I don't give two shits who I have to shoot between the eyes to do it.

36

ELLA

My head is screaming for some relief right now.

The drugs are starting to wear off, and my body doesn't feel as heavy as it did earlier, but in return, it feels like my head is attacking me from the inside out. The only thing I'm happy about at the moment is that all the lights in the building are off.

A headache should be the least of your worries.

Right. I should be thinking of ways to get out of this situation, but the pain is so bad, it's the only thing I can concentrate on. Until the pain is gone and the drugs are fully out of my system, nothing I do right now is going to help me.

A small movement to my right catches my attention, and I can't help but flinch as the figure gets closer to me.

"You don't need to be scared of me," Marisela lets out when she comes into view, a small, sadistic smile playing on her lips.

"From what you told Peter, I do," I say, using my voice for the first time since all of this started.

A laugh leaves her. "When it comes to men like him, you have to give them the words they want to hear. Just because I told him we should kill you doesn't mean that I'm actually going to follow through with it. I could think of a few reasons why keeping you alive could be beneficial."

She slides her finger down my face, and I try my hardest to move away, but I'm still tied to a chair. I can't really move much.

"Why are you doing this?" The question has been plaguing me since my eyes met hers earlier. I've tried to come up with an answer, but my head hasn't been clear enough to figure it out.

"Why are you still tied to a chair?" She smirks down at me. "Or why am I working with Mr. Hill to take down Bennett?"

I don't answer. She knows I'm asking.

Her smirk grows even more. "Well, you're still tied to a chair because I don't know what you are capable of. For all I know, you are a trained assassin, and the second you are free, you'll come for my throat."

How can she be joking right now?

"As for the other question, Bennett took something from both of us, and we think it's time for him to pay for his actions."

Anger starts to boil inside me. "His actions? What did he do? Besides raise your children and treat them as if they were his own?"

A slap lands against my cheek, and for a few seconds, the pain in my head is forgotten.

"You don't know what you are talking about."

"I know you'd rather kidnap someone and work with a slimy bastard like Peter Hill than go to your children and make things right."

A sharp pain radiates from my scalp as Marisela grabs me by the hair and starts to pull. She snarls down at me, her face so close, I can smell the minty gum she is chewing.

"If I were you, I would keep that pretty mouth of yours shut and not mention my children again."

My head snaps back with so much force, it takes a second to stop the dizziness.

As my head settles, I come to the realization that if I ask the right questions, there is a chance Marisela might actually talk. I just have to make sure I don't say anything that is going to make her mad. The kids are off the table, and I'm guessing so is Bennett's brother, but I'm sure there are other topics she would be more than willing to talk about.

Peter seems like a good place to start.

"How do you and Peter even know each other?" I ask.

The two of them together seem like a very odd pairing. It's unexpected and definitely not something I saw coming.

If the rumors about Marisela are true, then she is known to run with the cartel. As far as I know, Peter is nowhere near that level of shadiness.

For a second, I think that Marisela is going to ignore me, but then she starts talking.

"I guess you can say we met by chance."

A wave of pain hits my head, making me groan, but I try to ignore it. "What does that even mean?"

"It means that when someone puts out a call to bring down a powerful billionaire, people come from all over the place to answer. I was one of the people."

I don't know if it's the drugs, but I'm having a hard time following.

"A call? What do you mean by 'put out a call'?"

I swear, I could hear this woman roll her eyes. "It means that Mr. Hill put out a hit."

That's why he hasn't been as vocal about taking Bennett out as CEO: he has been planning to take him down behind the scenes.

He couldn't do it as a Lane Enterprises employee, so he decided to do it for himself, hoping that everything would work out in his favor and the title would fall to him.

Bennett was right. Peter Hill is a conniving bastard.

And Marisela is right there next to him.

"How did you even know about the call Peter put out?" I ask, trying to piece everything together.

Marisela turns to face me, giving me another smirk. "Just because I've been in hiding for years doesn't mean I don't keep tabs on people. The man who took my children away from me has been at the top of my shit list for years. So when his name popped up, I took the opportunity. I would be dumb not to. And when Peter found out about my personal connection to Bennett, he was excited to get started."

Her personal connection.

Something clicks in my mind.

"You were the one behind the number, weren't you? The one that kept calling him?"

Please say no. Please say it wasn't you.

The way she grins tells me everything I need to know. She was behind it, and she has no regrets.

"Of course, it was me. I had to get Bennett's attention somehow. What better way than a number that would trace back to his brother."

"You're a cruel bitch."

She closes the distance between us and once more runs her finger along the length of my face. "Honey, you haven't seen cruel. That was just me getting started."

I'm able to pull away enough to let her finger fall, but even with the distance, I can still feel her skin against mine, as if it was burned to my flesh.

As much as I don't want to hear what she and Hill had planned for Bennett, I have to keep Marisela talking.

"What's in it for you? If you succeed in taking down Bennett, Hill gets the title of CEO, but what do you get?"

The first thing that comes to mind is the kids. They are old enough to see their mother for who she really is, but what if she gets to them?

Her children are the only logical thing I could think of her wanting, especially if she has the mindset that Bennett took her children from her.

The bitch should be fucking grateful he took them in and raised them as if they were his own. Not a lot of twenty-two-year-olds would have done that.

"What I get is a little more complicated. Where Peter's

part of the deal is a little more straightforward, mine comes in sections."

I know I'm going to regret asking, but I have to know. "How?"

Marisela looks down at her nails, as if she is bored out of her mind. "The plan was fairly simple. We take out Bennett first, and since you are now married, you would be next, followed by Henry. That way, the only individuals left are my kids, and the family fortune would fall to them. Peter gets to be CEO of every company the Lane family owns, and I would do everything in my power to repair my relationship with my kids."

I hate this woman.

I hate her so fucking much.

Just the thought of her using her four kids to get the money meant for them and them alone makes me sick. They deserve more than a mother who is going to use them. They deserve a mother who will fight for them, who will help them through life and love them wholeheartedly, and Marisela will never be that.

For the first time since I met her, I feel bad for Marisela.

She will never get to know the amazing humans her children have become.

She will never know that Elliot loves to explore the world and help people in need.

She will never know that Samantha is loyal beyond comprehension and loves to work on cars because it's something she did with Henry when she was younger.

She will never know that Grayson's love for hockey

runs so deep that there is no doubt in my mind he will make it to the professional level one day and hopefully play for the Dark Knights.

She will never know that Drake is obsessed with computers and has a love for math like nobody else.

She will never know her children and see how great they are, and that's okay. They don't need her in their lives.

Which makes getting out of this all that more important. If I can't make it out of here for myself or for Bennett, then I will try for them. They may not be my kids, but I love them, and like Bennett, I would do anything for them—including protecting them from a mother who is greedy and power hungry.

"They deserve more than just being used for their money," I say out loud, my inner thoughts slipping through.

Marisela throws a snarl in my direction. "They also deserved to grow up with a mother, and look how that worked out. Sometimes, you don't get all you deserve."

If only I had my hands free, then maybe I could wiggle myself over to her and strangle the shit out of her.

I hate this woman beyond measure.

For the next few minutes, we stay silent. She walks around me, still in her expensive heels, and I continue to sit here, just letting the drugs seep out of my system.

"Why don't you just kill me already?" I find myself asking during her fifteenth lap around my chair.

"I could, but I fear if I have one of my men kill you now, Peter is going to freak out and call this whole thing off. I think I will wait it out."

"Where is Peter, anyway?"

I haven't seen him in a while. He was panicking a bit ago about there being a change in plans, but he disappeared after that.

"He's trying to convince himself that going back to the penthouse and grabbing Bennett would be a good idea."

I can't help but let out a snort. "Bennett knows I'm gone. That penthouse probably has more security than the White House right now. Hill toys with going anywhere near there, he's dead."

"That's exactly what I told him, but men can be stubborn."

As if he heard us talking about him, Peter walks into the room, looking like he just took a hit of whatever drugs they gave me, but instead of relaxing his body, they're having the opposite effect.

When he takes out a gun and points it in my direction, I know he has gone off the rails.

"What the fuck do you think you're doing?" Marisela asks, looking at the man as if she is tired of his crap.

"We need to get rid of her," Peter growls, his eyes hard and never leaving mine.

I've never seen him like this. Sure, there were times he let his anger get the best of him in board meetings, but this on a whole different level.

"You're fucking insane. I told you I could use her for something."

"I don't care. She knows too much already. If we let her go, she's going to talk and screw everything up. We need to get rid of her before she does that."

Tears roll down my face as I try to look anywhere but at the gun pointed at me, but I can't.

This is it. The second Peter pulls the trigger, I'll be gone.

The only thing saving me right now is the fact that Marisela is still talking to Peter, buying me more time.

"What makes you think they don't already know who took her? Do you really think you can kill her and walk away without facing any consequences? Newsflash, Peter: they are going to know who pulled the trigger, and they are going to come after you no matter what."

Peter's grip on the gun tightens.

"They won't come after me," he states with so much confidence.

"And why is that?" Marisela asks, her stance combative.

"Because I'm going to make them believe you did it. Lane will be so damn distracted with the fact that you're here and that you killed his wife, he will just hand the company over."

Does he live in a delusional world? If that was to happen, if Peter killed me right now and made it seem like Marisela pulled the trigger, he would definitely go after her, but he wouldn't hand over the company to someone like Peter. Bennett would rather let the company burn to the ground than hand it over to him.

Apparently, I'm not the only one who thinks this man's plan is insane, because Marisela actually lets out a laugh.

"You're more stupid than I thought if you think that is going to happen."

"It will. Just you watch."

Marisela shakes her head at him. "It won't. Want to know why? Because you won't make it out of this room alive."

"What the hell are yo—"

A shot rings out, and Peter's question is stopped abruptly.

For a few seconds, there is silence, no movement. It's just me and the two people in the room, too stunned to even do anything. But the second that blood starts to gush out of Peter's mouth, it's pure chaos.

Screams leave me as people start yelling, more people storming into the building, shots fired, people running for cover. So much happens, and the only thing I can do is sit here and hope a bullet doesn't hit me.

Eventually, all the chaos starts to die down, but fear is still running deep through me, more so when all the new faces now surrounding me don't look familiar.

This is truly where I'm going to die.

I don't realize I'm hysterically crying until a figure crouches down in front of me. I don't register his face until he says my name.

"Elizabeth."

As soon as I hear my name and the voice it's coming from, a different type of sob escapes me. A relieved one.

"Bennett?" I ask, the stars in my eyes making it hard to see.

"Yes, baby. Let's get you out of here."

The ties holding me to the chair come loose, and I'm finally able to move.

The tears clear, and as soon as my arms are free and

I'm able to see his face clearly, I wrap my arms around Bennett's neck and hold on to him for dear life.

His arms wrap around my body so tightly, I know I will still feel them when he lets go. "I got you. I got you."

His words are soothing, but when I look over his shoulder and see the body only a few feet away from us, all comfort is gone.

"Peter is dead," I say, not being able to believe what I just lived through.

"He is."

"What about Marisela?" I ask, pulling myself away just a fraction to look around the room for her, but she is nowhere to be seen.

"She ran as soon as the shots started. We don't know where she went, but we have men searching for her."

They'll find her. And if it's not tonight, it will be soon. I just know it.

"Let's get out of here. We need to get you to a doctor."

Bennett pushes himself up and brings me along with him. All I can do is nod at his suggestion and snuggle myself into his arms as he walks us out of the room.

It's not until we get to the car that I'm finally able to speak, and I try to give Bennett the words I wish I was able to say earlier.

"Bennett?" I ask as I rest against him in the back seat of the SUV.

"Yes, my sweet Ella?"

"I love you."

His words come quickly. "I love you too, baby. I love you so damn much."

37

BENNETT

It's close to four in the morning, and the house is completely silent. The only noise seeping through the walls is the birds starting to chirp outside.

Even though the birds are nice to listen to and the silence helps clear my head, I can't help but wish for some noise.

Kids screaming.

Laughing.

Anything would be better than the silence right now.

But the ones who make noise are sleeping, and after the night they had, they are going to be sleeping for a while longer.

Taking my eyes away from the night-covered property I've been staring at for the past hour, I turn to look over at the bed behind me.

Once the doctor I have on call gave Ella the "all clear," we went back to the penthouse to grab the kids and Henry to return to the manor. Ella was tired and wanted to sleep, but she didn't want to do it where she was reminded of the night's events.

After having some tea Henry made, she came to bed, and quickly after, Charlie, Drake, Samantha, and Grayson climbed into bed with her and haven't left her side. As much as I wanted to sleep in the same bed as my wife tonight and make sure she was safe in my arms, I let the kids have their time with her.

I look over at each one of their faces, and they don't have to be awake for me to know Sam, Grayson, and Drake love Ella dearly. If we hadn't gotten to the office building when we did and something had happened to her, they would have been devastated. To them, she is family.

Knowing the kids love Ella makes my anger about this whole thing even worse. Marisela and Peter almost took someone out of my kids' lives who they care about, and it wasn't even a second thought. For that, my hatred for them will never disappear. I will hate them for the rest of my life. Hill will be easy to forget now that he's dead, but Marisela is still out there, and when she inevitably pops up again, I will try my hardest to destroy her.

Feeling my anger come to the surface, I decide to take a break from my watch duties and head downstairs, but before I do that, I walk over to the bed and place a soft kiss against Ella's temple. I tried not to wake her, but when I pull back, I see her beautiful eyes staring back at me.

"Go back to sleep. I'll just be downstairs," I whisper.

She gives me a nod and cuddles deeper into the hold Charlie has on her.

When I get downstairs, I'm met with a familiar scene: Henry sitting at the kitchen island with a cup of coffee in his hand. The last time we had a morning like this, I had a nightmare and had a snoring ten-year-old in my bed. It's crazy how much has happened since then. The only difference now is that Elliot is sitting right next to him.

"Couldn't sleep?" I say, walking over to the coffee maker and pouring the first of many cups I know I'm going to drink this morning.

Elliot is the one who answers. "Never actually went to sleep."

"That would make three of us," I say, taking a long gulp of coffee.

"How is Mrs. Lane doing?" There is sadness in Henry's eyes, and I hate it.

"Sleeping, but she's still shaken up. It might be a while before she can be herself again."

What she went through was fucking traumatic—not only the kidnapping part but also watching someone get shot and die in front of you. That stays with you forever. I just have to hope she is able to get through it.

"I'll go into the office and help out while she adjusts," Elliot throws out, catching me by surprise.

He never wants to work at the office, and that he is offering to do so now is surprising.

"I appreciate that."

He gives me a nod and goes back to drinking his coffee.

Henry is the one to speak next.

"Sir," he starts, clearing his throat a few times before getting the words out. "I would like to apologize again for not telling you about the tracking device. Once you got older, I should have. Maybe then we would have known Ms. Serrano had resurfaced."

When I first learned about the tracking device, I was angry. Henry had a way of finding Robert, and I didn't know. But I've spent the last four hours in my head, and that tracking device was front and center. I realized I had no right to be angry.

Robert left when I was eight. At that age, I wasn't looking for my brother. I was just hoping he would come home one day. I'm sure I didn't even know what a tracking device was, so Henry telling me would have made no sense, especially if the device stopped working after three years. Would it have been nice to know when the kids came to live here? Yes, but even then, nothing could have come from it.

"You don't have to apologize, Henry. I understand why you kept it from me. I had no right to get angry last night."

He gives me a nod and takes a sip of his drink. His eyes are still filled with sadness, which tells me he is going to continue to beat himself up over all this.

"What happens now? What are we going to do about my mom?" Elliot asks after a few minutes of silence.

I wish I had an answer. I wish I could tell him I will stop at nothing to find his mother and make her pay for her part in last night's events.

But Marisela is unpredictable. It could be a few years before she pops up again. We can't be sitting around waiting.

"There's not much we can do. We know she's out there,

and she knows we will be on the lookout, so she isn't going to try anything soon. We'll just have to up security and be vigilant. If anything happens, we have to communicate it, otherwise, she will catch us by surprise again."

He doesn't say anything. For a few seconds, he just sits there and takes my words. Eventually, he gives me a nod.

"How did she and Peter Hill even team up for this? That seems like the most unlikely pairing," Elliot throws out, asking the same questions that came to my mind.

Thankfully, Ella filled in some of the blanks on the way home last night.

"Apparently, the dark web connects people in the most unexpected ways."

I would have never put the two of them together, but I guess it made sense. Now I know what Marisela did before showing up at my office. She was plotting with Hill.

I should feel bad that the man is dead, but I can't. I feel bad for his family, enough to ask Henry to pay for the funeral so they don't have to, but not for him.

For a few more minutes, we sit in the kitchen and finish our coffees. Sometime around five in the morning, Elliot excuses himself, saying he's going to try to get a few hours of sleep, and a few moments later, Henry does the same.

Not me, though.

Instead of going upstairs and going to sleep in Drake's bed, I head into the study.

Now that I know what Marisela was after, I have to move things around to make sure the kids are protected, including planning what happens to the title of CEO if something ever happens to me. I'm going to make sure the title falls to someone who will protect the company, not a slimy bastard like Hill. If his plan had worked, he would have destroyed the company within a year.

I'm in the middle of sending an email to my lawyer, asking him to make a few changes, when the door to the study opens. Given the time of day, I half-expected it to be Henry, but to my surprise, it's Ella standing at the door.

"You're supposed to be sleeping," I say, leaning back in my chair and taking her in.

She's not hurt. There aren't any cuts or bruises on her face, but I know what she went through took a toll on her.

"Little snores woke me, and I couldn't go back to sleep."

The damn snorlax. We've taken him to the doctor, but we have yet to make another appointment for the recommended surgery.

"How are you feeling?"

"Okay," she says as she walks over to me and settles herself on my lap.

I press my mouth to her hair. "I'm going to need more details than that."

She lets out a sigh. "Even though I was just strapped to a chair, my body feels like it was put through the wringer. That, and my head still feels cloudy."

I wish I could give her something for that, but I have no idea what the fuckers gave her or how much.

"It will go away soon, I promise."

She hums against my chest and doesn't say anything. She doesn't even move for the next few minutes, so I start to think she fell asleep.

But of course, that isn't the case.

"Bennett?" she says, lifting her head from where it rests against my chest and looking up at me.

I can tell she has something on her mind. "What is it?"

She almost looks scared. "Marrying you was the best decision I've ever made."

Her words make my heart beat faster, and I give her a smile. "Why are you telling me this?"

"Because it's what I wanted to tell you while I was strapped to that chair. That, and I loved you. Since I already told you those words in the car last night, I wanted to give you the rest."

I place my hands on either side of her face.

"Choosing you as my wife was the best decision I ever made." I give her a chaste kiss.

The way she smiles at me when I pull away is one I will remember forever.

"You never had any doubts?" she asks, as if she wants to believe me, but something is telling her not to.

"I did. Last night, some even tried to slip through. I kept thinking that if I hadn't married you, you wouldn't have been put in the situation you were in. If I hadn't married you, then you would have been safe. But the more I thought about it, the angrier I got with myself. I hated thinking that, because when it comes to you, there aren't any regrets, and there never will be."

Her lips land on mine for a soft kiss.

"There is also something else that I wanted to tell you. I thought about it the whole way home, but I didn't know how to bring it up."

"What is it?"

Tears spring into her eyes as she prepares herself. "I don't want this arrangement to end at the two-year mark like we agreed. In such a short time, you've made me feel like I'm actually worthy of something. You make me feel safe, wanted, and I don't want to let that go. I don't want to let you go. I want to stay a Lane and be a part of this family and go to work with you every day and go on trips and everything that comes with being your wife. I don't want the two-year mark to come and have to walk away. I don't know if I'd be able to. It would break me, and I would never recover."

She wouldn't be the only one who would break if we ended this when we said we would.

My whole fucking life would be shattered into a million pieces, and there would be no way to ever put it back together.

I need Ella in my life. Now and until the end of eternity.

"Baby," I say, looking into her eyes. "Two years with you would never be enough. When the time came, the only way one of us would walk away would be if we wanted to. But if you don't want to and neither do I, then we can throw that agreement out the fucking window."

"Really?"

"Really. You've been mine since day one, Ella Vincent. I just hope you are ready to belong to me forever."

Her hands land on either side of my face. "I'm ready."

"Thank fuck."

My lips smash themselves to hers with urgency. Even

though my lips were on hers a few minutes ago, it feels like I haven't kissed her in forever.

And forever it will be for us, none of this two-year shit.

The only thing I have to worry about now is making sure she and the rest of our family are taken care of for the same length of time.

38

BENNETT

I'm in the study looking over the documents my lawyer sent over when a soft knock lands against the door.

When my eyes move up, I'm met with one of the most beautiful sights in the world.

Ella is standing in the doorway, her chestnut brown hair in waves, the blue silky dress she's wearing absolutely perfect against her skin. I want to tear it off her.

But tonight is the one night I have to hold off. She has to look presentable for her date.

"How do I look?" she asks, walking into the study and giving me a twirl.

My eyes immediately go to her ass. That fabric does wonders for her body.

"Like you're going to be the hottest mom at this dance."

A small laugh leaves her. "More like the youngest. I bet you a date that the second Drake and I walk in, people are going to start whispering."

I give her a smirk as she walks closer to me. "They will

no doubt be staring, but it will have nothing to do with your age."

"What would it have to do with, then?"

Placing the paperwork on my desk, I close the distance between us, placing my hands on her hips.

"You are a Lane. The second you walk into that room, everyone is going to be looking at you because you are a Lane. You did the one thing all of them wish they could."

Her arms go around my neck, and she brings her face closer to mine. "And what is that?"

"Married the billionaire bachelor."

"Hmm. I wonder what they would say if they knew he paid me to marry him?"

I narrow my eyes and let my hands travel down to her ass. I grip on to her globes until she yelps.

Quickly, the yelp is replaced with a giggle. "I was kidding."

She leans up and places her lips against mine, and just as I'm about to slide my tongue into her mouth, she pulls away and looks over my shoulder.

"I thought you said you were done with work for the day." Her eyebrows raise in question.

"I am. That's some personal stuff."

"Oh?"

Might as well tell her. She's going to find out either way, but if I hold it in, she's going to think it's something that it's not.

I let go of her ass, putting space between us and walking back to the desk.

"I talked to my lawyer a few weeks ago about making a

few changes to my estate, and he finally sent everything for me to look over." I grab the paperwork and hand it to her.

She looks up at me with concern. "Your estate?"

"Just in case something happens to me, I want to have everything in order."

Her eyes grow sad at my words, but she nods in understanding. Death is always a difficult subject, but it's one of those things in life that just happens.

From a young age, I always knew I needed to plan for when my death came. I needed to make sure everything was in line in case something bad happened to me and my family was left with nothing.

Nine years ago, I added the kids to the estate, leaving almost everything to them. But now that Ella and Charlie are here to stay as part of our family, I needed to make some changes. Now more than ever.

Peter Hill is taken care of, but there are plenty of people out there just like him who will want to come after me or my family, and I need to be prepared.

"What changes did you make?" Ella asks, doing a quick scan of the papers.

I don't answer her; I just let her continue reading the paperwork.

When she looks up at me and starts shaking her head, I know she found it.

"No."

"Ella."

"You're not leaving me fifty percent of your fortune." She shakes her head again, as if doing so is going to change the outcome. She's cute when she gets like this.

If it wasn't for the kids, she would be getting a lot more than fifty percent. She is also getting all my shares of Lane Enterprises.

Sensing that she is seconds away from freaking out, I place my hands on either side of her face and stop the shaking, making her look into my eyes. "Too late. It's already done. If anything ever happens to me, you are taken care of. For life."

Tears start to form in her eyes, but she does her best to not let them fall.

"Can I reject it?" she lets out, almost defeated.

I can't help but smirk at her. "Sure, but only after you're taken care of."

"Fine."

Not being able to help myself, I place a chaste kiss on her lips before I pull back.

"I also took care of Charlie. A trust fund is set up in her name."

A small gasp leaves her, and it takes her a second to formulate words. "Why would you do that?"

"Because she's family, and my family deserves to be taken care of. I did it for all the kids, and if any other kids come, they will get the same treatment."

As she looks up at me, her eyes gleam with love. I think she is just now realizing I meant what I said. This is real between us. No more agreement. No more timeline. Just fucking love that neither one of us wants to let go.

I married her to get the CEO title, but I will stay married to her forever. She is it for me. She is the one woman who changed my perspective on marriage, the one who has captured my attention from day one.

"You want more kids?" she asks, a small smile playing on her lips.

"There was a point where I didn't. I already had four who talked back; I couldn't imagine more of them. But now, with you, I think it would be nice to have some."

Another kiss lands on lips. "Maybe we can add one more."

"However many you want."

She smiles so bright, it lights up the whole room.

"Thank you," she lets out, shifting until her arms are around my waist and her head is resting against my chest.

"For saying yes to more kids?" I say through a small chuckle, wrapping my arms around her.

"No." She pulls away, just enough to look up at me. "For giving me the life I always wanted and never thought I would get. For making every one of my wildest dreams come true. For taking care of both me and Charlie."

I place a hand on her cheek and run my thumb along their skin as she leans into my touch.

"You told me once that your goal was to make sure you gave your sister the life she deserved. I have the same goal for you. I plan on giving you the life you deserve and more for the rest of mine."

This time, when the tears come, she lets them fall. "I love you, Bennett Lane."

Hearing her say those words does something to me. I want to hear those words and only those words for the rest of my life.

"I love you too, sweet Ella."

And I do. This woman owns my whole heart in a way no other woman ever would.

Not giving a shit anymore, I slam my mouth against hers, one of my hands moving into her hair and holding her face to mine.

Her mouth is fucking delicious, and if we had more time, I would explore it, memorize every single inch as if it were the first time, before making my way down the rest of her body.

But there's a chance that a ten-year-old is going to be storming in here any minute.

My tongue slides against hers, and she lets out a hum that goes straight to my cock. My hands itch to slide between her legs and see if she is drenched for me.

The only thing holding me together is that I know she'll be in my bed tonight, her pussy mine for the fucking taking.

Having some self-control.

I pull away from my wife, and an idea springs to mind.

"Tomorrow, you're mine. No kids. No interruptions. Absolutely nothing that will take you away from me."

A smirk forms on Ella's face, and it's the sexiest thing in the world. "Yes, husband."

If my cock wasn't rock-hard before, it is now.

I've heard Ella call me her husband. She has said it here and there when talking to people, but she has never said it in that tone. I like it way more than I should.

It's just a word, but hearing it in a sultry manner has

me wanting to say fuck whatever prior commitments she has, bend her over the desk, and fuck her brains out.

Control.

Have fucking control.

"You're going to be repeating those words nonstop tomorrow night."

"Hmm. Can't wait." The way her smirk grows tells me she knows exactly what's happening to me with her words.

Before I do something stupid and have her cancel on the excited ten-year-old who had Henry order a corsage, I take her hand in mind and walk us out of the room.

As we walk to the front of the house, I hear a giggle coming from the living room. Drake is laughing at something Henry is saying, and it's one of the best sounds I've ever heard.

As we get closer, my mind goes back in time.

If my parents hadn't died and Robert hadn't left, would that sound exist? Would I know what it's like to raise four kids who aren't mine and what it's like to hear them laugh or see them smile? Would I know what it's like to be a father and raise kids as if they were my own?

There are more days than I can count where I wished my parents were still here. That I wasn't orphaned and didn't have abandonment issues that can't be repaired. But then the what-ifs come to mind, and those wishes vanish.

I miss my parents, no doubt about that, but I don't know what I would have done without the things their deaths brought. I don't know who I would be, and I truthfully don't want to know.

When we reach the living room, Henry is pinning a

boutonniere on Drake's suit jacket. The kid may only be nearly eleven, but he looks so damn grown-up. He reminds me of Elliot when he was the same age.

"I have your date for you, bud," I say to the room.

Drake turns to us with a big smile, and once his own flower is situated, he grabs the one sitting on the coffee table and walks over.

"This is for you." He holds up the small box for Ella, his smile growing.

My wife takes the box from my nephew before bending down a bit and placing a kiss on his cheek. "Thank you. It's beautiful."

The kid watches with excitement as she opens the box and slides on the corsage.

To some people, this may just be another mother-son dance, but to him, this is everything. He has never had a mother figure in his life. Hell, he doesn't even know his own mother, so having Ella do this means so much to him, and I know he will never forget it.

Part of me wants to kick myself for not bringing a woman the kids could look up to into our lives sooner, but I guess I was just waiting for the right assistant.

Because they love Ella just as much as I do.

"Are you ready to go? We can't be late," Drake says, nearly bouncing on his toes.

Ella lets out a laugh and holds out her hand. "I'm ready if you are."

With an excited nod, Drake slides his hand into Ella's and waves to me and Henry as they make their way out of the house.

Henry and I watch from the front steps as they get into the car, and we stay there until the car disappears down the long drive.

"Henry?" I say as the car fades into the distance.

"Yes, sir?"

"I'm going to need my mother's ring." I turn to find him with a smile on his face.

"It's a good thing I just had it cleaned."

Good.

Now it can go where it belongs.

On the finger of my wife.

When Bennett told me I was going to be his tonight, this isn't what I expected.

I thought that when he said no interruptions, we would be going to the penthouse and have a night to ourselves, maybe a candlelit dinner and then no clothes for the remainder of the night.

But I was wrong. Big time.

Because instead of us going to the penthouse, he brought me to a club. And not just any club, but Perversa.

Walking in was a bit of a shell shock. Even though I'm almost twenty-six, I've never stepped foot in a place with a club atmosphere. A dive bar, sure, but never a club, let alone a strip club.

Not just anybody can get in. You need to be a member to be able to walk through the black door—I just don't know if Bennett is a member because he's friends with Dante, the owner, or because he bought a membership.

As much as I want to ask, I keep that question to myself

and try not to think of anything else but the dancer performing in front of us. She's beautiful, her body moving with so much fluidity and conviction.

"She's beautiful," I whisper to Bennett as the dancer brings her performance to an end.

"That she is," he agrees, and I'm about to make a joke about commenting on the beauty of other women in front of me when I notice he isn't looking at the woman whatsoever. His eyes are on me and me alone.

Have they been on me all night?

My body is telling me yes.

As I stare into my husband's eyes, I conclude that I don't want to be here any longer. I want to go home and get lost in the way he makes me feel.

"I think that I'm ready to get out of here," I say with a smile I hope is sexy enough to convey what I'm dreaming of him doing to me.

He throws me a smirk before giving me an understanding nod, then hishand wraps around mine and quickly pulls us out of the private room.

We move through the club quickly, so quickly that I didn't even notice Bennett had called our driver until we're already sliding into the back seat. As soon as the door is shut behind us, Bennett pushes the button to put the partition up and doesn't waste a single second to pounce on me.

My tongue slides along his as I let out a moan. I had his mouth on mine not even an hour ago, and I was already missing it.

Needing to feel him everywhere, I hike up the dress I'm

wearing and close the distance, climbing up until both my thighs are straddling him.

Immediately, one of Bennett's hands goes to my hair and pulls my mouth even closer to him, as if even when we're connected, there is still too much room.

Our tongues dance, and my body grinds against his.

I don't know if it was the club or the promises he made for the night, but my need for this man is on another level. I'm close to tearing our clothes off just to get closer to him.

Bennett must have read my mind, because the hand that isn't in my hair slides up my bare thigh until he makes contact with my core.

His fingers slide against my panties, and for the first time tonight, I wish I had gone bare. With no material in the way, his fingers would have been inside me already.

I let out a whimper as his knuckle grazes my clit. My hips buck, wanting more.

"Such a greedy little thing," Bennett says before taking my bottom lip between his teeth.

"Only when I really want something," I say when he lets it go, grinding myself onto his lap.

"And what is it that you want, sweet Ella?" His mouth moves away from mine to my jaw and then to my neck.

Would it make me desperate if I pushed his face down until he took my breasts out of my dress and placed his mouth on one of my nipples?

"I want you," I say, bucking my hips against his hardening cock.

"You have me. Now, what else do you want?"

I'm frantic now as I circle my hips. "I want you to fuck me before we get home."

"And how would you want me to do that?"

This man is asking way too many questions right now.

My need for an orgasm building by the second, I decide to find my inner CEO and get shit done. I slide my hand into Bennett's hair and pull until his mouth is off my body and his eyes are looking into mine.

"You either fuck me with your fingers or your cock. I don't care which, but you will do it, or I will take matters into my own hands and make myself come while you watch."

The smirk that lands on his face is so fucking sexy. If I wasn't already dripping for him, I would be now.

"Are you bossing me around?"

"Someone has to. The CEO needs to be reeled in sometimes."

"Baby, you can reel me in whenever the fuck you want." He thrusts his hips up, and I can't help but let out a moan.

Bennett shifts a bit, and I think that maybe he is finally going to move my panties to the side, but no. Instead of my panties, he starts undoing his belt, and within seconds, his cock is out.

My mouth waters as I watch him slide his hand up his length.

"You should come first before I give you my cock."

"Trust me when I say, Mr. Lane, that my pussy is plenty wet for you. Fuck me now; we can think about foreplay later."

"That mouth of yours is going to get you in trouble, Mrs. Lane."

"You can take it up with my boss on Monday. I need you to fuck me now."

His hand lands between my thighs once more, his knuckles gliding over the now-soaked fabric before he slides it to the side. When his fingers touch my bare skin, I swear, I see stars.

I lift myself up until I'm hovering over him, his cock lined up with my entrance. I slide myself down until I'm taking most of him.

Having his cock inside me makes me feel so damn full. I swear, I will never tire of this feeling.

"My wife feels like a damn dream," Bennett groans, his hands going to my hips, moving me ever so slightly.

"You feel like a dream."

I start bouncing up and down without a single care in the world. I don't care that there's a driver on the other side of the partition. I don't care that we're driving through the city and that there's a chance that, even through the dark tint, someone could see us. I don't care whatsoever.

The only thing I care about is that my husband makes me feel like a damn goddess and that I'm about a minute or two away from exploding around him.

Bennett's fingers dig into my hips through the fabric of my skirt, and for a split second, I'm afraid he's going to rip it, but then I realize I don't care. He can rip whatever article of clothing he wants. I'll just add it to the stockpile I have going on back home.

Our moans and groans fill the back of the car, and

hearing them has me moving my body harder. When Bennett's mouth meets my neck, I don't know how much longer I can hold off.

I need to come, and I need to come now.

"I'm close," I pant, grinding my pussy against him.

One of the hands gripping my waist moves to where we're connected. I feel his fingers on my clit, and my panting gets louder.

He feels so damn good.

"It's like you were made for me, Ella." Bennett's words vibrate from my ear all the way to my toes. He knows how to make my body sing. "Come for me, baby. Cover my cock in everything you have, and I promise I'll reward you when we get home. Come, sweet Ella. Let me hear you moan out my name."

It's as if my body was waiting for his orders, and I come so damn hard that dark spots start to cover my vision.

I continue to ride his cock through the high until my body falls limp and he takes over.

The way Bennett uses my body is absolutely delicious, and I feel another orgasm flood my system as he digs his fingers into my skin and thrusts *hard* into my pussy. When the wave of my second orgasm hits, Bennett lets out a groan in my ear, releasing his seed into me.

His forehead lands on my shoulder, and for the remainder of the drive to the penthouse, we try our best to catch our breaths.

When the car comes to a full stop, I begrudgingly get off him, causing the mess that we made to not only slide down my thigh, but to also cover his dark slacks.

I can't help but smile a little bit when I see the stains.

I'd happily buy him a new pair of pants and add these to the pile of ripped clothes I have in my closet.

The smile stays on my face as we get ourselves situated, Bennett tucking his cock back in his pants and me fixing my dress and sliding my panties back into place before getting out of the car and heading upstairs.

Since we are still reeling from the incident, we wait for Bennett's head of security before getting off the elevator. When we have the all clear, we head in, and Bennett wastes no time pulling my body to his.

"You look like you could use a relaxing night," he whispers in my ear before tugging my lobe between his teeth.

My body melts against his, as if the two orgasms I just had in the car weren't relaxing at all. "What do you have in mind?"

His face leans in until his lips are pressed against my ear. "I was thinking maybe a massage. Go to the bedroom and strip. I want you completely naked in the middle of the bed."

His words elicit a shiver.

With a nod, I follow orders as he trails close behind me.

When I reach the bedroom, I go to turn on the lights, but Bennett's hand stops me. All he does is shake his head and nod toward the bed.

He's up to something, but I don't question him.

Walking deeper into the room, I start sliding off my dress and let it drop until it's a pool of material at my feet. I feel Bennett's eyes on me from behind, but I don't turn to look over at him. I just continue ridding myself of my panties and bra, dropping them to the floor with my dress and shoes.

As I walk over to the bed, stripped down to a black fitted sheet, I sense Bennett moving behind me. When I turn to face him, I see him lighting candles across the room. He must have brought them here earlier, because there wasn't a single candle in this room the last time we were here.

About twenty candles are lit, lighting up the room in the most sensual way.

When the last candle is lit, I finally take my eyes away from the man who owns every part of me. I follow orders and lay in the middle of the bed.

I lay there, face down, for the next order to come, but Bennett doesn't say anything for a minute or two. He continues to move across the room until the bed shifts under me, and I feel his body hovering over mine.

"Seeing you like this is a glorious sight," he whispers in my ear before placing a kiss just behind it.

The kisses don't stop there.

He continues to kiss his way down my body until he reaches the inner part of my thighs. A small kiss lands on my pussy, and, as if my body knows what's coming next, my legs fall open.

Bennett lets out a small chuckle and places one more feather-like kiss against my lower lips before he pulls away.

The bed shifts again, and this time, instead of hovering over me, he straddles my body.

It's then I realize he is just as naked as I am.

"I know we've talked about it, but I need assurance. Are you still curious about wax play?" His hands start to massage the globes of my ass.

I try not to get lost in his actions and answer his question. "Yes, I'm still curious."

"Would you be willing to try it tonight?"

I nod against the mattress. "Yes."

His hands move to the upper part of my ass, and it feels like heaven.

"We'll start off slow. If at any point you want to stop, say the word and I will. You are in control here, not me."

"Okay."

A few seconds after I say the word, something cold hits my skin, and Bennett starts to move it around my body. His hands slide with the oil, kneading my muscles. I thought what he was doing to my ass felt good, but this is a whole other level. His hands press into me hard, and I continue to melt into the mattress.

I don't know how long he massages my back and ass, but by the time he tells me to turn around, my body is so relaxed, I feel like I'm more asleep than awake.

When I shift to lay on my back, Bennett turns his focus to my front. He takes his time with my breasts, making sure my nipples are taut when he moves his hands down my belly. He continues to move down until his fingers glide through my pussy, making sure no part of me is left uncovered.

My legs twitch when his fingers meet my clit, and when he pulls his hand away, I miss it.

The bed shifts under me as Bennett climbs off and goes to grab one of the candles that sits on top of the dresser.

As much as I want to concentrate on what he's doing, I can't pay much attention with him standing only a few feet away, fully nude. With the glow of the candles he lit and the moonlight streaming into the room, his body is lit up, every single inch of him glowing, including that delicious V that I want to slide my tongue down, his cock at half-mast.

This man is gorgeous, perfect in almost every way. I can't believe I'm married to him. I can't believe that an agreement for two years of marriage has brought me to this moment, where my heart is so full and owned by someone who was just supposed to be my boss. Never in a million years did I think taking a job as an assistant would get me here, but I'm glad it did.

My eyes go back to Bennett when I notice him tilt the candle just enough to drop some wax on the inside of his wrist.

He's testing it.

I find it insane that this man, this billionaire of a man who has so many other important things to do and think about, took the time to do this, to learn how to do it properly. Any other person would have jumped in headfirst to both of our detriment, but not Bennett.

It's even the little things he does that leave me in awe.

When Bennett is satisfied with the temperature of the wax, he walks back to the bed, but instead of joining me, he stands close to the edge.

"Give me your wrist," he orders, holding out one of his hands to me.

With butterflies of excitement swooping through my belly, I sit up and give him my wrist. Ever so slowly, he drops a few bits of wax onto my skin, and the sensation is surprisingly a good one. Actually, it's better than good.

"Is that too hot?" he asks, his eyes on my face, making sure I don't lie.

I shake my head. "No, it's perfect."

He's perfect, and I lean up to tell him just that.

"Lay back down," he says when I pull away, and I gladly oblige.

With my back to the mattress and my eyes on Bennett, he holds the candle just above my body, dropping the first few bits of wax onto my skin.

This wax feels different from the kind waxers use for body hair. This one feels lighter, softer in a way, and I think I like it more.

Bennett continues to spread droplets all over my body, starting with my arms before moving to my belly, and when he drops a few droplets on my chest, covering my nipples, I let out a moan. The heat feels perfect against my skin. He moves back down my body again, and this time he doesn't stop until he has the candle just above my pussy.

My eyes stay on his face as he licks his lips and drops a few splatters of wax on my mound. Another moan escapes me when the hot droplets meet my bare skin. When a few land against my clit, I let out a yelp, but it's quickly replaced with a moan.

Never in my life did I think this would be something I

liked, that I even enjoyed, but I do. I guess it takes the right person, one who makes you feel safest, to try something like this.

After dropping a few more beads of hot wax across my thighs, Bennett places the candle down and takes a look at his handiwork.

"How do you feel?"

I can't help but give him the dopiest smile ever. "Really good."

"I'm about to make you feel even better."

And he does.

He wastes no time getting back onto the bed and massaging in the wax so it mixes with the oil already covering my body. His hands move against every inch of my skin, leaving nothing uncovered. The massage quickly turns into a sensual one when he takes one of my nipples in his mouth, and his fingers strum my pussy as if I were his personal instrument.

My body feels glorious, and when he widens my legs and slides his cock into me, I feel like I've earned a trip to heaven.

His eyes lock onto mine as he pounds into me, and I can't help but wrap my limbs around him, bringing our bodies as close as possible.

As I look into his eyes, I feel it. I feel the type of love I never thought I would get to experience.

For the last five years, my life has been centered around one thing: giving my sister the best life possible. She was the priority, and I didn't care if I had to suffer. I didn't think about dating or finding someone to spend my life with. As long as she was taken care of, I'd worry about myself later.

But then came Bennett. What started as a simple arrangement has turned into so much more. He has taken care of me and Charlie, protected me, and for the first time, I feel safe and loved in a way I never thought I'd feel.

Yet, here I am, feeling every single ounce of it.

Sliding my hand into his hair, I bring his face down to mine until our lips meet.

"I love you." The words come out as a whisper, but it's the most powerful whisper ever spoken.

"I love you too. So damn much."

And he continues to show me just how much he means those words.

"I HAVE SOMETHING FOR YOU," Bennett says as we lay in bed an hour after we made love.

He starts to move away from me, but my body is so wrapped around his that he lets out a chuckle as he shifts just enough to reach the bedside table.

He shifts us so we're both sitting up, my limbs no longer wrapped around him like a spider monkey. With our backs to the headboard, he holds a small box between us: a ring box.

I look up at him with curious eyes. "What is it?"

"Open it and find out."

I take the box from him and do just that. Nestled inside on a black cushion is a beautiful cushion-cut diamond with other small diamonds surrounding it, all sitting on a gold band. It almost looks like a flower in bloom—unique and absolutely gorgeous.

"This is beautiful," I say to Bennett, not taking my eyes off the piece.

"It was my mother's. It's the ring that my father proposed with. She didn't wear it much after they got married, so it's almost in perfect condition."

"I'm sure it would have looked beautiful on her," I say with a smile.

"It did," Bennett agrees, a small smile forming on his face.

I look back to the ring, and that's when his words finally make it through my mind.

"Wait. You're giving this to me?" I ask, sounding a little shocked.

One of my favorite smiles spreads across his face.

"I am."

"But I already have a ring."

He takes the box from me. "And that ring is yours to keep." His eyes don't leave the ring as he twirls it around his long fingers. "I never wanted to get married. I never wanted to go through the possibility of losing someone I loved like I lost my parents, but I always thought that if there was a woman out there to change my mind, then I would give her my mother's ring. When I picked out yours, I thought about it. I thought about asking Henry for this one and giving it to you. I knew you'd cherish it even though our agreement was only for two years. It would have been an easy thing for me to do, but for some reason, I decided against it."

"It wasn't the right move at the moment," I voice out loud.

And it wasn't. I don't know how I would have reacted if he had given me his mother's ring all those months ago. I probably would have freaked out.

Bennett gives me a nod. "No, it wasn't. But things changed, and I finally asked Henry for it. It's yours if you want it."

Words don't form on my lips, so I give him a nod while I try to hold back tears.

With a smile on his face, he takes my hand and places the ring at the tip of my finger.

"Are you sure?" I ask just before he slides the ring above the one he gave me on our wedding day, the one I know I will cherish just as much as the one that belonged to Catherine Lane.

"One hundred percent sure. Not only do I love you more than I can ever comprehend, but you take the nightmares away. The bad memories don't come when I'm with you. You are my light in the darkness, and I'm never going to give you up. No matter how much the fear of losing you may affect me. You own my damn heart, and now you can carry something that symbolizes it wherever you go."

A tear escapes the corner of my eye, and Bennett reaches over to wipe it away just before he adjusts the ring so it faces correctly on my finger.

The ring is absolutely beautiful. I never want to take it off.

"Thank you for trusting me with it," I say before leaning in to give him a kiss.

A smile forms on his lips when I pull away. "Thank you for agreeing to marry me."

"I'd marry you a thousand times over if I could."

"Is that so?"

"One hundred percent."

He stays silent for a second, but when he speaks again, he takes me by surprise. "Then let's get married."

"What?"

"Let's get married again, for real this time. No arrangement or timeline in place. No satisfying of any clause. Let's get married again because we truly want to."

I think about it. It would be nice to have a wedding I can look back on and think about how happy I was instead of how scared because I didn't know what two years married to a practical stranger was going to do to me.

Not even two minutes into thinking about the idea, I'm giving Bennett a yes.

"Okay, let's get married again."

Bennett pounces. One second, I'm sitting next to him, giving him a smile, and the next, I'm on my back and he's on top of me, giving me a look like he is ready to devour me for the rest of the night. But hunger isn't the only thing floating through his eyes.

There's also *love.*

He loves me just as much as I love him.

It's crazy to think that eight months ago, we were just

strangers. I needed a job, and he needed an assistant. The job was just a much-needed paycheck for me, but it turned into so much more.

Love and commitment. Safety and protection. Family and forever.

Bennett Lane gave me so much the day he hired me, and I will forever be indebted to him. I will spend the rest of my life making sure he knows just how thankful I am for him.

Who knew taking a job in the corporate world would be so good to me?

I run my fingers through his hair. "Thank you for changing my life. I will never be able to thank you enough."

He turns his head and places a kiss against my palm. "Thank me by never leaving me."

"I would never dream of it."

I will hold Bennett tight and never let go, fighting all his nightmares along the way.

EPILOGUE

BENNETT

I walk to the gravesite and place a bouquet of flowers right in the middle.

Twenty-five years.

That's how long it has been since my parents died, since I've stood only feet away and watched as their caskets were lowered into the ground. That's how long it has been since the last time I've visited.

Though I haven't been here since the day of the funeral, the plot is clean, and I'm sure that's thanks to Henry.

I don't know what spurred the decision to come here, but for some reason, it felt necessary, like it was something I needed today.

"I don't know if I'm supposed to talk out loud or keep all the words in my head," I say to the headstone in front of me. I'm not usually one to speak what's in my head out loud—that's an Ella thing—but keeping things in seems like it would be a lot more emotionally damaging than the alternative.

So talking out loud it is.

"I'm sorry I haven't come as often as I probably should. I guess I got so used to feeling you two around the house that I didn't feel the need to come here. But now thinking about it, I can see how that would be wrong."

Why is this so damn hard?

"Anyway. I wanted to come today, because I guess I wanted to feel close to you guys. I'm getting married today. Well, I'm getting married again. The first wedding was just so I could become CEO, but this time, it's the real thing. It's to the same woman, but we thought it would be nice to start anew. I even gave her your ring, Mom. She loved it. I don't think she has taken it off since. Same goes for the bracelet Henry gave her. I think you would have loved her. I never thought I would find someone like her, but I did, and I couldn't be happier. She completes me on all levels. I don't know if I'd be CEO without her. She is absolutely everything."

Why is this so damn hard? Is this what other sons do when they visit their dead parents—just ramble a bunch of nonsense?

"And you would have loved your grandkids too. It's crazy to think how big they've gotten. It was like one minute, they were cute kids, and the next, they're teenagers with attitudes."

I wonder what my brother would say if he saw just how much the kids have grown.

"They remind me so much of Robert and me when we

were younger, especially the boys. They each have their own personalities, but there are times where I swear I'm looking into a mirror or watching a home movie because they are just like us. It's crazy. Samantha reminds me of you, Mom. There's a fire in her that I hope she never loses. That girl is going to be coming after my CEO title, I'm freaking sure of it. She's as beautiful as you, too. There is this picture of you in the study, and I swear there are times I look over at it and see Sam. It's uncanny."

A lump starts to form in my throat, but I push it down as best I can. I've cried at this gravesite before, and I don't want to do it again.

"I've been trying my best at raising them. At least, I think I have. I haven't had a door slammed in my face in a few months, so I see that as a good sign. They're good kids, and I'm trying to be the parent you two taught me to be. Hopefully, I'm making you proud."

Something wet lands against my cheek, and for a second, I think it's raining, which would be ironic, but when I wipe the droplet away, I realize it's a tear.

I guess crying while I'm here is inevitable.

"As for Robert, I'm still looking, and I won't stop until I find him. He's out there, I know he is. I just have to keep looking. I will find him, and I will bring him home. I promise you that."

More tears roll down my face, but this time, I don't move to wipe them away.

"I miss you guys. There are days I truly wish you were here. That you could see this family that I have and be happy here with me, but that can't happen, and I'm okay with that. I am okay. I promise you that I am. I'm happy, and I'm okay."

I don't know if those last five words are for them or for myself.

For another ten minutes, I stand there just looking at the grave, letting the emotions take over. I don't say anything else until I'm ready to head back to the manor.

"I should get going. I don't know if I can promise I will be back more often, but I will try. I love you both. Thank you for being the best parents in the world. I will continue trying to make you proud."

I needed this. I needed to come here today and talk to them, let everything out. I needed to feel my parents close by, and I feel stronger for it.

Most of my life has been defined by losing my parents. And while that is a part of me, it's not who I am.

I'm not just the kid who was orphaned and raised by his caretaker.

I'm not just the kid who had his brother walk on him a month later.

I'm more than that. I will always be more than that.

I'm a son. A brother. An uncle who stepped up as a father. A husband. A damn CEO. I'm just getting started with life, and soon people will know me to be something other than the orphaned eight-year-old. They will know me as the man who will stop at nothing to get what he wants if they don't already.

And I won't. I will not stop at nothing to build myself a life my parents would be proud of, corrupt or not.

I look back at the tombstone one last time, giving the

names a smile, and for a second, I swear I feel Thomas and Catherine right next to me.

"I love you both."

With one final look, I head back to the car.

It's time to marry the woman who makes me the best man possible—again. I may be a little corrupt at times, but she loves me.

She fucking loves me and drives all the nightmares away.

Ella Vincent Lane is mine, and I will never let her go.

People are going to have to pry her from my cold, dead hands.

PLAYLIST

Dark, Twisted and Cruel - Alan Wake, Paleface
Lose Control - Teddy Swims
Beautiful Things - Benson Boone
Too Sweet - Hozier
Desperado - Rihanna
Say Yes To Heaven - Lana Del Rey
Constellations - Piano Version - Jade LeMac
HEARTBEAT - Isabel LaRosa
Lust For Life - Lane Del Rey, The Weeknd
Heartburn - Wafia
After Hours - The Weeknd
Falling - Harry Styles
Swim - Chase Atlantic

MORE OF THE LANE FAMILY IS COMING

Book 2 in the Lane Family Series will be releasing
February 14, 2024!
Are you ready for Elliot's book?
If you want more Muertos Cartel, you will definitely want
to check out his book.
Pre-order Elliot's book today!

ALSO CHECK OUT...

If you enjoyed Dante Rosetti in this book, be sure to check
out his story in Powerful Deception!
Read Powerful Deception today!

ACKNOWLEDGMENTS

This book was a fever dream. Never did I think that this book will ever come out. I know I've been known to say that a book has been in my head for a while and it's has finally come to life, but believe me when I say that this book, at least this family has been in my head for years. And by years, I mean well over a decade.

This started out as my love for something blossoming into something more.

For a while, I debated if I should write Bennett's story, but after much thinking I decided that his story was necessary. His story is the start of everything, and why not kick off this new series with a little marriage of convenience?

This story definitely took a different direction than what I had intended, but the end result is perfect.

Thank for reading it.

Thank yous also go to....

Readers - for taking a shot on my books, time and time again. You have no idea how much I appreciate your love and support.

Becky - for helping me get through this book and texting me almost every day and making sure I was getting words in.

The Author Agency and Good Girls PR - Thank you

for helping get this book out there and helping me spread the word.

Haya - The covers that you made are absolutely everything and more. Thank you for taking on this project and making the coves come to life.

Alexa and Ellie - For dealing with my chaos of tight deadlines and making this book what it is!

Now, who's ready for some Elliot? A reader (@annahbiotics on instagram) gave me the idea for his leading lady. Any idea as to who it may be?

Here's a hint.... They were in Las Vegas when Leo and Serena got married ;)

BOOKS BY JOCELYNE SOTO

One Series

One Life

One Love

One Day

One Chance

One for Me

One Marriage

Flor De Muertos Series

Vicious Union

Violent Attraction

Vindictive Blood

Lane Family Series

Vows In Corruption

Promises and Deception

Chicago Dark Knights Series

Skating the Blue Line

Passing the Red Line

Hitting the Goal Line

Standalones

Beautifully Broken

Worth Every Second

Powerful Deception

Fake Love

Salutis Meae

ABOUT THE AUTHOR

Jocelyne Soto is an independent author living in California. She loves reading romance and discovering new authors. She comes from a big Mexican family, and with it comes a love for all things family and food. Jocelyne has a love for her mom's coffee and writing. In her free time, you can find her reading a romance novel on her kindle while writing heartwarming and chaotic romance stories in between. From sport romance to dark romance, there is no limit as to the type of stories that will come to Jocelyne's mind.

Check out her website for ways to connect with Jocelyne!
www.jocelynesoto.com

bookbub.com/authors/jocelyne-soto

goodreads.com/jocelynesotobooks

instagram.com/authorjocelynesoto

tiktok.com/@authorjocelynesoto

facebook.com/authorjocelynesoto

pinterest.com/authorjocelynesoto

threads.net/@authorjocelynesoto

JOIN MY READER GROUP

Join my ever-growing Facebook Group. You get first looks, sneak peeks and giveaways!

NEWSLETTER

Sign up for my Newsletter!
You will get notified when there are new
releases to look out for, giveaways and more!

www.ingramcontent.com/pod-product-compliance
Lightning Source LLC
Chambersburg PA
CBHW061542190726
48289CB00004B/1130